A Season for Solitude

MATTESON WYNN

For Michael and Steven

Chapter One

Every time I watch a movie, I love how I find myself magically transported to a different world.

Until, of course, someone breaks the movie's spell by interrupting.

This time, I was ejected from the film noir universe of dames and gumshoes by Bayley kicking up a ruckus.

The house creaked and groaned at me so loudly that I paused the movie with an alarmed, "Bayley, what's up?"

An image of the Knack Shack, my mental practice room, popped into my head.

"You want to talk to me?" I abandoned my popcorn, sitting up straight as I scanned the property for problems.

Frowning, I said, "I don't see anything wrong. What's going on? Are you okay?"

Through our bond, Bayley's emotions roiled.

The image of the Knack Shack started flashing in my head.

"Okay, okay, I'm going."

Even though I couldn't detect anything overtly wrong, I reached for my magic and poured a protective bubble around the couch, shielding both me and Fuzzy in the process.

Fuzzy, who had been snoozing next to me, lifted his head, looked at the bubble, then looked at me.

I shrugged. "Just in case. Better safe than sorry. If Bayley's going to all the trouble of an unscheduled mental meetup, something big must be going on. While I'm distracted, keep an eye out, all right?"

"Meow."

After last fall's fiascos, I'd told Bayley, "I need an easier way to talk to you. The only way you can speak actual words to me is if I'm unconscious, and you meet me in a mental projection through a dream link. There's gotta be a better way to do this that doesn't involve me being Coma Girl."

Bayley had groaned in agreement, so I'd continued on with, "What if we create a more permanent mental meeting room that we can go to when we want? I can shift my mental state on purpose, thanks to my work with Carmine, so I don't need to be knocked out. We can use the new room not only to talk to each other but also to help me get the knack of working magic with you."

Now, as Bayley creaked and squeaked around me, urging me to hurry up and meet him, I was grateful all over again that we'd built the Knack Shack.

Settling back against the couch, I regulated my breathing until my brain shifted into the right state. Then I carefully called up my magic, one branch at time, combining a teaspoon of green Foster earth magic, blue Murphy water magic, red Smith fire magic, tan Best animal magic, and purple Guthrie air magic, and then stirring them together in my mind until they were evenly mixed. I took the resulting "batter" and shaped it in my mind into a bridge.

The first few times we'd done it, it'd taken me a while to carry out each step. But now, I had the whole process down.

In seconds, I was mentally crossing the bridge to the Knack Shack. I opened the door and walked into the room.

Instead of a glittery magical princess playroom, the Knack Shack was monastically simple. That was kind of the point. We needed a distraction-free zone to allow for focus without wasting any energy. Like a black box theater, the room featured just four black walls, a black ceiling and floor, and a black box sitting in a corner. A kitchen island holding a stack of bowls provided a working space in the middle of the room. The only "decoration" in the room was a set of five thermometers on the wall. Except, instead of measuring temperature, each thermometer gauged how much of each type of magical energy I had at my disposal.

Bayley said, "Finn!" He'd kept the British accent he'd adopted, and it was even thicker now than usual, showing his distress.

"What's wrong?" I asked as I turned toward the golden ball of light bouncing up and down in the middle of the room. Bayley had let my brain choose the form of his avatar. For some reason, it interpreted his presence as a golden ball of light.

I, on the other hand, looked and felt like my real-world self. Although the space was virtual, all my senses reacted like I was in the real world. Which was great sometimes, and not at others. Like now, when Bayley's jouncing was making me dizzy.

I was about to ask him to hold still when conflicting emotions poured through our bond from Bayley to me. I caught excitement, worry, and uncertainty all underscored by a sense of urgency.

"Bayley, seriously, what's wrong?"

"Your birthday—"

My shoulders relaxed, and I groaned. "Oh is that all? You're spending a ton of energy on a mind-link to talk about *my birthday?*"

"When you said that it's in three weeks—"

"I know you're upset that I didn't mention it until tonight, but it's no big deal, I swear. Honestly, the only reason it even occurred to me to bring it up was because of that movie we were watching."

His voice had a frantic edge as Bayley said, "I need to prepare—"

"No, you don't. Really. I'm planning on treating it like a regular day. I mean, I haven't even told Nor that it's coming up." I scuffed the floor with my foot and mumbled, "It's only my second birthday since my dad died. Birthdays were hard enough without Mom, but with him gone too, I still don't feel much like celebrating. No offense."

"You mistake me. I need to…" he paused, searching for the right word, then said, "Power down. To have some downtime. Sort of."

I blinked in surprise. "Wait, what?" With a confused laugh, I asked, "How does *my* getting older make *you* need a rest?" I couldn't suppress my grin as I teased Bayley, "Downtime? I mean, I'm not planning a big party or anything, but that doesn't mean it'll be so boring you need to sleep through it. Though, I gotta be honest, that does sound kind of appealing."

"Finn, this is serious."

"I kinda got that from the whole mind-link thing." I sighed, grin fading. "Okay, explain, please."

Bayley's voice shifted, much more uncertain. The imaginary room creaked around me, reflecting Bayley's anxiety. "Your magical knowledge has been growing very rapidly. And because of the bond, it's affected me as well. I'm also supposed to grow, on my own. In theory, I should grow with every Housekeeper."

Anger sparked a slow burn in my chest as I thought of all the years Bayley had been neglected by his Housekeepers. "And the last several Housekeepers haven't helped you grow at all."

"Even if they had, there's only so much growing that can be done before my time with a given Housekeeper is up."

He meant before we went and died on him. I winced at the thought.

Bayley continued, "But if I can take the birthday shortcut, I might be able to grow in ways I haven't before."

"What birthday shortcut?"

"It's a…loophole, of sorts. If I have a particularly special bond with the Housekeeper, there's a chance to…grow…all at once. And our bond…well, it's unlike any of the others." I was about to thank him, but he added in a rush, "The catch is that the only way I can take advantage of the loophole is for my main functions to go dormant while I…process. It'll feel like…well, I'm not sure what it will feel like exactly. But I would guess it will feel like I'm not here."

My brain stuttered. *Feel like Bayley wasn't there?* Our bond was so strong that it'd be like losing a piece of myself.

As I tried to squash my rising dismay, Bayley added, "There's more."

"Of course there is. Alright, lay it on me."

"It has to happen before the first birthday of the Housekeeper. I need to go…right now."

Chapter Two

"What? Why?"

"It takes time to do properly, and it can't be done unless I'm not functioning the way I usually do."

I said slowly, "So, like a computer upgrade? That's when the main systems have to be shut down—to go offline—while all the changes are implemented."

"Offline, yes, like that." He sounded close to panic as he added, "Six weeks. If we're going to attempt this, we're supposed to allow *at least* six weeks before the Housekeeper's birthday so that I would only be unavailable in short increments. We're down to three weeks. I'm already so behind I have to do it all at once."

I stared at him, speechless.

Bayley blurted, "I made a mistake. It's been so long since I had a Housekeeper with more than a surface bond that I had all but forgotten about this chance. When you told me tonight that your birthday is nearly upon us, it triggered my memory. I am ashamed that I let something so important go unremembered." If Bayley were a person, he would have been wringing his hands. "This is supposed to be a carefully planned process where we have time to get ready and…I've bungled it. I am sorry, Finn."

My first instinct was to calm Bayley, so I said, "It's okay, we'll figure it out." But then the rest of what he said registered and I said as calmly as I could manage, "Three weeks? You're leaving for three weeks? *Right now.*"

"Not necessarily three weeks. If it goes smoothly, I could be back much sooner. I'm just supposed to allow as long as possible in case of…issues."

And that didn't sound worrying at all.

Bayley hesitated, his anxiety so palpable that it was raising *my* blood pressure.

I rubbed my forehead. "You might as well tell me the rest."

Bayley listed a bunch of details, starting with the fact that the property would be on lockdown as soon as he went offline. While I tried to cope with what he'd just laid out, he put the final nail in the coffin by adding, "Once I start, I have to finish. You won't be able to get me back until I'm through."

He couldn't stop once he started? "Bayley, that sounds dangerous."

"It is…not without risk," he said.

I had the feeling that was an understatement.

"But it is a risk I am…excited…to take." I must not have been doing a good job of hiding my concern because he said, "It will be okay Finn. I have total trust that you will care for me while I'm offline."

Bayley sounded confident. And so eager. He reminded me of a kid staring at a pile of presents, twitching to open them.

I was anything but.

What if he was gone the whole time? Replays of the various threats we'd fended off played on a loop in my head. Sure it'd been calm the last couple of months, but that didn't mean we could just relax. And Murphy's law said that a new disaster would park itself on the front lawn the second that Bayley left.

A vision floated through my mind of me standing on the front lawn trying to fend off an invading horde with a frying pan.

My mind spun, trying to work out the possible complications.

"I know you have more questions, Finn. But time is so short. If I am to be a success, I really do need to go."

The urgency pouring off of Bayley made it nearly impossible to concentrate. "What I'm getting is that this is really, really important to you."

Bayley said, "Yes." In a quiet voice he said, "I think this is my only real shot. There will never be another you."

How could I say no to that? With a sigh, I said, "Well, this isn't optimal. But of course, I want to help you be all you can be." And I would deal with whatever the consequences were when the time came.

A surge of hope and pride poured through Bayley, bringing a small smile to my face.

Shunting my worries to the side, I rubbed my hands together, and put on my best cheerleader voice. "Okay! Let's do this. Uh, *how* do we do this?"

"We leave the mind-link. Then you try to relax."

Because that didn't sound ominous.

However, I didn't fuss at him. Closing my eyes, I felt the room swim around me as Bayley and I disengaged from the mind-link.

A gentle head butt from Fuzzy confirmed I was back in the real world, and I opened my eyes to find him peering at me.

Fuzzy leaned into me, and I slowed my breathing to try and calm my racing heart.

Bayley's mix of worry for me and excitement over his adventure flowed through our bond.

What he needed from me was support, not doubt, so I did my best to give it to him. "You've got this. I'm sure your, er, upgrade will be a big success! Just do your thing, and don't worry about anything while you're away. Fuzzy and I will hold down the fort," I said with as much enthusiasm as I could muster.

I closed my eyes and said, "Sweet dreams Bayley," then added quietly, "I'll miss you."

The house made a crooning sound around me.

I felt a sense of anticipation, like Bayley and I were holding our breath.

Then he was gone.

Chapter Three

It was like someone flipped a switch.

One second, I had a roommate in my brain. The next, I was home alone.

I'd barely registered that thought when a wave of fatigue rolled through me as my body registered the absence of Bayley's energy. The edges of my vision went gray and dizziness swamped me. Squeezing my eyes shut, I clutched the edge of the couch cushion and waited it out.

When I opened my eyes, I realized I must've passed out. The clock told me an hour had passed.

"Meow?" Fuzzy pawed at me.

"Hang on, I'm a little out of it."

Disoriented, I sat up from where I'd flopped over on the sofa. I felt like I'd woken up in a strange place.

Tentatively, I called in my head, *Bayley?*

No answer.

I reached for him and felt…nothing.

I couldn't feel Bayley.

Panic swamped me.

Bayley?

Still nothing.

Just a big, echoing emptiness where he usually was.

He'd warned me he'd be gone, but I hadn't realized how… *quiet*…it would seem without him in my brain. I realized that I'd been expecting this to feel a bit like other times when he'd pulled back to the edge of my consciousness.

It wasn't.

It was like he'd totally left.

Fear squirmed through me.

Had he somehow miscalculated and disconnected us? Was he okay? What if he was really gone-gone?

I realized I was panting and made an effort to slow my breathing.

This is ridiculous, I chided myself. *You've spent your whole life Bayley-free up until six months ago. There is no reason to feel panicked because he's on hiatus for a bit.*

Fuzzy squished himself closer. Although he couldn't easily fit on my lap anymore, that didn't stop him from draping his front half on me.

As Fuzzy nuzzled my hand, I let the feel of his soft fur sifting through my fingers calm me. I tried to put emotion aside and think logically. There must be a way I could check on Bayley to make sure he was all right.

Closing my eyes again, I focused inward, feeling for my connection to Bayley.

I reached for my magic. To my delight and relief, my magic came when I called it, even without Bayley. I started with my Foster magic, figuring I could use it to trace the energy link between me and Bayley, the way I traced a plant's energy.

I visualized my mind as a dark void with me standing on one side of it. Reaching out with my Foster magic, I sighted the connection between me and Bayley almost instantly and let out a breath I hadn't realized I was holding.

My mind interpreted the connection between us as a sort of *Tron*-esque bright electric highway, similar in some ways to what I saw in plants. It connected me to a gold, glowing spot in my brain—Bayley.

Two things popped out at me. The gold spot was dim, and the energy flowing back and forth between me and Bayley was extremely sluggish. Every now and then, a single spark traveled the highway between us. The actual highway, the connection between us, was bright and unbroken. But the back-and-forth was almost nonexistent.

I thought about it for a minute. When I looked at a healthy growing plant, there were usually lots of flashes darting back and forth as energy traveled around the plant. What I was seeing between me and Bayley reminded me of what happened when a plant was hibernating for the winter.

I opened my eyes to find Fuzzy staring at me with concern.

"Bayley's okay, I think." It took me a second to realize I actually believed that. I added, "Our connection is still nice and strong. But he is, uh, offline."

Fuzzy pawed at me.

Guessing he was worrying about how I was doing, I responded, "Me? Um, I'm still not totally sure. What about you? I know you and Bayley talk all the time. Is this going to mess with you at all?"

Fuzzy said, "Meow meow," then groomed a spot on his coat.

Two meows in a row like that meant "no" so I said, "Glad you're okay. Hmm. I wonder what this is going to do to me."

A quick body scan told me the dizziness I'd felt earlier was gone, but I was way more tired than usual.

Slowly, I sat up. Fuzzy shifted so I could get off the couch.

I stood up carefully, took a few cautious steps, then proceeded to walk around the room a bit. "Well all my parts work." Yawning, I added, "But I feel like I want to sleep for a year."

I stopped pacing and did a mental check. I felt...weird. Expectant. Like a part of me was waiting for someone, keeping an eye on the spot where I expected them to arrive. Except instead of watching the door at a party, I was monitoring a part of my own mind.

Fuzzy chirped at me.

"I think I'm actually okay." I heard the surprise in my voice and qualified, "It just feels...different."

Fuzzy padded over to rub against my legs.

"Thanks for the support, Fuzzy. I think it's going to be really strange without Bayley around, so extra cuddles are much appreciated."

The wind gusted, rattling the window. Stepping closer, I was greeted by a curtain of falling snow. Snowflakes were racing each other to see who could reach the ground the fastest.

Part of the reason for the film noir marathon earlier was

because we'd tucked in to wait out the blizzard.

This was my first blizzard—not just my first blizzard in the house, but my first blizzard ever. I knew they could wreak a lot of havoc, downing trees and power lines. I caught myself wishing Bayley were around and then scolded myself. It wasn't like he could do anything about the weather even if he were online.

"I'm perfectly capable of monitoring the property myself," I said aloud.

Fuzzy gave me a look.

"Yes, I'm talking to myself. What? Lots of people talk to themselves. It doesn't mean I'm going crazy or anything."

Fuzzy blinked at me.

Ignoring the very catlike judgy look he was giving me, I decided to do a survey of the property.

I called up my mental map and did a double-take.

The more time I'd spent with Bayley, the clearer my mental map had become. Now, the high-def map with all the details I'd managed to fill in was gone. In its place was a basic, pixelated version.

"Well that's not great, but it could be worse," I said to Fuzzy. "My map may be eight-bit instead of high-res but at least I'm still connected."

Continuing to scan the mental map, I felt reassured that I could see the entire property. My map was still working, albeit not at full capacity. With the blizzard, I couldn't imagine anyone stopping by, but it was a relief to know that if someone tried to enter the property, I'd see them coming.

A sudden wave of fatigue washed over me.

Did simply looking at my mental map make me more tired?

If so, that wasn't good news.

I looked down at Fuzzy. "It's late. Why don't we try to get some rest?"

I was already in my pajamas so I dragged myself upstairs and flopped into bed.

Fuzzy bounded up and settled beside me.

I fell asleep trying to adjust to the feeling of life without Bayley.

Chapter Four

Falling snow feels as magical to me as falling stars.

At least, that's what I thought when I was awake.

My subconscious must not have agreed with this assessment because in the dream I was having, the snowflakes looked more like little ghosts that laughed at me as they flew by.

As their low, raspy laughs continued, some part of my brain realized that I was actually hearing something in the real world and incorporating it into my dream.

A thought floated up.

Why is someone in my room laughing at me?

Adrenaline kicked my conscious brain into gear, ripping me from my dream. Before I was even fully awake, I'd already slammed a magical shield around the bed.

My pounding heart sprinted me the rest of the way to consciousness so that I went from dead asleep to sitting straight up, wildly swiveling my head to identify the source of the emergency.

I thought I heard another chuckle, quieter this time. But a wide-eyed search of the room revealed no one but me and Fuzzy.

He should have been asleep. Fuzzy was still snuggled tight against me, but he was staring toward the window. Following his gaze, I caught movement outside.

Frost coated the windowpane, making it difficult to see. I'd almost convinced myself that there was nothing there, when skeletal fingers raked against the window.

I gasped, flinching back.

As I stared, the fingers turned into a branch, rattling and scratching against the glass, as though trying to break into the nice warm house.

The rest of my sleepy senses finally kicked in and registered the seething wind just as it chucked a fistful of snow that splatted against the window with a raspy hiss.

I let out a shaky laugh as I realized I was ducking like the snow could hit me. Shaking my head at myself, I said to Fuzzy, "False alarm. It's just the storm." Scrubbing my hands over my face, I swallowed my heart back down my throat and dropped the shield.

My mind might have sorted out that the wind was the source of the weird "laughter," but my body wasn't having it. I still felt like something was terribly wrong.

Only when Fuzzy gently nosed my hand did I notice my death-grip on the quilt. Forcing myself to unclench my hands, I tried to figure out why I felt so freaked out. I loved snow.

"Bayley, I—oh."

And with a stomach-clenching jolt, I remembered.

"Bayley?" I said tentatively.

Silence answered me back.

With a hollow feeling, I checked our connection, then murmured, "He's still gone. Guess it was unrealistic to hope that he'd be back so soon."

Fuzzy rested his head on my lap with a soft meow.

Unfortunately, a good night's sleep had done little to ease the shock of Bayley being gone. I tried to think about last night, but trying to sift through all the details Bayley had laid on me made my head buzz. When a headache started to build, I gave up dwelling on what had happened and focused on the present.

A cold gray light filtered in through the snow-crusted windows, but my room was plenty warm. And when I reached over to turn on the light, its cheery glow dispelled some of the gloom. "Bayley promised all his normal functions would still work. Looks like he was right."

I must've looked as lost as I felt because Fuzzy nudged me and said, "Meow?"

"I'm fine," I said automatically, then paused to think about it. "I'm tired. And I've got a bit of a headache." I shook my head.

I was a little medicine-heady, my mind kind of muzzy. I guessed it was my brain chemistry trying to adjust to its new state. "Overall, I just...feel a little weird. Okay a lot weird. Do you?"

"Meow," Fuzzy said, placing a paw on my leg.

I sighed, running a hand through my hair. "Between the weather and being Bayley-less, it's gonna be a really strange day all the way around. Might as well get up and get on with it."

I climbed out of bed and got dressed. I seriously considered staying in my pajamas, but I figured keeping to my normal routine was probably a good idea.

The clock told me that it was already nine a.m.

"Wow, we slept late, Fuzzy. And I'm already looking forward to taking a long nap. Guess it's a side effect from Bayley's absence."

Wondering what other fun aftereffects I should be expecting, I dragged my tired butt downstairs to the kitchen in search of some desperately needed coffee.

On my way through the mudroom, I noticed a small puddle of water around my boots. A quick check told me nothing was leaking, and I realized I must not have stomped all the ice off yesterday.

The puddle really bothered me, and at first, I couldn't figure out why. Then, I realized that if Bayley were around, he'd have whisked the water away so I wouldn't need to deal with it. The puddle was an example of what I suspected would be a constant set of reminders of just how integrated my and Bayley's lives had become and how much his absence would affect me, in big and small ways.

I fetched a towel from the kitchen, dried the floor, then went about making breakfast.

As I set the coffee to brew, I had a hankering for a Shake-It-Off.

I said to Fuzzy, "Do you think unusual cravings are a normal part of this separation?" While I put food in his bowl, I puzzled it through. "I usually only drink a shake to recover from using too much magic. Maybe without Bayley here, my body feels the difference in our bond as a kind of magical drain. I mean, I've got a full party-girl-the-morning-after thing going on, hold the actual party."

Fuzzy stared at me. I had the sense that he was trying to communicate something to me, but without Bayley to interpret, I wasn't sure what Fuzzy wanted to say.

With a small huff, Fuzzy gave up on staring in favor of nudging me toward the fridge. When I started taking out the ingredients for the shake, he stopped glaring at me and chowed down on his own breakfast.

"As usual, you're right, Fuzzy. If I'm craving it, I should just go ahead and drink it. It's not like it'll do me any harm."

While my coffeepot chugged away, I made myself a Shake-It-Off and took it to the kitchen window to drink.

Greeting my lavender plant, I said, "Good morning, Sprout. Looks like the storm's almost done getting its ya-yas out." The snow had calmed from mosh pit to slow dance, and the wind was only half-heartedly tapping at the windows. "Still Sprout, I bet you're glad you're in here all toasty and not outside today."

Sipping my shake, I turned my attention to studying the yard.

I barely recognized it. Mounds of snow had redesigned the landscape into a foreign territory. The normally flat, grassy backyard had been transformed into a series of hills and valleys separated by stretches of empty, white plains.

"Look at this, Fuzzy. Isn't it amazing that tiny little snow-flakes can gang up like this to totally rewrite the world?"

Fuzzy hopped up on the counter next to me and stared out the window.

In some places, only the tops of the garden's fence posts were visible, peeping out from under their rumpled snow hats.

"Geez guys, I wonder how deep it is?" I realized I was including Bayley in the conversation and sighed. It was going to be an uncomfortable day for sure, despite the cozy weather. I redirected my conversation to Fuzzy, pointing as I said, "If the snow stops, maybe we can go out later." My gaze snagged on the greenhouse, and I felt a sudden concern for the Grack.

"I hope the Grack and her babies are okay. I know we've got the backup spell in place to make sure the greenhouse doesn't lose any heat, but I can't help being a little concerned. I mean, even you have to admit those Gracklettes are cute."

Fuzzy gave me a look that told me I was nuts.

I could see his point. The Grack looked like a big, craggy rock, and the babies looked a bit like pebbles. I still thought they were cute.

My coffee gurgled at me, cheerfully signaling its readiness. I sucked back the last bit of the Shake-It-Off and poured myself a cup of steaming java. As I enjoyed my first sip, I said to Fuzzy, "Looks like it's going to be a nice, quiet, relaxing day with just the two of us."

Chapter Five

I should've known better.

Instead of finding the quiet relaxing, the longer I stood drinking my coffee, the more I hunched up, until I was curled over my mug like I was trying to keep someone from stealing it.

I shook my head. Usually, I liked the calm, but today it was like Quiet had gone on vacation, and its mean older brother Silence had taken its place. I couldn't shake a sense of anxiety, like I was missing something, like I should be doing something.

Truth was, I had plenty to do. I had mounds of magical textbooks to study, and there were always TV, movies, music, the Internet, or a novel to distract me. Yet I couldn't seem to motivate myself to do any of those things. I stood frozen in the kitchen, clutching my mug like it was a lifeline.

With a huff at my own silliness, I tried to walk off some of the itchiness by pacing around the kitchen. But I couldn't shake the tightness in my stomach that made me feel like something was off. Logically, I knew that it had to be a reaction to my lack of contact with Bayley, but telling myself that did absolutely zippo to ease my anxiety. If anything, it made it worse.

"Nope," I said out loud. Hearing my voice bouncing back to me in the empty kitchen helped shatter the oppressive spell. "I'm not doing this. I've been alone in the house—okay, not this house, but the diner—plenty of times. And I actually love that feeling of having the run of the place. So I'm going to enjoy my Bayley-free time too and not get freaked out by it."

But I couldn't help checking my connection to Bayley. I was a little ashamed at the amount of relief that poured through me when I saw him still there, faintly, in the far corner of my mind.

With a little more clanging than strictly necessary, I cleaned the kitchen. The clattering of pots and pans soothed me enough that my stomach unclenched.

But the second I stopped, the silence slid back into the room. Its presence was so visceral that my shoulder blades started to twitch like I was being watched. I found myself looking over my shoulder to see if someone was behind me.

Of course, no one was there.

Fuzzy looked at me, then looked at the empty spot behind me, then back at me.

"Yes, I know nothing's there. I'm just jumpy. I suppose it's to be expected."

But the third time I caught myself checking behind me, I decided maybe I needed to ease my way into my new solo time.

I started with the person most likely to understand what Bayley was doing. I dialed my neighbor Zo, who answered with, "What's wrong?"

"Nothing's exactly wrong."

She waited in silence.

"Well, Bayley's sort of offline for a bit. Actually, I'm surprised you didn't call me or show up here. Usually when something new happens on the property, you pop up."

"Mmm," Zo said. "What happened?"

I repeated to her all the stuff that Bayley had explained about him leaving.

"And after he left, what happened?"

"I went to sleep." I thought back to the night before. "Ugh," I said, rubbing my temple.

"Problem?"

"No. At least I don't think so. It's some kind of reaction. When I try to think about Bayley leaving, I get a headache."

A pause, then, "What do you remember?"

I recounted my conversation with Bayley before he left, ending with, "Bottom line is that the property is on a basic lockdown for now, which will increase in severity the longer he's gone."

Zo grunted then said, "Beside the headache, how are you feeling?"

"I think I'm okay. I'm a little cotton-headed and tired. And it's…odd…being here without Bayley." Hastily I added, "I totally support what he's doing. It's just a big adjustment."

After a pause she added, "I'm not surprised Bayley decided to try an upgrade with you as Housekeeper." There was an odd resignation in her voice. Before I could ask her about it, she said, "But the piece I'm missing is why now? You've got plenty of time. Your birthday isn't until September."

"No it isn't. It's in three weeks."

"What? You're sure?"

"Well, yeah," I laughed. "I think I know when my own birthday is. And I didn't even tell you yet the part about Bayley leaving as a result of my birthday. How did you know?"

"I just do." There was a brief silence, followed by a half-muttered, "Three weeks. No wonder Bayley took off so suddenly."

"Why did you think my birthday was in September? We've never even talked about it before."

"It's in your file."

"My file?"

"Your Foster file," she clarified.

"How did *you* get a look at my Foster file?"

"That's your question? The more interesting issue is why your birthday is listed wrong. That's…unlikely." Her voice went distant, like she was talking to herself. "The Fosters must have found out your mother was pregnant, and she must've fudged the details around your birth. Interesting."

"She did *what?*"

"I'm just guessing here, but it seems fairly obvious that your parents obfuscated the date of your birth."

I said sarcastically, "Sure they did. That makes perfect sense."

Except when I thought about it for a minute, it sort of did. It fit with the whole "hiding Finn from the magic world" thing my parents had had going on.

Like a bunch of loose sheep, all my unresolved questions

about my parents started baaing loudly and running around my mind. Unwilling to be distracted, I shooed them all to the side and forced myself to focus on the matter at hand.

"We can discuss my parents' hijinks later. Right now, I'm wondering what else I need to know about this situation. Bayley explained everything before he left, but he was in such a hurry, I want to make sure I really understand what's happening to him. Can you tell me anything more about what he's doing?"

"What makes you think I know?"

"Because you always seem to know stuff."

"Mmm."

"Okay, well, do you at least know if there's anything I can do to help Bayley?"

Zo sighed. "Bayley is on his own."

I groaned. "I hate that. Okay. Is there anything I should avoid doing?" A frisson of panic sliced through me as I blurted, "I'm still okay to practice magic, right?" I'd been making so much progress. The thought of losing ground made my heart skip a beat.

"Yes, doing magic is fine."

"Anything to avoid?"

"Don't die." And she hung up.

I looked down at Fuzzy. "I'm not sure if that was helpful."

Fuzzy rubbed his head against my leg, and I patted him.

We stood like that for a few moments.

The silence came strutting forward like a gangster ready for a shakedown. It was like it had been leaning against the wall, arms crossed, watching me and biding its time. Now it stepped up and glared at me.

I glanced toward the basement door. If it weren't winter, Sibeta and her people would likely be in the pool in the basement, and I could go hang out with them. But since it had gotten really cold, they'd all stopped coming by. From what I could gather from Sibeta, they were sort of hibernating, and though she didn't say it explicitly, I got the feeling that I shouldn't bug them unless it was really necessary.

Thinking about Sibeta's absence just made my headache worse.

Between the headache and the offness of everything, my nerves jangled.

"You know what I need, Fuzzy? I need to continue on like I normally would." Glancing out the window I said, "The snow has finally stopped. Let's go practice some magic."

Chapter Six

Fuzzy stepped in front of me, blocking me from going to the mudroom.

I frowned at him. "Zo said it's okay for me to practice magic while Bayley's offline. I'll be careful—I won't pull any energy from him or overdo it to the point where it might worry him."

Fuzzy hopped up on the kitchen counter next to where the dishes were drying. He batted at the cup I'd used to drink the Shake-It-Off earlier.

"Oh! You're not worried about Bayley. You're worried about me." I chewed my lip. "Okay, you have a point. I am a lot more tired than usual. But," Fuzzy laid his ears back slightly and started swishing his tail, so I held up a finger and said, "hear me out. This is a really good opportunity to see what I can do without Bayley. I mean, when am I ever going to have this kind of opportunity again? Never. And he could be back any minute, so I should take advantage of this chance to do magic without him while I can. Right?"

Fuzzy looked at the ceiling, like he was praying for patience.

"I promise not to overdo it. Really."

With a little huff, Fuzzy leapt down from the counter and padded toward the mudroom, chittering softly the whole way.

Following him, I said, "Thank you for looking out for me." As I donned my winter gear, I said, "It's supposed to be my day to practice Foster magic, so let's go to the greenhouse." As soon as I thought of the greenhouse, the need to check on the Grack tugged at me. "Besides, like I said earlier, we should look in on the Grack and the Gracklettes after the storm."

Fuzzy gave a firm, "Meow." The Grack wasn't his favorite person—their relationship was tolerant but not warm—so I was a little surprised by his prompt agreement.

We headed outside, but we didn't get very far. Normally, Bayley would have kept the porch clear. But now it looked like a bunch of snowdrifts had partied too hard and passed out. Everywhere I looked, there were waist-high snowbanks drunkenly listing this way and that.

As I eyed the snow, I realized that a section was way less deep than the rest. Looking more closely, I spotted a sort of trough running from the door, across the porch, and in a straight line to the greenhouse.

"It looks almost like someone cleared a path halfway through the night," I muttered, "and now it's partly covered over with snow." Squinting at the path made my headache worse, so I turned to face Fuzzy. "Bayley isn't here, and I'm fairly certain I didn't sleepwalk and shovel a path. Do you know if the Grack did this?" I asked, rubbing at my temple.

"Meow."

"Did you tell her that Bayley is gone?"

Fuzzy stared at me.

I shook my head and said, "Doesn't matter. Whatever her motivation, it was really nice of her to make a start on a path. It'll make clearing the rest of the snow that much easier. I'll have to thank her when we get to the greenhouse."

Gauging the distance between the porch and the greenhouse, I said, "Guess it's going to be a Smith day today. I know today is supposed to be a Foster day, but this is a good practical exercise. I can use my Smith magic to melt the snow. You should hang back, just in case I mess up."

Maybe it was the fatigue or the headache, but instead of slipping into my usual focused state, as I began to call on my magic, my mind drifted back.

I was sitting in the kitchen with Neil Guthrie on one of his mandatory "make it up to Finn" days. A few months back, Neil had stalked me with the intention of hurting me. But it hadn't exactly been his fault. Someone had brainwashed him into thinking I was responsible for his father's death and that he must get revenge.

Only sixteen, Neil had been an easy target. They'd manipulated Neil's grief and anger at his father's death into full-blown homicidal rage. The fact that Neil's form of Guthrie air magic allowed him to cast top-notch illusions made him an excellent weapon. We'd managed to stop Neil from doing me—or himself—any harm. However, we hadn't caught the jerk who brainwashed him.

Neil had needed a lot of help. So my friends Lou, Pete, and Zo had been working with Neil to deprogram him and help him heal.

Part of that was the "make it up to Finn" days, where Neil, an incredibly powerful magic user, tutored me, a newbie. It gave him a chance to see that I wasn't the Root of All Evil, not to mention that it also helped him to grow skills like confidence and patience. On my end, I got the chance to learn from a powerful Guthrie. So far, it seemed to be working. I was learning, and his feelings about me had ratcheted down from murderous wrath to teenage disdain.

On this particular day, as usual, he'd been scowling at me. "I don't get what your problem is."

I was holding onto my patience so hard that even my fists were clenched. Trying not to growl back at him, I said for the hundredth time, "It's easy for you. I don't have the years of experience you do."

Neil shook his head, crossed his arms, and leaned his chair back until he was balancing it on two legs, then rocked the chair as he spoke. "I don't think lack of experience is the real problem here. I mean, that's part of it. But there's something basic about magic that you're just not getting."

"Oh yeah, and what's that?"

He shrugged, "Hell if I know." With another shrug, he added, "Maybe you're just not a very good student."

Before I could censor myself, I snapped back, "Maybe you're just not a good tutor."

Neil snorted. "Like you've got a lot of options."

As much as it pained me, he was right.

Bayley sighed around us.

Taking a deep breath, I rolled my shoulders until they unhinged from my ears and tried again. "I get that you pull on your Guthrie magic to cast an illusion. The part where I'm getting stuck is understanding how you manipulate your magic to create certain effects. So, for example, can you make this," I pointed to the book in front of me, "look like something else?"

Still balancing on his chair, Neil glanced at the book, and it suddenly looked like a bowl of fruit.

I said, "Okay, so how did you get the magic to work?"

"How do you get your plant magic to work? Or your magic with Bayley?"

"Those are kind of the same thing. Carmine taught me to look for the energy in plants. And I see the, er, magical energy between me and Bayley. But they're alive. Air isn't. Neither is water or fire, really. So I don't understand how you guys do what you do." Neil didn't know I could wield any of those magics, so I added, "I need to be able to do more with my Foster magic than just play with plants. Some Fosters can do things with dirt and rocks. I want to be able to do that too."

Neil chewed his lip. "So you're visualizing your magic?"

"I guess."

"I can work with that." He thumped the front legs of his chair onto the floor and leaned his arms on the table. "What does your Foster magic look like?"

"It's green."

"Does it have a feeling?"

Surprised, I said, "Actually yes. It's...sort of tingly."

He nodded. "Okay, when I work with my Guthrie magic I can both feel it and visualize it too. So it's not that different."

"But how do you get it to do stuff?"

"I tell it to. It's like..." he stared at the ceiling as he searched for an analogy, "sculpting, I guess. I sculpt images with my magic." He looked proud of himself for putting that into words, nodding to emphasize his point.

"Argh!" I thunked my head onto my notebook. "I understand

that works for you, but it doesn't work for me. I need something more specific."

Neil nodded vigorously. "Now you're getting it. You need something specific to *you*. Your relationship with your magic is personal. So what's second nature to you?"

"I don't know. Cooking?" popped out of my mouth. I was being sarcastic, so I was surprised when he started nodding again.

"Sure, why not? Cook with your magic."

And oddly enough, that had worked. Something had clicked in my brain. I started working with my magic the same way I worked with recipes.

A snowflake landed on my nose dragging me back to the present.

"Right, focus Finn." Centering myself, I set up a "stew" spell. I'd been using this framework for anything that needed to stay actively "simmering" for a while.

I called up a strand of my Smith magic as my "batter." It felt sluggish, which wasn't totally surprising given my overall low energy.

Starting with a small stream the width of my pinkie finger, I began "pouring" the magic into the air around me. Next, I "kneaded" it into shape, pushing and pulling the magic where I wanted it, using a combination of my mind and my will.

Usually I made a rough ball around me when I worked a heater spell, but now I made a wedge, with the pointy end facing forward. Finally, I set the whole thing to a medium "simmer," drizzling a slow but steady trickle of Smith magic into the wedge around me and Fuzzy.

I stepped forward, moving my wedge with me. The snow started to melt, but reluctantly.

"Hmm," I said to Fuzzy. "I'm going to have to ramp up the heat level to scalding to melt the snow. That's a ton of energy." I pursed my lips. "Okay, let's try Guthrie instead."

I released my Smith magic, and I called up my Guthrie magic. Maybe it was just me getting warmed up, but it seemed to come much easier than the Smith magic had.

I made the stream of magic about a thumb's width, and

then whipped the magic until it was a nice, frothy batter—light, like a meringue. I shoved forward, and the snow scattered into a cloud in front us, blinding me.

Dropping the magic quickly, I swiped at the snow on my face.

"Mrrwrrwrr!" complained Fuzzy, as he shook snow off his fur from behind me.

"Sorry! That didn't go as planned. I think I need a different stirring method. I can see now where whipping would…well, do what it just did." I thought for a few seconds. "Mmm, so a meringue is the wrong way to look at this." What I wanted was to push the snow up and off to the side of the existing path.

"Okay, instead of whipping, I think what I need is kind of like folding an omelet. Scoop up the bottom, fold it over the top. Yes, that'll do it."

Starting again, I folded in waves of magic. To my delight, the Guthrie magic shoved a gust of wind into the snow in front of us, then swept it to the left, thereby mostly re-clearing the porch section of the path that the Grack had made. I sent a second, gentler wind to shift the remaining snow. Stepping to the edge of the porch, I repeated the same action, and cleared a small part of the path onto the lawn.

As we worked our way across the backyard to the greenhouse, I experimented with the size of the Guthrie magical energy I was pulling and the amount of wind I was gusting.

By the time we made it to the greenhouse, my feet were dragging, but my success had painted a huge smile on my face.

Stepping into the warm greenhouse, I released my hold on the Guthrie magic with a thank you. I didn't really think the magic was sentient, but it felt important to treat it with respect and not take it for granted.

"What do you think I should call this recipe, Fuzzy? The 'eggscellent snow shovel' maybe?"

Fuzzy shook his head and stalked off.

"Everyone's a critic," I mumbled, heading for the back to have a look at the Grack and the Gracklettes.

"Hi there," I called as I approached.

The Grack waved an appendage at me. I took it as a huge

compliment that she felt comfortable enough with me now that she didn't feel like she had to get up and formally greet me. Poor mama was probably tired with all those little ones to look after, and I was glad she stayed resting where she was, with all the Gracklettes gathered around her. Better yet, she let me approach her babies without feeling the need to get between me and them.

With Bayley's help, we'd worked out a rudimentary sign language to help us communicate. I held out both hands, palms up, while out loud I asked, "How are you?"

She gave me a single wave above her head indicating that she and the babies were fine.

"Glad to hear it." I gave her a thumbs-up. I took a moment to admire the Gracklettes. Pointing to the babies, I used the American Sign Language sign for "pretty," swiping my fingers down my face. "Gosh, they sure are cute."

The Grack rocked back and forth a bit, which I'd come to recognize as her Proud Mama reaction.

She looked at me and waved two appendages, bottom side up.

"Me? No, I don't need anything," I said, signaling "no" by shaking my head and signing "no," and then I signed "thank you" by touching my chin.

"Fuzzy?" I called.

Fuzzy padded over to stand slightly behind me.

I looked over my shoulder at him. "Fuzzy, can you make sure the Grack understands that Bayley is offline temporarily? And let me know if she has any concerns?"

Fuzzy gave me a long look, sighed, then turned to face the Grack.

They sat there, conversing silently for so long that I started to worry. A few times, Fuzzy looked at me, then back at the Grack. At one point, his tail started swishing back and forth, and then his ears went back, and I thought maybe they were arguing for some reason, and I was going to have to intervene. The Grack wasn't Fuzzy's favorite person, but they hadn't argued in months.

I was just about to interject when Fuzzy mumbled, followed

by a chuff, and the Grack signaled me, "I'm fine," again.

I looked down at Fuzzy. "That took a lot longer than it should've. Is she really okay?"

"Meow."

"And she understands about Bayley?"

"Meow."

"Okay." Looking at the Grack, I said, "Glad you're fine with everything. I'll be over here if you need me," I said pointing.

The Grack waved goodbye, and I headed to my usual workbench at the front of the greenhouse. Fatigue pulled at me, and I could practically hear my coffeepot calling to me, so I only did a quick check on the plants, watered those that needed it, and headed back out calling a, "Have a nice day!" to the Grack as I left.

As Fuzzy and I trudged along the path toward the house, my Best magic tugged at me. This happened sometimes when I used more than one magic—the others sometimes seemed to want a turn too.

I felt another tug and stopped in the middle of the path, looking at the woods to the left. I used my meringue setting again—light and fluffy as a cloud, gentle and sweet—to search for animals.

I didn't see anything obvious that would have tweaked my Best instincts. In fact, the only real thing of interest on that side was the graveyard, though as far as I knew, my Best magic had zero interest in dead people.

As soon as I thought of the graveyard, for a brief flash, something nagged at my mind. But when I tried to catch the thought, it disappeared again. Of course, any time I thought about the graveyard, my mind got squirrelly. As though taking my thoughts literally, my magic detected a squirrel tucked up tight in a nest just inside the tree line. Almost immediately, I found another squirrel and a couple of birds.

I spent a few more minutes searching the woods, relieved when nothing unusual popped up on my radar. By the time I released my Best magic, I felt happy and satisfied, though tired. My stamina had increased enough over the last few months that even tired, I could work multiple branches of magic without harming myself or Bayley.

Smiling in satisfaction, I said, "C'mon Fuzzy. Let's go have some dinner and watch one of Bayley's favorite film noir movies."

Chapter Seven

Fatigue walloped me about halfway through the movie, and I passed out on the couch.

I found myself standing in the snow outside of a house. I became aware that I was dreaming, which was unusual for me. I'd been having lucid dreams more often since becoming Housekeeper, but they weren't a regular thing.

Staring at the house, somehow I was sure it was Bayley. Although, in the way of dreams, he looked different than usual. Instead of the three-story house I was accustomed to, Bayley was a small, single-floored cabin. There was still a seating area out front, but it was on the ground—more of a covered deck than the current raised porch.

Surveying the area around me, I saw that I was in the front yard. It looked weird too. Same shape and size, but around the edges of the grove, the trees staring down at me looked unfamiliar.

I tried to turn around to look at the sentinel trees, Todd and Libby, that guarded the entrance to the grove, but I fell over. As I landed with a crunch, I realized I'd been standing in several feet of snow.

Slowly, I sat up. I was dressed in a t-shirt, jeans, and sneakers, and as soon as I realized it, the cold began biting at me.

Clambering awkwardly to my feet, I chuckled to myself as I brushed the snow off my torso. I would've thought that my brain's way of dealing with the snow outside would be to conjure the nice, hot desert in my dreams. Instead, it just created more snow for me to deal with.

Rubbing my arms to keep warm, I trudged toward the house. It was harder than I anticipated. My legs sank into the snow well past my knees, forcing me to wade through it like an awkward robot.

After several minutes of intense slogging, I was panting with effort. I looked up at the house and stopped short.

Bayley wasn't any closer.

Looking over my shoulder, I could see the trail I'd blazed from the center of the lawn to where I stood. I turned back to face Bayley, frowning. Given how far I'd walked, I should've already been at the porch.

"Hey Bayley, a little help please?"

Something niggled at the edge of my mind—something I was supposed to remember.

"Bayley?"

He didn't respond, but for some reason, this didn't seem odd to me.

With a huff, I started walking again, this time keeping my eyes on the house as I plowed my way forward.

I kept moving, but the house never got any nearer.

A shiver ripped through me. This winter, I'd quickly learned that you could work up quite a sweat exercising in the cold. Given how hard I was working to hike through the snow, I should have been sweating by now.

Instead, I was getting colder by the minute.

And then I realized my hands and feet were nearly numb.

I tucked my hands under my armpits, hunched over to try to conserve as much warmth as I could, and redoubled my efforts to make my way to Bayley.

I went twice as fast as before, huffing and puffing with the exertion.

Bayley remained where he was at a distance.

I had a sudden image of me becoming an ice sculpture on the front lawn.

"Bayley," I called. "I could really use some help."

The house remained dark and impassive.

Dimly, my waking mind tried to remind my dream brain

that Bayley was currently unavailable, but dream me wasn't having it.

"Bayley!" I called, struggling toward him.

No response.

Suddenly the snow was chest high, and I felt like I was trying not to drown. Swimming through the snow, cold gnawing at the skin on my arms, I frantically tried to make it to the porch.

Turning sideways, I tried shouldering a path. But when I stopped and looked up, the snow in front of me had grown into a huge wall that totally blocked my view of Bayley.

For a fraction of a second, dismay froze me in place, but it quickly changed to horror as the wall toppled on top of me.

Gasping for air, I sat straight up. It took me a second to realize that I was still on the couch, and I'd been dreaming. A shiver rocked me, and I realized I was drenched in sweat.

"Meow?" said Fuzzy, standing next to the couch, front paw on my leg.

"Bad dream," I said, scrubbing my hands over my face. "Weird, bad dream." Images from my nightmare flickered through my mind. "I think," I said slowly, "that it's an anxiety dream. I'm having separation anxiety from Bayley."

Great. Did that mean I was going to have nightmares the entire time he was gone?

This Bayley downtime was getting better by the minute.

Chapter Eight

I tried to go back to sleep, but I was too riled up and sweaty. A glance at the clock told me that it was nearly my usual time to get up anyway.

"I guess I'm getting my day started a little early," I said with all the enthusiasm of a student about to take a pop quiz.

I peeled myself off the couch, took a shower, and then went through my usual checklist of making coffee, feeding Fuzzy, and making breakfast for myself. Where yesterday, I'd missed Bayley's external presence, today I was noticing how strange it was to be alone in my own head.

Although I was used to Bayley retreating to a corner of my mind to give me space when I needed it, he'd never been quiet this long. It'd been six months of sharing mind space with Bayley, and being alone again felt abnormal.

I told myself that was ridiculous, but it didn't make me feel any less out of whack.

So instead of eating in the kitchen per usual, I went to the living room and turned on the TV for company.

It helped. Right up until the forecast came on.

When I groaned, Fuzzy came padding into the room.

"Fuzzy, it's going to be super cold today with a wind chill well below zero. I think we need to stay inside."

Fuzzy muttered at me.

Now that Fuzzy had grown to be mid-calf high, he hated being inside all day even more than he had when he was smaller. He reminded me of a German shepherd—he needed to get out in the fresh air, get some exercise, and check the perimeter while he was at it.

"If you really want to go out, you can, but it'll have to be quick, or you'll have to wear the booties."

If Fuzzy turned the look that he gave me on the frigid air, it'd be summer outside in no time.

"It's not my fault the weather sucks. We're just going to have to do the best we can."

Still muttering, Fuzzy stalked to the edge of the room and lay down in the doorway, his butt facing me.

Who says you need words to communicate?

I tried to watch the morning TV programs. I did. But the fourth time I looked at the clock and only fifteen minutes had passed, I chucked that idea and decided the better thing to do would be to keep busy in a more usual way.

"Fuzzy, I'm going to do some baking. You're welcome to come with me if you like."

Fuzzy didn't respond, but he did follow me into the kitchen and settle down in a corner.

Before I began, I pulled my necklace out. "Percy?"

A pause then, "What?"

"I'm doing some baking. What music would you like today?"

Another pause, then a hesitant, "How much time do you have?"

"Well, I'm going to make several batches of cookies, so I'll be at least a couple of hours. You have time to listen to any number of things all the way through."

"I need a moment to think."

"No problem. Take your time." As Percy contemplated his music choices, I began setting out all the things I'd need for the cookies. While I worked, my mind drifted back to my recent discovery about Percy.

That day, Percy had opened a door to return Carmine home after a visit. It was no different than any other time I'd asked Percy to help out. I'd placed the necklace against the pantry door, the seed sprouted into a handle, and Percy used his magic so that when I opened the door, I was looking into Carmine's bedroom instead of the pantry.

But on this particular day, I'd noticed that Percy seemed more unhappy than usual. For some time, I'd been pondering his ongoing tendency to treat me like I had cooties. At first, it was understandable that he'd be reticent. He didn't really know me. I mean, he'd been with my family for years, but he'd never interacted with us, so far as I knew. He'd only started talking with me when I accidentally woke him up by bleeding all over him—something he referred to as me "feeding him my blood," which squicked me out big time.

But since he'd been awake, he'd had plenty of time to observe me and Bayley and our friends. We were a friendly group, so I didn't understand why he was still so avoidant. I tried to give him privacy—not everyone is an extrovert. But he took the whole misanthrope thing to a level that would have Oscar the Grouch raising an eyebrow.

I hated that a key member of my household was so unhappy all the time. And on that day, his extra level of misery pushed me over the edge.

After Carmine was safely home, and we'd closed the door again, I said, "Percy, we need to talk." When he didn't respond, per usual, I added, "I actually mean 'we.' You need to be a part of this conversation." When he still didn't say anything I shook the necklace, repeating, "Percy, Percy, Percy," until he growled, "Alright!"

"Good. Let's chat."

"I'm atwitter with anticipation."

Putting the necklace down on the kitchen table, I sat in front of it.

Now that I had his attention, though, I wasn't sure how to start.

Choosing my words carefully, I said, "So remember that one time when you mentioned you weren't in the necklace by your own choice?"

No answer.

I poked the necklace, "Percy."

An irritated, "Yes."

I sighed. I really hoped he wasn't going to be monosyllabic

the whole conversation, or we wouldn't get very far. "Do you want to tell me how you came to be in there?" I asked, gently nudging the necklace.

"No."

Well, at least that answer came fast.

My fingers drummed the table. "Percy, this may come as a surprise to you, but it bothers me that you seem so unhappy. Today, in particular, you seem extra miserable. Is there anything I can do?"

There was another long pause, and I was just about to poke him again when Percy said, "I don't understand."

He did, indeed, sound confused. But more than that, he sounded suspicious.

"What is it you don't understand?" I said, using the soothing voice I use for skittish animals that might bite.

"Why? Why would you want to do anything?"

Now it was my turn to be confused. "I'm sorry?"

Percy made an aggravated sound. "What's your angle?"

"My angle?"

"What do you want, Finn," Percy said, exasperated. "Just tell me what it is that you want. That's what you usually do. No need to go changing things up now."

Guilt crawled up my throat and choked my voice for a moment. I did usually boss Percy around, mostly because it was the only way to get him to respond to me.

"I'm truly sorry if you feel used," I began.

"Don't be. I'm a tool. That's what you do with tools." He was so matter-of-fact that I was stunned into silence. I couldn't tell if he was lashing out at me, or if he was just being honest. But there was some truth to what he was saying, and it made me feel ashamed.

Bayley felt my discomfort, and the house growled around us.

I shook my head. "He's right Bayley, at least in part. We do treat him like a tool."

My mind scrambling, I said, "Percy, you are more than just a thing to be used. I'm so sorry if I made you feel that way. You're a person, of sorts. I'm not sure what kind of sorts because you won't tell me what you are, but you're certainly a sentient being." I folded my hands in front of me on the table. "I've come to think of you as part of our team. You'd given me the impression that you were okay with that. Has that changed?"

"No."

Relief loosened the knot of guilt a little. "Okay then. To be clear, you're still fine with opening doors?"

"Yes."

No hesitation there. He sounded certain.

"Do you enjoy it?"

I didn't think he was going to answer when he muttered, "It's the only time I get to do what I do. Just a little. But it's better than nothing."

I waited, but he didn't elaborate. I felt lucky that he'd shared that much, so I didn't push him.

"Well it sounds like it's mostly a good thing for you then. Which brings me back around to my initial question. I'm trying to figure out what we can do to make your life a little more enjoyable." I chewed my lip. "I don't know if it's possible, but did you want to, I don't know, try and leave the necklace?"

"No! No no no. Put that out of your head!"

I held up my hands in surrender. "Okay, okay. No problem. If that's a nonstarter, then what else can I do for you?"

"Like what?"

"I don't know!" I threw up my hands in frustration. "I know almost nothing about you! Are you a catlike creature and I should be leaving the necklace in the sun periodically so you can bask? Are you part vampire, and I should leave you in a drawer once in a while so you can lurk in the dark? I literally have no idea here. Help me out Percy."

Mentioning vampires made me think of how I'd woken him up. I really, really hoped he didn't say, "You know, actually, it'd be great if you fed me some more of your blood."

Ick.

"I don't know," said Percy crossly.

"Is that true? You really don't know? Or do you not want to say? I swear I have no hidden agenda here, other than the fact that I'm a little worried about you. You seem, I don't know, sad or something."

"You're making a colossal deal out of nothing," said Percy irritably.

Ah hah! So there *was* something bothering him. "Well if it's nothing, then you won't mind telling me what the deal is then, right?"

Percy gave me a sigh so long and so put upon that teenagers everywhere were probably taking notes.

"Fiiiiiiine. I just..." and he mumbled the rest.

"I'm sorry I didn't catch that," I said leaning over the table.

"This is dumb."

"Yup, you said that already. And?"

"The song. I didn't get to hear the end of the song. Alright? Happy now?"

I furrowed my brows. "What song?"

"Oh for the love of Pete," said Percy, using one of my favorite expressions. "There was music. In the greenhouse. When you were with Carmine. You shut it off when you left."

My eyebrows shot up. Of all the things I could have imagined Percy would say, this was not even on the list.

Carmine loved classical music. In fact, he loved it so much that we'd installed a sound system in the greenhouse so he could listen to music while we worked together.

I asked, "You like classical music in particular or music in general?"

"Classical music? Is that what you call what Carmine listens to?"

"Yes."

"Then yes, that. The other musics are interesting as well. But the classical. The intricate structures," Percy said, longing in his voice. "I find studying the structures...appealing."

"And you were...studying the structure...of whatever was playing, and we shut it off?"

"Right near the end. At least I think it was near the

end," he grumbled. "I don't know for sure how the structure resolved! I can posit a guess to its completion, but I will never be sure now."

"Percy, that sucks! Why didn't you just tell us? We would've been happy to wait till the song ended."

Percy sniffed, "And owe you a favor? I think not."

I blinked at him for a moment. "You think I'd make you owe me a favor just for letting you finish listening to a song?" His silence was its own answer. "Oh Percy," I shook my head. "That's...heartbreaking. That's no way to live." And I added quietly, "Not to mention I thought you'd have a better under-standing of me as a person by now."

I sighed deeply. "Well, I can't do much about your char-acter judgment skills, but I can help with the music thing. If you like classical music so much, it's not a big deal to play it in regular rotation for you. Heck, we can even try to set up regular listening times so you have something to look forward to. And if you tell me which bits you like particularly, I can find out who the composers are and find other works by them. We can branch out from there."

Percy sounded agitated. "Why would you do this?"

I tried for patience. "Percy, don't be an idiot. You're a lot of things, but I don't think that obtuse is one of them. You live here. You know that everyone here gets to do stuff they like without owing me or anyone else any favors. Why should you be any different?" I leaned forward and said, "Like it or not, pal, you're part of this little family we've got going. I'm not sure if you're the grumpy uncle or what, but you're part of the group nonetheless. If I've learned anything from talking to you today it's that I need to be more considerate of you and more inclusive."

And I'd kept my word. For the past couple of months, I'd started playing classical music at regular intervals. Percy was still grouchy, but now, once in a while, he'd speak up without being prompted, to comment on the music.

Percy interrupted my musing when he said, "I'd like to listen to that Boston Symphony Orchestra concert again, this time the whole way through."

I set aside my mixing bowl to put the music on for him as I said, "Sure thing."

After a short pause, I heard a quiet, "Thank you."

"You're welcome," I said, then settled into making cookies as the music swelled around us.

Chapter Nine

As the last cookie batches came out of the oven, I gathered the ones that'd already cooled and went to freeze them.

"Oh dear." A full freezer stared back at me. After a couple of minutes of brainstorming options, it occurred to me that I had an enormous second freezer at my disposal.

Dashing outside, I stowed the containers of cookies in a snowbank on the porch, then returned to the kitchen to make lunch.

While I sat at the table eating, the same somebody's-watching-me sensation I'd had yesterday came back. Once again, I kept looking over my shoulder. And once again, Fuzzy followed my gaze, looked behind me, then stared at me, which I took to be his way of saying, "Human, there's nothing there. What's so interesting?"

I tried to ignore my discomfort, but after I finished the lunch dishes, I caught myself standing in the middle of the kitchen, hand pressed to my chest like a damsel in distress.

Maybe something really was wrong, and I was missing it.

Fuzzy wound his way around my legs and asked, "Meow?"

Shaking my head, I said, "You know what? I'm being silly. If something feels off, I'm perfectly capable of checking it out by myself."

Plopping myself back down at the kitchen table, I closed my eyes and settled into the breathing pattern I used to access my magic. My thoughts wanted to dash around like overexcited puppies, but I eventually managed to get them to sit and behave.

I called up my mental map. It still looked pretty janky, but I could see enough to make sure nothing had gone haywire.

I started where the driveway met the road. If someone was going to cause trouble, that was the most likely spot for them to enter.

Nothing seemed out of place.

I followed the driveway all the way back to the house.

Still nothing.

But I couldn't shake the something-is-wrong sensation crawling up the back of my neck, so I continued to scan, moving methodically from one section of the property to another until I'd scanned the whole thing.

I didn't find anything out of place. Still, I finished my scan by focusing on the house.

Starting in the basement, I worked my way up to the top of the house.

By the time I got to the attic, I was half-heartedly scanning, my mind already partly on what I should do next.

But then I jerked upright, my eyes flying open.

"What the—? Fuzzy, we have to go to the attic. Something's there."

At a fast trot, I took the back stairs to the second floor. Fuzzy followed on my heels.

"I know there's a lot of things in the attic. But the thing that popped up on my map isn't like the others."

I stopped short outside the attic door. "Can you feel that?"

Now that I'd noticed the strange sensation coming from the attic, I couldn't seem to un-notice it. It was like some kind of weird high-pitched ringing, more felt than heard.

Fuzzy didn't respond, but when I opened the attic door, he bounded up the stairs ahead of me.

When I reached the top of the stairs, he was nowhere to be seen.

"Where'd you disappear to?" I called as I looked around myself.

At one point, Bayley had stacked everything in the attic so that it was tightly packed, ceiling to floor. I was relieved to find that sometime in the interim, he'd returned the assorted bits and bobs to their usual state of flagrant disarray. This way, I had space to clamber over and around stuff, and I could poke into the nooks and crannies.

Which might have been easier said than done.

I'd flipped on the light switch on my way up the stairs, but it did little to chase away the gloom. On the best of days, the sparse windows didn't let a lot of light in through their grimy panes. But the clouds outside made it even dimmer in the attic than normal. What was usually a soft twilight had deepened into late dusk, with deep shadows pooling in the corners. Twisting silhouettes from the shivering trees outside writhed on the walls and ceiling, giving the impression that the room was shifting.

"Jeez, Bayley's gone for two seconds, and the attic decides to moonlight as a haunted house." My tone was sarcastic, but I couldn't help the little shiver that went through me as I took in the coiling shadows.

I looked around for the mysterious interloper, but nothing immediately popped out at me. A quick check of my map didn't help—I couldn't seem to drill down any further than "attic"—and I couldn't pinpoint the direction of the ringing.

A massive armoire hulked on my left, so I figured that was as good a place to start looking as any. I circled it once before prying the doors open. Dust billowed out, but otherwise the armoire was empty.

I called out to Fuzzy, "Strike one on finding the weird noisemaker. In other news, no Narnia for us today." Though on second thought, given how much fun I'd been having dealing with DeeDee, maybe not having another magical doorway in my life was a good thing.

Stepping back to assess the surrounding area, I had a sinking feeling. "Oof, this is a lot. I mean, look at all this stuff. How am I going to find whatever is making that ringing sound?"

A rustling noise had me turning to the right where Fuzzy appeared from between some boxes.

"Meow," he said, then headed off into the shadows again. He paused to look back at me, and I realized he wanted me to follow him.

"Of course you found it first, you clever boy. Coming!"

As I clambered after Fuzzy, the wind let loose a long, creepy moan, adding a Halloween soundtrack to the twisting shadows.

The hair on the back of my neck stood up, and I had to remind myself that I liked the attic. I absolutely took out my cell phone and turned on the flashlight to see better and not at all to dispel the feeling that the shadows were staring at me.

Turning my attention to Fuzzy, I focused on wending my way through the obstacle course.

The farther I went into the attic, the colder I got. I was about to complain that Bayley wasn't there to warm things up when I stopped myself and smiled.

"I've totally got this."

Calling on my Smith magic, I coated the air around me until I'd formed a heat bubble that I tethered to myself, so that it moved with me while I walked. Then I set the spell to keep simmering in the back of my mind.

I called into the darkness, "Hey, if you're cold Fuzzy, I've got a nice warm spot over here."

"Meow," Fuzzy called from deeper into the attic.

Following his voice, I made my way through the debris until I found myself all the way on one side of the attic, standing next to Fuzzy, squinting into the darkness. Shining my flashlight, I discovered that I was standing in front of a trunk that was tucked up tight under where the roof met the wall. I quickly realized there was no way to open it where it was—it was really wedged in there.

But this was definitely where the ringing was coming from.

I tried reaching out with my magic. Since I didn't know what I was dealing with, I pulled just a pinch of each type of magic and put it into my magic batter. Then I allowed a single drop to gently touch the trunk.

The second the magic touched the trunk, the ringing stopped.

Fuzzy and I looked at each other.

"Not sure if that's a 'yay help is here; I can stop yelling for someone to let me out' or a 'yay dinner is here; I'll just look extra innocent until she opens the lid.'" I stared at the trunk. It didn't disclose any further information no matter how hard I stared at it. "Well, I can't just leave whatever it is in there. It's obviously not happy."

Several minutes of tugging and shoving later, I managed to slide the trunk forward.

Fuzzy came and sat next to me, leaning forward to sniff the closed lid. His tail started twitching, and his ears went back.

"That good, huh?" Well, at least he wasn't hissing.

I frowned at the trunk. "You know, Fuzzy, it occurs to me that Bayley stuck this in the corner for a reason."

A sudden sneaking suspicion bloomed in my mind. It was a sign of how discombobulated I was that it hadn't occurred to me first thing.

"Do you think I should open it?" I asked.

Fuzzy cocked his head. After staring at the trunk for a long moment, he poked at the lid with his paw.

"Okay then. Me too. Hopefully Bayley won't be irritated with us for doing this without him."

As I leaned forward to open the lid, my necklace swung free from where I had it tucked in my sweater.

I pried open the lid and looked inside.

"I was afraid of that," Percy and I said at the same time.

Chapter Ten

"Jinx," I said.

"I beg your—"

"You owe me a coffee," I told Percy distractedly.

Percy harrumphed and then went quiet.

But staring at Percy meant staring at my necklace, and I was once again struck by the similarities between it and the star sitting in the trunk in front of me.

The trunk's star was like a six-inch, 3-D rendering of my necklace's star, and it looked like it was made of the same type of tarnished metal. Like my necklace, the trunk's star resembled the inside of a cut apple, each arm concave, with an oblong-shaped "seed" in the top arm while the other arms were empty. But unlike my necklace, all the arms connected to the penta-gram in the middle to form one solid star that could stand up on its bottom arms.

I reached in and picked the 3-D star up, pulling it away from the ancient brown cloth it was nestled in.

As soon as I touched the star, I felt the same odd sensation I'd felt the first time I'd held it. I searched my memory for when Mila had brought it to me after stealing it from a super-secret Foster magical library.

Mila had noticed the funny feeling it gave off too. She'd said, "It's magic. Of some sort. It was tucked away in a cubby behind one of the books. I figured since it looked like your necklace, and you're the Housekeeper and all, maybe it should come and hang out here for a while."

Looking at it now, I agreed that it was definitely magic,

but my Best magic was tingling, telling me that the star felt sort of alive.

"Hey there," I said.

It didn't say anything back.

As I turned the star slowly, it gleamed dully in the dim attic light, but it didn't *do* anything. It just sat there.

"You know," I said to it, "Wil went kind of bonkers trying to get his hands on you." I added, "Wil and I used to be friends... or so I thought."

I only noticed how wistful I sounded when Fuzzy rubbed his head against my leg.

I scritched between his ears with one hand while I contemplated the star in my other.

"Wil insisted I let him have you—whatever you are—erm... oh yeah, he said you're an artifact. Of course, he wouldn't tell me what kind of artifact, or what you do, or anything useful— apparently you have 'lore' surrounding you. Lore only he knows, according to him. But he wouldn't tell me why he wanted you, so I told him he couldn't have you. Then he resorted to bribery. Then he tried threats. That butt even tried to nab you for himself and walk right out of here with you!" I said shaking my head. "Bayley and I kept him in line, but it got a bit ugly."

If the artifact had any opinions on its near-abduction, it didn't choose to share them with me and Fuzzy. It continued to sit quietly in my hand.

But I couldn't shake the feeling that it was somehow...aware.

"So anyway, sorry you've been stuck up here—Bayley has you tucked away to keep you safe, and I'm sure he's been keeping an eye on you. And you haven't seemed to want attention...until now that is."

And suddenly I was very certain that it did want my attention because as soon as I said it, my Best magic began bouncing around like a dog that had just sighted a squirrel.

Fuzzy stretched his neck toward the star. When I lowered it to his eye level, he chuffed out a warm breath that tingled across my hand and over the surface of the artifact.

It glowed dimly as a soft chime rang from it, vibrating

my hand.

I nearly dropped it.

As I fumbled to hang onto it, the glow and chime faded away. When I had a good grip again, I looked at the star, and it looked the same as before—dull and static. It was as if the chiming glow had never happened.

"Can you do that again, Fuzzy?" I said, lowering the star to him.

Fuzzy let out a longer breath this time, and the star chimed and glowed longer.

"Well that's neat," I said. "I wonder if—"

As I blew on the star, Percy called from my necklace, "I wouldn't—oh no."

The star lit up even brighter than when Fuzzy had blown on it, and the chime was a different pitch and steadier.

This time, when I stopped blowing, the chime faded, but the glow didn't totally go out.

I sent an angel-hair-pasta-sized tendril of my Best magic toward the artifact, stopping just short of touching it. When it didn't seem to object, I let my magic gently brush the edge of the star.

At first, it didn't react.

Then I felt something. It felt as though the star had moved slightly, but I could see plainly that it was sitting still in my hand. When I focused, I realized that I could feel some kind of energy inside the star slowly stirring. I had that sensation that it was studying me again.

"I'm Finn. I'm the current Housekeeper. Nice to meet you."

After a breathless moment, it started to glow brighter. The light's intensity built until it lit the attic. Then it winked out.

"Oh great," Percy complained.

"What?" I asked.

"It likes you," he said, sounding utterly disgusted. Then he muttered, "Of course, it likes you. You're—" he stopped abruptly, and I got the sense he was about to say something and then changed his mind and said, "*you.*"

"Um, who else would I be?"

I didn't expect him to answer, but I heard a soft, "Literally anyone else would be better."

"Rude! What does that even mean?" I looked away from the star to glare at my necklace.

Percy sounded resigned when he said, "Never mind, it doesn't matter. You've done it now."

"Done what? What did I do? It's only polite to introduce yourself." With a bewildered gesture to Fuzzy, I added, "And if you're talking about the breathing thing, he started it!"

Fuzzy gave me a look and I said, "What? Well you did."

"Don't you understand that that just makes it worse?" Percy said. "The Orret and the Housekeeper have just touched it."

"So?"

"I can't explain it to you."

"Of course you can't," I sighed. Wishing I had Bayley to consult for more info, I said, "Well look. Bayley was fine keeping it here, and in fact seemed kind of fond of this thing. So I'm fine with making friends with it."

Percy had no further response.

I looked at the artifact and said, "Well despite what Percy said, it's nice to meet you. When Bayley gets back, I'll definitely check with him about you."

When the star didn't respond, I decided it seemed fine with that plan, and I bent to put it back in the trunk.

But the second I put it down, it let loose a discordant chime that sounded like a small wail of dismay.

I reached for it, and as soon as I touched it, the noise stopped. Taking my hand away resulted in more wailing. I tried closing the lid of the trunk, and the wailing got louder.

"Oh dear," I said.

Fuzzy pawed at the lid, and I opened it for him.

He immediately stuck his head in and nosed the star. It stopped making the bad sound and pulsed a soft glow at him.

Fuzzy looked at me, then back at the star. He nudged it toward me and trilled, "Mrrrw."

"You want me to pick it up?"

"Meow."

As soon as I touched the artifact, it pulsed a happy glow.

It seemed to want company. A lightbulb went off in my head. "Oh! I think I get it. You reacted when I probed the attic using my mental map. Did you reach out because you felt me poking around, and you're missing Bayley's company? Is that why you're sounding off?"

The star glowed once.

The wind picked that moment to scrape against the windows, and the shadows glowered around us.

"I get it. Being alone up here with all the creepy noises must be unsettling. Believe me, it's weird having Bayley gone for me too. But Fuzzy and I have everything under control. And Bayley will be back before you know it. There's no need to worry."

The artifact apparently wasn't going to take my word for it because as soon as I leaned toward the trunk, it started the discordant chiming again.

Fuzzy batted me away from the trunk.

"I get that you both think the artifact should come with me." I looked down at the star and added, "But I can't carry you around all day. You're too big."

The star gave another pulse of light. Then it glowed so brightly I had to look away. At the same time, it vibrated in my hands so hard I could barely hold onto it. The glow and the vibrations died at the same time. When I looked back at my hands, the star was the size of a silver dollar.

"Okay. I guess you're coming with us," I said. I tried tucking the star in the pocket of my sweater. When it didn't fuss, I took it as a win. "You can hang out at least until Bayley gets back."

"Meow," Fuzzy said.

Chapter Eleven

With the star tucked in my pocket, Fuzzy and I backtracked toward the attic door. Fatigue dragged at me, so I released my heat bubble to save energy. Immediately, the chill started nipping at me.

As I made my way to the door, I scanned the mounds of stuff that I passed. "You know, Fuzzy, if Bayley's gone the whole three weeks," I cringed a little, "it might be a good time to make some progress on sorting out this mess. Maybe we can come back here and inventory everything." A shiver rippled through me, and I added, "Not now though. Later. When I bring coffee and a heavier sweater."

Fuzzy leaned into me as another shiver ran through me and I said, "Is it just me, or are you cold too?" As I spoke, I was startled to see a vapor cloud announce my words.

"Okay, so not just my imagination." The cold was just another tangible result of Bayley's absence. I reminded myself it was only temporary, but when I said, "Time to go," I sounded as tired as I felt.

Abandoning the attic, I headed down the stairs.

As I stepped off the stairs into the warmer air on the second floor, a giant yawn caught me by surprise.

I shut the attic door and made my way to the kitchen where I stood in front of the refrigerator, undecided.

I'd been planning on making something time-consuming for dinner, but I decided on quick and easy.

After I fed Fuzzy an early dinner and made myself a sandwich, we holed up in front of the TV until I couldn't keep my eyes open any longer, and we trundled off to bed.

As I tugged a blanket over myself, Fuzzy hopped up and cuddled in next to me, head on my arm.

As soon as I closed my eyes, I fell asleep.

And I found myself back in the same dream I'd had before.

I was knee-deep in snow in the grove in front of the house. As before, everything looked a little off. Bayley was again smaller, like a simpler deconstructed version of himself. And the grove had the same not-quite-right feeling to it.

I scrubbed my hands over my face and muttered, "Ugh."

I struggled a few steps forward, but as before, the house remained the same distance away.

"Really brain? You couldn't come up with anything more original?"

As I said it, I realized that like the last dream, this was also a lucid dream.

I tried walking forward again, but the house remained stubbornly at a distance.

Deciding to change tactics, I ran toward the house as fast as I could. Well, I tried to. I only made it a short distance before I face-planted in the snow.

Note to self: knee-deep snow is not made for running, even in dreams.

As I clambered unsteadily to my feet, I dusted the snow off my bare arms. But the second I acknowledged there was snow covering my bare skin, I felt how cold it was.

"Oh no. Not this again."

Stomping my feet as much in agitation as to keep them warm, I drew on my Smith magic and seared the area around me.

My mouth dropped open as a circle of fire erupted. Moving outward, it melted the snow in a ten-foot perfect circle, then died out.

"Whoa. I wasn't expecting that. I didn't know I could even use magic in a dream. And uh, that's not how my magic works." I pondered the circle around me. "Although, people do crazy stuff like flying in dreams all the time, so I guess it kind of makes sense."

Aiming this time, I sent a more targeted burst of heat to

melt the snow in front of me. A giggle escaped me as a line of fire shot from my hand. "Guess I'm hot stuff huh?" I could picture Fuzzy's reaction to my dad joke and that made me giggle harder.

Turning to the task at hand, I fired away at the snow, clearing a short path, then stopped.

Keeping an eye on Bayley, I walked to the end of the path. Though I could walk much easier now, the house remained the same distance away.

"The fire was kind of fun, but overall this dream is dumb. I'm literally getting nowhere," I told the dream. "I'm waking up now."

I closed my eyes, but when I opened them, I was still in the dream.

With a growl, I squeezed my eyes closed tightly and tried to force myself awake.

But when I peeked one eye open, I was still dreaming.

I kicked the snow a few times then started to pace.

Maybe I needed to make it to the house in order to leave the dream? But how was I going to do that?

I scuffed my foot as I thought, which brought my attention to the frozen grass that my heat spell had exposed.

The ground might be frozen but that didn't make a difference to my Foster magic.

Reaching for a spaghetti-sized green strand of my magic, I fed it into the ground. There was a breathless moment when I thought it might not work, but suddenly a Jack-and-the-Beanstalk-sized green vine erupted from the ground. It was as thick as a tree, but bendy like a vine.

Pointing toward the house, I instructed the enormous vine to grow across the lawn.

In real life, I didn't know if I could accomplish something like this yet. But in my dreams, it seemed I had the kind of magic normally only seen in movies.

The vine writhed its way over the snow. I held my breath as I watched, ready to pull back the vine if it kept growing but never got nearer the house.

When the vine reached the covered deck area in front of the house, I was so surprised that I almost didn't stop it in time. But I used my magic to halt the beanpole's growth just short of the house, not wanting to damage Bayley, even a pretend Bayley in my dreams.

The central stalk had grown straight up until it was about a foot above the snow, then bent at an unnatural angle and continued roughly parallel to the ground. Using the leaf stalks that sprouted from the central vine like ladder rungs, I carefully climbed up the beanstalk to the part where it bent. Stepping out onto the section that ran straight to the house, I teetered along it like it was a balance beam.

As I cautiously made my way across the stalk, I kept an eye on the house. I huffed out a pent up breath as I realized I was finally getting closer. Maybe if I could get inside I could communicate with Bayley?

A spark of excitement zipped through me at the thought.

Even moving slowly, it only took a minute to make my way over most of the snow-clad lawn. But as I was closing in on the house, a wind picked up out of nowhere. It gusted strongly enough to make me pause until it passed.

When the wind died down, I resumed walking. I was almost there.

I heard the second gust coming as it rattled its way through the trees, and I halted again. But the wind was much stronger this time and slammed into me, shoving me off the beanstalk.

Then I was falling, arms and legs flailing. I should have hit the snow immediately, but instead I kept falling and falling—

I woke up, arms and legs kicking and tangled in the covers. Fuzzy was on the floor next to the bed, meowing at me.

Hearing Fuzzy helped ground me back in the real word.

Panting, I ran my hands through my snarled hair. They were shaking.

Wrestling with my sheets as I tried to untangle myself, I muttered to Fuzzy, "Nightmares suck."

As soon as I had myself reasonably extricated, Fuzzy hopped up on the bed, pressing himself into my side.

Looping an arm around him, I said, "Thanks buddy. Oof, that was no fun."

Chapter Twelve

After the weird dream, it took me ages to go back to sleep. But eventually, my fatigue clobbered my insomnia over the head, and I dozed off. Fortunately, I slept so hard that I didn't dream again.

On the third day, I woke and immediately checked for Bayley.

Still no dice.

I glanced out the window. No falling snow, and the wind had died down, but gray clouds lounged overhead.

Another gloomy day.

Turning my gaze back to the bedroom, my eyes snagged on the artifact I'd stashed on the nightstand next to the bed. It must have trusted that I wouldn't abandon it because it hadn't protested when I'd stuck it there for the night.

"Good morning, Star," I said. "Hmm. We're going to need to give you a name. Stella? Is that too obvious?" I picked up the artifact. "Do you like the name Stella?"

It didn't complain, so I said, "Stella it is," and set it back on the table.

But when I went into the bathroom, Stella rang an unhappy sound.

I walked back to the nightstand. "You really don't like being alone, huh?" I didn't love the idea of taking a shower with Stella watching, so I tucked it under a towel before I went on with my morning routine.

After I got dressed and went to the kitchen, Stella now nestled in my sweatshirt pocket, I kept going with my usual tasks, feeding myself and Fuzzy breakfast.

But the longer I sat at the table sipping my coffee, the more the urge to leave the house pressed on me.

After checking the temperature, I said to Fuzzy, "Why don't we go to the greenhouse after breakfast? I'll get some Foster magic practice in and take care of the plants. You can stretch your legs."

After visiting the Grack and the Gracklettes, I worked away the morning in the greenhouse, but eventually I had to go home.

I trudged into the mudroom, took off my coat and boots, and then sat there on the bench, listening to the house. After the rustling plants and the gentle clicking sound of the Grack tending to the Gracklettes, the sudden quiet amplified Bayley's absence.

"Meow?"

"It's just weird to come inside and not have Bayley creaking and groaning to welcome us. Everything feels so...odd. It's almost like this is a different place—like I don't know the house at all. Which isn't true of course."

Fuzzy hopped up on the bench next to me, and I rubbed between his ears as I thought out loud. "Bayley's magic is so amazing. I guess a part of me thought he'd nail this and be back by now. But it's three days since he left, and he's still gone. I think I need to start planning for him to be away the whole time." I pondered my next steps, and it was pretty obvious where I needed to start. "I think it's about time I call Nor and tell her what's happening."

Although she'd originally been my competition as a Housekeeper candidate herself, Nor had become a close friend and ally. Nor was one of the smartest, most strategic thinkers I'd ever met, and I regularly counted my lucky stars that she was my friend—and that her girlfriend Mila was an equally awesome badass. Mila ran some kind of secret organization and could get her hands on anything—information, goods, people, you name it.

I dialed Nor's cell phone, but the call went to voicemail.

"It's Finn. Call me when you can." It said a lot about the last six months that I felt it necessary to add, "Uh, nothing's on fire or anything," before I hung up.

I could've left her a more detailed message. Our phone calls were super secure, both magically and technologically protected, but it made me nervous to leave recorded info about weirdness at the house.

Glancing at the clock, I realized it was time for lunch.

I fed Fuzzy and ate my sandwich standing at the sink, looking out the window at the snowy yard. As soon as he finished his own lunch, Fuzzy hopped up next to the sink and joined me, grooming himself as I nibbled.

He stopped grooming at the same time I stopped eating.

At first, I thought it was so quiet in the kitchen that I could hear my chewing echoing off the glass.

Wincing, I said, "I had no idea I chew so loudly! Sorry Fuzzy," but then I realized that I'd stopped chewing, and I could still hear the sound.

I tilted my head to listen harder, only to realize that Fuzzy was doing the same thing. "What is that?" I asked.

Fuzzy shook himself and looked at me.

"Yeah, I'm with you. It's sort of unsettling." I paused, trying to figure out what I was hearing. "It's...kind of like a humming? But super soft. It's there, then not." I shook myself, just like Fuzzy had. "Ugh, seriously what *is* that?"

I pulled the star out of my pocket. "Hey is that you?" I asked as I held it up to my ear. Nothing. "Sorry, Stella. It was you the last time, so I had to check."

Stella had no comment.

Pocketing the star, I prowled around the kitchen trying to find the source of the sound. The longer it went on, the more it got on my nerves, and I paced around the kitchen looking for the source, becoming more and more agitated as I tried to find out where it was coming from.

Fuzzy jumped down off the counter and left the kitchen.

"Meow!" he called from the hallway.

I followed after him to find him standing at the back door.

"It's coming from outside?" I frowned. "Maybe it's the wind rubbing some branches together in the most annoying way possible?"

Hurriedly, I put my outdoor gear back on and went outside. Fuzzy followed at my heels.

The noise seemed to echo around the yard, coming from no specific source.

It was definitely louder outside, but I was momentarily distracted by the open, empty food containers strewn in my path.

"Uh, who ate all the cookies?"

Whoever had the munchies must've been super hungry. There wasn't a single crumb left.

As I gathered the food containers and stacked them by the door, I looked around for tracks in the snow.

The only tracks were Fuzzy's and mine.

"Well, at least it's not a bear," I muttered.

I didn't have time to puzzle it out any further because the noise became even more irritating.

"Ugh! I feel like my teeth are vibrating. Can you tell where it's coming from Fuzzy?"

Fuzzy turned to face the woods on the right, lifting a paw and pointing in that direction.

Closing my eyes, I reached for my mental map and searched that section of the forest. Nothing seemed amiss, but the longer I stood there, the more certain I became that I should go check out the woods. The only reason I hadn't headed straight for them yet was because of the ocean of snow barring the way.

"Okay, let's work the problem. What could be wrong in the forest? Maybe the trees, but it doesn't sound like branches rubbing together to me. And it doesn't sound like any kind of animal I've heard before—oh no! You don't think one of the Talers is having a problem because of the storm do you?"

I'd dubbed the unusual folk living on Bayley's property "Talers" because they reminded me of creatures you'd find in a fairy tale. I had no idea how many different types of Talers lived on the property, but I knew for sure I hadn't met them all.

With my luck, since Bayley was offline, of course it would be a Taler—one I hadn't met yet.

The noise seemed to intensify. I nearly stomped off the porch and headed to do a physical search of the woods, snow be damned, but Fuzzy pawed at my leg.

Looking at his bare paw made me reconsider. "Are you warm enough?"

"Meow."

"It's probably not a great idea to spend too much time out here just standing around in the cold. But I want to try again before we go inside." I wasn't sure if it was my stubbornness kicking in or some weird reaction to Bayley being gone, but I was more determined than ever to figure out what it was we were hearing.

Closing my eyes, I called up my mental map again. This time, I sifted a blend of Foster and Best magic over the map, coating it thoroughly.

An overpowering sense of déjà vu flooded me, so strong that my head started aching.

As quick as it had come, it passed, leaving me disoriented for a moment.

"Meow?"

"I think the noise is distracting me."

Returning to my map, I felt my magic and the map sync together. Since I wasn't sure exactly what I was looking for, I moved slowly from the section of the woods closest to me outward, keeping an eye out for anything that felt off or unusual. I was starting to despair when I reached the pond deep in the woods.

There was something…

I focused on that section of the map and tried to understand what I was feeling. I'd been to that section of the woods just once, last fall, and the pond had seemed very nice but unremarkable. It was similar in size to the one in the woods on the other side of Bayley, near Zo's house. Unlike the Zo-side pond, the pond on this side of the woods was surrounded by boulders on one side, just like the lake at the back of the property was.

If I hadn't been studying the map so closely, I might not have noticed the tiny foggy dot by the pond. The one time I'd visited, no Talers had come out to meet me. But my map was telling me that right now, some kind of Taler was hanging out by the pond. Maybe they were doing some ice fishing?

The sound pulled at me again, rousting me from my thoughts.

I surveyed the distance between me and the forest. "That's a lot of snow to hike through," I said to Fuzzy, "though it looks like the Grack went through there at some point, so I know I can at least clear off whatever path she made." Squinting was making my head hurt so I turned to look at Fuzzy.

"If I'm going to try to investigate, I'd better do it now. It gets dark early, and the last thing I want is to be caught in the woods at night, especially with that new storm front moving in," I said, gesturing to the sky.

I started back toward the porch stairs, but Fuzzy scooted around me and got in my way.

Stopping suddenly on the snowy porch wasn't a good idea, and I skidded forward.

With what looked suspiciously like amusement, Fuzzy watched me pinwheel my arms as I flailed for balance. Despite my efforts, I toppled over and wound up in a snowdrift. I landed on my side which had the added benefit of causing the star in my pocket to dig in to me.

"Ow," I muttered. The snowbank was relatively comfortable, kind of like a really cold beanbag chair, and part of me wanted to just stay there. That tipped me off to how tired I was. Given my lack of sleep and lack of Bayley, staying outside and letting the cold sap my energy probably wasn't the smartest thing.

But the noise gnawed at me, and I decided I didn't care if I was tired. I needed to figure this out.

I clambered unsteadily to my feet and was about to head off the porch when Fuzzy stepped in front of me again. Frowning at him, I said, "I get it if you don't want to go with me. I've got boots, and you've got bare feet. Maybe you should stay here while I take a quick trip into the forest."

Fuzzy chittered at me but didn't move.

"You're in my way, pal," I said, moving to step around him.

Fuzzy shifted to block me.

We had a staring contest for a moment.

Crossing my arms, I said, "I take it you don't want me to go?"

"Meow."

"I know I said I'm a little tired. But if I don't leave now—"

Fuzzy nudged me in the direction of the house.

"You want me to go inside?"

"Meow."

A sudden gust of wind hissed through the trees, making me shiver.

Fuzzy tipped his nose into the air and sniffed. He looked at the sky and then looked back to me. Muttering, he shoved me again, less gently this time, toward the door.

I was about to argue with him when another visitor from the Wind Department shoved past me, causing me to stumble back a step. As I was catching my balance—again—I caught a glimpse of the sky.

"Uh, is it getting darker?" I asked, taking a step toward the porch stairs. I was really going to need to get a move on to make it to the pond before it started snowing again.

The star in my pocket started to vibrate. I tried to ignore it, but the vibration was even more distracting than the noise.

"Ugh, Stella. Not you too. Is this because I fell on you? Because that was totally Fuzzy's fault."

Stella vibrated harder.

"You want to go inside?"

The vibrating stopped.

"Meow." Fuzzy grabbed my hand in his mouth and started tugging me toward the door, careful not to chomp through my glove.

"Okay, okay, I'm coming." I shook my hand free of his mouth and went to the back door.

I briefly considered letting him in first, shutting him inside, and then going for the hike on my own. Although I wasn't sure if scratching my "find that noise" itch was worth upsetting him.

Thinking of scratching, I suddenly realized I wasn't itchy anymore. Startled, I turned toward the forest. Beside the occasional wind gust hissing across the snow, it was quiet.

"It stopped," I said to Fuzzy in surprise.

A brief check of my mental map told me the foggy spot was gone from the pond too.

"I really hope that means whatever that was, it managed to fix its own problem," I said. Worried I'd let a Taler down, I trudged inside.

Chapter Thirteen

Inside, the warm air wrapped around me like a hug as I thunked down on the bench and pried my feet out of my boots.

Blowing on my hands as I wriggled my toes, I said, "I didn't realize how cold I'd gotten, but boy can I feel it now. My feet feel like they're dangling icicles instead of toes, and my hands aren't in much better shape. It's a good thing you got me to come in when you did, Fuzzy, or I might have gone full popsicle. Thanks—I don't know what I was thinking. Too stubborn for my own good, I guess."

I pulled on my slippers, stomped around a bit to try to bring some feeling back into my toes, and made my way into the kitchen.

The tiredness I'd felt outside grew as I got warmer, until I felt like I was dragging lead blocks with my feet.

I was inhaling a cookie as I brewed fresh coffee when the phone rang.

Looking at the caller ID, I smiled.

"Hi Nor."

To the point as always, Nor said, "What do you mean nothing's on fire? Was that code for you accidentally burned something down?"

I heard a female voice in the background.

Nor said, "Mila would like to know if she can listen in."

"Sure thing," I said. "It'll save you having to explain things to her once we're done."

I heard a faint click then Nor said, "You're on speaker."

"Hey," said Mila.

"Hi Mila. You're back in town? How was your latest trip?"

"Oh you know, the usual," said Mila.

"Blew up a palace and deposed a dictator?" I suggested.

She snorted, "No palaces, no dictators." She paused then added, "There *may* have been a little exploding."

"Sure, sure, very restrained, I bet," I said. "Gotta keep things tasteful. You wouldn't want to go with gaudy, over-the-top exploding." I supposed I should be alarmed, but I couldn't help but giggle. Mila was a lightning storm, and I thoroughly enjoyed the show.

Nor got us back on track and said, "So what's happening?"

I recounted the situation with Bayley.

When I finished, there was a short pause where I guessed Nor and Mila were exchanging questioning looks because Nor said, "I thought your birthday was in very early September. It's in the Foster database file on you. Mila did you know it was her birthday?"

"No," said Mila sounding extremely put out. "Man, are you sure your Mom and Dad weren't spies? They sure did a hell of a job obscuring information about you."

"Nope. They spent too much time in the diner to be secret agents. They were plain ole folks, sorry. Well as plain as magical people can be. Except for the whole hiding me from the magical community thing, we were a boringly normal family."

Of course, I suspected that at least part of the reason my parents hid me was because they knew that I had an exactly balanced amount of each branch of magic. Eventually, I needed to tell Nor and Mila about me being a balance. I trusted them both, but I had this feeling like the longer I could keep me being a balance under wraps, the better it would be. Certainly, Reese and Zo thought it was important for me to hide it for as long as possible.

Mila said, "It's disturbing that even I didn't know your birthday is coming up. So it's on the 28th?"

"Yup."

She hesitated and then asked, "You're sure?"

I said, "Yes," but then I paused. "Why?"

"Well, your parents lied about when you were born to the

Fosters. I was just wondering if it's possible that they decided to fudge the details with you too."

I wanted to say that she sounded crazy, but I couldn't ignore the fact that I didn't know my parents as well as I thought I had. Reluctantly, I admitted, "I mean, I suppose it's possible. I honestly have no way of knowing for sure. But my birthday has been on February 28th for my entire life, so in my mind, that's my birthday, and that's what I'm going with."

"Fair enough. The 28th it is then. Well, we'll have to celebrate," said Mila, "seeing as it's your first birthday in the house."

When I hesitated, Nor said, "Unless you don't want to."

"Can I think about it? It's not that I don't appreciate the offer. It's just that it's…complicated. With Bayley being gone."

And if we did have a party, it'd be my first big celebration without either of my parents. It had to happen sometime. I just wasn't sure if that time was now.

"No pressure," Mila said.

Nor added, "And if you decide you want to do something, it doesn't have to be a big production. We can have dinner and some cake. I'll arrange everything, so all you'll have to do is be there."

"That…could be really nice. Thanks. Let's see what happens with Bayley and go from there."

Mila said, "Speaking of Bayley, not gonna lie. I'm worried about the sitch over there. Is everything, you know, working?"

"Yes, but on low power."

"Meaning?"

"Well, I can see my map of the property, but it's pixelated. And the house has power and heat and all that stuff, but it's all normal now—no magical tweaking from Bayley. For example, the attic is colder than the rest of the house. That's totally normal for a regular house, but if Bayley were here, he'd adjust the temperature because I was in the room."

"Why were you in the attic?" asked Nor.

I told them about Stella. "My best guess is that Stella felt Bayley's absence and that somehow woke it up. I know this sounds weird, but it seems lonely to me."

Mila said, "Interesting. Well, we know that at least Wil is

interested in getting his hands on that star. Are the property's defenses going to work with Bayley offline?"

I groaned. "It's like they've already been tripped. The whole property went into a kind of lockdown mode when Bayley left. So, nobody in or out for the time being." Except maybe for Zo because she seemed to be the exception to all of Bayley's rules.

"Well, that's smart," Mila said, "but that limits what I can do to offer you extra protection."

"Yeah, you were right to have me install those extra defensive measures. I thought it was overkill at the time, but now I'm glad they're there." Something tugged at my memory, but it was there and gone in an instant. I wondered if not being able to hold onto a thought was another fun side effect of Bayley being gone.

Mila interrupted my musing when she said, "Told you so."

"Yeah, yeah, yeah," I laughed. "Though even without the extras, I'm not totally defenseless. In addition to Bayley's automatic defenses, I've got my magic."

"How is practice going?" asked Nor.

"You still doing your magical baking thing?" asked Mila with a smile in her voice.

"Yup," I said. I couldn't keep the pride out of my voice as I said, "And it's going great now that I have an approach that works."

Mila chuckled. "I love it—it's so you."

We chatted a few more minutes then wound down the call. Before we hung up, Nor said, "I'm still concerned about you being all alone in the house without Bayley there. That's a great deal of alone time."

"He probably won't be gone very long," I said. "Plus I have Fuzzy to keep me company. And Percy." Sort of. Even though he'd warmed up a little, he wasn't exactly chatty.

Nor said, "Percy! I should have thought of him sooner. He can open a door like usual, and we can use it to visit."

I shook my head. "Nope. Bayley said Percy can't work his magic while the lockdown is in place."

Nor sounded worried, "Well, at least we can talk on the phone regularly so I can check in with you and see how you're doing."

"Um, about that," I said. "Bayley warned me that the longer

he was gone the more things might get fritzy. The lockdown will stay in place for sure, but other stuff might get a bit wonky."

"Other stuff like what?"

"The phones. The TV. The Internet, that kind of stuff."

"That's…not optimal. You'd be really cut off." I could picture the frown on Nor's face as she spoke.

"I doubt it'll come to that. And even if it does, I really do have plenty to do. I've got books to read, magic to practice, and things to bake. Plus, without Bayley here, for once I'm going to need to be a regular housekeeper. Have you seen the size of this place? It'll take me a whole day just to dust."

Completely ignoring my teasing tone, Mila said seriously, "I don't love it, you being there without any backup. I have total faith in your abilities, Finn, but it's always better to have contingencies in place."

"Don't worry, it'll be fine," I said with way more confidence than I actually felt. "As soon as Bayley's back, I'll call Nor right away."

Nor sighed. "Well, it's a max of three weeks, right? Bayley said one way or another that he'd be done by your birthday. Three whole weeks may get tricky for any number of reasons, but I'm sure you can handle it Finn.

Mila added, "And if you need us, we'll figure something out to get around the lockdown. Heck if you get really stir crazy, I can meet you at the property line, and we can have a picnic."

I appreciated the thought, but it was February in New England. No one was having picnics if they weren't abominable snowmen.

"No worries, you guys. I've got this."

Chapter Fourteen

I so did not have this.

Five minutes after I got off the phone with Nor and Mila, I found myself standing in the middle of the kitchen again, staring off into space, thinking about the night Bayley had left, and running through everything he'd told me.

I only snapped out of it when Fuzzy started pawing at my pants leg.

"Ugh," I said, rubbing at my temples to dissuade the headache that had popped up. "I have got to get my act together."

I refocused myself on making a nice dinner. I quick-thawed some shrimp, boiled some pasta, then sautéed the shrimp with butter, capers, and lemon. When the pasta was done, I combined it with the shrimp and topped the whole thing with lemon zest, parsley, and freshly-grated Parmesan.

By the time I finished cooking and eating, I was yawning so hard that even though it was only-toddlers-go-to-sleep-this-early o'clock, I went to bed and passed out. It didn't last. I woke up in the middle of the night having had the exact same dream as the night before.

For the rest of the night, I was a piece of flotsam, bobbing in and out of sleep, until it was time to start my day.

At breakfast, Fuzzy scarfed his food and then parked himself by the sink, watching the snow drift lazily to the ground. I was poking half-heartedly at my cereal wondering if I was ever going to get a real night's sleep again when Fuzzy went rigid, his gaze riveted on something outside.

Abandoning my cereal, I joined him at the window and

asked, "What do you see? Is it a bird?" I peered outside. "Tell me it's a cardinal. That would be so New-England-winter postcard."

I scanned the yard but found no splash of red breaking up the monochromatic view. "Well bummer. Though I suppose it's a good thing the birds are tucked in rather than wandering around in the cold." Fuzzy jolted to his feet, inching closer to the window in a low stalk.

I leaned forward too, frowning. "Fuzzy? What is it? All I see is falling snow."

Fuzzy propped his front paws on the windowsill and stared even harder.

A gust of wind blew some of the snowflakes in our direction. At least, at first I thought it was the wind. But then I realized that just a few of the snowflakes were moving toward us. The rest continued heading straight for the soft, white blanket on the ground.

Then I noticed that the rogue flakes were bigger than they should be. They were still tiny overall—maybe the size of an acorn—but they were definitely larger than the rest.

As the rogues sped toward us, defying the laws of gravity, I reflexively asked Bayley, *Do you see this?* in my mind.

Of course, he didn't answer.

Shaking my head at myself, I refocused on the objects approaching the window. I patted Fuzzy and said, "Okay, I see them now."

Fuzzy growled a warning just as the four rogues landed outside on the windowsill in a row.

I blinked, stared, then blinked again.

Those weren't snowflakes.

But I had no idea what they were.

They were white like snowflakes, but that was pretty much where the resemblance ended. They had central, oval-shaped bodies with two big wings sprouting near the top. Overall, their shape kind of reminded me of the helicopter seeds that came from the maple trees outside.

Peering closer, I could see that their central bodies were more the size and shape of cannellini beans than an acorn.

Except that in the general area where a human head would be, these "beans" had two tiny eyes and a mouth slit.

They had no legs, but they did each have a foot with a claw on the end, kind of like a single, large bird's toe. The toe/foot stuck out from underneath the oval body like the foot on a Mr. Potato Head.

I leaned closer to get a better look and instead of backing away, the four critters on the window crowded forward to study me as well.

Fuzzy whacked at them, hitting the window glass with a gentle "bam."

They didn't flinch. In fact, one of them looked like it was laughing, one of them waggled its wings, and I was pretty sure another one of them stuck its tongue out at him.

As they jostled themselves closer, they used their wings to maneuver. When they came to a standstill, they each positioned their wings so they stuck straight up in the air like antennae. I realized that the wings had something like hands on the ends when they started waving at me.

"Fuzzy, these guys must be another type of Taler!"

Fuzzy gave me a look that I translated as, "No duh. You think?"

I groaned, "I wish I knew what, exactly, they were."

I suddenly remembered what the "helicopter seeds" from the maple trees were named. "Well, for now, I'm going to call these guys Samaras, like the seeds. What do you think?"

Fuzzy flicked his tail, more concerned with watching the Samaras than with their name. Suddenly, he leapt down from the counter and dashed to the back door. It only took me a few seconds to reach him, but apparently that was too long because Fuzzy was standing on his hind legs, batting at the doorknob with his front paws. He was so big now that standing that way made him tall enough to see out the door's window.

The second I opened the door a crack, Fuzzy shoved his way through and bounded out onto the snowy porch.

"Wait!" I called fruitlessly, realizing too late that I should have put my boots and coat on before I opened the door.

A gust of cold wind blasted in, chasing me back a step as Fuzzy dashed forward, scattering the Samaras who'd flown over.

I slammed the door shut and ran into the mudroom, yanked on my boots, then hurried outside, tugging on my coat and gloves as I went. I heaved a frosted breath of relief when I saw that Fuzzy hadn't gone far. He was sitting on the cleared path, surrounded by the Samaras.

They were fluttering around above him, dancing in the air. Their wings made a soft, high-pitched tinkling sound every now and then, and I wondered what their feathers were made of to create that noise.

Fuzzy sat in cat pose, very still, with only his tail twitching occasionally, watching them intently.

It reminded me of how he looked when he watched the birds.

"Don't eat them!" I said as I walked cautiously over to join him. I was hoping that my poofy coat would make me look comical and friendly, like a Macy's Parade balloon, instead of menacing, like a Macy's Parade balloon up close.

Fuzzy looked over his shoulder at me, then returned to watching the Samaras.

Sotto voce, I said to him, "Thank you for your restraint."

Fuzzy gave me a long-suffering look then returned to his vigil.

One of them separated from the others and headed for Fuzzy.

With a shooing motion, I said, "I'm not sure that's a good idea—"

It ignored my waving hands and landed on Fuzzy's nose before I finished.

The other three Samaras clustered together, floating in midair, and waved at their compatriot. I couldn't tell if they were showing alarm or excitement. If I were them, I'd be yelling at my buddy to get off the thing with the big teeth.

Fuzzy sneezed.

The reckless Samara on his nose twirled into the air, then settled back where it was.

Fuzzy looked at it for a moment, slid a side gaze to me, then looked back at the Samara and sighed.

I stepped closer to Fuzzy and ran a hand down his back as I

said, "Thanks for being so patient, Fuzzy."

Using my coaxing voice, I said, "Um, hey there pal. How about you don't try Fuzzy's patience? Why don't you come over here with me?" Slowly, I reached out a hand toward the Samara on Fuzzy's nose.

It turned to look at my hand.

Its fellows stopped waving and turned as a group to watch me.

I held my hand still, palm up, and waited. The reckless Samara looked between my hand and my face for a moment then fluttered over to land on my hand.

I could barely tell it was there, it was so light. Slowly, I lifted my hand toward my face.

The reckless Samara lowered its wings so they were pointing down, reminding me of long, droopy dog ears. It used the hands on the ends of its wings to grab hold of the fabric of my glove and balance itself in my palm.

When my hand was about neck high, I said "Hi there," my breath puffing out in a white fog.

Unfortunately, I had my hand too close to my face, and the fog enveloped the Samara.

It shook itself like a wet dog then waved a wing at me agitatedly.

"Sorry," I said, moving my hand back a few inches and out of range of my breath.

It waved at me more calmly. I took that as a sign I hadn't caused any damage.

Apparently so did its buddies because the other three Samaras glided and spun their way over to land on my hand.

Even with all four of them taking up most of my palm, they weren't any heavier than holding four big beans.

"Hi there everyone. I'm Finn. The Housekeeper."

With my other hand, I gestured and said, "This is Fuzzy."

Fuzzy looked at the Samaras and said, "Meow."

The reckless Samara hopped to the edge of my hand and gestured at Fuzzy.

Fuzzy stared at it, then blinked slowly.

I reached for Bayley, huffed in frustration, then said to

Fuzzy, "Let me guess. You can understand these guys, just like you understand Sibeta and the Grack."

Fuzzy gave me the same slow blink he'd just given the Samara.

"I can't decide if that's awesome or frustrating, since they can talk to you, but without Bayley I can't understand what either of you is saying." I shook my head.

Fuzzy tipped his head as though he were thinking.

The reckless Samara turned back to me. As it started waving at me, its buddies joined in.

I had a palm full of waving Talers, and I had no idea what they were saying, what they wanted, or why they'd chosen to show up now.

I missed Bayley so much it was a physical ache.

But he wasn't available, so I hiked up my Housekeeper pants and said, "Welcome to Bayley House. It's freezing out here. Would you like to come inside?"

The reckless Samara turned to Fuzzy. There was some waving while Fuzzy tilted his head and stared at the little guy, having a silent conversation. Then the Samara turned to its friends, and after some group waving, it turned back to Fuzzy.

Fuzzy looked up at me.

"What?" I said.

Fuzzy padded over to the back door.

I looked between the Samaras and the door.

"Okay, I guess we're going inside then."

Chapter Fifteen

The Samaras didn't seem to object, so I took them with me into the house.

Plunking down on the bench in the mudroom, I lowered my hand next to me and said, "Okay you guys, hop off for a minute. I need to change to inside mode."

They all turned to look at me when I started speaking, but instead of hopping down, they turned to each other when I finished. There was a lot of waving again, and I wondered if they were speaking in some kind of sign language, or if there was some kind of telepathy involved. They were so small, maybe their voices were too high-pitched for me to hear.

Wishing I had Bayley to advise me, I gently shook my hand to try to encourage them to get off.

They just clung on tighter.

Fuzzy intervened. He leaned forward and nose-nudged them off my hand. Unfortunately, then they all took to the air and scattered around the room.

"No, wait!" I called. If they got loose in the house, tracking them down would be a nightmare.

Like he was worried about the same thing, Fuzzy meow-barked at them. They flew back to us, hovering in a group.

"Thanks Fuzzy. Can you please do me a favor and let them know that I don't want them to go wandering? They need to stay with us."

Fuzzy turned his attention to the Samaras.

After a moment, the Samaras all waved at him in unison.

Fuzzy looked at me and chirruped.

"I'm going to take that to mean we're all set," I said. "Thank you, Fuzzy. You're a lifesaver."

I hastily took off my coat, gloves, and boots, donned my bunny slippers, then stood up to face the flock.

"Okay you guys. Come on," I gestured with a "follow me" motion and led the way to the kitchen.

They flew in a group trailing behind me, wings occasionally tinkling, with Fuzzy bringing up the rear.

"Please, make yourselves at home," I said, pointing to the kitchen table.

Of course, the Samaras didn't need chairs. They alighted on the table top, the butcher block, and the counter top. The reckless one landed on the water faucet.

"Fuzzy, I'm going to try to find out what they need. Can you please help me?"

Pacing over to me, Fuzzy gave my leg a nuzzle and sat next to me, waiting.

I started with the reckless Samara who'd landed on the faucet.

"Hi," I said.

The Samara launched itself off the faucet, diving, swooping, and whirling around in the air. I had the sense it was trying to communicate.

Looking down at Fuzzy, I said, "Too bad Sibeta is hibernating. I mean, I could wake her up to translate and do her Diplomat for the Talers thing, but I'd rather not do that unless I absolutely have to. Let's see if we can't figure this out ourselves." Pointing to the swooping Samara, I glanced at Fuzzy and said, "Is it excited?" He didn't say anything so I tried again. "Agitated?"

"Meow."

"I was afraid of that. Any chance you can tell me why it's upset?"

Fuzzy gave me a look.

"Yes, I know without Bayley we're severely limited. But anything you can do to help me communicate with these guys would be super helpful."

Fuzzy looked thoughtful. Then he turned and trilled at the

reckless Samara. It came to hover at eye level in front of Fuzzy. They stared at each other, with the Samara occasionally waving at Fuzzy.

While they were in conversation, I scanned the kitchen to see what the other three Samaras were up to.

I was startled to find they'd all flown to the butcher block and were lined up, watching the conversation between Fuzzy and the reckless Samara.

Something must've happened because they all leapt into the air at the same time. The reckless Samara flew over to join them, and there was a bunch of twirling, waving, and diving. It looked to me like they were having a lively debate.

"Are they arguing?" I asked Fuzzy.

"Meow."

"Should I be worried?"

"Meow meow."

"Okay, if you say so. They look like they're really going at it though."

The amount of waving and flitting back and forth had doubled. But I had to admit, it also looked really pretty. It was like watching a bunch of odd snowflakes dancing around the kitchen.

Abruptly, the three Samaras returned to their positions on the butcher block, and the reckless one flew back to Fuzzy.

"I'm guessing the argument's over," I said.

"Meow."

"Okay. Any chance you can give me any idea what's going on?"

"Meow."

"Really? How?"

Fuzzy gently took hold of the edge of my hand in his mouth, being careful not to poke me too hard with his sharp teeth.

I followed his lead and allowed him to shift my hand so it was palm up.

Fuzzy held on as the reckless Samara landed on my index finger. It looked at me then looked at Fuzzy.

I tried to move my hand to bring the Samara closer to my face, but Fuzzy tightened his grip.

"Okay, I got it. You want me to hold still. Why?"

I didn't have to wait long for an answer.

The reckless Samara lowered one wing so that it stretched above my finger. When I leaned in a little closer, I could see that the wing feathers didn't look soft and downy like bird feathers. They looked stiff and spiky, like they were made of lots of little bones instead of little hairs. If they really were made of some kind of bone, no wonder they clinked.

Using the hand on the tip of the opposite wing, the reckless Samara plucked a hair-thin spoke off one feather, turned to me, and jabbed it into my finger.

"Ow!" I yelped, jerking my hand in response. But Fuzzy held onto it, keeping me clamped in place.

The Samara swooshed its wings in an intricate pattern over my finger. A small glow emanated from where it'd stabbed me, then the Samara stopped flapping and turned to stare at me.

I had a split second to be confused before I got so dizzy that I nearly fell over. Fuzzy let go, and the Samara leapt into the air as I slid down the sink cabinet to the ground.

Fuzzy nuzzled my face as I concentrated on taking slow, deep breaths.

A weird buzzing filled my head that coalesced into "...told you it wasn't a good idea."

Fuzzy stopped nuzzling me to glare at the Samara.

It waved at him. "Well look at her! At least before she was working. Now she's all broken."

"I'm not broken." At least I didn't think I was.

"You can understand me?"

I nodded, found that was a bad idea, and used my words instead. "Yes." I looked at Fuzzy. "I take it this is why you let it stab me?"

Fuzzy nodded.

"That glow...was some kind of magic?"

"Meow."

The reckless Samara sounded disgruntled. "It was his idea. Frankly, I wasn't sure it'd work at all. I'm still not sure it was a good idea. I mean, you humans are so weird, it could give you brain damage for all I know." It fluttered its wings. "You don't have brain damage do you?"

"Probably not if Fuzzy said it was okay," I said, hoping my brain wasn't melting. I tried shaking my head again and found that the dizziness had abated, so I slowly climbed to my feet.

I heard a chorus of cheers from behind me and turned to see the other Samaras were jumping into the air and twirling back down to the kitchen block.

"I can hear them too," I said, thumbing at the Samaras behind me.

The cheering cut off abruptly and was replaced by a bunch of low muttering as the Samaras all flocked over to join the reckless guy who'd landed by the sink.

They huddled together, and there was a lot of whispering and gesticulating. I realized with a start that none of their mouths were moving and all the "whispering" I was hearing was in my head. As I watched, the Samaras gestured when they "spoke," just like people did, but the actual communication seemed to be taking place telepathically. Even so, their voices rose and fell the same as if they were speaking out loud.

I was a little nervous about having a bunch of strange telepaths accessing my brain, so I checked my mental shields and was startled to find them super reinforced. Maybe I'd upped my mental armor while I was sleeping as a reaction to Bayley leaving? Or was this my magic protecting me from the bond with the Samaras? I didn't have time to contemplate it, though, because the reckless Samara separated itself from the others and turned to me.

"You being able to hear all of us? This is not normal."

"I get that a lot," I said. When the Samara glared at me I said, "I take it I'm only supposed to be able to talk to you?"

"*If* this worked, which was a big if, no matter what the Orret said—"

"Fuzzy."

"What?"

"The Orret. That's his name."

One of the other Samaras said, "You call the Orret *Fuzzy?*"

"Yup."

There was a pause where they all stared at me, then the Samara on the end whispered loudly, "Maybe her brain was damaged beforehand."

"That'd explain a lot," said a Samara in the middle

"I do not have brain damage! He likes his name. Ask him."

They all turned to Fuzzy, as the reckless one asked, "This is truly your name?" Fuzzy must've backed me up because the Samara on the end said, "Maybe the Orret has brain damage too."

As the others muttered in agreement, I said, "No one has brain damage!"

"Well, whether you have brain damage or not—"

"I don't—"

"—I did the exchange. You should only be talking to me." The reckless Samara pointed its wings straight down and said direly, "This isn't correct."

"Do you do this often?"

All the Samaras twitched their whole bodies as if they were shaking off cooties.

"No," said the reckless one.

"Has this ever been tried with a Housekeeper?"

"Only once. A very long while ago," it admitted.

"That guy was a real…dung beetle," volunteered the Samara on the end.

There was a pause before "dung beetle" popped into my brain, which I guessed was my brain trying to translate what the Samara was saying into something I could understand.

"I take it things didn't go well with the, er, dung beetle?" I said.

"He tried to cage us. For study he said."

"He thought we were some kind of unusual insects! Insects!"

One of the Samaras in the middle added, "He thought maybe Bayley had some kind of effect on the local wildlife. He wasn't able to grasp the concept of…us."

"That's awful!" I said.

"Dung beetle," one of the Samaras muttered.

"I'm so sorry. Well, look, I'm a different Housekeeper, and

I'll do my best to treat you all with the same respect I give any other guest. Okay?"

"Okay," said the reckless Samara. "But this still isn't normal."

"How about we take the fact that I can talk with all of you as an unexpected bonus?"

The reckless Samara grumbled, "Fine."

The one on the end said, "It's too late now anyway."

"Great, so now that we've got that out of the way, how about we introduce ourselves, and you guys can tell me why you're here."

Chapter Sixteen

"Oh that's easy," said the Samara on the end. "We want to—"

"Introductions first," interrupted the reckless Samara.

I said, "I'll go first. I'm Finn the Housekeeper."

The Samaras all spoke over one another.

"We know that."

"Why else would we be talking to you?"

"Oh great. Another one who thinks we're brainless insects. I told you this was a bad idea."

And what seemed to be the now obligatory, "…brain damage. Or maybe she's just not very smart."

"Hey! That's not very nice," I scolded gently.

They all stopped talking and stared at each other. There was a bunch of wing shrugging followed by a begrudging chorus of, "Sorry."

"Just because I'm trying to make sure we're all on the same page, does not mean," I eyed the one on the end, "that I have brain damage. It just means I'm trying to be polite and respectful. Okay?"

The reckless one rocked back and forth in place and said, "Of course." It looked at the other Samaras who also rocked back and forth and echoed, "Of course."

"Now how about you introduce yourselves. And um, what exactly are you?"

"What do you mean?" said the reckless one.

"I'm human. Fuzzy is an Orret. What are you?"

I saw it gesture, there was a delay, and then my brain told me that it'd said, "Pumpernickel."

That didn't seem right, so I asked, "Could you say that again?"

Again, there was a delay after the Samara spoke, but this time my brain came up with, "Purple pickle."

I shook my head. "That didn't translate."

It shook its wings in agitation. "That's because it's not a word in your language."

I sighed. "Well, I've been calling you Samaras." I explained what samaras were, and they agreed that that designation was acceptable for the time being. "Okay, good. Now, what are your names?"

In unison, they all said, "Our cluster is called 'Look Up in the Air! It's a Bird, It's a Plane, It's Those Males.'"

I blinked at them.

The reckless one said, "It didn't translate again?"

"Oh it translated. I'm just not sure it made sense." In fact, I was concerned my internal magical translator had a sense of humor.

"It'd be easier if we just show her," said the one on the end.

"Agreed," said the reckless one.

At the same time, they all launched into the air. It looked like they were all going to crash together, but instead they linked their feet in such a way that they formed a single cluster. Working as a unit, they turned and swooped through the air, linking and unlinking their wings, forming stunningly intricate designs. Their grace and visual prowess would make human aerialists green with envy.

They broke apart again and returned to their spots on the edge of the sink.

"That was beautiful," I said. "It's like you're air-dancing!"

They all puffed themselves up and ruffled their wings, filling the air with tinkling clinks.

"We can do more!" said one in the middle.

"We could show her—" said the one next to it.

"I don't know—" said the one on the end.

The reckless one waved its wings. "Not now! Will you focus?"

All their wings sagged slightly.

"Maybe you can show me later," I said, which caused their

wings to perk back up a bit. "How about we do names for now."

The reckless one waggled a wing to get my attention. "I am," and then all I heard was my brain humming "One of These Things Is Not Like the Other."

I definitely needed to talk to Bayley about debugging my magical translation program when he got back.

I frowned. "Whatever your name is, it isn't translating."

"I am not surprised," he said.

I thought for a moment. "Can you describe to me what your name means?"

He said, "Our names are related to how we work in our cluster. I am that who directs the movement of my cluster."

I pictured the aerial ballet in my head and asked, "Like a choreographer?"

"I do not know this word." He looked at the other Samaras, and they all seemed clueless as well.

"Do you know what dancing is?" I asked.

A couple of the Samaras launched into the air where they darted and dashed, spun and flipped, all in a way that looked reminiscent of a dance.

"Like this?" one called.

They did indeed look like dancers. "Yes, though the people version generally involves music and is on the ground. Like this." I danced around the kitchen a little but stopped when I was greeted with howls of laughter.

"She's like a fish out of water," gasped one between peals of laughter.

"No, it's like she had too much maple juice," said another, who started twitching madly, inducing even more laughter from the others.

I resisted the urge to topple them into the sink and instead returned to stand in front of them, hands on hips. "Hey, not all of us can fly."

The reckless one made an effort to stop laughing and said, "You are correct. That was not bad for a flightless being."

"With a broken leg," the one on the end mumbled.

The reckless one shot them all a look, and they muffled their laughter into the occasional rogue giggle.

I said to the reckless one, "Back to my point, do you know what I mean by dancing?"

This caused a new round of giggles, but the reckless one managed to hang onto his laughter and said, "We do."

"Okay, well, a choreographer is someone who directs the dancers in their group. They tell dancers what kind of movements to do and when to do them. Does that sound like you?"

It thought a moment, looked at the others, who nodded, then looked back at me and said, "Yes that is close enough. I am leader of this cluster."

"How about I call you Corey, for short?"

All the Samaras suddenly stood very still and stared at me.

The reckless one said, "You wish to bestow names upon us?"

I thought the word "bestow" seemed like an odd translation choice, but I said, "Only if it's okay with you. Since I can't understand your real names for now, I need something to call you. Think of them like nicknames."

I wasn't sure if "nickname" was going to translate but I guess the Samara got the gist because he said, "A moment, Housekeeper."

The Samaras took to the air and huddled together in a clump, talking quietly.

I said to Fuzzy in a low voice, "I'm not sure why nicknames require a conference. I think I'm missing something here."

Fuzzy tipped his head, looking thoughtful, but didn't comment.

Before I could talk with Fuzzy further, the Samaras returned to the lip of the sink.

The leader said, "We will receive your naming, Housekeeper. With thanks." He leaned forward, sweeping his wings down and back, in what looked like a formal bow. The others did the same.

That feeling that I was missing something got worse, but without Bayley to clarify, I had to wing it. "Okay then. So you will be Corey?"

"Kuh-or-eee," it repeated back slowly. "I accept, Housekeeper.

For you, I shall be Corey."

The Samara next to Corey stepped forward. "Do me! In our cluster, I do this!" And he leapt into the air, executed a series of spins that made me dizzy just watching, then landed gracefully.

"You do turns?" I asked, making a twirling motion with my finger.

"Yes!" He said, twitching his wings with pleasure.

I said, "Well a dance term for a turn is called a pirouette. What if I call you Rou for short?"

"Roooo...yes, I accept. With thanks," he said.

Next up came Jet, named after jeté, because he did a series of spectacular darts into the air that reminded me of leaps.

And finally, my "maybe she has brain damage" buddy on the end got dubbed Shay because he did a series of dives that reminded me of the way a ballerina plunges toward the floor in a penché.

"Great, now that I know your names, how can I help you?"

Corey said, "Can you keep a secret?"

Chapter Seventeen

"Yes, I can keep a secret," I told Corey and the other Samaras, who'd clustered around him.

Corey folded his wings forward and started using the hands at the end of each wing to fuss with the feathers on the opposite wing. It took me a moment to realize that Corey was fidgeting.

"Corey," I said gently, "there's no need to be nervous. It's okay to tell me whatever is going on."

"We would like some more of the soft, brown—" my brain paused and came up with "trash seeds. Please," Corey added hastily.

The other Samaras echoed, "Please!"

"I think we're having a translation glitch. Soft, brown trash seeds? Fuzzy, do you know what they're talking about?"

Fuzzy leapt up onto the kitchen counter and batted at the stack of food containers that I had washed but not put away yet—the ones that had held the cookies I'd put outside.

"Oh! Did you guys eat all the cookies?" I asked, astonished, taking in the tiny size of the Samaras and comparing it to the dozens of cookies that had gone missing. Maybe they were like hummingbirds and needed a ton of sugar to fuel their aerial acrobatics.

Corey must have thought I sounded accusatory because he folded his wings all the way across his body and began wringing his hands. "We took the—" a pause, but this time I got "cookies" when the translation kicked in. Adding in a rush, he said, "They were outside. We thought you did not want them."

Well, that explained why my translator had come up with "trash seeds."

I said, "It's okay. You guys aren't in trouble. I had no specific plans for those cookies, and I'm happy to share."

Wings perking up a bit, Corey said, "We hoped you might have more you do not want."

I realized they must be really hungry to come and ask me for help. The Talers were notoriously shy and for them to reveal themselves to me…well, they must've been bordering on desperate.

"I do have extras, and I'd be happy to make some more." I did a quick mental tally of the baking supplies that I had stashed. I'd planned ahead in case we got snowed in, so I had plenty of ingredients on hand. "Was there a particular flavor you liked better?" My heart lifted at the thought of being able to bake for them, and I felt better than I had since Bayley left.

Corey and the other Samaras looked back and forth at each other. "Flavor?" Corey asked.

I went to the freezer and pulled out some of the cookies I had stashed there. After I fished out one each of oatmeal raisin, peanut butter, chocolate chip, and plain sugar cookies, I brought the pile to the butcher block and laid them out in a row for the Samaras.

"I don't remember which of these I left outside. Do you like one type more than the other?"

With a cheer, the Samaras flocked over to the first cookie and surrounded it.

Corey held up a wing and the others stopped. They all turned to me, wings twitching, as Corey said, "May we have them?"

"Of course, but they're still frozen. Do you want me to warm them up?"

"No need," said Corey as the Samaras, in a totally coordinated motion, each grabbed a tiny chunk of cookie and ate it at the exact same time. Then, they moved from cookie to cookie, staying in perfect sync, tasting each cookie in the row.

The decision was split. Corey liked the oatmeal raisin best, but Jet liked the chocolate chip, Rou liked the peanut butter, and Shay liked the plain sugar.

"We would be grateful for any," said Corey, bowing, and the others followed suit.

"I'll tell you what. I can put together a mix of what's in the freezer for starters. How many would you like?"

"We would be glad of any number," said Corey. The other Samaras fluttered up and down on the butcher block in what I thought was excitement.

I had about four dozen in the freezer, so I sorted out two dozen for them. "Um, how are you going to carry these?"

We decided a baggie would work best. I was zipping it shut when all the Samaras suddenly froze. Shay darted to the window over the sink and said, "Uh oh."

The others joined in. I followed and peered outside. All I saw was snow falling sleepily to the ground.

I was about to ask what we were looking at when Corey spun to me, rising up so he could look me straight in the eyes. "The cookies. They are our secret?"

I had no idea why I needed to keep cookies a secret, but it seemed important to Corey, so I said, "Um sure. In fact, if you'd like me to bake you cookies regularly, we can probably work something out. I'd just like to get Bayley involved, but I can't do that right now. Bayley—the house—is, er, sleeping."

"We know."

"What do you mean you know?" That brought me up short. Was that why they were here? Because Bayley was offline, and they were somehow trying to take advantage of that fact?

Shay was signaling frantically from the window, so Corey flew over. After a glance out the window, he said, "We must go. Do you mind leaving the cookies in the same way as before?"

"Sure that's fine—"

The whole cluster sped out of the kitchen. But instead of taking a left for the back door, they turned right.

Fuzzy and I dashed after them as I shouted, "Hey!"

They ignored me, hurling straight for the front door. They stopped short, right before they smashed into it, and then dropped to the doorknob.

I reached the door just a few seconds after them, and they were already working at opening the door.

"Here, I can get that for you," I said. They scattered as I reached for the knob. When I yanked open the door, a cold wind pushed its way into the hallway, causing me to take a step back.

It didn't seem to bother the Samaras at all. Jet, Rou, and Shay clustered in the doorway, while Corey zipped outside. Stopping to hover above the porch, Corey spun around this way and that, then waved a wing, and the others dashed out to join him.

They formed a line, chorused, "Thank you" as they dipped once, then dashed off, disappearing into the falling snow.

Another gust of wind convinced me to shut the door rather than stand there gawking.

Returning to the kitchen, I looked out the window to try and identify what I'd missed that had caused their abrupt departure.

The sleepy snow continued to head for its napping spot on the ground. But nothing in particular looked out of place.

Fuzzy hopped up on the counter, looked out the window, then back at me, then out the window again.

I stared at the world outside and said, "I don't see it."

With a little huff, Fuzzy reached out a paw and gently batted my jaw until I turned my head.

I obliged and stared in the direction he indicated toward the tree line.

"Meow," he said.

"I am looking."

I stared harder. Finally, I got it. "That clump over there right at the edge of the trees. It's moving in a different direction than the rest of the snow."

"Meow."

Now that I knew what I was looking for, I scanned the tree line again. "I see at least two others."

"Meow...meow."

"More? There's more?"

"Meow."

"Are those more Samaras?"

"Meow."

"Huh." I hadn't had a chance to talk to Corey and the others about their species at all, and now I was wishing I had.

I stood watching the Samaras in the distance for a few moments. None of them approached the house.

I said, "Given our little dance troupe's hasty exit, I'm going to hazard a guess that maybe they weren't supposed to be here."

Fuzzy just looked at me.

"And if they weren't supposed to be here, what do you want to bet that they're not supposed to be eating cookies?"

Chapter Eighteen

Fuzzy and I watched the miscellaneous Samaras until they faded back into the woods.

"That's a lot of little guys," I told Fuzzy. I could see why the former Housekeeper had thought they might be insects. "I wonder how many there are altogether?"

Whether my little troupe of Samaras were supposed to be eating piles of sugar or not, I'd told Corey and his group that they could have more cookies, so I dumped the cookies in the baggie into the plastic food tubs and placed them on the porch as promised.

"I'll check with Bayley when he gets back to make sure I'm not breaking some kind of rule. But in the meantime, I don't see a big problem with sneaking the Samaras some cookies," I told Fuzzy.

Happy for an excuse to spend the rest of the day in my happy place, I skipped magic practice and baked more cookies, played music for Percy, and puttered around the kitchen.

That night, I still felt unusually tired, but I felt calmer, and I fell into a dreamless sleep.

When I came downstairs the next morning, I popped outside to check to see how many cookies were still left.

There weren't any.

After I hustled back inside, I said, "Those are some hungry guys. I may need to up my baking game."

That day and the next few passed by in an almost *Groundhog Day* fashion. Wake, put Stella in my pocket, breakfast, practice magic, lunch, bake stuff while I played music for Percy, dinner, try to stay awake and fail, put Stella on the nightstand, bed. At some point during the day, Nor and/or Mila would call or text to check on me.

Although it wasn't that easy. Every day, I'd hear some random noise, like the house creaking or groaning, and I'd start to talk to Bayley, then stop mid-sentence when I re-remembered he wasn't there. Or I'd think I heard a whisper or a laugh behind me and whip around, only to realize that the wind was sighing past the window.

And every night, the recurring nightmare ripped me from my sleep.

All the while, there was no word from Bayley.

That's how I finished out the first week.

As I trudged into my second week, my magical practice started to falter.

I was in the greenhouse, working some Foster magic on a plant that was struggling, and my mind wandered. One minute I was in my magical meditation zone, and the next, I was back in the night that Bayley had left, reliving the memory of him leaving and me waking up the next morning Bayley-less.

I snapped out of it to find myself standing over the plant. Fortunately, I'd let go of my magic the second my mind wandered, so I was looking at a healthy, blooming plant rather than a dried flower arrangement.

My head was starting to hurt, and I felt vastly uneasy that I'd lost focus, so I ended practice early that day and had an early lunch.

But the same thing happened when I tried to work Murphy magic the next day, and Guthrie magic the day after that. The following day was Smith magic, and when my mind started down memory lane before I'd even begun to call up my Smith magic, I decided that maybe I needed to rethink my plans before I barbecued the back lawn.

I called Zo.

"Something weird is happening."

"You don't say."

"I mean beside Bayley being offline. I'm having trouble

concentrating." I told her about my magic practice and asked, "Do you think it's related to Bayley being gone so long?"

Zo said carefully, "What do you think?"

I wanted to snark, "I don't know, that's why I'm calling you," but instead I hazarded a guess. "He didn't intend to be gone the whole three weeks. Maybe the longer he's gone, the more of a strain it is on him if I do magic?"

"Mmm."

I nodded. "Actually that kind of makes sense, if you think about it. It's got to be more of a strain on him, the longer he's gone."

"It is."

She sounded so certain that I wondered what she wasn't telling me. "Okay. Well in that case, maybe I should lay off practicing until he gets back. It's only a couple of weeks—not enough time for me to lose any ground." I tapped the counter as I thought. "I can switch to studying the piles of magical texts I have and pick up the practical part when he gets back."

"Sounds like you have it all figured out then," Zo said and hung up.

I stared at the phone then looked at Fuzzy. "Is it me, or is Zo even more terse than usual since Bayley left?"

Fuzzy said, "Meow, meow," and shook his head for emphasis.

"Well, good to know it's not just me, I guess. But I wonder why Bayley being gone has her out of sorts. If that's even what's bugging her. With Zo, it's hard to tell."

Fuzzy stared hard at me for a long moment, then sighed and shook his head again.

"Well whatever. I figured out what I needed to know. No more magic practice for me till Bayley gets back."

The next day, I tried out my new "study only" plan, and to my relief, I was able to focus just fine.

"I think this will work out well," I told Fuzzy.

But I was washing dishes after lunch when a sudden lurch caused me to drop my dish into the sink with a clatter.

Fuzzy bounded over and pawed at my leg.

Shutting the water off, I looked around the kitchen,

disconcerted. "Did you feel that?"

"Meow."

It took me a minute to locate the lurching feeling. It had come from my connection with Bayley, but I could feel something different about the property.

"Bayley?" I called. When he didn't answer, I dove inside my mind to check on him.

He was still offline, gleaming dimly in the distance, but when I looked at the connection between us, I did a double-take. The energy flowing from Bayley to me was still sluggish, but the energy going from me to him had picked up speed.

I opened my eyes and looked at Fuzzy. "Something is happening. Bayley is pulling energy from me. Just a trickle, but he's definitely using me for backup."

I called up my mental map and scanned the property, including the house. The property's magical boundary grabbed my attention.

"Uh oh," I said to Fuzzy. "There's an extra layer of lockdown barriers in place. It's like the magical walls around the property thickened. A lot. You can feel that?"

"Meow."

I paced. "What do you want to bet that Bayley needing extra energy is related to the extra lockdowns." I stopped as I said, "Oh no. What else got affected?"

I grabbed my cell phone and dialed Nor. When the call went through and the phone started ringing, my shoulders slumped in relief. At least I wasn't totally cut off yet.

I left Nor a message saying, "Hey Nor. More lockdown protocols just snapped into place. For now, my cell phone is still working—obviously—but I'm not sure how much longer that's going to last, so I wanted to make sure to touch base with you and let you know what's going on." I paused and tried to put some cheer in my voice as I said, "Don't worry. It's fine. It's only another week and a half of this, max, so if we get cut off, don't stress."

For a second, I thought about telling her about Bayley needing energy from me, but I decided that would definitely stress her out, so instead I ended the call with, "Okay, hopefully we'll talk soon. But at the very least, I'll call you when Bayley gets back. Take care."

I hung up and just stared at the cell phone. While a tiny part of me still held on to the hope that Bayley would show up any time now, the rest of me had resigned myself to the fact that he'd be gone the whole time.

I checked the energy flowing between me and Bayley again. It was small enough that I couldn't feel its effects over my ambient level of fatigue. But still, I'd have to be super careful that I ate regularly and didn't overextend myself, or I'd definitely feel the drain.

I looked at Fuzzy. "Well, we knew this would probably get weirder before it got better."

I made us some dinner, and then we trundled off to bed.

As had been the case since Bayley left, I passed out the second my head hit the pillow.

But I didn't dream.

Chapter Nineteen

The next few days blurred together as I followed my new routine. The main change was that I was actually sleeping every night now. Maybe because Bayley had been gone more than a week, my brain had finally adjusted. Well, somewhat. Even with the extra sleep, fatigue continued to plague me. And I was still jumping at sounds, constantly looking over my shoulder.

As I was nearing the end of the second week, I ran out of eggs. The next day I ran out of milk.

With the lockdowns in place, there was no way for me to get new groceries, so I was stuck with what I had on hand.

I checked the Internet to see what kind of recipes I could download for limited-ingredient desserts, but my connection was slow and spotty. It reminded me of how crappy our service was in the desert. I'd come to take a good Internet connection for granted, and now I was seriously resenting my lack of access.

I surveyed the cookies I had already made, figured out how many more batches I could make with what I had on hand, and shook my head.

"Well, I'm going to have to dole out what's left a little at a time and hope the Samaras don't get mad at me."

Fuzzy sniffed.

"Yes, yes, I know I don't *have* to give the Samaras anything at all, but I don't want to cut them off with no warning. Maybe if I taper them down, they'll figure out I'm running out of stuff. Or they'll come and talk to me again, and I'll be able to explain."

Fuzzy huffed and muttered. Apparently I was looking

forward to seeing the Samaras again a lot more than he was.

While I made the cookies, the classical music swelling around me, I drifted into my happy place. At first. But my thoughts drifted back to the night Bayley left and the next morning when I woke up without him. I only realized I'd wandered off into the past when the kitchen timer went off and jarred me back to the present, heart racing. Shaking my head at myself, I managed to finish making the remaining batches without losing focus.

When I set the last batch out to cool, I had about an hour till sunset. As I donned my outdoor gear, Fuzzy materialized next to me.

"Yes, of course you can come out with me. It's chilly though, and it'll be night soon, so you know the rules. Don't go taking off on me, please."

Fuzzy gave me an affronted look and went to stand in front of the back door.

I went out onto the back porch and surveyed the yard. "Do you see the Samaras anywhere?" I asked.

Fuzzy shook his head.

I sighed. "Okay let's try the front."

Fuzzy and I went through the house and out onto the front porch. I'd cleared off a small path, so I was able to walk to the edge of the stairs and look out over the yard.

A pristine snowscape had replaced the grove I knew and loved. It was so flat and round that I had the urge to use my Smith powers to liquify the snow and turn it into a giant ice skating rink. Not that I knew how to skate. Yet. But it was on my list of things to learn. I sighed. Too bad I hadn't thought of it before I'd cut off my magic practice.

Staring at the grove in front of the house usually made me sigh with pleasure. Even though I could see Todd and Libby, the sentinel trees that marked the entrance to the grove where Bayley lived, I didn't feel my usual sense of comfort from them.

Instead, flashes of my recurring nightmare swamped my mind.

Cold bit at my lungs as my breathing quickened, and I put

a hand on the porch post to steady myself.

Fuzzy trilled at me, ears back in concern.

"It's the stupid nightmares," I said.

They were bad enough at night. No way was I going to let them dominate my waking life. Gritting my teeth, I carefully plodded down the porch steps and waded a little way out toward the lawn.

I hated that my heart was pounding, not just from exertion, but also from anxiety.

When I'd made it a little ways from the house, I turned and stomped my way back to the porch.

Something inside me eased as I made it up the steps with no trouble.

"Hah! Take that subconscious." I hadn't had any nightmares the last few nights, but I was still haunted by them, and I had the sinking feeling that as long as Bayley was gone they could pop up any time.

Fuzzy was looking at me strangely, but I ignored him.

I walked back and forth a few times, porch to driveway and back, until all of the anxiety faded, and I started to laugh at myself.

"Much better," I giggled.

Fuzzy shook his head and followed me as I walked down off the porch to the edge of the snow path I'd made.

A rustling in the trees to the left caught my ear. Fuzzy and I swiveled at the same time, looking over to investigate.

"Samaras?" I asked Fuzzy hopefully.

Fuzzy's ears were partway back, and he said, "Meow meow," and shook his head for emphasis.

Still, I thought I heard something, softly whispering through the forest.

I cocked my head and listened harder. When I looked down, Fuzzy was doing the same thing.

"I don't see anything. Do you?"

Fuzzy shook his head, then started to walk to the porch.

"Wait, let's have a closer look," I said, wading toward the woods. I kept going until I'd reached the edge of the house.

Moving closer didn't help. I still couldn't see any movement. But the same soft whisper came again. I was listening so hard that I felt like my ears were ringing.

I started forward. But Fuzzy lodged a claw in the bottom of my right pants leg, causing me to slip. As I windmilled for balance, I splashed snow all over my parka.

Stella started chiming.

"Jeez Fuzzy. Now see what you've done," I said.

Unrepentant, Fuzzy clawed both of my pants legs and tugged.

"I take it you're done snow trekking for today?" I asked.

Fuzzy yanked on my pants again at the same time that Stella chimed.

"Both of you have had enough of the cold huh? Well, two to one—you win. Let's go inside." With another quick glance over my shoulder, I trudged back through the snow to the house. I clomped up the porch, but before I went inside, I paused for another look at the tree line. The shadows were starting to deepen as the sun headed off for its dinner plans. Squinting, I scanned the trees one last time, but I still didn't see Samaras or anything else.

"Meow!" Fuzzy shifted impatiently.

"I'm going to assume that your better eyesight and hearing ruled out anything interesting happening in the woods?"

Fuzzy huffed.

"Okay then, let's go in and get dinner started," I said.

The rustling sound came again, but I slipped inside and closed the door.

Chapter Twenty

The next day, not having enough ingredients on hand to blithely bake away the afternoon put the kibosh on my newfound routine.

I studied my magic books in the morning, but then after lunch, the afternoon yawned before me.

And all at once, everything sort of hit me.

I paced as I thought.

It'd been nearly two full weeks without Bayley, and I'd had no word. What if he was hurt or in trouble? Worse, what if he didn't come back at all?

I was already short on basic baking supplies and would eventually run out of food. My phone and Internet service were spotty and likely to disappear altogether any second, leaving me truly isolated. I couldn't even use Percy to get help. I had no backup.

What the hell was I doing with my life anyway? Had becoming the Housekeeper been a terrible idea?

And that was the thought that put an end to my spiral. Because the one thing that I knew for sure was that given the same choice, I'd choose being Housekeeper again.

So I did what I always did when I needed to think things through. I made coffee and sat myself at the kitchen table.

I'd been there sorting through my feelings long enough to nearly finish my coffee when Percy interrupted the quiet. "Aren't we baking today?"

"I ran out of ingredients. No more baking till Bayley gets back."

"Hmph."

"Not to worry, Percy. I can still put on music for you to enjoy.

Would it be alright if I play it for you while I'm studying in the mornings?"

"Yes. That would be...acceptable."

A grin teased the corners of my mouth as I said, "Just 'acceptable'?"

Percy huffed, "Fine. It would be...nice."

I smiled but didn't continue to tease him.

I'd been sitting there sipping my coffee for another few minutes when Percy asked, "What are you doing?"

"Drinking coffee?"

"Well, yes, but you're just sitting there. In silence. You never sit still for long, much less in silence."

I couldn't tell whether I should be offended or not. "I don't think that's entirely true. But anyway, I'm just thinking." And I went back to drinking my coffee and pondering.

Another few minutes passed and Percy said, "About what?"

I set my coffee down and pulled my necklace up so the pendant was even with my face. "Are you alright?"

"Why do you ask?"

"You've never asked me or anyone else what we're thinking before."

I thought maybe I'd offended him when he didn't reply right away, but then he said, "Things are not...usual...at the moment."

I snorted. "When is my life ever 'usual'?"

"You know what I mean."

"I do." I released the pendant and walked to the coffeepot to get a refill. "To answer your question, I was thinking about what it's been like the last couple of weeks alone here—well, not alone—I've got you and Fuzzy—but, you know, without Bayley." I refilled my cup and returned to the table.

"And?"

I stared into my coffee and fiddled with my mug. "I was really worried when Bayley said he was leaving.... When I agreed to be the Housekeeper, I knew it'd come with a degree of isolation— that's part of the deal. And I've been feeling it, particularly since winter came, and we get snowed in every other week.

"But this," I waved my hand around vaguely, "this is a kind

of isolation I've never experienced before."

"You weren't ever really alone at the diner."

"Not really, no. Sure my parents had a date night once in a while, but I was never alone for any length of time before."

"And?"

I blew out a breath. "And, I'm okay." I was surprised to realize that I really was. "Sure I've had a few bumpy days. And some full-on panic moments," like the one I'd had earlier.

When I didn't continue, Percy prompted, "But?"

"Well, that's what I've been thinking about." I took a sip of coffee and then tried to explain. "The hard part was agreeing to be Housekeeper. And yeah, it's been a huge adjustment. But every time I start to panic, I think about being Housekeeper, and I calm down."

"And?"

"And I think that maybe I'm settling into life as the Housekeeper." I felt superstitious about saying it out loud, like I might somehow jinx it. "Does it suck having Bayley gone? Yup. But am I coping? Yes. Yes I am."

"You sound surprised."

"Well yeah. This whole thing has knocked me for a loop." I took another sip of coffee before I added, "But it hasn't knocked me out. And I'm not going to let it."

Percy was quiet for a minute, then he asked, "Do you like being Housekeeper?"

Startled, it took me a few seconds to respond. "You've never asked me that before either."

"What would be the point of asking when Bayley is around? You're too soft-hearted. Even if you hated it here, you'd never say so in front of him because you wouldn't want to hurt his feelings."

Alarmed, I said, "Have I done something that makes you think I hate it here?"

"No...but time without Bayley gives you a rare chance to assess the situation...privately."

"And you think that with him gone I'm going to find that I have second thoughts?"

Percy said quietly, "Yes."

"Why?"

"Why wouldn't you? You're trapped in this place. It's a nice enough place. But you're trapped nonetheless." Bitterness tinged his voice.

I wasn't sure we were really talking about me anymore. "Is that how you feel? Trapped?" When Percy didn't answer, I said carefully, "It's different for me, Percy. I chose this. Do I have days when it's hard? Hell yes. Some of them are really hard. Like when Nor and Mila went to Fiji over the new year. Had I not been Housekeeper, I could have gone with them and spent two weeks playing in the ocean." Although if I weren't Housekeeper, I probably wouldn't be such close friends with them. But still.

Percy said, "Exactly my point. This is a pretty prison. But it's a prison nonetheless."

I shook my head. "I don't feel imprisoned. Restricted, yes. Even disheartened sometimes. But never like I'm in jail." I paused then added. "It's my choice. And...I like my life."

Percy sounded disbelieving as he said, "And you have no regrets?"

I laughed. "I didn't say my life is perfect. But in terms of the this-is-your-life big picture? No. Not really. I wanted an adventure. And I got one. Mostly, I feel lucky."

Percy sounded even more incredulous as he said, "Lucky?"

I smiled. "Well, in awe a lot. And surprised a lot. And worried about becoming Ensign Red Shirt way more than I anticipated. But mostly lucky." I waited, but when he didn't respond, I said gently, "I take it you don't feel lucky. Being in the necklace."

Percy sounded exhausted as he said, "This *is* the lucky option."

If being in the necklace was good luck, and he hated it as much as he seemed to, what had the bad luck option been?

Chapter Twenty-One

As the calendar clicked over to week three, the final set of lockdowns fell into place. The magical boundaries doubled again in thickness, the Internet went out for good, and so did my cell phone.

As I did every morning when I made coffee, I checked on Bayley. Like every other day, nothing had changed.

Thinking of Bayley, my mind immediately returned to the night he left. I managed to avoid getting sucked into the memory and then huffed at myself in frustration.

My unscheduled trips down memory lane were getting more and more frequent. At first, the memories had only plagued me when I was in my meditative magic-using mental state. Then they started interrupting me when I was baking. Now they were interfering with me concentrating on my studies and even doing basic tasks like making coffee. And every time I snapped out of the memory, I was on edge, my whole body like a coiled spring, my heart double-timing it.

I was starting to get worried.

With a sigh, I reminded myself that this was the last week, and Bayley would be back soon. Then I started reorganizing the kitchen. Again.

Fortunately, Zo showed up.

I was drinking coffee, looking out the back window, when I felt her blip onto my mental map. She was on the back porch.

As I moved through the kitchen, I heard her tap at the door.

"Hi Zo," I said, letting her in.

Zo stepped into the hallway and stopped.

"Would you like to have some coffee?" I asked, heading for the kitchen.

"No thank you." Zo hadn't moved, so I stopped in the kitchen doorway and turned to face her.

"Your phone is dead?" Zo said.

I nodded. "Yes. And the Internet. It's week three, so I suppose it's to be expected. You know, since Bayley isn't back yet." I sounded disappointed, even to myself. "Um, how did you get past the magical lockdown barriers anyway? If you can do that, any chance you could bring me some groceries? I'm out of milk and eggs—"

"No. I can't. I can, however, get you one phone call," said Zo. She pulled a phone out of her pocket and handed it to me. "This will work once, and only once, so choose wisely."

Before I could comment, she spun on her heel and walked out the door. Within moments, she had blipped off my mental map.

I stared after her, blinking. "Uh," I waved at the closed door, "thanks for dropping by?" I looked down at the phone in my hand, then at Fuzzy, who had been watching from the kitchen.

"That's weird, right? Even for Zo?"

Fuzzy sighed.

I went back to the kitchen and put the phone on the counter. "I wonder who she thinks I'm going to need to call. And why."

Chapter Twenty-Two

As it turned out, it didn't take me long to figure out what to do with the phone.

The next morning, studying was nearly impossible. Every time I tried to read, my mind wandered back to the night Bayley left. Finally, I gave it up and went to the greenhouse to visit the Grack and the Gracklettes, thinking a change in scenery would help clear my mind.

The visit gave me the warm fuzzies, and I left with a smile on my face.

But as I was walking toward the house, my mind wandered again, drawing me back to the night Bayley left.

The next thing I knew, my ears were ringing, Stella was chiming, and Fuzzy was howling and stabbing me in the butt with his claws.

"Ow!"

I looked down to find that I was thigh-deep in snow and had waded past the edge of the house toward the forest.

"What the…?" I blinked, shaking my head groggily, which I immediately regretted when my head ached in response.

"Okay Stella, you can turn the claxon off," I said, wincing as my head throbbed in time with the chiming. She stopped as I turned around to face Fuzzy, who meow-scolded me.

Shakily, I said, "Thank you both." My face was so cold that I was having difficulty talking. "I…I don't know why I'm zombie walking across the yard, but I can tell you this definitely is not a good thing. Thanks for stopping me."

Fuzzy trilled at me worriedly.

"Let's go inside before I do anything else stupid."

Fuzzy led the way, stopping every few feet to make sure I was following. I waded back to the shoveled path then hurried inside the house.

When I fumbled with the zipper on my coat, I realized my fingers were numb. And my feet.

"Fuzzy are you okay? If I'm this cold—" Frantically, I grabbed for his front paw. He let me, and I was relieved to see that there was no sign of frostbite. Tears in my eyes, I said, "I could have hurt you. This is bad. Are you really okay?"

Fuzzy nuzzled me and purred softly.

Shivers shook me as my body started to thaw out. While I made a fresh pot of coffee to help warm me up, Fuzzy stayed glued to my heels. I was anxious enough that I didn't need the caffeine, but I was so freaked out that the comfort factor outweighed any concerns about the jitters.

As I waited for the coffee to finish, I gripped the edge of the counter and tried to think through what had happened. "Okay, so what we know is that I've been having the memory flashbacks. And they're getting worse. It's definitely related to Bayley being gone. The only thing I know of that can cause flashbacks is PTSD. Is it possible to get magical PTSD?"

My gaze landed on the cell phone. I wondered who I knew that could talk to me about PTSD-type flashbacks and if finding out was what I should spend my one phone call on.

Fuzzy rubbed against my leg then hopped up on the counter so he could nuzzle my face. I wrapped my arms around him and buried my face in his fur. Not only had I put myself in danger, but I'd also endangered Fuzzy, and possibly even Stella.

"Yeah, this isn't a wasted call. It's necessary at this point," I said, pulling back from Fuzzy and grabbing the phone.

I dialed the phone and breathed a sigh of relief when the call went through.

"Yup?"

"Hey Lars. It's Finn." I'd briefly thought about calling Nor or Mila, but discarded the idea because my calls almost always went to voicemail. But Lars almost always answered.

"What's wrong?"

"What makes you think something is wrong?"

"I may be your favorite mercenary, but I'm pretty sure you're not calling to invite me to tea. And I'm guessing there's a reason you're calling from a number I don't recognize."

I laughed and said, "You're right. I need your expertise." And I explained about Bayley being offline.

When I finished, he let out a whistle. "This must be a big adjustment for you."

"No kidding."

"So what's the problem?"

"I, um, think I might have some kind of magical-backlash PTSD-ish situation. Something is wrong with me. At first I was having recurring nightmares. And now, I can't stop thinking about Bayley leaving. I keep flashing back and reliving when he left and when I woke up after. It started off just happening once a day or so, but now it's happening more."

"That's understandable, given your circumstances."

"Well maybe. But just now, while I was stuck in a flashback, I wandered off into the middle of the yard—in the snow and the cold—like I was sleepwalking. Whatever is going on with my brain is getting worse, and I'm worried I'm going to do something dumb and hurt myself or Fuzzy." I clenched the phone like a lifeline as I added, "Given your profession, and how much action you guys have seen, I thought you might have some insight—maybe some ideas how to chill out."

"Mmm. Is there a particular point in the memory that you're stuck on?"

"Yes! How'd you know?"

"It's not unusual. Do you feel comfortable telling me about it?"

"Okay, but it doesn't make any sense. I keep remembering going to sleep, then waking up the next morning."

A pause. "Tell me about the waking up part."

"There's not much to tell. I went to sleep, I woke up, remembered about Bayley, and then got up."

"Can you tell me how you feel when you think about it?"

"The going to sleep part after he left? I feel sad and a little scared. But the waking up part," my breathing got short and tight, and I started to pace, "I think about it, and I feel like I need to run," I sounded breathy, and my pace picked up as I strode back and forth, "like I'm in trouble, and I need to...something."

"Slow, deep breath Finn."

I forced myself to stop pacing and did as he instructed. "I. Can't. Stop. Thinking about it! That moment when I woke up. And the more I think about it, the more of a headache I get."

Lars was quiet for a long moment. "Do you get a headache when you think about the night when Bayley left?"

"Huh. Actually, no."

"What happens when you try to think about when you were asleep?"

"I don't have any memories from then. I was *sleeping.*"

"Humor me. Try and remember something—being woken up by the wind briefly, a dream fragment. Anything."

I searched my memory but, "There's nothing there."

"Mmm. How's your head feel?"

"My head? Oh. I've got a little headache forming."

There was a long pause before Lars said, "Who's there with you?"

"It's just me and Fuzzy."

"I'll call you back."

"No, wait! This is the only call I get—it's complicated—"

A grunt then another long pause. "Let me talk to Fuzzy."

I turned to see that Fuzzy was moving toward me. "I guess you can hear him."

"Meow."

To Lars I said, "Fuzzy is sitting at my feet. Do you want me to put you on speaker?"

"No."

I looked askance at the phone, and it was like he could see me as he said, "Just go with me here. I know you can talk with him. How does the 'yes' and 'no' work?"

"One meow is 'yes,' two is 'no.'"

"Great. Can you hold the phone next to him? Please?"

The urgency in his voice let me know that he was taking all this seriously, so I did as he asked.

After a series of "yeses" and "nos," Fuzzy nudged the phone toward me, which I took to be my cue.

"Do you remember when Nor talked to me and RG about signing the confidentiality agreement?"

Confused by the non sequitur it took me a moment to say, "Yes."

"Do you remember that we were happy to go ahead and sign because we wanted to avoid a hex?"

"Uh huh."

"Do you remember why?"

"Something about side effects?"

"Yes."

He seemed to be waiting for me to elaborate, so I searched my memory. I said slowly, "RG said you'd rather avoid a hex because too many hexes could clash with each other."

"And even if they don't clash?"

"They give you headaches." I went cold. "You think I've been hexed?!?"

"That's what Fuzzy says. Whatever happened, he was there. He doesn't think you're in any immediate danger from the hexer though. I asked."

Mouth agape, I looked at Fuzzy, who pawed at my leg.

Lars said, "Try thinking about the night Bayley left again, but try harder to remember the period when you were 'sleeping.'"

I concentrated, remembering falling asleep and then searching for—"Ow!" An arrow of pain stabbed through the base of my head.

"Stop!"

As soon as I focused back on Lars, the pain evaporated.

"What hurt?"

"My head."

"Where?"

"The back of my head, near the bottom."

Lars sighed. "Okay, this is really important. Don't go digging for the memory."

"But you just said…"

"That was just to do a quick test. Someone has messed with your memory. We don't know who or what they did, exactly, but they did it while Bayley was gone, so they wouldn't have him as a witness."

"It was right after he left," I said. Mind racing, I added, "Lars, it's worse than you think. With the lockdown protocols in place, no one should be able to get in or out of here. And worse, nothing unusual is on the property. I've been checking carefully."

"Well, someone found a way around the lockdown because someone tampered with your memory as soon as Bayley was gone."

Chapter Twenty-Three

I didn't know whether to start with who, why, or how. So instead of saying anything, I just stood there, mouth flapping open and closed, like a fish out of water.

"Maybe I should come by. I'm nowhere near you physically, but can you use the necklace thing again?"

I shook my head, "No. It's part of the lockdown. You know, the part where *no one goes in or out*," I growled, resuming my pacing. "Oh this is bad. This is bad right?"

"Well, it's not great."

"Is there a way around the memory block?"

Lars said, "I wouldn't," in a way that made me think he was shaking his head "no" really hard. "There's too many unknowns. Who placed it, what kind of magic they used, if they set any booby-traps in place in case you attempted to disarm it—"

"Booby-traps!"

"It's a possibility."

"Well, bugger."

"Seriously, Finn. You're there alone—"

Fuzzy howled.

"Sorry Fuzzy," Lars called. "But you both know what I mean. There's a limit to what Fuzzy can do to help. And with this lockdown in place—"

"Lot of good that's doing," I muttered. "Only thing it seems to be stopping is me."

"—and no Bayley to provide backup," continued Lars, "it's not worth the risk. Are you listening Finn?"

"Yeah, yeah," I muttered.

"You wouldn't perform brain surgery on yourself would you?"

"I mean, it wouldn't be my first choice, no."

"Okay then," Lars said, sounding relieved. "So you can just try to deal with the flashbacks until Bayley comes back. There's not a lot you can do, other than being aware of when you start to slip away and having Fuzzy keep an eye on you. When Bayley drops all the extra safety protocols, you can get someone to deal with the hex. I bet Mila will know someone, and if she doesn't, I'll get you a recommendation for a good hex breaker."

"Okay, thanks Lars. Really. I appreciate the help. At least now I know I'm not going crazy."

"No problem. Call me any time."

We hung up, but I stayed where I was, lost in thought.

"Meow?"

"What are the chances Zo already knows I have a memory block on me?"

"Meow," said Fuzzy, then he bobbed his head for emphasis.

I squinted my eyes at him.

"And you knew I have a memory block."

"Meow."

"Do you know who did it? And why?"

"Meow." Fuzzy paced around me, agitated.

"That bad, huh?" I ran my hands through my hair, tugging at it. "It really sucks that I can't communicate with you clearly without Bayley. I'm part Best, for Pete's sake, I should be able to do better than this." I pointed at him, "Just as soon as Bayley comes back, we're going to improve our communication skills, okay?"

I reached out a hand to pat him, and he gave me a quick nuzzle then said, "Meow."

I blew out a breath. "Okay, that's a tomorrow problem. For right now, let's work with what we have. So, 'yes' and 'no' questions." I paced around the kitchen. "Let's see. You know how my memory got messed up—also the who and the why." I stopped short. "And Lars said you were there?"

"Meow."

"Well yeah, it was sometime late at night, and it had to have been on the property, so it makes sense that you would have been there." It seemed like a long shot, given the time and location, but I asked, "Was anyone else there? Other than the memory thief, that is."

"Meow."

"Seriously? In the middle of the night? In the middle of a blizzard?"

"Meow."

"Worst lockdown protections ever. I'm gonna have to talk to Bayley. Just how many people were able to get in?"

"Meow meow."

"What do you mean 'no'? You just said there were other people."

"Meow." He stared at me.

I thought over what I'd just said. "I said something about how people were able to get in."

He kept staring at me.

"They weren't able to get in…they were already here?"

"Meow," Fuzzy pawed at me.

"Talers?"

"Meow."

"Talers I know?"

"Meow."

"The Grack?"

"Meow."

"So the Grack saw what happened. That's…good? Except I can communicate with her even less well than I can with you. Too bad Sibeta isn't around."

Fuzzy paced in front of me, tail swishing. "Meow meow."

" 'No'?" I frowned. " 'No,' as in it isn't bad she's not here?"

Fuzzy gave me an exasperated look and walked out of the kitchen. I followed him to find him standing in front of the basement door.

"Wait, was Sibeta there?"

A loud "Meow," accompanied frantic pawing at the door.

"But she's hibernating! Ugh, what is even happening?" I scrubbed my hand over my face. "Well, maybe I can get some answers. And it looks like you get to go swimming."

As soon as I opened the basement door, Fuzzy darted ahead of me, and before I was halfway down the stairs, I heard a splash.

When I reached the bottom of the stairs, I laughed at Fuzzy paddling around the pool. But my laughter choked into a startled, "Oh!" when I realized Sibeta stood on the surface of the water at the far end of the pool.

"Hi Sibeta, I was just coming to find you," I said as I walked toward her. An image of a giant-sized Sibeta superimposed itself over the Sibeta in front of me, causing me to slow as I tried to make sense of the double vision. But focusing on what I was seeing brought a bolt of pain stabbing through my head, stopping me in my tracks.

"Are you well, Housekeeper?" asked Sibeta, her chorusing voice echoing around the basement.

I glanced toward her, relieved to only find one, regular-sized Sibeta wavering on the top of the pool, gliding toward me. The pain disappeared as quickly as it had come, leaving me shaken.

"No, I don't think I am," I said.

Chapter Twenty-Four

Sibeta didn't react to that statement, which was surprising. Over the last six months, she'd become fairly adept at mimicking human expressions, so she was capable of expressing a wide range of emotions when she wanted to. Instead, she wore her default, inscrutable face.

Usually she was deeply concerned about me and eager to help. Now, she seemed to radiate aloofness.

I studied her as she halted at the edge of the water. The weird overlaid image I'd seen before was gone, and she looked like she usually did. She was semi-translucent, brown like the pond water she stood on, wrapped in a watery cloak that rippled. She looked human-ish—she had a face, torso, and limbs in all the right places—but no one would mistake her for an actual human being.

I walked toward her and made it two whole steps before the double-image reappeared, along with the searing pain. Disoriented, I sat down, hard. I closed my eyes and as soon as I couldn't see Sibeta anymore, the pain went away.

"Huh."

I cracked one eyelid open experimentally, and the two Sibetas returned, along with the pain and disorientation. They shut off abruptly the second that I closed my eye.

I decided the floor was my new friend, and a perfectly reasonable place from which to conduct a conversation. Keeping my eyes closed, I asked, "Sibeta, is there a reason I'm seeing two of you? It's making my head hurt."

"Yes, Housekeeper."

When she didn't elaborate, I prompted, "Does it have

anything to do with my memory loss?" My head hurt in the same place it did when Lars asked me to try and remember, so I was pretty sure the double vision was related.

There was a long silence. It sucked that I couldn't study her expression, but given her epic poker face, I tried to comfort myself with the idea that I probably wasn't missing much.

When she continued not to speak, I ventured, "Let me guess. It's complicated."

"It is indeed, Housekeeper."

There was another silence, and then I heard splashing near the edge of the pool, followed by soft footsteps approaching. I yelped when Fuzzy brushed his wet face against mine. "Ugh, Fuzzy! I appreciate the love, but the wet fur, not so much."

He chose to ignore my opinions and plunked himself right next to me, leaning in so that his body touched as much of mine as possible. Within moments, we were both soaked.

"Geez, thanks," I muttered.

Fuzzy sighed and leaned in a little more.

That's when I noticed the tingling. Everywhere the water had soaked through my clothes, little tingles erupted, shooting outward, until my whole body felt like a buzzing bee.

"Sibeta, did you magic the water?" I asked.

"Not I, Housekeeper."

A garbled, "Housekeeper!" came from the direction of the middle of the pool. I opened an eye to see Mari waving an arm-shaped appendage at me. Unlike Sibeta, she kept most of her body under water, so that I could only see her head and shoulders. Like Sibeta, she had a pond-water brown, humanish face, but it was different enough from Sibeta's that I could easily tell them apart.

As I waved back, it dawned on me that Sibeta had felt it necessary to summon her ace healer. Not only that, but she'd had Mari waiting on standby, so she'd be available the moment I showed up.

So Sibeta had expected me.

I didn't know if I should feel proud that she had that much faith in my ability to figure stuff out or worried that she was sure I'd need a master healer.

"Thank you for being here to help, Mari," I called.

Sibeta translated my thanks into her own language, and I heard Mari's clicking and clacking reply. "She is happy to be of assistance," Sibeta explained.

I risked another peek at Sibeta. Whatever Mari did to the water was working. "Ah, there's only one of you now Sibeta. We seem to be making progress." I looked at Mari, who still didn't move, and then back at Sibeta. "Why do I have the feeling that this is going to end up with me in the pool? Should I just get in now?"

"That would be wise, Housekeeper."

I kicked off my bunny slippers and climbed slowly to my feet. The world stayed nice and still like it was supposed to, and none of the pain returned, so I took advantage while it lasted and scooted over to the pool.

"Fuzzy, I think Stella will be fine staying in my sweater pocket, but would you take care of my necklace for me? I don't want it soaking in the pool needlessly. Percy, I'm giving you to Fuzzy."

Fuzzy muttered, and Percy grunted, "Fine," at the same time, so I slipped Percy over Fuzzy's head.

After stripping down to my bra and undies, I stepped into the water. Some underground source heated the aquifer which filled the pool. Even though it was winter, the water felt as balmy as it always did. The heat soothed me as I sat on the underwater seating area that Bayley had built for me inside of the pool. The bench was just deep enough that my shoulders remained submerged, but my head stayed above the water.

Mari and Sibeta had a quick conversation, then they both approached me, Sibeta gliding along the top of the water, and Mari flowing through the water so smoothly that I wondered if she had formed a mermaid tail I couldn't see.

They stopped a few feet away, Sibeta standing in front, Mari a bit behind and to the side of her.

In a hushed voice, Sibeta said, "I may not speak with you about that which you are unable to recall on your own."

I wasn't sure why we were suddenly whispering, but I replied quietly, "Why?"

She looked like she wasn't going to respond, but then she said carefully, "It is the way of things."

"But you can break my memory block. Or Mari can. Right? That's why she's here?"

"If that is what you want, then you must do so yourself," said Sibeta, "if you are able."

I chewed my lip as I thought it over. Sibeta wasn't trying to talk me out of it. In fact, she must've been pretty sure that I'd try to circumvent the hex because she had Mari on standby. "Mari is here to, what, heal my brain if I accidentally melt it?"

"She will help as much as she is able."

That didn't sound particularly reassuring, but I'd experienced Mari's healing powers once before, and I knew she could work miracles.

I thought of Bayley. I hadn't wanted to do any more magic while he was away unless necessary. But my gut was sure this was necessary.

The timing of the hex concerned me. If I were a bad guy, and I wanted to get at Bayley, what better way than to mess with his Housekeeper when he wasn't there? The more I thought about it, the more I was sure I had to fix this before Bayley returned. Someone had gone to a lot of trouble to mess with my head, and I needed to know why for both my and Bayley's safety.

"Okay, let's get rid of this hex."

"You are certain this is what you require?" asked Sibeta in a hushed tone.

"Yes."

Sibeta stared at me. "There are dangers."

"I talked to Lars—my mercenary friend?" When she nodded, I said, "He explained it to me. I know this could go south in a bad way." I glanced at Mari, "But that's why Mari's here. Even if my brain gets a little scrambled, I'm betting she can keep it from getting totally fried."

Sibeta took that in for a moment. "An...unusual way of stating your circumstances, but more or less accurate." She looked to Mari, who clacked at her, then back at me, "Shall we begin?"

I rubbed my hands together. "Yeah. Time to make this hex an ex."

Chapter Twenty-Five

As I leaned back against the edge of the pool, Fuzzy lay down on the edge, next to my head, careful to keep Percy out of the water. Mari shifted closer—close enough to easily reach out and touch me. Sibeta kept her distance, but I could feel the weight of her stare as she floated nearby.

With the three of them surrounding me, I took a deep breath and closed my eyes.

Right away, I pictured myself standing in my Knack Shack.

I glanced at my energy thermometers. All were glowing green, but if I had to work multiple strains of magic at the same time, which seemed likely, then I would burn through my reserves. I didn't want to affect Bayley, so I needed to be strategic in my use.

"Good thing we planned for this."

I trotted over to the black box sitting in the corner near the thermometers. When I pried off the lid, a pile of glowing coffee beans winked at me from inside. Each bean was a swirl of colors representing Bayley's and my magics: green, blue, purple, red, tan, and gold.

In my first few months as Housekeeper, there were so many emergencies that I kept getting whammied by draining my magic. So Bayley and I had decided we needed some backup batteries. We'd spent the last few months gradually sequestering caches of both of our magical energies for emergency use.

We'd decided the energy stockpile needed to look like something my subconscious would immediately associate with energy—thus the coffee beans.

Reaching a hand into the box, I plucked out a single bean. When I pulled gently, a second bean followed it. We'd linked the beans together with a strand of Bayley's energy so that when I pulled on a bean, the others would follow, like beads on a string.

I wound the beans around my right wrist like a bracelet, and kept the bracelet connected by the strand to the remaining energy beans in the box.

"I sure do hope this still works while you're sleeping, Bayley," I muttered.

With a mental nudge, the bean that rested against the inside of my wrist glowed brighter, turned translucent, and sank into my wrist. As soon as the bean was gone, the other beans shifted along the bracelet to fill the empty spot, adding a new bean from the dangling strand to make the bracelet complete again.

Checking my energy thermometers, I saw that I'd received a boost. "Yay, it still works!" I didn't need the reserve energy yet, but now I had it literally at hand if I did. Hopefully, it'd be enough.

I turned and faced into the room, the energy beans behind me on my right, and the thermometers to the left.

"Okay, hex. Let's see what you've got."

After a moment of thought, I called on my Best magic and summoned a glowing, tan ball as the main ingredient of my magic sauce. With their animal magic, the Bests were, well, the best at manipulating minds. People were, after all, animals, and over the last few months I'd learned that no branch of magic was better at understanding the human psyche than the Bests. Animal magic also worked well here because animals were very good at finding what they needed and getting into places they were supposedly locked out of.

I told my magic, "Find the hex. Find the block that's hiding my memory."

The magic flashed as it absorbed my intention.

Then I waited.

The waiting part I'd learned from Carmine.

"You need to be patient, Finn," he'd explained, placing his

hand gently on the plant I held. "You may think you have the right solution, but hold the intention in your mind and wait to see how the magic *feels*."

I'd done what he asked and stood there communing with my magic. With a surprised, "Oh!" I suddenly felt what he was talking about. "It feels...it feels...soupy?"

"Soupy?" Instead of mocking me, Carmine sounded curious.

Cheeks flushing, I said, "A tiny bit soupy, yeah. I...okay, I know this sounds nuts, but it...tastes...wrong?" I hastily added, "It's not like I'm over here licking my magic—I'd probably wind up like that kid with his tongue stuck to the flagpole—but when I try to figure out what's wrong, my mind is telling me the taste is off."

Carmine furrowed his brows and pursed his lips. "I know you're relating to your magic through cooking metaphors, but do you mean you can also actually taste it, like it has a flavor on your tongue?"

I shook my head. "It's not synesthesia, not like the way Reese can see smells." Closing my eyes, I reached for my magic. "When I touch my magic, and I think, 'Okay, what do you need,' the answer I get in my brain is that it's...soupy. Like, uh, too thin and watery." I winced at my analogy, then relaxed a little as I saw Carmine nodding, wearing an encouraging half smile.

"If you were cooking—if this was a batter, say—how would you fix it?"

"Depends on the batter, but usually it's some combination of adding a little more ingredients and then giving it a bit of a stir so that it blends properly."

Carmine waited patiently while I thought it through.

"I think, maybe, my magic is telling me that since I'm 'cooking' with my magic, I need to not only make sure it looks right, but I also need to make sure it 'tastes' good. Kind of like tweaking a dish until it's what I want."

Carmine looked delighted. "How fun! Everyone relates to their magic in their own way," he said. "Understanding your 'magical language' is key to deepening your practice."

Now, looking at my Best magic, I had the same "tastes

wrong" feeling, but instead of having a case of the soupies, I felt like I had a case of the blands.

The Best magic felt like the right base ingredient, but it needed a little something extra.

"What am I missing?"

Keeping the Best strand hovering, I called up my Murphy magic. While I visualized swirling the blue Murphy magic in with the tan Best, I told it, "You're here to help flow through and around the barrier. You'll not only help wash it away, but also heal any damage."

I sampled my magical concoction, and it still needed a tad more…something.

I was going to be dismantling a block, which had kept me under the illusion that I knew what was going on when really I didn't.

With a smile, I called up a strand of Guthrie magic and tossed it into the mix. "Your job is to help cut through any illusions and to blow away all traces of the invading magic."

I looked at my magical batter. Now it looked and tasted right.

"Ready to help me get my memory back?"

The ball flickered in response.

"Let's do this."

Chapter Twenty-Six

My swirling tan, blue, and purple ball of Best-Murphy-Guthrie magic twinkled at me.

"Now how do I want to deploy you?" Musing aloud, I said, "If I were treating a plant, I'd visualize the plant. Maybe I can do the same thing with my own mind."

Setting my ball of mixed magic to the side, I called up a linguini-sized string of my Best magic and whipped it into a light, airy mousse. Stepping back, I sent the cloud of magic to the middle of the room.

"Show me a map of my brain."

I wasn't sure it would work, but to my relief the cloud flickered and spread out, creating a giant holographic image. While I hadn't ever seen my own brain, what I was looking at certainly seemed realistic. Guess all those anatomy lessons my parents insisted on were paying off.

I checked the thermometers again. Definitely lower, especially the Best thermometer, but still fine. Even so, I used up an energy bean to be on the safe side.

Now how was I going to get my magic ball to interact with the brain hologram?

I stepped back from my magic ball and really looked at it. The thing that caught my attention immediately was that both the ball and the giant brain were mainly tan—Best magic.

Best magic was the key.

I thought about what I wanted my magic to do—to sniff out the hex wherever the little bugger was hiding in my brain and chase it out of there—and the answer came to me.

With a grin, I reconfigured my magic. As the ball swirled, I had the urge to yell, "Form of…!" like the old cartoon superheroes used to do.

The magic ball spread out, re-forming into a droopy-jowled, floppy-eared bloodhound that pranced around my feet. Its body was mainly tan, but it had a blue glow inside the neck and belly. Its face and nose had purple splotches, and it wagged a fluffy purple tail that looked like it had been stolen from a golden retriever. A long, blue tongue and shiny blue drool completed the look.

As a magical form, the bloodhound was mostly translucent, more like a ghost dog than a tangible canine. But it was so cute, I couldn't resist running my hand along its back. My magic sparked and glittered in response.

Refocusing on the task at hand, I studied the brain hologram. It was nearly as tall as I was, but I blew it up to fill most of the room so I could see inside it more clearly.

"Whoa."

Instead of the simple country lanes I'd see in a plant, the brain was populated by millions of ultra-fast highways with complicated interchanges, bridges, and tunnels.

Swallowing against a rising feeling of overwhelm, I tried to look for anything obviously out of place so I'd know where to tell my magic to start.

After a few minutes, I conceded that nothing looked obviously wrong.

Of course, anyone who could install a good mental block would have to be good at hiding it.

I looked down at the bloodhound. "Go find the hex!"

With its nose in the air, the bloodhound loped toward the brain. I had a sudden concern about how the two magical constructs would interact, but I needn't have worried. As it reached the hologram, the dog turned even more ghostly and flowed into the 3-D image. I caught glimpses of the bloodhound, head down, sniffing here and there, as it flowed methodically from one section of my brain to the next.

While the magic darted around the image of the brain,

I could feel a vague tingling in my own head. I had a moment of disorientation while I tried to reconcile watching the magic and feeling it work at the same time.

Suddenly, the dog stopped roaming. With a short, deep "Woof," it sat at the bottom back of the hologram. At the same time, I felt a knot of pressure forming in the same spot in my head.

"Good magical-construct doggie!" I told it. "Um. That's kind of a mouthful. How about I just call you Con?" The dog wagged its tail. "Okay Con it is. Con, stay."

While the bloodhound waited patiently, I walked around the 3-D brain, stopping in front of where the dog had parked itself. While I still didn't see anything amiss, I totally believed my magic when it said this was where the hex lurked in my brain.

Focusing on the spot where Con sat, I said, "Magnify."

Although I was standing still, I felt like I was zipping forward as the view zoomed in.

Suddenly I was staring at Con and a big blurry spot.

I tried walking around the spot, but no matter what angle I viewed it from, it remained the same, blurry smudge.

"Well, hello there."

Concentrating, I tried to force it into focus.

A bolt of pain shot through my head.

"Okay, I got it," I muttered. "No forcing if I don't want to break my brain."

I realized the blur wasn't totally solid. It was drifting and trailing, kind of like smoke or fog.

That gave me an idea. Wind dissipated fog and smoke.

Looking down at Con, I concentrated on the Guthrie magic swirling in it as I said, "Try to disperse the fog. *Gently,* please!"

After I pictured what I wanted, Con stood, walked a few steps forward, then turned around to face me. Con started wagging its tail—its purple, Guthrie-magic-infused tail. As the tail swept back and forth, the fog stirred.

"It's working!"

I imagined the dog redoubling its efforts and looked up to see Con's tail sweeping faster. Little purple shooting stars streaked from the tail, entwining with the swirling fog until the whole thing was glittering with tiny purple lights.

"Dissipate," I commanded, giving my Guthrie magic a little push.

The purple lights twinkled in response then drifted off in all directions. But as my Guthrie magic succeeded in pulling the fog apart, vertigo swamped me, and I fell to my knees.

From far away, I heard Sibeta murmuring. I had the vague sense that she was calling to me. That probably wasn't a good sign, but no way was I ready to stop.

A cool wave of relief washed through me. I recognized the feeling. Mari was working her magic on me. The Knack Shack came to a standstill again, and I climbed slowly to my feet.

Maybe ripping apart the fog hadn't been the best way to go, but it had worked.

As the Guthrie magic whisked the last of the fog away, an object came slowly into focus.

I groaned.

A door.

Of course it was a door.

"Someone has a twisted sense of humor," I told Con.

It cocked its head, waiting for my next command.

Walking around the door didn't help. It turned with me so that I couldn't get behind it.

I sent Con scratching at the knob to see if I could use magic to pry open the door.

That was a bad idea. As soon as the claws touched the doorknob, I felt an answering clawing sensation in my mind.

Clutching my head in my hands, I gritted out, "Stop!"

As soon as Con stopped, so did the pain in my head.

"I'm smarter than this. I know the direct approach isn't the way to go. We've gotta be sneaky like the hex, and do this in a way that heals any damage that I incur along the way. Healing…okay Murphy magic, you're up." I looked at Con. "I know you're not a real dog, you're just a manifestation of my magic, but forgive me for this nonetheless. I need you to go drool all over the door. In fact, it'd probably be best if you give it a good licking."

Happily, my magical bloodhound didn't take offense. It went where I pointed, slobbering blue Murphy magic all over the doorknob, down the side of the door, and under the bottom.

That's where we hit the jackpot.

If I hadn't been watching so closely, I might have missed it. But when Con got to the bottom right corner of the door, some of the sparkling blue "drool" slipped underneath and disappeared. But I could still feel it, pooling somewhere that I couldn't see beyond the door.

"Ah hah! Gotcha."

I concentrated Con on that one spot, feeding a little more Murphy magic under the door.

"Hold."

I'd learned my lesson with the clawing. Before I fed too much magic in at once, I checked in with how I was feeling. My head felt a little...swimmy. But it didn't hurt, and I could think clearly.

My attention jumped to the wall. The Best thermometer chart emitted a pulsing red light, and both my Guthrie and Murphy reserves had dropped.

"Awesome." With a sigh, I tapped my bracelet. Manually, I commanded an entire row of beans to absorb quickly into my wrist. After the first few sank in, the thermometer stopped flashing.

"Automatic drip, please." I set the flow of energy beans to a slow, steady absorption rate to supplement whatever magic I still needed to do.

Returning to directing my magic, I told Con, "A little more Murphy magic drool, please."

The bloodhound complied, and more blue magic flowed under the door.

"It occurs to me that I'm willingly coating my brain in dog spit. Sure this is all a visualization, but still. I live the weirdest life."

The door rattled, cutting me off.

"Come!" I pulled Con back to me just as the door opened

a crack.

A cloud of smoke oozed partway out then paused. It hovered at head height, and I had the odd sensation that it was staring at me, assessing. After a moment, it oozed onto the floor, and the door closed behind it.

The smoke twisted and turned, re-forming itself and solidifying.

When it was done, I stood there, blinking at it.

"A porcupine?"

I looked down at my bloodhound. "Oh, I get it. I bring a dog. The hex's magic blocks me with a porcupine."

I shook my head at the porcupine. "I have serious concerns about your conjurer's sense of humor."

The porcupine stared at me, rippling its quills.

The implicit threat in the porcupine wasn't lost on me. What better metaphor for "I can shred your mind into tiny pieces any time I want" than a razor-quill-wielding rodent?

Plus, the appearance of the porcupine meant the block was adaptive. Really, really not good. That was some seriously strong magic.

I knew the whole "look at my evil porcupine" thing was an attempt to scare me into backing away, but it backfired. If anything, it doubled my determination. No way was I going to leave a mind-shredding time bomb embedded in my brain.

I silently commanded Con to inch forward a bit and check out the porcupine.

The dog took a few mincing steps forward.

In response, the porcupine rotated its quills like a bunch of stabby missiles locking in on a target. But instead of launching the quills, the porcupine rattled them. It wasn't a normal rattling sound. The sound vibrated oddly, permeating my brain.

My ears rang, my head throbbed, and my vision swam, all of which caused my stomach to lurch.

I suddenly felt like I had a concussion.

Once again, I could distantly hear Sibeta, and this time Mari too. Both sounded urgent.

Again, cool relief poured through my mind, and my vision

stabilized as Mari flooded me with healing magic.

I didn't need to hear what they were saying to know that I was treading a dangerous line.

Eying the porcupine, I considered my next move. If just rattling its quills could concuss me, what would happen if it actually poked my brain with one? I didn't need to be a neurosurgeon to know that stabbing my brain was an express trip to No-More-Finn-Ville.

I wasn't sure if I was falling prey to a sunk cost fallacy, or if it was my innate stubbornness kicking in, but I told the porcupine, "I've come this far. I'm not giving up."

I took a step forward, and the porcupine immediately raised its quills. I stopped quickly before it started rattling. But the quills remained raised in clear warning.

"It's gonna be like that huh?" I shook my head at the porcupine. "Any chance we can talk this out like reasonable beings?" I said coaxingly.

The porcupine just stared at me, quills still raised.

So conversation was off the table, which left me with the obvious question.

How do you disarm a porcupine?

Chapter Twenty-Seven

The porcupine wasn't about to let me near it. Even if I could walk right up, I'd still have to deal with all those quills.

While the porcupine and I studied each other, I rifled through my knowledge of magical constructs.

One, they had a general function.

Well this guy was here to guard the hex. So check.

Two, the form could tell you something about what kind of danger the construct posed.

Between the quills' rattling and their lethal sharpness, mind-shredding capability noted. Check.

Three, the form could also give a hint to the limitations.

I frowned.

What was noticeable about the porcupine?

Well, the quills, obviously.

But was there anything special about them?

Peering closer, I realized the quills were all pointing in the same direction.

The porcupine was a giant metaphor, just like my bloodhound was. Were the quills an unintended clue about how the magic worked?

If the magic were directional—if it had to be aimed and pointed—then I needed to get around to the blind side.

It was worth a try.

I sent Con running to the left, making sure it maintained the same distance from the porcupine. As the porcupine spun both its body and its quills to track the Con's movement, I shrunk my avatar to half size, hoping a smaller target wouldn't alert the porcupine. I crept to the right, keeping low to the ground, trying to avoid catching the porcupine's attention.

I had Con bounce and pounce in place like a puppy. Since Con maintained a safe distance, the porcupine did nothing more than ripple its quills and glare menacingly. With an internal fist pump, I managed to scoot around the back of the porcupine unnoticed.

Keeping as quiet as possible, lest the quills get aimed at my avatar, I scanned them for some clue about the magic user who had cast the construct.

With a start of surprise, I saw that the magic wasn't from one of the magical families. Instead, an oily, slate gray sheen of magic coated each quill. Usually, unknown Talers showed up as a kind of foggy gray on my mental map. The most likely conclusion was that I was dealing with some sort of Taler.

Why would a Taler put the whammy on me?

Dealing with the magical block was bad enough, but dealing with totally foreign magic added a whole other level of potential disaster. I hadn't thought it was possible for this to get worse, but the stakes had just gone up again.

I calmed myself by thinking it through. The basic goal hadn't changed: disable the hex without damage. Or rather, without any more damage than I'd already caused.

A glance at my magic reserves told me I'd nearly run through my backup beans. I had enough beans left for one more big push, then I was going to be down to the dregs.

Yanking on my Foster magic, I whipped it over the porcupine in the form of a dense blanket of *Galium aparine,* aka sticky willy, an incredibly sticky weed whose leaves Velcroed themselves to whatever they touched.

The moment the blanket touched the quills, the porcupine reacted by shooting some of the quills outward. But the quills got trapped, sticking like darts in the leaves and stems of the weed blanket.

In a flash, the weeds wound themselves around and between the quills, then around the entire porcupine's body. With a tug, I rapidly contracted the blanket, forming a tight net.

The porcupine tried to rattle its quills, but to no avail. Then it tried to run toward Con, but its feet were trapped, so it just wobbled a bit and then stopped.

I'd effectively immobilized the porcupine.

But it came at a cost.

A wave of fatigue swamped me. My bracelet was gone. A glance at my energy chest confirmed it was empty.

Anything else that I did was going to come from my already-low personal energy reserve.

And I hadn't even opened the stupid door yet.

Expanding my avatar to its normal size, I summoned Con, and we approached the door.

I tried the doorknob, but it was still locked. Apparently defeating the porcupine guardian equated to me dismantling the tripwire guarding the hex, but I still had to dissolve the actual memory block itself.

I studied Con. There was an active pool of magic still swirling in the bloodhound construct. Maybe if I did this just right, I wouldn't need to fuel it with any extra magic.

The porcupine wiggled, trying to break free. I tightened the sticky willy blanket in response.

The porcupine kept trying to shimmy free, but it didn't have enough clearance to raise its quills and shred the blanket.

Still, it was actively pushing at my Foster magic. "I know you think you're all sneaky, but I see you over there. You're forcing me to expend magic to keep you contained. Kind of a dick move, but props for nefariousness."

The porcupine redoubled its efforts.

I looked down at Con.

"We need to get a move on."

Chapter Twenty-Eight

"What is it about being the Housekeeper that my life involves prying open closed doors?"

I faced off with the door. Having Con lick it had worked the first time to get it open, so I said, "You're up again, my friend."

Con plodded over to the weak spot it had found before and immediately started licking the bottom of the door.

I drew on the remaining Murphy magic swirling in the dog, directing it under the door in a slow, steady pour. I couldn't see it, but I could feel a pool of my Murphy magic sitting on the far side of the door. The new stream connected with the waiting magic.

Pausing, I stared at the door.

Nothing came out to confront me.

The porcupine, however, was struggling anew.

"Looks like you're the main defense mechanism," I said. "You stay put."

In my mind, I pictured the pool of magic on the other side of the door forming a giant wave. I gently pressed it against the door.

I could feel pressure building in my head, but instinct told me to keep going.

While maintaining the pressure on the door, I directed one section of the wave to reach out and cover the doorknob. I stirred the magic until it was spiraling, turning round and round over the door knob as it pressed against the door.

Magic from the "wave" began seeping back toward me from

around the sides and the top of the door.

The door began crackling, the sound somehow adding to the pressure building in my head.

I glared at the door. "You will *not* explode my brain like a blueberry in a microwave. You will let go. Now!"

At the same time, with one section of the magic I gripped and wrenched the doorknob, while I surged the wave against the door.

I cried out, staggering backward and falling to my knees as the pressure in my head became unbearable.

But then, the doorknob turned, the door swung open, and a tide of Murphy magic flooded through, pooling around me, Con, and the porcupine.

The door fell apart, chunks of it landing in the flood of magic.

My head felt funny. The pressure was gone, but my thoughts felt cloudy and muffled. In addition, everything had taken on a surreal quality, like I'd been up all night.

Both the Best and Murphy thermometers flashed crimson, and the Foster and Guthrie sections were near the red line.

I thought maybe Mari and Sibeta were talking to me, but everything seemed so dreamlike that it was difficult to tell.

All I knew was, I had to finish this.

I looked down, and to my surprise, the pool of Murphy magic had responded to my subconscious direction to finish this by starting to dissolve the door. The porcupine was also dissolving.

Within moments, the water magic had neutralized the remaining enemy magic.

"Thank you," I told my magic. With a wave of my hand, I let go of the Murphy, Foster, and Guthrie magic. I released Con and most of the giant brain hologram.

That just left what the opened door had revealed.

In front of me, where the door had been, an open archway appeared. Looking through the arch was like looking at a freeze-frame of a video image. It took me a moment to reconcile that I was seeing the view of my room that I had when I was lying in bed.

It dawned on me that I was seeing a paused memory. Likely, the memory that I was missing.

Murmurs buzzed at the edge of my hearing, calling to me urgently, but I ignored them. Dazed and so exhausted that even my avatar was swaying on its feet, I stepped through the arch and let the memory play.

Chapter Twenty-Nine

I sat straight up, trying to figure out why my heart was beating fast.

Fuzzy was awake too, standing next to the bed, his eyes gleaming at me in the darkness.

I asked, "Bayley, what's wrong? Why did you wake me—oh."

As I came fully alert and remembered what happened last night, anxiety welled up. Turning on the bedside light, I checked the clock and realized I'd only been asleep a few hours.

A thought bubbled up. *When was this?*

With an effort, I paused the memory. I visualized stepping back through the arch and found myself once again looking at a freeze-framed image from the memory. Except it didn't feel like a usual memory. It felt like I was living the events in real time. Maybe this was the process to regain my lost memory—I had to live it again to integrate the experience.

I stared through the arch at the frozen image of the clock. I'd been thinking that Bayley had just left, that I'd only been asleep a short while. So, as Lars had suspected, the missing memory was from the night Bayley went offline.

The hex had done its job well. This whole time, I thought I'd passed out and not woken up till the next morning. I remembered being exhausted that morning and chalking it up to Bayley's absence. It looked like there was more to it than that.

I felt a little nervous about re-experiencing something that had resulted in a memory block the first time around, but I didn't see a way around it.

Squaring my shoulders, I walked back through the arch and

went to relive my adventures.

I had a moment where I was aware I was remembering being in bed, but my awareness faded, and then—

The storm outside drew my attention. The wind moaned a hello as it scurried through the yard, rattling the trees and shaking the house. I was about to ask Fuzzy if the wind had woken us both when I stopped short.

Something was wrong.

I didn't hear the usual warning bells Bayley rang in my head, but a different sort of internal alert was sounding, causing my gut to clench and all the hairs on my arms to stand up.

My anxiety shifted to alarm, jarring me into problem-solving mode. Bayley was offline, and it was up to me to protect him and the property.

Scrambling out of bed, I went to the window. Outside, the snow hurled itself at the ground, so thick now that I couldn't see much. The wind snarled, throwing a fistful of snow that slammed against the window, obscuring my view further.

The feeling that something was wrong got stronger.

Since seeing out the window was a no-go, I tuned into my mental map. I spent a few seconds goggling at the fact that it looked super pixelated before the nagging, Houston-we-have-a-problem feeling forced me to focus.

A quick scan said that everything was as it should be. But my gut continued to insist that wasn't right.

Forcing myself to relax, I fed a tendril of my Foster magic into the map, tapping into the trees and plants on the property.

Same result. Nothing was out of place.

Frustrated, I automatically reached for Bayley's help. I fought off a wave of despair when of course he didn't answer.

"Okay, Finn," I said aloud to myself. "Chill. You can do this."

Taking a deep breath, I closed my eyes and studied the map again. Was I missing something because the map was pixelated?

If so, then to get the most out of the map, maybe I needed to use more magic than I normally would.

I sprinkled all of my magics across the map like I was dusting a cake with rainbow sanding sugar. The magics twinkled and sparkled as they sifted across the map, covering it entirely. For a moment I thought it wasn't working, as the sparkles disappeared, one after the other. But finally, there was a single section of glittering sparkles blinking to the right of the greenhouse in the backyard, near the woods.

I zoomed in on the backyard until I had a close-up of where the magics were centered. Releasing the magics, I tried to make sense of what I was seeing. There was a...smudge?

Yes, a semi-transparent black smudge.

It blended into the shadows on the map so well that I hadn't been able to pick it out without the aid of my magic.

Usually, when something new entered the property, my brain interpreted it as something being added to the map—it was one of the ways I quickly identified when something new had arrived.

The smudge didn't feel like something added—it felt like a void, a small empty space.

And it was moving in a straight line toward the woods.

Normally, I could tell who was on the property by the color they were on the map. I'd never seen an empty-feeling black smudge before. Maybe that was a result of this low-res version I was seeing while Bayley was offline?

I looked down at Fuzzy.

"I don't suppose you know what a black smudge on my map means?"

Fuzzy hissed.

"That doesn't sound good. I'm not exactly thrilled either. I'm particularly not loving the timing. Bayley goes offline and within a couple of hours we have a weird visitor—when we're supposed to be on lockdown, no less. Think that's a coincidence?"

Fuzzy shook his head vehemently.

"Yeah, me neither."

I decided to get a better look. Zooming in further on the mental map, I stared hard at the smudge.

It stopped moving.

Cold crept through me. I wasn't sure how it was possible, but I felt like the smudge was staring back at me.

"Um," I said.

The smudge started moving again. But instead of moving toward the woods, it changed direction and made a beeline for the house. For me.

"Crap," I said. "We've got company Fuzzy."

Executing a quick change that'd make a superhero jealous, I got dressed, shoved my feet into my bunny slippers, and dashed down the back stairs, Fuzzy following close on my heels. Normally, Bayley would've been turning lights on as we ran, but with him gone, most of the house remained dark. I felt a spear of longing and worry as his absence echoed through me. I sure would've loved to ask him what was going on.

As we reached the mudroom, Fuzzy slipped in front of me, a low growl emanating from his throat. His fur was standing up, which put me even more on guard than I already was.

Thump, thump, thump!

I jumped and stopped short as the mystery guest knocked on the back door.

If Bayley were awake, I wouldn't have hesitated to answer. But it was the middle of the night, and visions of magical serial killers danced in my head. Sure Bayley had said the property protections were fully in place, and sure, serial killers probably didn't knock politely first, but whatever was out there was doing an excellent job of cloaking themselves, which said to me they were up to no good. At the very least, the intruder warranted caution.

I inched forward on tiptoes until I could peek around the corner of the mudroom at the back door.

Fat lot of good that did me.

All I could see through the window was the vague outline of a figure.

I checked my mental map again. Getting closer to the stranger hadn't made the map any clearer. It still had the weird smudge where the visitor was.

Well, whoever it was, they didn't show any signs of leaving. And I couldn't leave them out there in the blizzard forever.

"Fuzzy, the door is locked. I think we should at least see who it is."

Fuzzy padded forward to the door, and I followed, flipping

on the porch light as I went.

It didn't help much. The figure was backlit, bundled up in a long coat with a hood, and dusted in snow.

"Who is it?" I asked.

"Hello Finley Foster. We haven't met yet. But you should let me in." There was a pause, then, "If you please."

The voice was muffled, but it was deep enough that I was pretty sure I was talking to a male. I said, "You realize it's the middle of the night? And there's a blizzard? Who are you, and what are you doing here?"

"If you would please allow me to enter, I can explain."

When I hesitated he added, "I am here because Bayley is... how should I put this...on leave. If you grant me entrance, I can explain more."

That did it. I opened the door.

The guy gave himself a quick shake, flinging most of the snow that had been covering him onto the porch, before stepping inside.

An icy gust followed him in. Shivering, I shut the door quickly and hopped back a few feet to get a look at the stranger from a safe distance. Fuzzy stayed glued to my side.

"Thank you," he said.

As the guy pulled the hood down on his floor-length coat, Fuzzy and I studied him.

He wasn't too tall—just under six feet by my guess. He wasn't particularly plump or skinny, but instead, somewhere in the middle. Even his clothes were nondescript. The faded pants, brown sweater, and battered boots combined into a bland, lived-in look. His hair, eyes, and skin were all different shades of brown.

Nothing about him, from his features to his clothes, stood out. I had the feeling that if he were standing in a crowd, my eyes would slide right over him. In fact, he was so middle-of-the-road that he looked like he should be the picture next to the word "average" in the dictionary.

Yet for some reason, I felt alarmed enough to take another step back. It wasn't because he was average looking—it was because he was *too* average.

I looked at Fuzzy. Usually, he approached strangers and gave them a good sniff to check them out. Instead, Fuzzy tipped his head back, took one sniff, shook himself, and leaned into my leg.

When I reached down to pet him, I realized he was trembling. Adrenaline flooded me.

Scooping Fuzzy into my arms with a grunt, I moved back farther from Too Average Guy, calling up my magic as I went.

As he finished brushing off his overcoat, I triggered the magic circle in front of the door.

That had been Mila's idea.

Over the last few months, she'd been training me in defensive techniques and helping me upgrade the protections in and around Bayley.

At the time, she'd said, "This might be overkill—Bayley can easily grab any intruders and send them packing. But I like redundancies—better to have it and not need it."

Then she'd had me and Bayley construct containment circles inside the front and back doors. Either Bayley or I could activate them by ourselves.

Now, as I reached out with my magic, the circle flared to life, snapping a containment bubble around Too Average Guy.

He smiled. "Impressive."

There was nothing impressive about it. It was a basic circle. Something that kids learned in their first lessons.

"You don't give yourself enough credit. You were not raised with the kind of magical training children from magical families usually have."

An icy, prickling sensation skittered across my skin. I hadn't said that thought about kids aloud, had I?

"No, you did not. I don't always eavesdrop, but this is a special occasion," he said with a conspiratorial grin.

My mouth dropped open. So much for being average.

As I jacked up the power in the magic circle, reinforcing it to block him from my thoughts, my brain whipped through my options. Should I run? Should I try to call someone for help? Could I find a way to shove him back out the door and out of the house? Rapidly, I discarded each option. I'd have to drop the circle to try and get him out of the house, and I did *not* want to do that. Even if I could call someone, I didn't think I had the time to sit around and listen to advice. And with the lockdown and the blizzard, where could I run to?

Most importantly, I couldn't leave Bayley alone with whoever this was. He'd be defenseless.

My protective instincts kicked in, and anger washed through me, galvanizing me. I put Fuzzy down behind me so my hands would be free and leveled a glare at the visitor.

Fuzzy paced around my legs, agitated.

No-Longer-Average-Guy seemed impervious to the oh-no-you-don't-mister stare I was giving him.

Instead, he was concentrating on running his hands along the barrier that the circle had created. "Strong. Solid. I don't detect any cracks. And you did this with no assistance from Bayley."

"Who *are* you?"

He smiled again, nodded his head. "Yes, of course. Where are my manners? Introductions are in order."

As I watched, he started to…blur. There was a low, almost inaudible humming sound. The edges of his body softened, like they'd gone out of focus, and he looked all smudgy. Suddenly my mental map made sense.

Then, he stepped through the boundary and out of the circle.

My brain locked up.

That wasn't possible.

Everyone had told me that wasn't possible.

Even the Talers couldn't get out of a circle. A circle could contain anyone and any kind of magic. Everyone knew that.

Except, apparently, this guy.

Fuzzy let loose a long howl.

Really-Really-Not-Average-Guy resolidified and held out his hand.

"Hello Finn. You may call me Amon. It is a pleasure to meet you."

Chapter Thirty

I was kind of afraid to touch him, but I didn't want to be unnecessarily antagonistic. In the end, manners won out, and I shook his hand.

It felt like a normal, warm, human hand.

Dropping his hand as fast as I could without being insulting, I said, "Hi?" I didn't mean for it to come out like a question, but it was the best I could manage with so much confusion swirling in my brain.

"I'm not insulted at all," Amon said. "I realize this is unusual."

"Is there anything I can do to get you to stop that? Listening in on someone's thoughts is really invasive. And if I'm being honest, rude."

"I don't know, Finn. *Is* there anything you can do to make me stop?" Amon asked, clasping his hands behind his back.

Fuzzy let out a string of kitty chattering.

Amon raised an eyebrow at him and said, "You stay out of this." Amon looked at me. "Well?"

What could I do to block Amon? My mind scrambled, paging through protection lessons. Both the Bests and the Guthries had versions of mental spells. Of course, if I used too many magics in front of Amon he might realize—

"If helps at all, I already know you are a balance, Finn."

"*What?!?*"

Fuzzy growled at Amon.

"Don't look so alarmed." He leaned forward and lowered his voice like he was sharing a secret. "It's one of the reasons I'm here," he said with a wink.

Apparently spooky winks were one thing too many for my overstimulated nervous system to handle because my anger came roaring back, and I slammed a mental barrier around my mind.

Amon gave me a delighted smile, clapping as he said, "Very good, Finn."

I felt him probe at my mind. A gentle nudge at first, followed by a knock.

The mental barrier held.

I thought maybe he was done, then he punched the barrier, hard. When that didn't work, he sledgehammered it.

It still held.

I'd been working on modifying the Best and Guthrie versions of mental barriers, molding their teachings to work together. While Bests relied on strength, muscling their mental fortifications, the Guthries relied on fluidity and flexibility. By melding the two, I'd been trying to create a magical barrier that could flex with any blow, but stay strong enough not to break. The combination actually felt very Foster to me, like a tree able to sway yet remain firmly rooted in place.

Of course, I'd only been practicing my shield in private. I hadn't had an opportunity to try it out for real. Until now.

Amon nodded, his face serious. "Very, very good. I will respect your boundaries. You have earned it."

Good because you're getting on my nerves, you big weirdo, I thought at him. When he didn't react, I felt a little better.

"Let's get this out of the way. I am not here to harm you," said Amon. He looked down at Fuzzy. "Nor you, young Orret."

"Fuzzy."

He looked at me questioningly.

"His name is Fuzzy."

Shock skittered across his face. "You accept this naming?" he asked Fuzzy.

Fuzzy stopped pacing, sat himself between me and Amon, and stared at him.

Amon looked thoughtful, then he started nodding. "Finn

found you in a dumpster? Eating old fish? Yes that does sound terrible."

Fuzzy wasn't making any noises, but I guessed that Amon could hear him the way that Bayley could. Thinking about Bayley set off an ache so strong I nearly flinched. But for his sake and Fuzzy's, I tamped down on my feelings and focused on what Amon was saying.

"Finn crawled through what to get to you?"

My nose wrinkled as I remembered crawling through dumpster goo to retrieve Fuzzy from where he was hiding.

"Ah, yes, I see." Amon looked up at me and smiled again. "It *is* a very Finn thing."

"How would you know what a Finn thing is?" I blurted. I'd never met him before, so the fact that he seemed to think he knew enough about me to know what a "Finn thing" was…well, that was just creepy.

Yippee. Just what I needed: another stalker.

A sharp rapping on the back door made me jump.

"Finn? Open up!"

It was dark-o'clock, and a blizzard raged outside. How had my house suddenly become the hot place to be?

Rapping harder on the door, she called, "Finn?"

At least I recognized this voice.

Amon sighed and stepped aside into the kitchen doorway so I could get by him to answer the door.

I dropped the now useless circle and opened the door to find my neighbor Zo glaring at me.

This wasn't the first time she'd shown up when someone new visited Bayley. In fact, she made a habit of it.

I gestured for her to come inside. "Come on in, Zo." I thumbed over my shoulder, "This is Amon. He showed up a few minutes ago."

Amon stepped forward from the kitchen doorway so that he and Zo could see each other clearly.

If I hadn't been watching Zo, I would have missed it. Shock followed by something else flitted through Zo's eyes, causing her to stiffen. It was slight, but she flinched back, away from

Amon, and I realized what the "something else" was that I'd seen in her eyes.

Fear.

Zo was afraid.

My heart stopped. If Zo were a perfume, she'd have a top note of power with a base note of danger. Even the most powerful magical people I knew were afraid of Zo. I thought of her as an apex predator.

And she was afraid of Amon.

I wanted to go back to bed and pull the covers over my head.

Glancing between Zo and Amon, I didn't think that was in the cards.

A cold wind gusted in through the open door, and I shivered. "Zo, do you want to come in?"

Instead of answering, Zo stepped through the door, closing it behind her.

Amon smiled at her. "Hello...Zo."

I had the feeling he was about to call her something else. I raised my eyebrows and looked at her.

Zo raised her chin, staring Amon in the eyes and said, "Amon is it now?"

He shrugged. "It was my naming the last time I was here." He looked at me. "Is it no longer appropriate?"

"Um," I said, "Amon is still a name, if that's what you're asking."

He nodded. "Very good." He switched his gaze back to Zo. "Why are you here?"

He said it in a mild tone of voice, with a slight grin, but it felt like a challenge. From the way Zo straightened and squared her shoulders, she thought so too.

"My agreement with Bayley is in place."

"Of course, of course." He nodded, that blandly amused look still in place. "But then, Bayley is...otherwise occupied. So I ask again, why are you here?"

Zo frowned and stalked a few steps closer to me, so that she was standing just behind my shoulder. "I claim the Housekeeper Finn Foster as a friend."

All semblance of joviality fled from Amon's face, and something cold and calculating assessed Zo. "Do you now?"

Zo met his cold gaze with one of her own. It was like watching two serial killers have a staring contest.

"I do," Zo said.

"Are you certain?"

"I am," said Zo.

There was so much weight behind those two little words that I felt like Zo had just accepted some huge burden. Why would being my friend be a burden?

Amon's smile returned, though it didn't reach his eyes. "So noted. You may go."

I sucked in a breath. He'd just dismissed Zo like she was some kind of peon. If anyone else had dared to speak to her like that, I was pretty sure their days would be numbered.

But Zo didn't look angry. If anything she looked...relieved.

"What's going on?" I asked, turning to face Zo fully.

Zo placed her hands on my shoulders and gave me a little squeeze. "Remember how I told you things were going to move quickly from now on?"

I nodded.

"This is what quickly looks like." She glanced at Amon then back at me. "I know this doesn't make a lot of sense right now, but just...go with it."

"Go with what?"

Another glance at Amon, who shook his head once.

Zo sighed. "With whatever happens next."

I thought I'd hit my max for creeped-outness when Zo did something that raised my internal threat level from "watch out" to "you're doomed."

Tugging me closer, Zo hugged me tightly.

Zo hugs were super rare. How bad was "whatever happens next" that Zo felt she needed to hug me?

I was so stunned, it took me a few seconds to hug her back.

She said, "Despite your doubts, you are ready." Pulling away from me until just her hands were on my arms, she shot a defiant look at Amon before adding, "And you are not alone."

Zo let go of me and walked to the door. Hand on the knob, she turned back and flicked a look at Amon, then said to me, "He must keep his promises. And he is required to be fair."

Amon's face went flat. "You question me?"

Zo said with a hint of smugness, "I do not. I simply state the rules."

Amon's eyes narrowed.

Zo must've decided she'd pressed her luck enough because she nodded once, looked over at me and said, "I'll see you soon," then left.

When the door thudded shut, the image of a cell door closing flitted through my head. Which was ridiculous, since this was my home. But I couldn't quite shake the image.

Amon shifted, drawing my attention.

"I must also go."

Chapter Thirty-One

"Go where?"

Amon said, "For a walk in the woods."

I blinked at him. "You realize it's four a.m.? And there's a blizzard outside that's getting worse by the second?"

He smiled. "I do."

"Also, you haven't explained what you're doing here. And I haven't given you permission to traipse about. So how about you slow your roll. Why don't we sit down in the kitchen instead, have a little chat about what's what? I can make us some coffee." I glanced toward my coffeepot with longing.

"Perhaps later." He took a step toward the back door. "I must go."

"Must you?"

I maybe didn't do such a good job of keeping the sarcasm out of my voice because when he smiled, I had to fight the urge to back away slowly. "Yes," he said.

"Can you at least tell me why you need to go into the woods this hot second?"

"I can."

I waited, but he didn't say anything else. I groaned. "Will you?"

"No."

I sighed and tried to use logic on him. "Look. I don't know you. I don't know why you're here. It is unreasonable for you to assume I'm just going to let you do what you want."

"Oh?" A dangerous glint lit his eyes. "You're going to try to force me to comply with your wishes?"

So much for logic. He went right for "just try and make me"

like we were five-year-olds on the playground.

I rubbed my forehead. I wasn't an idiot—picking a fight with him was not smart. If Zo was scared of him, he could likely squash me like a bug, particularly without Bayley to help me fob him off.

But I wasn't totally helpless, and no way was I going to let some strange guy wander around all by himself.

"Simmer down there, pal," I said. His eyes widened as I waved my hands at him in a calm down motion. "Just give me a second to get my boots on."

His eyebrows rose.

"What, you didn't think I was going to let you gallivant around by yourself?" I said as I headed into the mudroom. A look over my shoulder showed me that he was studying me, lips pursed.

Fuzzy followed me into the mudroom, staying close. As I sat on the bench to pull on my boots, he sat between me and Amon. I rubbed his head to let him know I appreciated him guarding me.

As I donned my outdoor gear, Amon said, "You insist on joining me?"

"Yup."

There was a pause, then he said, "So be it."

When I was finally bundled up, I asked him one last time, "You sure I can't talk you out of this?"

Amon said, as though he was making a great concession, "I promise no harm will come to you or Fuzzy, and you will both return here safely."

I choked back the "gee thanks, that's big of you" and instead nodded. I wouldn't have believed him, but Zo did say he had to keep his promises. And while I had no reason to trust Amon, I did trust Zo.

I looked down at Fuzzy. "You should stay here."

He said, "Meow meow," and walked over to sit in front of the door.

Okay then. Group field trip through a blizzard it was.

"After you," I said to Amon.

We stepped out into the cold. Even though the porch was covered, the wind was having a great time redecorating it with a variety of snowdrifts. I could see from the stack accumulating on the railing that the snow was already at least a foot deep.

Amon walked to the top of the porch stairs and stood looking out into the night. While he pondered the storm—and hopefully reconsidered this idiocy—I tried to game out the cost-benefit analysis of using fire magic in front of him. I wanted him to underestimate me. It might give me a little bit of an edge.

Next to me, Fuzzy lifted one paw then another, shaking the snow from them with a disgusted look.

"I'm not sure you should be coming with us Fuzzy," I said. "This amount of cold on your paws can't be a good thing. And it's not like you can wear boots. Though I still have the ones I bought you, if you want to give them a try."

Fuzzy glared at me—the same look he always gave me when I tried to suggest putting booties on his feet.

I opened the back door, gesturing for him to go back inside as I said, "Why don't you wait this one out? I can't imagine we'll be gone that long."

Fuzzy gave me the feline equivalent of an eye roll, then went back to shaking his paws.

I closed the door.

Well, that made my decision easy. It was one thing for me to turn blue like a Smurf. But if Fuzzy insisted on coming with us, then no way was I going to take a chance he'd get frostbite.

I checked my magic reserves and, even while maintaining my mental shield, I still had plenty of energy to do fire magic at the same time.

Reaching for my Smith magic, I let it flow through me as I exhaled. The heat from my breath spread in a cloud that enveloped me and Fuzzy.

I looked at Amon. Tempted as I was to let him freeze for dragging me out in the cold, I grudgingly asked, "Do you need me to keep you warm, too?"

He looked surprised. "How kind of you to offer. That would be appreciated."

I pushed the heated cloud out farther to encompass Amon as well and set my magic to simmer.

"It appears we are ready, then," said Amon. "Let us go forth, shall we?"

While technically I'd insisted on joining this folly, I still felt like I didn't have a lot of choice. I trudged after him. If he noticed my marked lack of enthusiasm, he didn't comment.

Fuzzy trailed right behind me, stepping in my footsteps, as we descended the porch steps.

The wind picked that moment to come racing by, nearly shoving all of us off the steps.

Amon grunted. "That will be enough of that," he said. With a wave, the air around us went silent.

I was still providing us with some heat, but Amon had somehow added a— "What is that?"

"What does it look like?"

Despite my annoyance at my current circumstances, my curiosity got the better of me, and I studied the calm space around us. "It's like it's some kind of a...buffer bubble, maybe?"

Amon looked please. "That is an excellent way of looking at it. It acts like a barrier between us," he gestured to the snow whipping around us, "and that."

"But what happens when we move?"

"It moves with us."

"Huh," I said nonchalantly, but secretly I was impressed. My awe was quickly replaced by suspicion as it occurred to me that anyone who could conjure a moving buffer bubble could easily have generated the simple warming spell I was using.

Great, I thought. *He's testing us. Or studying us. Or who knows what else. He's definitely up to something. What do you think his deal is, Bayley?*

Grimacing, I wondered how long it was going to take me to stop automatically talking to Bayley. Maybe instead of fighting it, I should go ahead and talk to him. I decided to give it some thought later and turned my attention to following Amon.

We crunched through the snow. By the time we reached the edge of the house, I knew this wasn't going to work.

"Amon, even with me keeping us warm, and your, er, buffer thingy, the snow is too deep for walking—and getting deeper by the minute. We can't stay out in this, never mind go for a stroll."

"You must find a way, Finn."

He said *you* not *we*. "What do you mean *must?*"

"Going back is not an option."

"What? Why isn't it an option? The house is right there!" I turned around, pointing to Bayley.

"You insisted on coming along. Come along you must," said Amon with a grim finality in his voice.

"What are you talking about? That is absolutely it. I have had it. You're going to tell me what's happening. Right. Now. Or Fuzzy and I are going inside, and you can just go back where you came from, blizzard or no blizzard."

Chapter Thirty-Two

Whatever Amon was going to say in response to my little outburst was cut off when a blur of movement shot out of the greenhouse.

All three of us spun to look at it.

Fuzzy sighed as the Grack sped over to us.

She was glowing orange, indicating that she was radiating a ton of heat. Sure enough, the snow melted under and around her, evaporating with little sizzles and a bunch of steam.

One advantage of her super-heated glowing state was that I could see her features more clearly. When she glowed, I could clearly see the thousands of tiny scales that covered her.

Her six stumpy but muscular legs gave her a surprising amount of speed. Melting a path as she went, she zoomed over to us in just a few seconds.

I frowned in worry. She was a heat creature, so if she was out in the freezing snow, there was probably an emergency. Even more surprising was her showing herself in front of Amon, a stranger. Usually, she hid from people she didn't know.

Stepping so I was between her and Amon, I gave a polite half bow. "Hello, Ms. Grack. Are you and the, er," I didn't want to mention her babies if Amon didn't already know about them, so I switched to, "Is everything okay?"

She gestured for me to follow her.

I looked at Amon and said, "You're going to have to hold on a minute. I'll be right back." Without waiting for him to respond, I hurried after the Grack.

As we entered the warm greenhouse, I dropped my heat

spell. Fuzzy and Amon trailed us, but the Grack didn't object, so I let them follow me as I hurried after her to her nursery in the far corner.

She gestured to the babies.

I did a quick count and breathed a sigh of relief. All nine of them were accounted for. I visited them nearly every day, and I'd learned to identify the small differences between them so I could tell them apart. Scrutinizing them now, they looked the same as they always did.

I turned to the Grack, "Oh thank goodness. Everyone is here and safe. But um, is everything okay? Are you okay? Did you need something because of the blizzard?"

The Grack signaled to Fuzzy, who padded over and sat next to me. He stared intently at the Grack, who made hissing, grunting, and clacking sounds at him, then lapsed into staring at him intently.

I already knew that Fuzzy could understand her. I just wasn't sure how much Fuzzy was going to be able to pass on to me.

Fuzzy let out a small sigh.

The Grack waved an appendage at me to make sure I was paying attention, then pointed.

I'd been so focused on making sure the Gracklettes were okay that I hadn't noticed the rocks that had been stacked around them.

I looked at Fuzzy.

"Am I supposed to notice the rocks?"

"Meow."

"Okay, good. Um, I see them. Is there something wrong with them?"

"Meow meow."

"No? Er, am I supposed to help move them?"

"Meow meow."

"If I may?" said Amon.

I turned to him with a questioning look.

"The Grack, as you call her, summoned you to her domain simply to assure you that the babies are well. She did not want for you to worry. She is grateful for your concern and is quite impressed with your attention and care over these months."

He and the Grack stared at each other and, after a moment, I realized they were talking.

"You can talk with her telepathically, too?"

Amon broke off his conversation to look at me. "Of course."

"Can you speak to anyone telepathically?"

"More or less."

"But what about when they speak a different language, like the Grack? Doesn't that make a difference?"

"I see that rumors of your curiosity were not exaggerated."

I wondered again how he knew how curious I was, or anything else about me. Who had been giving him information?

He continued, "For the moment, let it be sufficient for you to understand that I can speak to many different beings."

The Grack waved at me, then gestured toward the door.

Amon said, "She would like to come with us."

"What? Why? And how did she even know we were going anywhere?"

Amon frowned. "How indeed." Gesturing toward her, he said, "Regardless, the Grack has requested of me that she be able to aid you. As a friend." He eyed me. "Do you accept her aid?"

"Is it going to harm her at all? I mean, being out in a blizzard isn't good for anyone, but I can see it being particularly bad for someone who is all about heat."

Amon tipped his head slightly to the side, studying me. "Interesting."

My forehead scrunched as I asked, "What about what I just said is 'interesting'?"

"You chose to inquire after her welfare before considering your own."

My full face crinkled into a what-is-wrong-with-you squint as I said, "Who wouldn't? That's just common courtesy. Not to mention that she lives here, and as a denizen of the property, she is entitled to the consideration and protection of the Housekeeper and Bayley."

Amon made a noncommittal "mmm" sound.

The Grack interrupted us by gesturing toward the rocks again.

"She says that if you put your hands near the rocks, you will find she has heated them, so that her children are cared for in her absence."

Using rocks as babysitters. That was a new one.

As requested, I put my hand near one of the rocks and, sure enough, it was radiating a ton of heat.

"Ah, okay. Thank you, Ms. Grack, for letting me know."

The Grack shot around us to the greenhouse door, waving with a "follow me" gesture before coiling and stowing her appendages, tucking them under their flaps where they'd be warmer.

"Well?" I asked Amon. "Is this going to harm her?"

"No."

I looked past him to the Grack and said, "Then I accept your help. With sincere thanks." With a glare at Amon, I said, "I don't know how I'd actually get through the snow without some help clearing a path."

Amon gave me a bland look, then turned to stare at the Grack.

"I have given her instructions on where to go. Follow along." And he strode after the Grack out into the night.

I looked down at Fuzzy. "Are you having fun yet?"

Fuzzy muttered, "Meow meow."

"Me neither. Come on. Let's get this over with."

Chapter Thirty-Three

The Grack cut through the snow like a blowtorch through whipped cream, melting a clear path for us to follow. In fact, she was throwing off so much heat that I didn't need to recast my warming spell. As an added bonus, her bright orange glow acted like a lantern. Though the snow whited out any view outside Amon's buffer zone, the Grack's light kept us from tripping as we walked.

As insane as it was to be out in this weather, our little party of four was cocooned in a heated, glowing bubble, protected from the raging storm all around us.

The Grack stayed in the lead with Amon slightly behind her, followed by me and Fuzzy. I noticed that Amon was nodding periodically, and it dawned on me that he was carrying on a silent conversation with the Grack.

I was curious what they were talking about, but I was more curious about where we were going.

We were headed into the woods that lay beyond the greenhouse. If we'd gone the other way, we'd have been heading toward Zo's property. The woods on this side ended at a strip mall that had a small convenience store and a pub.

I sincerely doubted Amon wanted to get a slushie, though maybe getting him a beer would improve his disposition.

Wracking my brain, I tried to figure out where we were going. There was a pond on this side. A sudden image flashed through my head, of Amon dropping his long coat to reveal a sequined leotard underneath. Picturing him ice skating around the pond, sequins glinting, had me choking back a snicker.

Probably not going ice skating.

Fuzzy saw me grinning and gave me a questioning look. I shook my head and murmured, "Tell you later."

Peering around us, I tried to suss out where we were in the woods, but it was too dark.

I wasn't even sure which direction we were heading. Paging through my memories of this part of the woods, I tried to imagine features of interest.

The only thing beside the pond that I could think of was—

I figured it out just as we stepped into the grove.

I stopped short and squeaked, "Why are we at the graveyard?"

When I'd first become Housekeeper, I'd learned about the cemetery in the woods.

That's where they buried all the Housekeepers.

Apparently, it wasn't enough that once we agreed to become Housekeeper, we were bound to the house and the property for the rest our lives.

We had to be buried here too.

I realized I was shaking my head and made myself stop.

"We will need more light," Amon said. With a sweep of his hand, he extended the snow-free buffer zone around us so that now it wrapped around the entire grove.

A deep, unnatural quiet filled the area. Standing at the back of the dark cemetery, barely lit by the Grack's glow, the quiet and dark pressed down on us like a living thing about to pounce.

Goosebumps erupted along my arms.

With an odd hiss, Amon flung his arm. A large pile of snow catapulted into the air, hovered, and spread out, rearranging itself into a series of golf-ball-sized clumps. Amon gestured, whispering something I couldn't make out, and the snow clumps began to glow. Now I could see that they were spikey, like oversized snowflakes. With a wave, Amon sent them scattering about the grove.

Having snowflake lights overhead should have felt charming. Instead, the light they cast was cold and pale, giving me a fluorescent-lights-in-a-hospital-morgue vibe.

Of course, the location itself didn't help. Like every other time I'd been here, knowing all my predecessors lay underfoot gave me a sense of foreboding. It was a very "you're next" feeling. Suppressing a shudder, I surveyed the clearing in front of me.

Once when I was little, I'd dumped a whole box of sugar cubes out onto the table. A mix of rectangular cubes, broken cubes, and sugar crystals came tumbling out, the cubes landing willy-nilly among the drifts of loose sugar.

That's what the graveyard reminded me of. Over a hundred gravestones poked up from the ground, some weathered and misshapen, and some tilted at odd angles. Each was hedged with snowbanks at the bottom and frosted with drifts on the top. The Grack's glow tinged the nearest stones a sallow orange.

Standing in the quiet bubble behind all those gravestones, the storm raging outside, was like being trapped in a reverse snow globe designed by a member of the Addams family.

Fuzzy leaned against my leg and sang a long, mournful meow.

Kneeling next to him, I put my arm around him. "I know it's a bit macabre, but there's nothing here that can hurt us. It'll be okay," I said, hoping I was telling the truth.

Fuzzy and I swung our gazes to the Grack as she scooted a few feet away from us. When Amon and I moved to follow, she charged toward us, forcing us to stop.

Fuzzy stepped in front of me and meowed at the Grack.

After she clacked back at him, he sat himself in front of me.

Message received: I was supposed to stay put.

The Grack clicked at Amon, who raised an eyebrow but didn't say anything. Well, he didn't say anything I could hear. I had the feeling he was speaking to her mentally again, and whatever he and the Grack were talking about, he didn't look thrilled.

The Grack scooted away and set about shuttling around an open area to the left of where the gravestones started. First, she melted all the snow, then she continued to crisscross the ground until it became a steaming, slightly sunken hole. Next, she shoved some snow onto the hot spot, standing next to it until it melted into a small puddle. Back and forth she zoomed, shoving and melting, rapidly forming a pool of water about five feet across. It stayed liquid, despite the cold.

"What is she doing?" I asked Amon.

"She won't tell me," he said, irritation pinching his face.

Before I could ask any more questions, she caught my attention again by shuffling back a few steps and stopping.

The ground under us shuddered. There was a cracking sound, followed by some gurgling. The puddle began bubbling.

It stopped as suddenly as it had begun. The water was steaming now, little tendrils of vapor forming and evaporating along the surface. Reaching out with my magic, I realized that the puddle was connected with the heated aquifer beneath us, just as the pool rippled, and Sibeta floated to the surface.

I said, "Oh!" at the same time Amon sighed.

Fuzzy made a smug-sounding chirrup.

As usual, Sibeta looked more or less human.

That was all that was usual about her. Instead of the flowing, rippling robes she usually decked herself in, she was layered in overlapping scales. They still appeared to be made of the same brown pond water as her usual robes, but they covered her from the neck down, forming a tight bodice over her torso and arms, and cascading into a skirt that disappeared into the puddle. Even her head was covered. It was like she was wearing a swimming cap, but made of scales. The only parts of her that weren't covered were her face and hands.

After staring for a few seconds, I was pretty sure she was wearing some kind of armor.

Well, this can't be good, I thought.

Aloud, I said, "Hi Sibeta."

"Good morning Housekeeper," she replied, giving me a deep bow.

Now that I was adjusting to Sibeta's appearance, I realized how bizarre it was for her to be standing there at all. Between the snowstorm, the time of night, and the fact that she was supposed to be hibernating, it was just plain bonkers that she'd shown up.

My stomach clenched in worry. "Um, sorry to interrupt you." Bayley had told me that her disappearing in the winter was normal—it was a time of rest for her. What was so important that it dragged her away from her downtime? Would it be bad for her health? I tried to remember if it was harmful to wake hibernating bears. "Is it okay for you to be out here?"

"You are kind to be concerned, Housekeeper," she bowed. Then she shot a glance at Amon as she added, "As you always are."

Amon sighed again.

It didn't escape me that she hadn't answered the question, but I didn't want to make a big deal out of it in front of Amon.

Speaking of whom, I said, "Sibeta, this is Amon. Amon, this is Sibeta."

"Amon?" Sibeta stared at him.

"Amon."

I could hear the period after his name as if he'd added "end of discussion."

Sibeta said, "As you say."

I found myself waiting for something, and then it occurred to me that I was expecting Sibeta to bow. She always bowed. In fact, she had a whole array of bows at her disposal. She was one of the politest people I had ever met and was, without fail, polite to everyone I'd seen her interact with.

But she didn't bow to Amon.

Oh my.

I was coming to the conclusion that not only did Sibeta know who Amon was, but she also didn't like him.

"You two have met?" I asked.

Amon didn't respond but Sibeta said, "Yes, Housekeeper. We have met."

I waited, but she didn't elaborate, and I had the feeling that it wasn't a good idea to ask for more details just then.

I shifted uncomfortably. With the Grack farther away, her heat wasn't keeping me warm anymore. If I was chilly, everyone else was probably cold too. The Grack had been spending a ton of energy, and I didn't want to impose on her any further, so I asked Sibeta, "Would you two like some help keeping warm?"

Sibeta turned to the Grack. After a quick conversation, she turned back to me and said, "The Grack appreciates your offer,

Housekeeper, and gratefully accepts. She offers her thanks for your perceptiveness and intercession." Again, she shot a look at Amon.

He gazed back at her impassively.

While they had a staring contest, I recast my heat cloud, surrounding myself, Fuzzy, and Amon, and then nudging it outward until it included Sibeta and the Grack. I knew it was working when the Grack did a little wiggle and hunkered down with a happy-sounding sigh.

I didn't realize I was smiling until Amon said, "Why are you here Sibeta?" in a voice that chased my smile away.

I was wondering the same thing, but I wouldn't have asked so rudely.

Sibeta didn't appreciate his tone either because she said, "Do not expect to cow me with your games…Amon."

A ripple went through her body from bottom to top, and Sibeta grew. One second she was the same size I always saw, and the next she was half-again as big.

As Sibeta grew, she pointed to the puddle beneath her, which rumbled and crackled, then doubled in size. The Grack zipped back, avoiding the growing puddle, while I adjusted my heat cloud to accommodate Sibeta's expanding form.

Towering over Amon, Sibeta said, "As you well know, it is my right to be here. You have erred in not calling me forth."

"I do not recognize your prerogative," said Amon, sounding totally snotty.

Sibeta went still, like she'd frozen solid. She blinked once and said very quietly, in a silky voice, "You challenge my understanding of protocol?"

The lack of expression on her face made it look like Sibeta was calm, but I was pretty sure that she was monumentally angry.

Another ripple and she grew again. Now she had doubled in height.

I had a flashback to the *Star Trek* episode where they meet the Greek god Apollo, and he makes himself the size of a giant. Was Sibeta doing an Apollo and going to keep growing until she was bigger than Bayley?

We were gonna need a much bigger puddle.

I stepped between Amon and Sibeta, raising my hands in a placating gesture.

Craning my neck to look up into her eyes, I said, "Sibeta, I am so sorry that Amon here has forgotten his manners."

I glanced at Amon, who looked amused.

Sibeta looked past me to Amon and said, "Concede."

Fuzzy turned around so he was facing Amon and let loose a string of chitters and meows.

I turned to Amon. "I'm not sure what's going on here, but how about you back down a bit so we can have a nice civilized discussion."

Amon said, "Sibeta insists she has the prerogative to be here."

I nodded. "Okay."

"I disagree."

Out of the corner of my eye, I saw Sibeta go still again. Resisting the urge to wince, I said, "Since you still haven't explained to me why we're out here, I can't see a good reason why Sibeta can't be here. Sibeta is my friend. Not only that, she has proven to be a smart, honorable, and fair negotiator with a detailed understanding of a whole bunch of customs and rules that I didn't even know existed. She is an accomplished diplomat. So if she says she has reason to be here for whatever it is you're doing, I'd bet my last dollar that she is correct."

Amon said, "Not sufficient."

Fuzzy complained at Amon, and I huffed in aggravation. Time to pull out the big guns. "You won't listen to reason? Fine. How about this, then. Even with Bayley offline, I'm still the Housekeeper, so I make the rules here. As Housekeeper, I say she gets to stay if she thinks it's important to do so."

I felt a little like a parent saying "because I said so" to a child, but apparently treating Amon like a toddler was the way to go, because he paused then said with a nod, "As you say, Housekeeper."

To my relief, Sibeta began to shrink down to normal size. She kept the armor on, though.

A few months ago, I wouldn't have dared to pull out my

"I'm the Housekeeper" stick. But I'd been fending off the Foster Council and their rabid pack of lawyers for the past three months as I fought for my and Bayley's rights. With every curveball they chucked my way, I got better at whacking it right back at them.

And if swinging my Housekeeper stick was what it was going to take to deal with Amon? Well then, batter up!

When Sibeta was back to being person-sized, I said, "Now that we're all on the same page, could one of you please explain to me what is going on?"

Chapter Thirty-Four

Sibeta bowed and said, "My apologies, Housekeeper. It is not my place. The...Amon can explain. But I can—I *will* say if he does not speak truly."

Fuzzy and I swiveled to stare at Amon in time to catch the anger flashing across his face. No wonder he didn't want Sibeta here. If he lied, she was going to call him on it.

The question was, why would he want to lie? And about what?

"Well?" I said. "Let's have it."

"Do you know this place?" he asked, gesturing to the graveyard.

"Yes. It's where they bury the Housekeepers when we die."

He nodded, looked up at the sky, and said, "It is time."

I followed his gaze, but past our lit circle, all I could see was the dark forest, broken by the white slashes of snow dive-bombing the ground. Still, my internal clock told me predawn was approaching. If it hadn't been storming, we might be able to see the first hints of the sky lightening.

"Time for what?" I said.

Ignoring me, Amon narrowed his gaze at Sibeta and the Grack. "You—"

"We are staying," interrupted Sibeta. Amon opened his mouth again to speak and Sibeta added, "We are friends to Finn."

Amon gave Sibeta and the Grack a flat look. "You are certain? I will not ask again."

Sibeta spoke silently with the Grack then raised her chin defiantly and said, "We will stay," as she glared at Amon.

"Meow," howled Fuzzy.

"As will Fuzzy," Sibeta added.

"So be it," Amon said and turned to face the graveyard. Then he called out a single word in a language I didn't recognize. His voice wasn't loud, but it reverberated so hard that it made my bones ache.

Amon gestured, and a matte black staff appeared in his right hand. Like Amon had appeared on my map, the staff seemed a little...smudgy, as though it were blurring into the shadows around it.

He stamped the staff on the ground once, and deafening thunder rolled through the clearing.

Then as Amon swept his hands upward, he began humming a steady, low note that set my teeth on edge.

With a grating sound, all the gravestones began growing.

My mouth dropped open, and my shoulders came up around my ears, but it did little to stop the scraping sound scratching through the grove.

When the stones had reached about eight feet tall, they stopped, in unison. Somehow, even though they kept the same tipped angles as they started with, they all stayed upright.

Amon changed the pitch of his hum, and the back sides of the stones—the sides facing us, which had no writing—began changing. I reached for Fuzzy, hand gripping his fur, as the middle of each tombstone sank several inches, leaving a ring of solid stone around the edges.

The sunken sections vibrated, the stonework turning into a shifting, semi-opaque filmy substance that reminded me of a moist, oozing membrane. When I tried to peer into the surface, vertigo swamped me. My stomach seesawed, and my entire body broke out in a cold sweat.

As movement flickered around the grove, Fuzzy leaned against my leg. In sync, silhouettes coalesced behind the membranes. They were people-shaped, but they were obscured, wavering behind the strange filmy substance.

Amon stopped humming, and in the sudden silence, it hit me like a ton of bricks. Graveyard, pseudo-people standing in weird arches...

"Are those doors—"

"Closer to windows."

"Fine, doors, windows, whatever. But are they showing us the Housekeepers' *ghosts*?!?"

"Ghosts? That is a crude way to put it," he said, tipping his head back and forth, considering, before adding, "but yes."

"But, but," I sputtered, "that's not possible!"

He raised his eyebrows, looked at the arches, then back at me.

Shaking my head, I said, "I asked if there was a way to communicate with the dead and was told that was a hard 'no.'"

He said, "It would seem otherwise."

Fuzzy yowled a series of long, mournful notes.

I knelt down next to him again, hugging him.

"It's okay, Fuzzy," I murmured into his fur. "Don't be scared. I'm right here."

Sibeta said, "It is not fear, Housekeeper. The Travis Fuzzy sings his people's song of the dead."

"Oh." Fuzzy's people had songs for their dead? Not for the first time, I wished there were a book on Orrets so I could read up on this kind of thing. "Thank you, Sibeta, for telling me so I wouldn't worry." I rubbed between Fuzzy's ears and said, "Good job, Fuzzy."

If Amon hadn't been there, I would've sung along with Fuzzy to keep him company. Although, if Amon hadn't been there, Fuzzy wouldn't be wailing his lament in the first place.

I glanced at Sibeta. She didn't look even slightly perturbed by the appearance of the ghosts. "You seem pretty okay with this," I said.

Sibeta nodded. "It is as it must be."

Fuzzy finished his song, and I gave him another hug before standing up and facing Amon.

I felt clammy and ill. The fact that he could yank the Housekeepers from their place of rest—that he could yank *me* from death when I joined them—filled me with a crawling horror.

I scowled at him. "Why did you roust the Housekeepers, Amon? I mean, they sacrificed plenty to be Housekeepers when they were alive. It is totally not okay for you to just yank them from, er, wherever they were—hopefully on a beach somewhere enjoying a cocktail." Hands on my hips, I demanded, "What is the point of this? Why are you here, Amon?"

"Why do you think?"

I shook my head at him. "I'm not in the mood to play games. I've been very patient with you so far. But this?" I gestured to the Housekeepers wavering in the windows. "You need to explain yourself. Now." And since I'd realized that using my title seemed to mean something to him, I added, "So say I as the Housekeeper." Hopefully my you-stayed-out-past-curfew-and-you'd-better-have-a-good-reason-Mister voice would help him realize I meant business.

I guess they didn't have curfews where he came from because he ignored me and repeated, "Why do you think I am here?"

I gave him an aggravated sigh and said, "My guess is you're here because Bayley is gone, and you thought you could get away with sneaking around because I'm fairly new at this. But then you got caught."

Instead of looking guilty, he gave me a bland look.

I frowned. Definitely he didn't have a curfew where he came from. He seemed to be missing the important fact that getting caught sneaking in wasn't something to be blasé about.

I asked, "But I don't understand *why* Bayley going offline meant you had to come here and wake me and the rest of the Housekeepers up."

Maybe if I went full toddler and just asked "why" repeatedly, he'd get annoyed and accidentally spit out an answer.

Amon gave me a secretive little smile that made me want to kick him, then turned to peruse the new arrivals.

As freaked out as I was, a part of me wondered if this was an Amon-only thing, or if talking to the dead was something I could learn. Grief speared through me as an image of my parents smiling at me flashed in my head. What I wouldn't give to be able to talk to them one more time. Not only did I struggle with the constant ache of having them each taken away so suddenly, but I desperately wanted to know why they hadn't told me about my magical heritage.

Before I went too far down that rabbit hole, I forced myself to focus on the dead who were swaying in front of me in a phantom wind. They were all staring at Amon. He seemed totally fine with that, but if I'd been in his shoes, I'd have had the heebie-jeebies.

"Greetings, Housekeepers," Amon intoned.

Chapter Thirty-Five

In sync, all the Housekeepers replied, "Greetings." They sounded far away, and the echoing rasp of their voices left no doubt that they were dead.

"You know why you have been summoned," Amon said.

As one, they replied, "We do."

I raised my hand, "I don't!"

Amon ignored me.

"Here stands the newest of your number," he gestured to me with his staff.

All of the Housekeepers swiveled their heads as one to stare at me. I caught glimpses of noses and mouths, but the definition in their features swam when I tried to focus on them.

I nearly took a step back as the icy weight of over a hundred dead Housekeepers settled on me. Instead, I held my ground and bowed in respect.

Amon turned to me. In an officious tone that rang through the clearing, he said, "Housekeeper Finley Foster."

"That's me," I muttered. Inwardly, I groaned. It was never good when they used my name and title in such a formal tone.

Amon widened his stance, shifting the staff so that it rested on the ground in front of him, midway between his legs, and clasped his hands on top of it. "As we speak, Bayley attempts to evolve his abilities."

"Which is his right," I said.

Amon didn't even glance at me as he continued, "Bayley's well-being is of importance to us all."

I nodded and was startled to see the rest of the Housekeepers nodding along in time with me.

Amon glanced at me. "There are conflicting reports about the current Housekeeper. Concerns have been raised."

"Wait, what?"

Amon went on as if I hadn't spoken. "She is inexperienced. She lacks knowledge of magic—both in theory and practice. She has no diplomatic experience. She lacks battle experience. She is young."

"She is standing right here!" I waved at him. When he refused to acknowledge me, I stepped around him and stood right in front of him. "I can't do anything about my age. And that other stuff may have been true when I started, but not anymore. Your information is six months old."

Amon looked down his nose at me. "Six months is no time."

"Maybe for you. For us humans, a lot can get done in six months," I countered. I pointed and said, "Just ask Sibeta."

A flicker of aggravation flashed in Amon's eyes as all the Housekeepers turned to her.

Sibeta bowed deeply then said, "She speaks truly, Housekeepers. Her progress is substantial and ongoing. She is... unique...in both character and motivation. Her uniqueness," she slid a look to Amon, "is what makes it possible for Bayley to advance." Amon opened his mouth to speak, and Sibeta cut him off with, "Bayley believes in her."

The Housekeepers started whispering. The slithering sound sent cold tingles skittering up my spine.

Amon spoke over them, his voice stern. "Bayley's beliefs are not in dispute. We are here to assess the Housekeeper's purported deficiencies." Turning to me again, he said, "Finley Foster, you are and shall remain Housekeeper. That is not in question. But should Bayley evolve, there may be...consequences. If you are not up to the task, then for Bayley's sake, it is imperative that we wait for someone who is."

My brain spun as I processed what he was saying. "I think I get it. You're here now because you want to see what I can do without Bayley around to help me. You want to see where I'm at, skill-wise, on my own?"

Amon nodded.

"I have questions," I said.

Amon said, "I am sure you do."

Sibeta called out, "She may ask."

A warning in his tone, Amon said, "I am aware of my duties."

"What is it you want me to do?" I said.

"Nothing. You will go about your usual life, but observers will be paying attention."

"Observers?" When he didn't take the hint and elaborate, I prodded, "Are you one of them?"

"No."

A small puff of relief floated through me that Amon wouldn't be lurking over my shoulder the whole time that Bayley was gone. "Who are the observers then?"

"You may not know."

My gaze slid to the ghosts. Were the former Housekeepers going to be watching me? I couldn't decide if it'd be fun or creepy having ghosts following me everywhere. Swallowing hard, I asked, "What specifically are they observing?"

"You may not know."

"How is that fair?"

"It is very fair...from a certain perspective."

I scowled at him then growled, "And what happens if these mysterious observers find me lacking? How does that impact Bayley's attempt to level up?"

"A worthy question, Housekeeper. It impacts him greatly. Should Bayley earn his advancement, and should the concerns about you be found valid, he will retain his power, but he will be unable to access it until a suitable Housekeeper is bound to him."

I gaped at Amon. "That's totally unfair to him! He's waited so long to be able to grow. You can't take that away from him."

Amon shrugged one shoulder. "Nothing is taken. Only delayed."

I crossed my arms and tipped my head, calculating. "You didn't expect me to catch you on the property, did you?"

"I did not."

"So you never planned on letting me know that I was being spied on."

"Observed. And no."

"But I did catch you. And now I do know what you're planning. So doesn't that give me a choice in the matter? What if I refuse? What if I say 'too bad, so sad, but Bayley and I are just going to do our thing, and I won't let you mess this up for him?' "

Amon's face went carefully blank. "You may choose to do so."

Sibeta's armor rippled. "He does not speak the whole truth, Housekeeper."

I looked back and forth between Sibeta and Amon, who was giving Sibeta a dark look.

"Oh?" I said. "What happens if I say no? Or, what if I decide I'm not ready *now,* but I want you guys to come back later, when I've got more experience?"

Sibeta gave a scant nod, so I guessed I'd asked the right question.

Amon said, "You may decide only once."

"So if I say no, that's it? I've blown my chance to negate the obviously false reports you've been getting, and Bayley has to wait for another, more acceptable Housekeeper before he can truly finish leveling up?"

"Yes."

"And you didn't think it was important to mention that?"

"Either you would consider the consequences or not." A flicker of approval flitted through his eyes. "It seems you are more analytical than reported."

I could see why Sibeta felt her presence was so necessary. Amon slipped and slid around the truth like it was a greased pole.

I didn't like it one bit.

Also, who was reporting on me to Amon? Whoever it was, they'd gone out of their way to paint such a negative picture of me that Amon felt it necessary to drag himself here and wake all the Housekeepers.

I asked, "Why can't you just let me and Bayley do our

thing? Hopefully, we'll have many years to hang out and grow together."

Amon said, "That remains to be seen."

Did he just suggest that I was going to die soon, or that I was a hopeless case and was unlikely to improve?

I was about to lay into him when I saw Sibeta tense and glare pointedly at Amon.

He leveled a cold stare at her. "I speak truly. Nothing is certain."

Sibeta said, "But the signs are there. To ignore them is to deny the truth. And you must speak truly."

Amon's glare turned colder. "As you wish." He turned to me. "'Many years to grow' is not a certainty."

I tried not to look at the tombstones, as I said, "Well, it's possible any one of us could get hit by a bus tomorrow, but it's unlikely."

Amon blinked at that before he replied, "That is one possibility. But it is also possible that you both will evolve. Should you do so, there may be...ripple effects. They could come sooner or later."

"Good ripple effects or bad?"

"That depends on the ripple, and one's point of view. There are many, many possibilities," he looked at Sibeta as he warned, "and speculating at this juncture is unwise."

Sibeta's lips pressed into a hard line, but she didn't contradict him.

I was more focused on Amon than on Sibeta. When he'd talked about me and Bayley evolving together and the possible ripples, his hands had gripped his staff so hard that his knuckles had whitened.

Amon was worried. He seemed to be fine with Bayley leveling up, but something about both of us having access to Bayley's new skills worried him. Did he think I'd accidentally blow up the house or something?

I mulled things over for a minute, cognizant of all the Housekeepers watching me closely. It wasn't like I really had any options. While theoretically I could say "no, don't observe me," I'd be screwing things up for Bayley. And that wasn't an option.

I squared my shoulders and said, "Of course I'm going to do everything I can to make sure Bayley gets to be his best self. So, let's get those peeping Toms going. What happens now?"

Chapter Thirty-Six

Turning to face the assembled Housekeepers, Amon said, "We shall commence. You understand what is required of you?"

The Housekeepers sighed, "Yes."

The ghosts flickered as low, unintelligible whispering hissed through the grove, echoing in a way that sounded like the whole area was suddenly filled with snakes. I tried not to cringe as I wondered if ghost snakes were a thing.

Abruptly, the whispering cut off. "It is done."

"What's done? What's happened?" I asked.

Ignoring me, Amon said, "And so it is," then banged his staff on the ground again.

Thunder boomed around us, loud enough to make me want to cover my ears.

A second whack of the staff sent a hum through the grove. The Housekeepers stepped back all at the same time and disappeared. As soon as they were gone, Amon whammed his staff again. The gravestones resolidified, regained their original shapes, then shrank back to their original sizes.

All except one. It solidified, but kept the window shape, glaring at me from across the grove like a giant, ridged slab of death. Was it supposed to be some kind of warning that I should be on my best behavior lest I join my brethren?

Before I could ask him about it, Amon turned to the side, staring into the forest and said, "You may come forth."

I heard the new arrival before I saw him. There was a vaguely unpleasant, barely-there sort of ringing sound, like when my ears rang after listening to music too loud for too long.

A man walked into the clearing. At least, I thought it was a man. For a moment, he seemed to be slightly distorted around the edges, like he was part mirage, and I found myself wondering if he was casting some kind of illusion. As he stalked closer, the distortion disappeared, but it was still hard to differentiate him from the snow. He was so pale that he made the snow look like it had a tan, and the immaculately tailored white suit he wore made him blend in even further.

As he closed in on us, I could see that his white-blond hair was slicked back *American Psycho* style, revealing a face with sharp cheekbones, a thin, pointy nose, and a cruel slash for a mouth. As he walked, the snow vibrated out of the way before him, creating a clear path.

A ripple went through Sibeta at the same time that the Grack backed up a bit, alerting me that neither was particularly pleased to see the new guy.

He didn't acknowledge either of them, but he gave them both a wide berth as he approached. The guy made a show of giving me a blatant once-over then dismissed me like I didn't exist. To Amon, he bowed.

Ah, I thought. *I've got your number, Mr. Snotty Pants.*

Amon said, "Greetings Zah-von—"

"It's just Zav these days," the man said, shooting his cuffs.

"Zav, then. I see you are well," Amon said.

The ringing sound changed, becoming slightly discordant, as Zav replied, "As well as can be expected given the circumstances."

Amon said mildly, "You wish to issue a complaint?"

The soft ringing shifted tone again, now a bit shrill, as Zav said coldly, "I do not."

Amon assessed him for a moment before turning abruptly to me with, "Finn Foster, meet Zav."

"And he is?"

"I do not understand."

"I'm the Housekeeper. What's he?" I purposefully didn't direct my question to Zav. I'd found that sometimes the best way to treat people like him was to give them some of their own medicine.

Amon looked vaguely irritated. If that wasn't enough of a clue that I'd asked a good question, Sibeta smiled.

"He's an...associate."

I glanced at Sibeta. She'd narrowed her eyes, but didn't object, so I was guessing that "associate" wasn't technically a lie, but it was treading a fine line.

"So he works for you?"

"In a manner of speaking."

I said to Zav, "I'm guessing that, like Amon, you're not from around here."

Zav looked insulted. "Obviously not."

Turning to Amon, I said slowly, "So you've got Zav working for you...doing what?" Although I had the sinking feeling that I already knew the answer.

"I keep an eye on things," Zav answered before Amon could.

"Things here?" I asked, sweeping an arm to indicate the property.

Zav smiled smugly, "Here, there. Wherever I need to."

Well, at least now I had a pretty good idea of how Amon had so much information about me.

Amon gave him a look that told me Amon hadn't planned on Zav answering me quite so bluntly.

I needed to do something about the condescending, slightly amused look that Zav was giving me. I'd learned from dealing with the various magical families that the longer that look stayed on someone's face, the harder it was to adjust the attitude that went with it.

I shook my head at him and chided, "You've been spying on us? That's gross. Seriously, what is wrong with you guys? Don't they have boundaries wherever you come from? Yeesh."

Zav looked momentarily startled at being reprimanded by little old me, then regained his sneer. "Please. You are the least of my concerns. You are one tiny part of a much larger job. You're not special."

Amon was staring at Zav with a slight frown. "You really needn't divulge your purpose to her."

"Why not? It's not like she's going to remember it anyway."

"What do you mean I'm not going to remember it? Why not?"

Amon said, "As you noted before, you will behave differently if you are aware you are being observed. So you must not be aware—of me, of Zav, of any of this," he waved his hands to indicate the cemetery.

I blinked at him. It wasn't like I was going to magically forget everything that had happened tonight.

Unless...

I held up my hands and backed away a few steps. "I do not give you permission to hex me."

Zav laughed, and my skin crawled. "How cute. Kind of like a puppy barking because it doesn't want to go in its crate." He leaned forward, a mean gleam in his eyes. "Just like the puppy, you'll do what you're told."

I opened my mouth to push back at him, but Amon gestured with the staff, causing me to freeze.

"So easy," Zav said with an oily smile. He glanced at Amon and said with a little too much relish, "May I?"

Amon nodded once, then said to me, "Drop your mental shield if you wish to avoid unexpected brain damage."

I tried to move, but I couldn't. Sibeta, the Grack, and Fuzzy weren't coming to my aid, which meant that they couldn't.

I had no real options, no way out of this, so I dropped the shield.

All I could do was stare at Zav in horror as he winked and said jovially, "Don't worry. I've spent a lot more time around humans than Amon. My hex shouldn't mess anything up. Well, probably not. You never know."

And then sound flooded my senses. My vision went dark, and all I could hear was a shrill ringing, so strong that it made my whole body vibrate.

Then it stopped. I opened my eyes, and Zav was gone. Amon stared at me then nodded once. "I promised I would return you and Fuzzy home safely. You will have enough time to reach the house before the mind block takes effect. I suggest that you not delay."

He turned away and thumped the staff again, and all the floating lights he'd created flared until they were blindingly bright, causing me to squint and cover my eyes against the glare. When the light faded, I slowly looked around me.

Darkness had reclaimed the cemetery, broken only by the soft orange glow coming from the Grack.

Sibeta, the Grack, Fuzzy, and I were all standing in the same spots.

But Amon was gone.

Without him there, the bubble that had been protecting us from the falling snow disappeared, so we were suddenly greeted by a host of overenthusiastic snowflakes.

"I guess we can go home now?" I said.

Sibeta nodded.

"Sibeta," I said a little desperately, "is there anything you can do about the hex?"

Sibeta said, "I am sorry, Housekeeper. I am limited in this matter. I may not dismantle it for you. And I may not tell you about it once it takes effect." She must have sensed the pile of questions I had because she shook her head and said, "We must go."

I knew she was right, the clock was ticking, so I choked back my questions and said, "Thank you for coming, Sibeta. And for your help."

"My honor, Housekeeper," she said with a bow, then sank into the puddle and disappeared.

To the Grack, I said, "Thank you for your help as well. Can you lead us back?"

Fuzzy chirruped at the Grack, and she scooted in front of us, remelting the path we'd come in on. When we turned to go, I extended a heat bubble around us to help us on our way. Since the path was already partly cleared, we made much faster progress returning to the house than we had on the way out.

I tried to sort through what had just transpired.

One thought kept repeating. *What if I blow this?*

Bayley was so excited to finally be able to level up, and I couldn't help but worry about what would happen now.

If I thought about it logically, I was being watched and judged all the time as Housekeeper, so having Amon sniffing around with his judgy pants on wasn't that much different than what the Foster Council had been doing since I started.

But who was Amon anyway? What kind of person could summon the dead? And he hadn't just summoned one Housekeeper, he'd summoned them *all*. What kind of Taler could do that? If he even was a Taler. I had a feeling that he was something different, something I hadn't encountered yet.

And what about Zav? He didn't give me quite the same "something else" vibes I got from Amon. But Zav did give off serial killer vibes, and he was coming and going from the property? How come I hadn't detected him crossing on and off the property line? I frowned. Maybe Bayley had more "preexisting contracts" in play like the one he had with Zo than I'd realized. I'd need to have a serious chat with him when he got back.

We reached the main path linking the house to the greenhouse. The Grack turned left toward the house and quickly cleared a path for me and Fuzzy. Then she clacked once at us and zoomed off toward the greenhouse to see her babies.

"Thank you!" I called after her.

A gust of wind urged Fuzzy and me to hurry the rest of the way to the house.

Once we were safely inside, with the door shut and locked behind us, I peeled off my outdoor layers and got a towel to dry Fuzzy off.

"You okay, Fuzzy?" I asked as I checked his paws carefully. They weren't cut and felt nice and warm, so I guessed he hadn't been bothered by the weather.

Fuzzy answered me with a loud purr and a nuzzle.

I clutched him to me. A little desperately, I said, "Fuzzy, they didn't hex you." Thinking it through, I added, "Even if you could, I'm pretty sure it's against the rules for you to try to break the hex—I wouldn't put it past Amon to penalize you, Bayley, or me in some way for interfering. But if there's any way you can watch out for me, please try. I know it's a lot to ask."

Fuzzy placed his paw softly on my cheek and said, "Meow."

"Thanks for looking after me and Bayley. I won't be aware of Zav and his shenanigans, so please be careful."

Fuzzy chirruped.

Sudden fatigue tugged at me. I wondered if it was the events of the night catching up with me, the hex starting to work, or the combination.

Yawning, I said, "I don't know about you, but I'm ready for some sleep."

"Meow," Fuzzy said. He trotted toward the stairs.

Within minutes, we were both tucked in bed. As I drifted off, I said to Fuzzy, "I wonder what fun Amon's observers have in store for us."

Chapter Thirty-Seven

I opened my eyes to find myself with Mari's arms wrapped around me, and Sibeta leaning over me.

It took me a few minutes to reconcile where I was. Last thing I knew, I was in bed with Fuzzy—

No, that was a memory.

Water sloshed around me as I stirred. "Amon." My voice came out in a croak.

"Amon," Sibeta said.

Then she went all blurry, and everything went dark.

I must've passed out because when I woke up again, I was lying next to the pool.

I snuggled into the soft pile of blankets and started to drift back to sleep.

Fuzzy must not have approved of that plan because he stuck his cold, wet nose in my face.

Nudging him away took all the strength I had, and I fell asleep again.

Voices woke me the next time.

"It had to be done, Fuzzy."

I pried my eyes open in time to see Zo following Fuzzy across the basement.

She looked past me to the pool. I couldn't muster the energy to turn my head to see what she was looking at, but when she asked, "Was she successful?" Sibeta answered with, "She was."

"Well she's not dead, so we can call that a success," said Zo matter-of-factly. She looked down at me and said, "Ah, you're awa—Finn? Finn—" I missed whatever came next as I slipped back into dreamland.

"Drink this."

I wasn't sure how much time had passed, but Zo was holding a straw to my mouth.

I woke up enough to swallow.

"Erg," I managed. It tasted like she'd put Brussels sprouts in my Shake-It-Off.

"Stop complaining. It's good for you." Her voice was gruff, but she was gentle as she tapped the straw against my lips. "Just one more good swallow."

I did as she asked and promptly fell asleep again.

Next time I woke up, when I opened my eyes, I didn't feel like I needed a crowbar to get the lids open.

I spent a moment staring blankly at the ceiling while I tried to get my bearings.

Bayley?

All was still quiet on the Bayley front. A quick check of our connection showed it was still strong, which was a relief.

Slowly, I sat up.

I felt surprisingly good. Normal, in fact. I expected a magic hangover to come by and whack me in the head like a sledgehammer, but it must've been busy torturing someone else for a change.

Whatever Zo had added to her gnarly Shake-It-Off must've given it quite a kick.

Turning my attention away from myself to my surroundings, I realized the basement was empty. I looked down at the soft blankets covering me and was startled to realize I was covered in some kind of moss.

Twisting this way and that, I realized I was actually nested in it. A thick bed of it cushioned me from the hard earthen floor, and a woven net of it covered me.

Noise from the stairs distracted me as Fuzzy raced down the stairs toward me. Zo followed at a much more sedate pace.

Fuzzy yowled loudly as he dashed into the room, slowing as he reached me so that he didn't bowl me over. As he rubbed his face against mine, his purr was so loud that it echoed around the room.

"Hey buddy. It's okay. I'm okay." He rubbed against me harder, and I laughed. "I'm happy to see you too."

His yowl must've been a summons because both Sibeta and Mari appeared in the pool. Sibeta zipped to stand on the surface faster than I'd ever seen her. Mari stayed in the water, but came right to the edge of the pool, as close to me as she could get.

"Hi guys," I said. Pointing to my moss nest, I said, "I'm guessing I have you to thank for this."

Sibeta bowed. "We could not bring you to your usual sleeping place. Mari needed to be able to attend to you."

Zo arrived next to me and added, "The moss has healing qualities to it. Otherwise, you wouldn't be awake yet. How are you feeling by the way?"

"Fine," I shook my head. "Not even a headache." Looking toward the pool, I said, "Thank you, Mari. Thank you, Sibeta. I have no doubt I'd be in serious trouble without you."

"Dead," said Zo. "You'd probably be brain dead. Or dead dead. Some form of dead." All four of us looked at her, and she threw up her hands. "What? You're not any kind of dead, so let's move on, shall we?"

"If it'll get you to stop saying 'dead,' then sure."

Mari said something to Sibeta who turned to me and said, "Mari would like to know if you feel well enough to get back in the pool on your own, or if you require assistance."

"I take it she needs me back in the water so she can check me out?" Sibeta didn't need to respond because Mari bobbed her head so vigorously that there was no doubt what she wanted.

As Zo and Fuzzy hovered nearby, I slowly climbed to my feet. "Huh. I'm fine. Way better than I should be," I said.

Mari gestured me over and chittered at us.

Zo said, "I think you'd better let Mari be the judge of that."

With a nod I climbed into the water.

The second I was seated on the shelf, Mari sent a series of small waves rippling over me. I held my breath as they washed over my head, then swept over my body. It felt relaxing, though I had a strong urge to bust out singing "at the car wash, yeah!" By the time she was done, I felt way more energized.

Even the fatigue that had been plaguing me since Bayley had left was gone.

Mari reached forward and touched my head. After a moment, she said, "Good."

"Good?" I asked. "I'm guessing that means the porcupine didn't poke any actual holes in my brain. Yay to no Swiss cheese brain!"

Even Fuzzy was looking at me like I'd lost my mind, but Zo was the one who said, "Porcupine?"

I explained about my mental battle, pausing periodically for Sibeta to translate for Mari. By the time I finished, Zo was frowning so darkly she'd give an angry Hades a run for his money, and Sibeta was rippling so hard that looking at her made me feel seasick.

Mari must've noticed because she said something, and Sibeta went still.

"Yeah, I'm none too thrilled about any of this either. It was a dick move on Amon's part to allow Zav to mess with my mind. But hey. The block is gone. My brain didn't ooze out my ears—thank you again Mari—so we win. Go team."

"It's not that simple," said Zo.

"Zav will know the block has been broken," said Sibeta.

"Fine by me. I'm planning on having words with that asshat anyway."

Chapter Thirty-Eight

They all started talking at once.

Fuzzy meowed, Mari clacked and waved, and Zo and Sibeta talked over one another.

Nobody present thought me having words with anyone was a particularly good idea at that moment.

I held up my hand, and they all fell silent.

"I get that a certain amount of healthy caution is called for. But I'm not going to let Zav walk all over me, either. There's a level of sociopathy happening here that I'm not comfortable letting roam around free as a bird."

"He's not on the property," said Zo.

"You're sure?"

"Yes."

"How do you know?"

"I just do."

My stomach picked that moment to growl its displeasure, so I decided to get out of the pool and eat something, then tackle the Zav issue later.

Sibeta was kind enough to flash dry me, and I got dressed. A quick check of my sweater pocket assured me that Stella was still there, nice and cozy.

After I swore to Sibeta and Mari that I wouldn't do anything rash and then I thanked them again, Zo, Fuzzy, and I headed for the kitchen.

As we climbed the stairs, Fuzzy pushed past both me and Zo and out the open door at the top.

Following after him, I called, "The idea is to get me all

healed up, not to make me fall down the stairs and break more stuff. What's up—oh."

As I crossed the mudroom, I could see him standing on his back legs, front paws against the backdoor window. Fat white snowflakes hovered in front of the glass.

Except, of course, they weren't snowflakes. My flock of Samaras had returned.

I opened the door, and they came darting in.

As I shut the door, they caught sight of Zo behind me and came to an abrupt halt, clumping together in midair.

"Hi guys," I said. "Nice to see you again." They all seemed to be staring at Zo, so I added, "This is Zo."

"Zo?" said Corey, slowly, as though testing out the word.

"Yes, Zo." Hands on hips, she squinted at them. "What are you doing here?"

The whole group bobbed in the air, reminding me of someone swallowing nervously. Moving as a single unit, they backed up a few inches.

"I told you," I said. "I invited them in." That made Zo narrow her gaze even more, so I clarified, "They're welcome to visit any time."

Zo looked at the clump. "You knew she would invite you in."

It seemed more of a statement than a question, but Corey answered her. "Yes."

She raised an eyebrow. "Do the others know you're here?"

The group bobbed again, which was an answer in itself, but again, Corey spoke for them. "No."

"Mmph," said Zo. She shook her head at them. "It's a good thing you're young. Stay here." To me, she said, "You. Kitchen," and stomped toward the sink.

I started to follow her, but noticed Fuzzy hesitating.

"You don't have to stay here and watch them if you don't want to Fuzzy." I glanced at Corey as I said, "I think they're smart enough to stay put if Zo tells them to."

"We will stay, Housekeeper, Orret," said Corey.

Fuzzy gave them a long look then followed me into the kitchen.

Zo was banging around in the cabinets. "Where's your coffee? It's been a whole five minutes since you've had a cup, and I don't need you passing out from withdrawal."

From Zo, that was a nearly effusive expression of affection, and I smiled at her attempt to care for me. "Here let me. Don't look at me like that. I've got it—I'm fine. Would you like me to put some water on for tea for you?"

"I can make my own tea," Zo grumbled and took to filling the tea kettle herself.

As I started to make a fresh pot of coffee, I asked Zo quietly, "So what's bothering you about the Samaras?"

"They shouldn't be here," Zo said. She didn't bother to lower her tone. If anything, she was a little loud.

There was no doubt they could hear her.

Keeping my own tone low, I said, "Okaaaay. But this isn't the first time a Taler has shown up unannounced. What's bugging you?"

Zo folded her arms. "We don't have time to deal with children right now—"

"Children? They're children?"

Zo huffed, "Well not technically. But for their species, they are young. Very young." She squinted, calculating, then added, "Think of them as teenagers. Old enough to know better, but too inexperienced to realize how ridiculously rash they're being."

The flock of Samaras zoomed around the corner. "We did not give the Housekeeper a rash!" The flock bobbed up and down, fluttering their wings in indignation.

I resisted the urge to admonish Zo with a, "See what happens when you don't keep your voice down?" and instead I raised my hands in a calming gesture and said, "No one said you were giving anyone a rash. Honest."

The bobbing slowed, but didn't stop, so I wasn't sure they entirely believed me.

Zo turned to face them, arms crossed. "The Housekeeper is very busy at the moment. This is not the time for whatever," she waved her hand vaguely, "this is."

"Don't you think you're being a little harsh? They haven't done any harm, and they've been hungry—you have to admit, this winter has been especially harsh. Also, you know that all the Talers have an open invitation to pop on by any time they want."

"Yeah!" said one of the Samaras, the others quickly joining in, making them sound like the teenagers Zo had described them to be. The chorus of "Yeahs" cut off abruptly when Zo swung her gaze to them.

Zo ground out, "Don't test me."

I happened to glance at Fuzzy and found him looking distinctly smug. If I had to guess, the Samaras tried his patience, too, and he was enjoying watching Zo put them in their place.

Zo turned to me. "Don't you think you've got enough headaches without this added distraction? Trust me when I tell you that you need to focus. This," she thumbed toward the Samaras, "can be dealt with later."

"Why does the Housekeeper's head hurt?" asked Corey.

"Did she fall and hit it?"

"I bet she slid on the ice."

"She doesn't dance very well."

It took me a minute to parse that last one. I was pretty sure they meant I was uncoordinated.

"No I didn't hit my head." I swung to Zo. "How much is safe to tell them? I don't want to drag them into this mess or get them in any trouble."

"You're the Housekeeper. You don't need to explain yourself to anyone."

While that kind of attitude might work for Zo, it wasn't how I preferred to operate.

"What has happened, Housekeeper?" Corey asked.

I decided to keep my explanation simple. "I had a block in my mind that made it so I couldn't remember things."

The flock backed away from me.

Hastily, I added, "It's gone. Do you understand?"

The flock clustered closer together as Corey said solemnly, "We understand." Corey flew forward a few inches, then added, "It is, maybe, best in the future to avoid the bad noise. Most do," before returning to the flock, all of which was bobbing in agreement.

I looked at Zo. "I'm having another translation issue. I'm pretty sure 'bad noise' is not what they meant."

"They're talking about your new friend, Zav."

Because he used some kind of sound magic. "Bad noise" was actually a pretty good translation after all.

"Wait, you know about Mr. Bad Noise?"

"Yes," said Corey. The flock members shook themselves as if shaking off fleas.

Studying their reactions, I frowned. "Has he been...bad... to your people?"

No one answered, but the entire flock backed up another foot.

Frowning, I said, "Do you happen to know if he has been bad to any of the other Talers...er, beings living on the property?"

I thought I saw a ghost of a smile on Zo's lips.

"What?"

"You are very...you."

"Who else would I be?" Turning to the Samaras, I said, "Well? Has he been mistreating the others living on the property?"

The Samaras drooped.

"I'm not scolding you," I said, tempering my voice to a more pleasant register. "But as Housekeeper, I need to understand what's going on. Can you please help me?"

I wasn't sure if it was the "please" or the "Housekeeper" that did it, but after a brief confab amongst themselves, the Samaras rose back to eye level, and Corey said, "He is dangerous. To all. That is why it is best to stay away."

"Thank you for your honesty, and the advice. Under normal circumstances, I might agree with you, but that's just not an option anymore." I looked at Zo. "I have to figure out what to do about him so he doesn't wreak any more havoc on me or anyone else before Bayley returns."

Turning back to the Samaras, I said, "Zo is right. I have a lot to deal with right now. But real quick, I'm guessing you're here because there have been fewer treats lately, and none have been left outside in—" I turned to Zo "—how long was I out?"

"Nearly two days."

"TWO DAYS? I'm hungry, but I'm not *that* hungry. And why aren't I dehydrated? Oh wait. Let me guess." Zo and I said, "Mari," at the same time.

"You should definitely eat something though," said Zo.

"Speaking of eating," I said to the Samaras, "about the treats." I was having a hard time concentrating on them because I was keeping one eye on Zo, who had walked to the fridge and was hauling out sandwich makings. "Zo you don't have to—"

She waved me off with a gruff, "Deal with them."

"Er, okay." I looked at Corey. "Hey, so here's the deal. I'm running out of ingredients, which is why I haven't been able to leave you as much stuff. As soon as Bayley is back, I'll order more, and we can talk about what you guys need to help you get through the winter. Okay?"

The Samaras whispered together, then as a group said, "Okay."

Zo placed a sandwich on a plate in front of me.

"Would you like one?" I asked the Samaras.

They looked at Zo, and then Corey said, "No thank you."

The Samaras flew to the door, so I followed them and opened it to let them out. "We'll talk soon," I called after them as they exited. They didn't respond, and I lost sight of them almost immediately as they blended in with the snowy landscape.

Closing the door, I paced back to the kitchen. "It's bad enough that Zav's messing with me. The fact that he's messing with others on the property is not okay. The Talers are supposed to be under Bayley's and my protection." I crossed my arms and said, "Alright. How do we put a mute on Mr. Bad Noise?"

Chapter Thirty-Nine

Zo and I sat down over tea, coffee, and sandwiches, and Zo began outlining my options.

Stopping mid-sentence, Zo shook her head at me and said, "That is if you can stay awake that long."

My jaw cracked as I finished my giant yawn. "Sorry. My coffee isn't doing its job." I said through another yawn, "It's not the company, I swear."

"You've been through a lot," Zo said, standing. "This can wait. Not too long, but certainly long enough for you to get some rest first."

"A little more coffee should—"

"No. Get some rest," Zo said, heading for the door.

"But I was just asleep for two days!"

"You were unconscious, and you were working the whole time. That's not the same thing." Zo finished the last sip of her tea. As she put her cup and plate in the sink, she said, "By the way, I put Percy upstairs in your top dresser drawer."

I really was tired. I had totally forgotten I'd given Percy to Fuzzy for safekeeping. A quick check of my pocket showed me that Stella was still there, so at least I'd managed to keep track of one of them.

"Thank you," I said.

Zo nodded and headed out of the kitchen, calling, "I'll come back soon." Then she was out the door and, a minute later, blipped off the property map.

I looked at Fuzzy. "I guess it's nap time. You up for a snuggle?"

Fuzzy nudged me toward the stairs, which I took for his

agreement that nap time was a good idea.

I climbed onto my bed and settled the comforter over me. Fuzzy hadn't even finished settling in next to me when I drifted off to sleep.

And I immediately found myself back in my nightmare.

"You again," I growled. "Really? I need to get some actual sleep!"

This time, I started the dream already standing at the end of my beanstalk, near the house, right at the point where I usually got blown off.

When I surveyed the house, I did a double-take.

Smoke poured from the chimney of the sort-of-but-not-quite Bayley house.

Not only that, but the window in the front parlor had light peeking out around the edges of the shutters.

Hope speared my heart.

"Bayley? Are you back?"

He didn't answer, but I was more determined than ever to make it into the house. My mind scrambled for a way to ride out the wind so that I didn't take another header into the snow.

Inspiration struck. So far, my powers in my dreams worked on a grander scale than they did in real life. Maybe it was defeating Zav's hex, but I felt more confident than I had in the other dreams.

When I heard the wind coming as it rustled in the trees, I called on my Guthrie magic. As the wind reached me, I made a swishing motion with my hand, using the magic like a spatula to smooth and direct the wind under me. Then I rode the wind, surfer style, until it deposited me on the front porch.

Releasing my magic, I crouched, bracing myself, half-expecting the porch to try to toss me back into the snow.

When nothing happened, I straightened and stepped toward the door, grinning madly. To my delight, it opened easily, and I dashed inside.

And skidded to a stop.

"What the...?"

I should have realized from looking at how different Bayley

was on the outside, that he'd be different inside. But I'd been so busy trying to get this far that I hadn't thought about what to expect.

It looked as though the house had only two rooms: one on my left and one on my right.

The stairs were still there, but they were simpler and led to a small loft over the hallway. A quick check showed me that DeeDee still lurked in her same spot under the stairs—of course she did. But the hallway came to an abrupt end a short way past DeeDee.

It was like I was looking at a version of Bayley that was hundreds of years old.

I went a few feet into the room on my left. The room itself took up the space occupied by the modern sitting room and dining room combined. A fire roared in a hearth that was twice as large as it usually was, and a big steaming pot hung from a stick, filling the air with the scent of simmering stew.

Instead of the usual furniture I was accustomed to seeing, I spied a rocking chair next to the fire with a basket full of yarn next to it. A rough-hewn table dominated the middle of the room, accompanied by a couple of comfortable-looking handmade chairs. An animal-skin rug covered part of the floor.

Along one wall, a beautiful bookcase was crammed with books.

The rest of the place was empty.

No built-in cabinets. No couches.

Yet even though the room was way more rustic than I was used to, it still felt cozy.

I realized with a start that it still felt like *Bayley*.

"Man, am I glad to see you Bayley! I really missed you. And hey, thanks so much for the nice warm fire. For a dream, the cold outside has been unpleasantly realistic."

I wound down as I realized I couldn't hear anything but the fire crackling. No happy house noises. Not even a single creak.

More tentatively I asked, "Bayley? Are you here?"

My heart dropped when he didn't respond, and I admonished myself for assuming that he was actually back just because my dream showed the house all lit up.

I looked around the room again, trying to reconcile what I was seeing. Why would my brain present me with such a basic representation of Bayley?

I'd just come to a conclusion, when a whisper of movement made me turn, and I jumped when I found a woman standing behind me, arms crossed. She had long, auburn hair that framed a face that was stunningly beautiful, despite the hard stare and compressed lips she aimed at me.

I found my voice and stammered out an, "Um, hi?"

She snorted and pushed past me, her long layers of skirts swishing. "Timidity does not suit the Housekeeper," she chided, crossing to the rocking chair. As she sat, she gestured, and another chair slid across the floor, stopping opposite her.

Taking the hint, I walked to the chair and sat down. Tipping my head as I studied her, I asked, "Who are you?" For the last couple of weeks, my subconscious had been trying to tell me something with these recurring dreams, and I really wanted to know who it had conjured up to deliver whatever news it had for me.

"I am Ailith." After a pause she added, "The First."

I waited for her to tell me the first what, but she didn't explain. Maybe there was an Ailith the second, third, and so on? "Hello, Ailith the First. I'm Finn Foster. Nice to meet you."

"I know who you are."

I smiled. "Duh. Sorry. Of course you do. You're part of my subconscious. It's just habit to introduce myself."

Ailith had cocked her head and was looking at me strangely. "You think me a part of your mind?"

"Well, yeah. This *is* my dream. A really weird, recurrent, lucid dream. But mine nonetheless. I've had to fight to get into this house, and now here you are, so I'm guessing there's something important my mind wants to tell me? I wonder if speaking to your own subconscious is a Housekeeper thing... definitely something to discuss with Bayley when he's back."

Ailith looked like she was stuck somewhere between aggravation and disbelief. "And what do you think this is?" She swept a hand in a circle, indicating the room.

"Ah! Yeah that took me a minute, but I think I just figured it out. The getting into the house, that was your standard anxiety dream, obviously a result of my being separated from Bayley."

Ailith's lips twitched. "Obviously."

"And this here," I repeated her gesture, "this is my mind reflecting me being back to the basics."

"Back to the basics?"

"Well yeah. See, I've gotten used to a certain, uh, enhanced way of living since being bonded to Bayley. I mean, you're part of my brain, you know."

Her lips twitched again, and a glint showed in her eyes as she nodded slowly. "I do know."

"So without Bayley, now I'm back to basic me. Well, not totally basic. I can use magic now. But still, the concept is the same. This is like a very basic version of Bayley—it's my mind mirroring how I am. Classic bizarre dream stuff, really, once you think about it."

This time when her lips twitched, a little smile slipped through. "Classic," she said, and I nodded, until she added, "And of course, totally wrong." Her smile widened at my confused look.

"In fact, all of your conclusions are wrong." She leaned forward in her chair and stage whispered, "I'm not who you think I am."

She leaned back with a big grin and said, "You may not be very bright, but you are persistent. And amusing. I can see why Bayley likes you so."

"Hey—"

She shooed me with her hand. "Go. Rest. You seem to need it." She said that last bit with a heavy dose of disapproval. "Return to me once you've figured it out."

"Now wait—"

But she waved both hands this time, and I fell deep asleep.

Chapter Forty

When I woke up, I found that my "nap" had lasted through the night, and now it was already afternoon the next day.

Fuzzy lifted his head and looked at me.

"Sorry, Fuzzy. I didn't mean to sleep so long. At least I feel more rested."

I took a fast shower and got dressed. As I placed Stella in my current sweater's pocket, I went to the dresser and opened the drawer.

"Hey Percy, sorry you got stuck here. Ready to come on out?"

There was a pause, and then Percy said, "Actually, I'd prefer to remain where I am for now. If that is acceptable."

I blinked a few times. Percy had never asked for me to leave him alone before. "Are you okay?"

"Yes."

"But you want to stay in the drawer."

"Yes. Please."

He sounded even more serious than normal. "Any chance you want to tell me why?"

"No."

I didn't need Percy for anything, and I could live without my necklace for a day, so I said, "Sure thing. But you'll let me know if you need anything?"

Another pause. "This is it. This is what I need."

"Okay then, have a good day." And I shut the drawer, giving Fuzzy a "what's that all about?" look.

On my way downstairs, I pulled Stella out and asked, "Are you doing okay?"

It gave a little chime and glowed once.

Relieved that Stella seemed fine, I tucked it back in my pocket, saying, "Sorry I haven't been around the last few days. Just chime in if you need anything."

After making hearty breakfasts for me and Fuzzy, I sat finishing my coffee, and my thoughts returned to the previous night.

I only realized I'd been tapping the table when Fuzzy nudged my arm with a, "Meow?"

Reaching down to pet him, I said, "I had another weird dream, Fuzzy. But it wasn't the same—this time I met a woman. I thought she was a part of my subconscious, but she said I was wrong. She even had a name. Ailith."

Fuzzy stiffened, and a low growl rumbled in his throat.

I stared at him in surprise. "Ailith? Do you know that name?"

Fuzzy said, "Meow," then paced the kitchen chittering at me, tail swiping back and forth.

"How? She's just something my mind made up. She's not real—"

Fuzzy yowled.

I gaped at him. "She's a real person?"

"Meow."

"So, not a figment of my subconscious. Uh, that means she's what, somehow projecting into my dreams?"

"Meow."

I hid my face in both hands and shook my head. "What the hell? Did Bayley going offline send up some kind of Bat Signal? It's like open season around here—even worse than usual, and that's saying something."

Fuzzy gave me a look that I translated as, "No kidding."

"Is she a Taler?"

He shook his head and sneezed.

Fuzzy stalked over to me. Grabbing my sleeve with his teeth, he tugged me toward him. When I stood up, he trotted across the room, then looked back at me.

"You want me to follow you?"

"Meow."

"Okay, okay, I'm coming."

Fuzzy took me to the back door. I backtracked into the mudroom and geared up before following him outside. We didn't get very far because in the two days I'd been fighting the hex, it had snowed again, and any paths we'd cleared had been at least partly reburied.

After grabbing a shovel from inside, I began forging a path to the edge of the porch. Even under the protective overhang, the porch still had at least six inches of snow to clear—more where drifts had formed.

While I worked, I took the chance to study the yard. Snow was still falling, the flakes swirling in a lazy waltz toward the ground. It was late afternoon, and the diffused gray light added an otherworldly quality to the backyard.

By the time I shoveled my way to the edge of the porch, I was sweating and a little out of breath.

I leaned on the shovel and peered out across the yard. "I don't know, Fuzzy. I see where the path the Grack made is. But there's got to be a good half a foot of snow since the last time we cleared it. I'd have to use a bunch of magic to make a serious dent, and I don't think that's a good idea yet. I'm sorry, but I don't see how we're going to get anywhere with this much snow on the ground." To prove my point, I stepped down to where I thought the porch step was hiding under the snow. With a crunch, my leg sank through the snow, finally hitting the step when the snow was midway up my leg.

Fuzzy looked at me then stepped out onto the snow too. His paws skated across the surface of the snow, and I leaned over, ready to grab him as he fell through. But as he scrabbled, instead of sinking, he remained balanced on top.

Fuzzy and I shared a startled look.

"How are you doing that?"

Fuzzy looked down then shook a paw at me.

Peering closer, I saw that he had spread his toes, so that the webbing between them was clearly visible.

"Okay, that's really cool. You have built-in snow shoes. Did you just now figure that out?"

"Meow!" Fuzzy said proudly, walking around in a circle. I

noted that his claws speared the snow as he walked, keeping him from slipping.

Fuzzy walked back to me and headbutted me until I backed up and returned to the porch. Then he took off across the snow toward the greenhouse.

"Sure thing, I'll just wait here," I called after him. With all the gallivanting we'd been doing out in the snow since Bayley left, at this point, I was pretty sure that Fuzzy wasn't in any danger of frostbitten toes. But I still kept an eye on him until he pried open the greenhouse door and went inside.

While he was gone, I took the opportunity to clear off the stairs. As I was finishing up, Fuzzy and the Grack emerged from the greenhouse, with the Grack clearing a path as she went.

"Good afternoon!" I called.

The Grack unfurled a tentacle arm and waved it at me as she scooted toward me.

"Thank you so much for your help the other night with Amon," I called as she came closer. "We got rid of the hex, and I want you to know I really appreciate all you did. And thank you for helping me now too."

The Grack waved at me again as she and Fuzzy reached the stairs.

Fuzzy and the Grack conversed for a moment, then the Grack turned and faced toward the forest to the right.

My stomach clenched as flashes of the encounter with Amon and Zav flitted through my head, and my feet refused to move.

Fuzzy paused and looked back at me. "Meow?"

"It's okay. I'm just a little nervous. You know, after the other night and all." I shook my head to clear it and tromped down the stairs after them.

Fuzzy didn't respond and instead followed the Grack.

I hurried to catch up with the two of them. I siphoned a trickle of Smith magic, careful not to strain myself, and cast a lukewarm warming spell around us. The Grack waved a thank you.

"You're welcome," I said. "Thank *you* for clearing another path for us. I couldn't do this without you." Although I still didn't know for absolute sure what *this* was, I had a sinking feeling that it was going to involve the cemetery.

We continued on and sure enough, I saw the graveyard through the trees. I started to cringe, half-expecting to find the wavering host of dead Housekeepers waiting for me. To my relief, the clearing was quiet, gravestones sleeping under their blanket of snow as they should be.

Fuzzy must have said something to the Grack because she paused, turned to look at him, then entered the grove, continuing across the clearing, skirting gravestones as she went. It took me a moment to make out what she was heading for. I didn't see it at first because the gray-white stone blended into the snow, making it basically invisible from certain angles.

I stopped in my tracks, restored memories integrating with what I was currently seeing.

Amon had dismissed the Housekeepers. They'd left, and all the tombstones had returned to normal. All but one. The one we were walking toward.

Chapter Forty-One

Fuzzy and the Grack moved toward the giant gravestone with no hesitation, but I lagged behind, walking cautiously. They skirted around the front of it, but I stopped several yards away.

Fuzzy chirruped at me.

"No thanks, I'm good over here."

With an exasperated sigh, Fuzzy paced back to me and grabbed my sleeve in his mouth, leaving me no choice but to follow him.

Getting close to the morbid monolith didn't seem to bother Fuzzy or the Grack at all, but I cringed, half expecting it to activate again.

Fortunately, nothing moved inside the stone arch.

Fuzzy tugged me around to the front side, which didn't have the ridge around the edge and the sunken center that the back sported. On the front side, all I saw was a regular-looking tombstone, albeit a ridiculously big one.

I had barely processed that when Fuzzy's frantic scratching snagged my attention. He was on his hind legs, clawing into the snow and ice clinging to the front of the stone.

"Fuzzy! Don't use the scary death stone as a scratching post!"

Fuzzy turned and gave me an aggravated look, then went back to scratching. When the gravestone didn't seem to object, I moved closer to see what he was doing.

Fuzzy had partly uncovered the top of a word. The rest of the inscription was still caked with ice and snow.

"You want me to read what's on the stone?" I guessed.

"Meow!"

I stared at the writing. I didn't like where I thought this was going, but I said, "Okay, let me help you."

Hesitating, I touched the tombstone really fast and yanked my hand away. When nothing happened, I proceeded to swipe away snow as quickly as I could.

Finally, only a few clumps of icy snow remained, obscuring the writing chiseled underneath.

Carefully, I started to dig the snow and ice out of the letters. As my fingertips bumped in and out of the grooves of the words, I felt a tingle of magic tickle my fingers through my gloves.

I jumped back, clutching my hand to my chest. As soon as I stopped touching the stone, the tingling stopped.

"Meow?"

"Sorry. I'm not hurt. Just startled. There's some kind of spell on the writing."

Tentatively, I leaned forward to touch the writing again and felt that same tingle. Now that I was paying close attention, I could sense Bayley's magic at work in the writing.

Unlike the rest of the stone, the writing looked remarkably new, like it had been chiseled yesterday. "I bet it's some sort of preservation spell," I murmured. "I wonder if it's part of Bayley's basic maintenance of the property. It'd be just like him to make sure the names of his former Housekeepers weren't forgotten."

With a gentle blast of heat, I melted the remaining ice that was crusted in the chiseled words.

I stepped back and read:

Here
The First
Lies

Slowly, I said, "In my dream, Ailith said she was The First. You're telling me that Ailith was the First Housekeeper?"

"Meow."

Cold prickled the back of my neck. I folded my arms across my chest, tapping my foot.

My mind tried to insist that the First Housekeeper was centuries dead and therefore couldn't be interacting with me.

Except, now that I remembered Amon's visit, I knew that wasn't true.

Parts of my conversation with Amon floated up, along with his exchange with the Housekeepers, and things started connecting in my brain. "I'm being observed," I said slowly. "I bet Amon either made them pick a representative or asked for a volunteer observer. I guess it would make sense to have another Housekeeper give their opinion." I looked at the oversized tombstone. "And so, what, Ailith is the observer, and she's been Caspering around the property, watching me?"

"Meow."

"Can you see her?"

Fuzzy tipped his head back and forth.

"Sort of? What, really? Is she here now?" I spun around, searching the cemetery.

"Meow meow."

My shoulders slumped in relief. "Well, thank the goth gods for small favors." I paced back and forth a few times, walking off the adrenaline spike as I thought.

I turned to the Grack. "Can you see Ailith too?"

Fuzzy looked at her, and I could see they were silently conversing, then both turned to me and indicated, "No."

"And Fuzzy you can only sort of see her. What does 'sort of' mean?" As Fuzzy chittered disgruntledly at me I waved him off. "I know, I know. You can't explain. Let's see if I can figure it out. If she's not here now, that must mean that she's not around me all the time. Right?"

Fuzzy nodded.

"She comes and goes?"

"Meow."

I stared at the trees as my mind raced, memories from the last two weeks taking on new meaning. "Fuzzy, since Bayley left, I keep feeling like someone's watching me, and I keep hearing things, like someone laughing. Is that—"

"Meow."

"Oh man," I said, hiding my face in my gloves. "Anything else I didn't realize was her?"

Fuzzy tipped his head, then turned his back to me.

"Sorry, I know that wasn't a 'yes' or 'no' question—hey!" I yelped as Fuzzy used his back legs to kick snow at me, and some of it went down my neck. "Stop it! That's cold!" I said, shivering as I brushed myself off.

"Meow!"

" 'Yes' what?" I looked at the snow in my hands. "Cold?"

"Meow." Fuzzy sounded relieved.

Memories fit together like puzzle pieces in my brain. "Since Bayley left, I've been finding weird cold spots in the house. And, I've been feeling watched and hearing stuff. I just thought it was my mind playing tricks because of Bayley being gone. But at least some of it is Ailith? She's been haunting me?"

Fuzzy nodded "yes."

"How does that even work?" I stared at the gravestone.

Murmuring as I thought out loud, I said, "Fuzzy, you said you saw her. But the Grack and I didn't. So she's not solid, like we are." My eyes narrowed as I concentrated. "Mmm, she was in my dream. So at the very least, she can mentally project herself. Is it possible she's, I don't know, more projection than actual person?"

"Meow."

"Amon said 'Ghosts is a crude way to put it.' In what universe? This is standard ghost stuff 101." Staring at Ailith's grave, I played back my memory of the other night again. Peering around the grove, I mused, "Amon said the funky arches on the backs of the tombstones were more like windows than doors. You can see through a window, and some stuff like light and sound can go in and out, but the window still functions as a barrier if it's not open." I thought a minute and said, "Okay, all the other, let's call them Windows of Weirdness, went away. Except this one." I stared at Ailith's. "So I'm guessing she's able to project herself through the window, even though she can't fully be here herself. Sort of like astral projection, sort of like a hologram maybe, except she's tethered to, um, the Death Dimension, or wherever she is. What do you guys think?"

Fuzzy and the Grack conversed silently, then both turned to me and indicated, "Yes."

The thought of an ancient ghost invading my dreams and following me around the house made my skin crawl. "That's just...wrong."

Fuzzy nuzzled me.

I sighed and rubbed his head. "Well, now I know."

Fuzzy and the Grack had a quick interchange, then the Grack led us back the way we came.

When Ailith's window was behind me, I felt a prickly sensation between my shoulders, like someone was watching me.

Spinning around, I called, "You want to come out and have a face-to-face talk like grown adults?"

The Window of Weirdness remained quiet.

I muttered, "Of course you don't. It's way more fun to be creepy and sneak into my dreams."

I turned back around to find Fuzzy and the Grack watching me. "I'm pretty sure Ailith is watching us. Whatever. She can enjoy the view of our cute butts as we walk away. Let's go."

The Grack and Fuzzy started again, and I followed after them.

But I gave a little wave as I went and said under my breath, "See you soon."

Chapter Forty-Two

As I followed the Grack and Fuzzy, I ruminated on the cemetery we were leaving. Did the Housekeepers return to the grove by choice? I thought back to the day I bonded with Bayley, but I couldn't remember what Nor had said when she performed the bonding ritual—I'd been so consumed with the actual bonding itself that I couldn't focus on anything else. I needed to talk with Nor about the wording in that ceremony. As a genius lawyer, Nor would know if there was any fine print I was missing.

The thought that I might have condemned myself to some kind of eternal Housekeeper service sat like a lead weight in my stomach.

A single chime pealed from my pocket, echoing through the trees.

Fuzzy and I paused, but the Grack whipped around and zoomed up to me so fast that I took an alarmed step back,

She began clacking at Fuzzy, all four appendages uncoiled and waving frantically.

I was about to question Fuzzy when the Grack froze mid-wave and stared past me.

I turned around, but I couldn't see anything but dim forest. My attention shifted to my leg as the Grack wrapped a heated appendage around it and tugged.

I faced her, and she tugged again.

"You want to go?"

She tugged a third time and backed up a few paces.

I half-turned to look behind me again. The long late-afternoon shadows made it difficult to see anything, so I checked my mental map, but nothing stood out. "What's out there?"

The Grack grabbed me again. While issuing a few terse clacks at Fuzzy, she tugged harder this time.

I stumbled forward with a, "Hey!"

Fuzzy darted behind me and gave me a nudge.

"Okay, I get the message. Time to go," I said.

The Grack took off at a brisk pace, following the path she'd melted on the way in, and I had to jog to keep up with her. Given the slickness of the melted snow, it took all my concentration to keep from slipping while maintaining her pace.

Fuzzy followed behind me, as sure-footed as ever.

While I ran, I quickly checked my mental map again. I couldn't run and study it closely, but from my brief glimpse, I still couldn't see anything wrong. But this wasn't my first rodeo. If my friends told me we needed to run for it, I believed them.

By the time we cleared the edge of the forest, I was short of breath. We were halfway across the backyard when she finally slowed.

I stopped, bent over, hands on knees, trying to catch my breath. "Interesting…choice…stopping here," I gasped. "Would…prefer inside…but okay. Just give me a sec," I puffed, grateful that my warming spell was continuing to keep the worst of the cold at bay.

While I tried to catch my breath, the Grack sped around us in a circle, quickly clearing a spot big enough for us to stand in side-by-side. She came to a stop on my left, while Fuzzy moved to stand on my right.

Both of them stared into the trees, tense and unmoving.

I eyed the forest as I struggled to get my breathing back to normal. With dusk approaching, I couldn't see beyond the initial row of trees, as darkness cloaked the forest beyond.

I knew Fuzzy had better eyesight than I did, and I suspected the Grack had some kind of enhanced sense—maybe increased smell or hearing. I didn't have either, but I did have my mental map. I had the feeling that it wouldn't be smart to totally drop my guard and focus all my attention on the map, but I decided to do another super quick check.

As I was pulling up the map, a small burst of white snow-flakes gusted out of the trees. But instead of falling to the ground, they flew straight for us.

With a short laugh, I said, "Is this what you're worried about? Don't worry Ms. Grack. I've already met these folks. I call them 'Samaras.' They seem friendly enough. Tell her, Fuzzy."

Fuzzy did no such thing. Instead, he turned slightly so he could track the Samaras as they zipped toward me, while still keeping an eye on the tree line.

The Grack didn't acknowledge me or the Samaras. She kept staring at the trees too.

As the Samaras raced toward me, I could hear a high buzz as they chattered to each other.

It wasn't a happy buzz.

As they reached me, I started to say, "Hi Corey—" at the same time Corey cried out, "Finn!" But both of us stopped speaking as a flicker of movement in the trees pulled our focus.

One of the Samaras muttered something. It translated as "Potstickers!" but I was pretty sure it was a swear. The Samaras halted in midair between me and the Grack, turning to watch whatever was moving through the trees toward us. Bursts of snow gusted along the ground, like an invisible snowblower was whisking the snow away.

We all went quiet as a man sauntered out of the tree line, a low ringing sound accompanying him.

I took a step forward, placing myself in front of Fuzzy, the Grack, and the Samaras as I said, "You." I didn't mean to snarl it, but it hadn't been that long since I'd recovered my memories, and I hadn't really had time to process how angry I was about it.

"Hello, Housekeeper," Zav said with a smirk.

He stopped at the edge of the backyard, standing just enough in the light that I could see him, but enough in the shadows of the trees that I had to work at it.

He was dressed all in white again, which made him extra hard to distinguish from the snowy background. I squinted, and I realized he was wearing a suit again, slightly different from the last one, but still exquisitely tailored so that it fit him like a glove—which he wasn't wearing. Not only was he missing gloves, but he also had no coat, no scarf—nothing to protect him from the cold.

What I really wanted to know was why there wasn't an "intruder alert" alarm bell clanging in my head. I yanked up my mental map, took a quick look, and frowned.

Even with him standing right in front of me, I still couldn't see him on the map.

I could see the dots representing me, Fuzzy, the Grack, and the Samaras, but there was no dot for him.

I dropped the map and returned my focus to him, promising myself I'd figure it out later.

His smile widened as he surveyed our little group. "Book club meeting?"

"What are you doing here?"

"Oh, just out for a stroll."

"How about you take your stroll somewhere else? Preferably off the property."

"Ah, but you said that you wanted to share the property with more people." He tilted his head down a fraction so he was looking up at me from under his brows. "You did say that, did you not?"

A chill went through me that had nothing to do with the weather. I had said something to that effect to Zo when we were out in the yard a few weeks ago.

How did he know that? Had he been there?

He laughed softly. "Oh, it's so much worse than you think Finn." He leaned forward slightly, and like he was sharing a secret, added in a mock whisper, "You know you're never truly alone here. Isn't that right," and he said something that sounded like "alzahar."

I didn't know what "alzahar" meant, but I guessed he was calling me some kind of insult, because he was frowning and glaring at me.

I rolled my eyes. "Okay, creepy pants. How 'bout you ease off the bad horror movie dialogue and just tell me what you're doing here."

He stared at my chest and said in a menacing voice, "You're treading dangerously."

He was doing that thing again where he refused to make eye contact, and I was betting he was just trying to get a rise out of me by so blatantly staring at my chest. I looked down at my boobs then up at him and said, "Hey buddy. Eyes up here, okay? Not sure what the customs are where you come from, but here, it's considered impolite to stare at a lady's chest. Also, for the record, the boobs don't talk, so you can yell at them all you want, but it's not going to get you anywhere."

Zav's gaze narrowed, still focused on my chest instead of my face, and he growled, "How dare you?" and stomped forward.

As soon as he moved, I dropped to kneel on the ground, yanking off my glove as I went. When the Grack had cleared away the snow, I'd realized why she chose to stop us where she did. Ignoring the cold that nipped at my hand as I touched the frozen ground, I reached for the dormant circle under us, and I pulled, hard. I hadn't needed any of the circles that Bayley and I had made since we'd first used them, but boy was I glad to have them now. Fortunately, even without Bayley awake, the circle we were standing over responded to me immediately.

A ring of small stones flowed up through the ground, forming a perfect circle around us. I reached out with my Foster magic, and the circle activated, light flashing from the stones, creating an impenetrable perimeter.

"Stop," I ordered.

Zav stopped, though I wasn't sure whether it was because I told him to or because he was surprised by what I'd done.

As I stood back up, he looked around me, studying the circle, a frown growing.

"If you're looking for cracks, there aren't any. This is a diplomatic-grade circle."

His frown hardened, smashing his lips into a thin, flat line.

Zav squinted, thinking, then suddenly he relaxed. He tipped his head to the side, crossing his arms as a slow smile oozed across his face. "Are you certain you want to hide behind your little circle? I can understand why you're scared," he taunted. "It was ridiculously simple to hex you." He winked as he added, "And that kid? Taking apart his mind was so easy it was comical."

I froze as understanding struck. "Neil. You brainwashed Neil."

He grinned. "Guilty as charged. What are you going to do about it?"

Images of Neil's tormented face flickered through my mind, and all the rage I'd felt when Zav first stepped into the clearing came back two-fold. I took a step forward, intent on removing the smug look from Zav's face.

I might have blindly crossed right out of the circle, taking it down from the inside, if Fuzzy hadn't jumped up, dug his claws into my coat, and growled at me.

I stopped short.

Closing my eyes, I did my best to tune out Zav's chuckling and took a slow deep breath. He was baiting me, and I'd almost fallen for it. But if he was trying to make me come out, that must mean he couldn't break in. I relaxed a fraction. He might be in league with Amon, but he apparently wasn't as powerful.

I shook myself, muttered, "Thanks," to Fuzzy, and faced Zav. "You say *we're* weak?" I said slowly. "I'm sorry, who can't figure their way past a little old circle? Oh wait! That's you."

Zav's smile shattered, and he took a menacing step forward, the odd ringing sound becoming discordant.

I leaned forward, mimicking his earlier posture. "And this circle? It's not the only one." I gave him an evil smile. "Keep right on coming buddy, if you think you can get all the way across the yard without stepping on one. Even if you happened to see all of the circles when you were spying on me, how sure are you that you remember where they were?" I folded my arms across my chest. "Say what you came here to say, or better yet, just get the hell out."

While he contemplated his options, I did the same, my mind racing. I could try to remove him from the property. Even with Bayley asleep, and my energy being low after breaking Zav's hex, I could rally my resources to eject him. That'd drain me back down to the dregs, but it would almost be worth it for the satisfaction of literally dragging his ass across the property.

But a niggling doubt stalled me. Zav might not be Amon-level strong, but he was still Amon's associate. As much as it pained me, the best option at the moment was to get him to back down and then formulate a plan to deal with him later.

With the extra light from the circle, I could see him calculating. The math must not have been in his favor because without a word, he turned around and walked back into the forest.

After a few moments had passed, and I couldn't hear any ringing anymore, Fuzzy relaxed slightly.

"Can you see him?"

Fuzzy shook his head, and the Grack indicated "No."

Corey said, "The bad noise has gone."

Kneeling again, I deactivated the circle, thanked it for its help, and returned it to the earth, the stones sinking back into the ground.

Fatigue washed through me.

"I don't know about you guys, but I'm ready to go inside."

Chapter Forty-Three

The Samaras flocked off into the trees without so much as a word. I called, "Bye!" after them, but they just kept on going. I hoped they weren't too freaked out to come back soon.

While the Grack returned to the greenhouse and her babies, Fuzzy and I returned to the house. I fed him and defrosted myself some dinner, hoping to fend off the weariness that plagued me.

Absently inhaling the stew, I sorted through what had just happened.

Zav had intimated that he'd been creeping around for a while. If that was true, then did Bayley know? What other bad guys were lurking unseen that I didn't know about? The thought made me squirm in my chair.

I forced myself to think rationally. Bayley knew all about the Talers, but he only shared his knowledge as the Talers introduced themselves to me. So it made sense that he hadn't mentioned Zav.

But Zav had been actively messing with me since Bayley had been gone. With the hex lifted, the events of the last couple of weeks were rearranging themselves in my mind. Twice I'd wound up outside, drawn by a weird sound, not to mention the time I'd blacked out and zombie-walked halfway to the woods. Now I was wondering if Zav was the cause, and if he was trying to check on his hex or cause me harm. I suspected it was the latter. But did Amon know Zav had been hounding me, and did he approve?

I wasn't going to get any answers about Zav this hot second. But the more I thought about it, the more it became clear that

I needed to have some kind of warning when he was nearby so that I could be prepared when he showed up.

And I was sure he'd be showing up again soon.

Fuzzy rubbed against my calf, distracting me.

"Hey buddy."

He rubbed my leg again.

I leaned down and petted his head. "Want some cuddle time while I have a think?" I put my bowl in the sink, grabbed my coffee, and headed to the sitting room.

I plopped down on one of the couches, snagged a blanket, and curled up. Normally, Bayley would have had a fire going by the time my butt hit the cushions. Longing speared through me, and I did a quick check. Yup, he was still there, safe and sound, so far as I could tell. And, of course, still offline.

Fuzzy hopped up and snuggled in next to me.

Stroking his chin, I said, "I have to sort out why Zav isn't showing up on my mental map. The last thing we need is to have him sneaking up on us again."

Closing my eyes, I called up my mental map.

Show me Zav.

The map blurred for a second, but instead of refocusing on his location, it returned to the overview of the property, showing me the foggy bits that represented all the Talers.

I pursed my lips, trying to puzzle it out. The map was telling me Zav was some kind of Taler. But Zav was in cahoots with Amon, and Amon barely showed up on my map at all. So maybe Zav was also cloaked in some way? If so, maybe there was another way to find him.

As I scritched behind Fuzzy's ears the way he liked, I explained my problem to him. "I'm pretty sure I'm missing something. I can't see Zav on the map, but I'm not convinced that he isn't here. I think I'm looking for the wrong thing."

Fuzzy chattered at me.

"You sound as disgruntled as I feel."

Fuzzy puffed out a sigh. He pawed at me until I looked at him.

"What?"

Fuzzy sang a long, high "Meoooooow" that made me scrinch up my eyes at its shrillness.

My brows beetled as I stared at him. "I get that you're trying to tell me something. I'm just not sure what it is."

Fuzzy pawed at me again, then sang another "Meooooow."

I opened my mouth to tell him I didn't get it, but then stopped short. Something about the meow was nagging at my brain. It seemed familiar. What did it remind me of?

As I finished my coffee, I thought about the sound. I hadn't heard anyone meowing recently other than Fuzzy, so I didn't think it was the meow I should be focusing on.

I hummed a "Meow" back at him, and a lightbulb went off in brain.

It was the pitch.

When Fuzzy had meowed and chattered at me, he'd done it using a single note.

And as soon as I figured that out, I remembered the sound I'd heard when Zav first appeared. When he'd entered the cemetery, he was making a weird ringing sound. In fact, every time I'd seen him, I'd heard something too. On the heels of that thought, the porcupine's rattling replayed in my head. I flinched before I could stop myself, even though it didn't cause me pain anymore.

Fuzzy nosed me.

"Sorry. Just a bad memory. I'm fine. I think I get it Fuzzy. It's about the sound, isn't it."

"Meow," he said, leaning into my hand.

I'd looked at my map a whole lot, but I'd never tried *listening* to it.

Refocusing on my map, I asked, *Where's Zav?* while I lightly dusted the map with a pinch of Best magic to give it a little oomph.

For a long minute, nothing happened, but then I heard it. Faint at first, there was a ringing sound coming from near the main road at the front edge of the property.

Mark the person who is making that sound, I told the map. A slate gray dot with an oily sheen to it appeared on the map.

"Hah! Found you!" I crowed. As I watched, Zav stepped out onto the road and vanished off my map.

Opening my eyes, I looked at Fuzzy. "Thanks again for the assist. I know how to see Zav on the map now. He just left. Now I just have to figure out what to do about him if he comes back."

Chapter Forty-Four

I shouldn't have been relieved that Zav was out in the world bothering someone else, but I was. I really hated the idea of him lurking around the property.

A yawn escaped me, and I snuggled deeper into the blanket. Expending extra magic on the map and the circle, not to mention trekking around in the cold while casting a warming spell, was catching up to me, and it felt good to have a quiet moment on the couch to think.

I was daydreaming when the room shifted around me.

I was back in the old-timey Bayley cottage. In Ailith's domain.

It took me a moment to realize my daydreaming had turned into actual dreaming. I must have fallen asleep on the couch.

When I looked down, I found myself sitting in a chair in front of the fireplace.

"I see you're here again."

I jumped as Ailith was suddenly in the chair across from me.

"Did you figure it out?" she asked.

"Right to it then? No 'Hey Finn, how was your day?'"

When she just stared at me I said, "Fine. Have it your way. So you're the first Housekeeper, huh?"

Her lips twisted into a ghost of a smile. "I am."

"And is this part of the whole observation thing? I thought you were just supposed to spy on me and report back to Amon. Is this some kind of Housekeeper hazing that you do with your successors?"

She cocked her head. "I'm not certain what 'hazing' is, but

no, not all my successors receive the benefit of my company."

I'd been taught to be polite to my elders, and she was *really* elder, but I had my doubts about whether her company was a benefit. So far, it'd resulted in a bunch of weird dreams and restless nights.

My lack of faith must've shown on my face because she glowered at me for a long moment before giving a little sniff and looking into the fire. "You should count yourself lucky."

I wasn't so sure about that, but I nodded.

"So to what do I owe the pleasure of your company?"

She whipped her gaze back to me, but when she saw I was sincere, she relaxed slightly.

"I am here to observe, as is my right. Should Bayley succeed, you may be a first as well."

"Is that why you're here? Because this seems like a lot more than just observing."

I guess she didn't like me questioning her because with the look she gave me, I wondered if she were actually trying to set fire to me.

"Look, I'm not trying to be difficult or challenge you in any way. It never crossed my mind that at any point in my life I'd be dealing with the long-dead First Housekeeper. See above re: *long dead*." My arms waved as I said, "I was assured *multiple* times that dead is dead. And yet here you are."

"Here I am."

"Again, I don't mean to be rude, but why did you want to talk to me? And while we're at it, how?"

Ailith pursed her lips. "The how is not for you."

I opened my mouth to argue, but she cut me off.

"The why is," she pinned me with a piercing look, drew herself up, her voice taking on a note of command, "I am the First. I have rights."

That was as clear as mud. "Such as?"

"Such as," she looked down her nose at me, "assessing those who come after."

I groaned. "What is it with you Fosters and your tests? Is it genetic? Maybe it's genetic. That'd explain a lot."

"No tests."

"Then what? What am I doing here? Why did you want to interact with me?"

"First, there was the matter of whether you could even access this liminal space." She gave me a nod. "A point in your favor. One that Amon will find interesting."

Sounded an awful lot like a test to me, but I nodded. Obviously, I'd jumped that hurdle, though it'd taken a few tries.

"Now, you must permit me to aid you."

I restrained myself from pointing out again that she was dead. How much aiding could she do? Instead, I said, "I don't understand."

"Permission. I require your permission."

"Permission? To aid me with what? Aid me how?"

She spoke slowly. "Per-mih-shun."

"Yeah you said that. Again, to do what?"

"I am…limited…from here. With you, I will be…less limited."

"With me?"

"You may take me with you when you leave this place."

A prickle of alarm ran through me. "And how would I do that?"

"You have space while Bayley is…otherwise occupied. I can temporarily use that space."

"You want to what? Move into my head?"

"In a basic sense, yes."

I clamped my jaw shut to stop the "oh hell no" that tried to come screaming out. I wrestled my emotions under control until I finally managed a more measured, "There's two people in here already. I don't think adding more is a good idea."

"Bayley is not currently…present. There is space."

That didn't sound right—Bayley was offline, not totally gone. But even if I conceded that it was momentarily quieter in my brain, "Why would I do that?"

"You will likely need my aid. This is the way to obtain it."

I couldn't think of anything that would make me want to have a ghost living in my head. Just the idea made my stomach roil.

"I'm sorry, Ailith. I appreciate the offer, but no thank you. I have enough going on, and I don't need to complicate matters."

Ailith's whole body went tense, and her fists clenched. I thought she was going to start yelling, but instead she stared into the fire, eyes calculating. Finally, she looked back at me, her mouth twisted, and she said through a clenched jaw, "When you change your mind, you may return here. But do not take too long. There will come a point when this option is no longer available to you."

Dread poured through me as I wondered what she thought she knew that I didn't.

"Sure thing. Uh, thanks again."

She waved a hand, the room went hazy, and then everything went black.

Chapter Forty-Five

When I woke up, I was still in the sitting room, on the couch, with Fuzzy snoozing next to me. My watch told me that a few hours had passed, and my body told me that at least some of that had been spent actually sleeping. My fatigue thermometer had dropped from "keeling over" to "low-level tired."

I lay staring at the ceiling, thinking about what Ailith had said.

Fuzzy lifted his head. "Meow?"

"I saw Ailith again."

Fuzzy sat up and stared at me.

"She says she wants to help me while Bayley is gone. And to do that, she wants me to let her into my head."

Fuzzy growled.

"Right? That was my reaction too. She seemed very sure that I was going to need her. It's making me nervous." I patted Fuzzy while I thought it through.

I sighed and said, "I'd love to talk to Nor about Ailith. I wish I could get you to open a door, Percy," I said to my chest. Remembering that Percy was still in my dresser drawer, I shook my head and said, "Awesome. Now I'm talking to my chest, and no one's there."

I stopped short as my brain made a sudden connection.

I remembered the way Zav was demanding that I answer him. At the time, I'd thought he was being purposefully rude and staring at my chest. Now, my brain served up a different interpretation.

"Oh. Oh no. I really really hope I'm wrong."

I hopped off the couch and jogged up to my bedroom. Fuzzy followed behind me.

When I got to my room, I retrieved my mother's necklace from the top dresser drawer.

"Percy," I said. When he didn't respond, I shook the necklace vigorously and said louder, "Percy!"

After a moment, a sleepy-sounding, sullen, "What?" came from the necklace. "Is it over?"

My gaze narrowed as I asked, "Is what over?"

Percy must've noticed the terseness in my voice because he paused before saying carefully, "Is Bayley back already? That didn't seem very long."

"How long have you been working with Zav?" I held my breath as I waited for him to answer, hoping he'd go off on me, telling me I was paranoid.

After a long moment, Percy said, "Who told you that?"

"Zav did." Which wasn't entirely true. But I was clenching the necklace so hard it was digging into my hand as I hoped that Percy would revive the spark of hope dying inside me.

"I don't work for Zav, at least not directly." Disgust dripped from Percy's voice when he said "Zav."

I froze. I just stood there, staring at the necklace, as the ramifications of his admission overwhelmed me.

Fuzzy's growl shook me free from my paralysis, and my mind started to race.

"You've been spying on me this whole time?"

Fuzzy winced at my shrill tone, but Percy didn't respond.

My logic circuits went into overdrive as I worked it through. "Oh it's worse than that isn't it? You've been in my family—in the Foster family—for generations. For how long exactly?"

I didn't really expect him to answer, but Percy said, "Since the beginning. Since the first."

Ice poured through me. "Tell me you haven't been spying on us this whole time."

When Percy made no attempt to deny it, my dismay bloomed into outrage.

"So if you're not spying directly for Zav…." I'd only seen

Zav act deferential once. I bit out, "Amon. It's Amon."

Percy heaved a long, defeated sigh, giving me the confirmation I dreaded.

If he'd named one of the other magical families, that would have been bad enough.

But having all-powerful Amon keep tabs on us?

That was so much worse.

"Why? To what end?"

In a dull voice, Percy said, "Does it matter? What is done is done."

"Yes it matters! What does Amon have to gain by keeping tabs on the Fosters?"

"It was only supposed to be the Housekeepers. Things got… confused when I was passed to one who left the house." He added deriseively, "A gift. I was a gift."

So Amon had planned to keep tabs on the Housekeepers, but it had gone awry at some point, and he'd lost his spy. I guessed, "You were gone, so Amon called in Zav to what, fill in where you left off?"

"Something like that."

"How long did you report on the Housekeepers?"

"A long time."

"How long have you been away from Bayley?"

"A long time." That meant Zav had been wandering around for a disturbing number of years.

I glared at the necklace.

If Percy cared about my glare, he didn't show it.

I asked, "While you were gone, did you still report on the Fosters?"

"What would be the point?"

"What's the point of spying on the Housekeepers?" I countered. I found it concerning that Amon was so interested in what the Housekeepers were doing.

Percy didn't comment.

"Come on Percy, don't clam up on me now."

After a pause, he said, "I am limited in what I can say."

Maybe I'd been spending too much time with Mila, but

that made sense to me. If you were going to embed a spy, it'd be prudent to limit how much they could expose you if they were caught.

I tried to puzzle it through. For Amon to place a spy in the house, either Bayley or the Housekeepers themselves must have special importance to him. I played back my recovered memories. I was pretty sure it was the former. Amon had shown up right after Bayley took himself off on his self-discovery retreat.

"Is it Bayley or the Housekeepers that Amon is interested in?"

Percy answered, "Yes."

I groaned. "Yeah, okay, the two are intertwined. Bayley's well-being depends in part on the Housekeepers, so it's hard to separate the two. How about this: which is more important to Amon?"

Percy said, "You already answered your own question."

I thought about what I'd just said. "The Housekeepers are interesting because of how they interact with Bayley. So really, this is about Bayley. I thought so."

I mulled over the situation, trying to figure out what I should do next. I could simply take Percy out of play and keep him in a drawer. Of course, that had its own problems.

Would Percy be hurt by being shut in a drawer? As mad and betrayed as I felt, I didn't want to hurt him.

The more I thought about it, the more problems I saw. First, I didn't know how Amon would react. Would he retaliate? Second, if I locked Percy up most of the time, he might refuse to open doors for me anymore, which would definitely suck. Third, a pang shot through me at the idea of not being able to wear my mom's necklace anymore.

Thinking about not wearing my necklace set off the memory of Zav yelling at my chest. I frowned. "He tipped his hand."

Percy said, "What?" and Fuzzy looked up at me.

"Zav. He tipped his hand. He demanded that you answer him—in front of not just me, but Fuzzy, the Grack, and the Samaras as well." I started to pace. "I mean, he was mad. From what I've seen, though, 'Daffy Duckish low-boil rage' seems to be his baseline state." I stopped pacing to look at Fuzzy. "Percy has been this secret for centuries, and Zav just outed him, in front of all of us, like it was no big deal."

Fuzzy blinked at me.

"Percy, what happens if Amon finds out that we know your real purpose?" When he didn't answer me, I gave the necklace a shake. "Percy!"

"I'm thinking." After another minute, Percy said in an exhausted voice, "If I have completed the task that I've been assigned, then he will...reclaim me...and assign me elsewhere."

I frowned at him. "You've been assigned to other places before?"

Defensive this time, he said, "I have."

"How many?" I demanded.

"I lost count."

I wasn't sure I believed that, but Percy's stubborn, angry tone told me it was not a good idea to push him on that topic just now. So I stuck to the subject at hand.

"Does Zav know you'll be reassigned?"

"He does."

"So, by revealing you to us, he's pretty much making sure you'll get the boot. In effect, he's making a play to take you off the board." Why now? It must have something to do with Bayley being away, but I wasn't sure exactly what.

I sat on the edge of the bed next to where Fuzzy sat on the floor. Resting my elbows on my knees, I held the necklace in my hand, studying it.

I really didn't want Amon to take my necklace away.

And if I were honest, it wasn't just the necklace I'd be missing. Percy might be a snarky pain in my butt, but I'd come to think of him as a part of my team. Practically, he was super useful. But more than that, we'd been making slow progress at becoming, if not friends, then at least friendly.

"You know Percy, if you wanted to get more info out of me, you should have been sucking up this whole time, instead of being the prickly delight that you are," I said half-heartedly.

Percy said, "Perhaps that was not my wish."

On a half-hearted laugh, I said, "If you didn't want to ferret out information, why did you choose to be a spy?"

"Who said I chose anything?"

I jerked back at his snarled response. "What do you mean you didn't choose?"

Being Percy, he didn't answer, so I tried to figure it out on my own.

"You're not from here…so it stands to reason that the rules where you come from are different from the way we do things. So maybe spying isn't a volunteer job, it's more of a draft situation? Like the military here sometimes does?"

Percy said grudgingly, "Well reasoned."

"Thanks," I said.

"But incorrect."

I sighed. This was feeling like my conversation with Ailith all over again. I had the right pieces, but the wrong big picture.

"Okay, I gave it a shot. I don't want to sit around here guessing all day, so how about you just tell me why you're spying if you don't want to."

"No."

I waited, but he didn't elaborate.

I prodded, "No? Just no? That's it?"

"I don't want to talk about it."

Fuzzy and I looked at each other. He had heard it too. Percy sounded really upset. In the six months that I'd known Percy, he'd sounded annoyed, snarky, superior, disgusted, resentful, resigned, and very occasionally, amused. But he'd never been upset.

"Okay, Percy. I'll drop it for now."

He didn't respond.

"One more thing though."

I waited him out until he finally said, "What is it?"

"Do you *want* to be reassigned?"

I waited, but Percy didn't answer.

Chapter Forty-Six

After putting Percy back in the dresser, I headed to the kitchen with Fuzzy.

"I don't care if I have no ingredients, I need to bake something. This thing with Percy is...I don't even...I need to bake something. Right now."

I'd just made it through the kitchen door when a sharp, tugging sensation yanked at my magic. I staggered to one of the kitchen chairs and dropped into it.

When Fuzzy darted over, shoving a concerned nose in my face, I said, "Something is up with my magic. Hang on."

I tried to make sense of what I was feeling. The pulling sensation was familiar—it was similar to what Bayley did when he needed to borrow my magical energy. But instead of Bayley's usual gentle sip from the top of my energy pool, this was like someone had stuck a straw in and slurped as hard as they could.

Frowning, I closed my eyes and studied the link between me and Bayley. While Bayley's energy moseyed toward me at a sleepy pace, my magical energy poured toward him with the enthusiasm of a troop of ants that had just spotted a picnic.

The sharp pulling sensation abated, and my energy slowed down some, but continued to flow toward him at a faster rate than usual. It was like Bayley had turned my magic faucet on, it had come blasting out at first, and now, he'd turned it back down a bit, but not all the way back to its usual dripping rate.

Bayley? Are you okay?

He didn't respond.

Opening my eyes, I said to Fuzzy, "I think something is up

with Bayley."

Fuzzy cocked his head.

"He's siphoning magical energy from me faster than usual. It feels like he sort of reached out and grabbed for it, then relaxed his grip a bit. I don't mind him borrowing magic if he needs it—we share all the time. But he always checks with me first, and he's always been more controlled about it."

I studied our connection again, following it to the glowing ball in the corner of my mind that represented Bayley. Did Bayley's glow look different?

"Fuzzy, I'm worried."

I retrieved the last of the chocolate chips from the pantry. Instead of trying to find a recipe that could use so few, I stood at the butcher block eating them as I fretted about Bayley.

I'd just polished off the bag when Bayley yanked on my magic again.

This time I was more ready for it and managed to grab the counter and keep my feet.

Fuzzy twisted around my legs, chirruping anxiously.

"It's happening again. Give me a sec," I said. The pulling sensation passed, and I sat back down, put my head in my hands, and took slow deep breaths. "I don't feel so good."

Fuzzy rubbed his head against my leg.

"Thanks for the comfort, pal. I appreciate it."

As I stroked Fuzzy's head, I searched my own to see what was going on with the bond now. The energy flow from me to Bayley was even quicker than when I checked a few minutes ago, but not turbo fast. But when I followed the connection to Bayley's corner of my mind, I gasped.

My eyes popped open, and I looked at Fuzzy. "Bayley's getting dimmer. Something is definitely wrong! Hang on, I'm going to try and figure out what's happening."

As I closed my eyes again, I zoomed along the energy highway until I reached Bayley's glowing spot and called out, *Bayley, can you hear me?*

I reached through our bond as I called, but I couldn't get a response from him. It was as though he was really far away, though clearly we were still joined.

I retreated back to my own corner of my mind and opened my eyes.

Fuzzy trilled at me the second I opened my eyes.

"I can't get through to him." I bit my lip. "I'm going to have to try something else." I got up and started pulling out Shake-It-Off ingredients, trying not to panic as I saw how low they were getting.

"Whatever is happening, he obviously needs a magic boost."

I stopped short, closed my eyes, and popped into the Knack Shack. The magic thermometer told me my reserves were not completely topped off, but not bottoming out either. Opening my eyes again, I started to put the Shake-It-Off together. "Okay, my magic has bounced back some since I broke the hex, so I'm not totally burned out. When I suck this down," I pointed to the Shake-It-Off I was assembling, "that should help me recover even more." I looked at Fuzzy and said, "Then I'm going to try actively pouring a little more magic into Bayley than he's already pulling. Give him a booster shot."

Fuzzy stalked back and forth behind me, chittering at me as I finished the Shake-It-Off.

"What I'm getting is that you're worried," I said.

"Meow!" He headbutted me.

"Yeah, me too. It's not great that I'm not at full strength, but making sure Bayley is okay is literally the definition of my job. Let's just see what happens."

As I chugged half the shake, I made my way back to the kitchen table. Settling into the chair, I focused on my link with Bayley.

I took a moment to feel the flow of magical energy moving from me to Bayley. As I concentrated, I pulled on my magic and sent more of it flowing through the bond. I didn't know which branch of magic would serve Bayley best, so I poured an equal amount of each type of magic into our connection.

The lane of the highway between us that moved from me to Bayley pulsed brighter and faster, so I knew that what I was doing was working.

At first, there was no change in Bayley.

But after a few minutes, Bayley's glow in the corner of my mind began to brighten.

I monitored everything for a few more minutes before returning my focus to the kitchen.

"Whatever is going on, that seems to be helping him for now."

"Meow?" Fuzzy pawed at my knee.

"Me? Um," I did a quick survey and frowned at how leaden my body felt. "Well, I was tired before I started, and now I feel like I just worked a double at the diner. No headache yet, probably thanks to the shake, but it's going to be an effort to keep this up." I polished off the rest of the shake and stood slowly, legs shaking slightly. "Probably a good idea if I go back to sleep again, maybe hedge my bets a bit," I said.

I was suddenly so tired that I didn't even try to finish my coffee.

Chapter Forty-Seven

I trudged up the stairs to my bedroom, Fuzzy following closely behind me.

"I swear there's some kind of chaos magic that makes staircases grow longer when you're tired," I huffed. When we reached my room, I collapsed on my bed.

"This is definitely not sustainable," I mumbled to Fuzzy as he curled up beside me. "But I think I helped Bayley with the extra energy boost. I'm going to turn the flow back down again so I can regain some energy while I rest. Hopefully, what I gave him will hold him awhile."

Before I could discuss it further, I fell asleep.

And found myself sitting across from Ailith again.

I bit back my groan.

This was not what I wanted. I'd hoped to recoup my energy with some quality time in dreamland, not to go toe-to-toe with Ailith again, which I was pretty sure would suck the life out of anyone.

"Ailith," I said, with a little wave.

"Now are you ready to see reason?"

A part of me wondered if I asked to get some sleep and come back after my nap if she'd let me go. Somehow I doubted it.

She said, "You realize your current solution for Bayley is a temporary fix."

Of course I did, but I wasn't sure I should concede that point so I asked instead, "Fix for what?"

Ailith lips twisted in a smug look that reminded me of the Grinch smiling right before he stole everyone's presents. "As I said, you do require my help."

This time I couldn't stop the groan from escaping. "Can we not? I'm really tired. How about you just, you know, give me a show of good faith and tell me what's going on. Then we'll see about you 'helping' me."

Ailith pursed her lips, studying me, then nodded once. She got up to poke the fire with a stick. Keeping her back to me, she said, "What do you know of the creation of the...houses?"

"Hou*ses*? As in plural?" I'd wondered if there might be others like Bayley, but hadn't been able to find out. "How many are there? Where are they?"

She glanced over her shoulder. "Not here."

"By 'here' you mean 'our world,' right?"

She nodded and poked the fire a bit more. Since this was a dream space, I figured she was doing it to stall for time. When it was roaring, she sat back in her chair. "Do you know anything of how Bayley came to be here?"

I shook my head, "No. I'm sorry to say that most of his history has been lost. The Fosters did a crappy job of keeping records."

The irritation on Ailith's face matched the irritation I was feeling. She'd probably lose her mind if I told her they'd even forgotten Bayley's name for a while, so I decided to keep that tidbit to myself.

Ailith's irritation morphed into a calculating look, and I braced myself for whatever was coming next.

"For now, all you need to know is that for Bayley to complete his task, he must gain the approval of those who oversee the houses."

"Amon?"

"At the very least."

A sick feeling lodged in my stomach. "How many others are there? Who are they? *Where* are they?"

She waved away my questions. "Not here. And it matters not who or how many they are. What matters is that they are powerful. And that Bayley is failing in his task."

"The power drain," I said.

"Yes. He did not adequately prepare. *You* did not adequately prepare him."

How was I supposed to prepare him? I'd had zero notice that he was even going to attempt this.

I said, "I can't fix what's already happened. The question is, what's the best way to move forward? How can I help?"

Ailith's eyes turned flinty as she said, "I have had dealings with these beings before. I can help Bayley. You must host me in your mind so I may go and advocate on his behalf."

How would that even work? Go where? And why did she need my permission? If she was as powerful as she was implying, why didn't she just help and tell me about it later?

Not only that, but so far, I hadn't been impressed with Ailith's people skills. She made Oscar the Grouch look like a beam of sunshine. I wasn't convinced that sending her and her cranky pants to deal with anyone, never mind people in charge of Bayley's fate, was a good idea.

I hedged, "Well, I've met Amon. If it's just a matter of having an 'in,' then I'm fine."

Her eyes narrowed as she tried to stare me into submission.

I kept my expression mild as I held her gaze, but on the inside I was laughing. She might be a hardcase, but I'd been hanging with Mila and Lars—two people who put the "Ha don't even try it" in hardass. If I could stand up to their intimidation, no way was she going to get me to squirm.

She must have realized it because she changed tactics. "I thought you genuinely cared for Bayley. Perhaps I was wrong."

Okay, so she was serving me guilt with a side of shame. Instead of taking the bait, I said, "You're trying awfully hard to convince me. What is it that you get out of this?"

With an affronted look, Ailith said, "I answer my calling. Once a Housekeeper, always a Housekeeper. Especially for me, since I was the first. My relationship with Bayley is…special. Different from the others."

The unsaid "different from yours" hung in the air.

I would have given a lot to ask Bayley how he actually felt about his first Housekeeper and just how "special" their relationship really was. Without Bayley to corroborate or explain,

I had only Ailith's word to go on. Six months ago, that might have been enough. But after Wil had turned on me, I wasn't as apt to take people at face value anymore.

Still, I didn't want to openly antagonize her. As usual, I fell back on my manners.

With a conciliatory smile, I said, "Again, I thank you for your offer to help, Ailith. And indeed, the information you've given me has helped me understand the situation a little better. But I still think I can handle this."

Ailith shook her head. "You must give me permission to intercede on Bayley's behalf!"

"And you would do that by moving into my head—because there's space." She nodded, and I said, "And you'd be like Bayley? A voice in the back of my mind?"

She avoided my eyes, and a chill ran through me as an ugly thought broke through. I was pretty sure that Ailith didn't just want to hitch a ride. She needed my permission because she wanted control. She wanted to possess me.

Staring into the fire, she said, "You need me. I can do what you cannot. When the time comes, I will make sure they give Bayley his due." Her voice was taut, her hands fisted, her jaw clenched, and her mouth pinched in a way that looked like she'd swallowed something bitter.

It suddenly occurred to me that Ailith might not be pushing so hard just because she wanted to help Bayley. She looked and sounded like she had some kind of score to settle. She said she'd had dealings with Bayley's overseers before. Maybe there was some truth to the theory that ghosts came back to deal with unfinished business.

Viewed through that lens, it made sense that Ailith had been pushing me so hard to let her "help" Bayley—especially if she became the one in charge, and I wound up as a backseat driver, at best. I'd suspected that Ailith had her own agenda, and I was pretty sure taking on Bayley's overseers was near the top of that list.

When I didn't respond to her, Ailith looked up at me. "If I am there, I can guarantee they will listen. I can make them."

She smiled, but the expression in her eyes twisted her grin into something dark, like there was violence just under the surface.

Any benefit of the doubt I'd been willing to give Ailith about her diplomacy skills evaporated. She was definitely spoiling for a fight.

Giving a polite bow that I'd learned from Sibeta, I said, "You have my sincere thanks. But what kind of Housekeeper would I be if I let someone else do all the hard work?"

Ailith started to protest, but I cut her off with, "Look, if I get into trouble, I can request your aid. In fact, it's kind of you to have my back should I need it."

Ailith opened her mouth to argue, but something in my face changed her mind. She snapped it shut and sat back in her chair. "So be it," she said.

As I said, "Thank y—" the room faded, and I slipped into a deep sleep.

Chapter Forty-Eight

When I woke at four a.m., I realized I'd managed only a few hours of sleep, leaving me disoriented. I would have gone right back to sleep, but my stomach was complaining.

"Right, right. I need fuel if I'm going to replenish my energy properly. I know," I mumbled, as I tried to convince myself to get out of bed. A quick check on Bayley made me want to pull the covers over my head. He was back to being dimmer than usual, but not as bad as yesterday.

"Meow?" Fuzzy's eyes gleamed in the dark.

"I'm trying to talk myself into getting out of bed. I need to eat. Bayley looks a little dimmer again, so I'm betting I'm going to need to spare some more energy."

Fuzzy yawned, got to his feet, stretched, then leaned over to stick his face near mine.

I couldn't help but laugh. "Okay I get it. Get up or get the cold, wet nose in my face." Still chuckling, I climbed out of bed, donned my bunny slippers, and headed downstairs.

Fuzzy darted ahead of me so that by the time I entered the kitchen, he was already sitting by his food bowl.

I fed him first, and then sat at the big kitchen table by myself, drinking a Shake-It-Off and shoveling down a bowl of dry cereal. Today the house seemed extra solemn, and the quietness pressed in on me.

After I finished eating, I leaned back in my chair, hands wrapped around my coffee mug, and inhaled the vapors deeply. Nothing like the smell of coffee to chase away the gloom.

I did a body check. Between the rest, the food, and the

Shake-It-Off, I felt functional. Still more tired than usual, but not direly so.

Then I went to check on Bayley. I nearly dropped my mug. "No."

Fuzzy appeared beside me.

Clenching my mug so hard my knuckles turned white, I looked down at Fuzzy and said, "It's Bayley. He's even dimmer than when I first woke up. Worse than yesterday."

Fuzzy's dismayed meow echoed how I was feeling.

I checked on Bayley again, hoping maybe I'd just looked at him wrong, but if anything, on a closer look, he looked even fainter than I'd thought. It was like he was fading from my mind.

Panic tore through me. Our bond was still intact, but when I reached through the link, I had to work hard to find any sense that Bayley was still there at the other end. When I finally connected to him, he seemed small and distant. And as before, when I tugged at him, he didn't respond back.

I thunked my coffee cup onto the table and hung my head in my hands. "This feels really wrong, Fuzzy."

I forced my rising panic to the side and put my logic brain to work. "I'm going to try feeding him a quick boost of energy and see if that makes a difference."

As Fuzzy leaned against me for support, I reached for my magic and sent a burst through my bond to Bayley.

I waited several minutes, but there was no change. He didn't get any dimmer, but he didn't get any brighter.

"Meow?"

I opened my eyes and looked at Fuzzy. "Nope, nothing."

I got up and poured myself some more coffee and then stood at the counter sipping and thinking.

When I'd fed Bayley energy, not only did it not perk him up, but also it didn't cause him to grasp for more, like that gulping sensation I'd felt yesterday, so maybe he didn't need more energy? Of course, that meant I had no idea what he *did* need. But it was clear to me that I'd better figure it out and find a way to help him.

A seed of an idea began to sprout in my mind, and by the

time I finished my coffee, I had a crazy plan.

"Fuzzy...this might sound strange, but hear me out. Bayley sort of hangs out in my mind—it's like he's got guest quarters in my brain. But it's a reciprocal bond...so who's to say I can't set up my own guest quarters in his mind? I mean, I've never been over to his place before, but that doesn't mean I *can't* go there... just that there hasn't been a need to yet."

Fuzzy switched his tail as he stared at me, head tipped, ears cocked. After a moment, he nodded his head once and gave me a tentative, "Meow."

I set my empty coffee cup down. "I bet you're wondering how that would help anything. See, I'm thinking that if he can't be here with me in my mind, then if I go to where he is instead—if I 'go to his house for a visit'—then maybe I can talk to him. And maybe I'll even be in a better position to help him with whatever he's dealing with." I nodded to myself. "I mean, it's worth a try. Bayley usually comes to me, but this time I'm going to go to him. Or at least try to."

Fuzzy didn't look convinced, but he didn't complain, so I took that as a sort of, "Okay, I guess so."

He trotted out of the kitchen, pausing over his shoulder to look at me, so I followed him. In the mudroom, he came to a stop by the basement door.

"Ah, you want me to tell Sibeta? Good idea. Let's see what she says."

When we got to the pool, I knew Fuzzy was worried, because he didn't even try to go swimming. He just sat on the edge and howled.

A brief time later, Sibeta rose to the surface of the pool. "Housekeeper," she said with a bow.

"Hi Sibeta," I said.

She turned to Fuzzy, staring at him in a way that made me think he was talking to her. As her gaze darted from me to Fuzzy and her brow furrowed, I said, "I guess he's filling you in on my plan?"

"He is."

"Do you have any thoughts?"

"Many."

When she didn't elaborate, I said, "And?"

"And I am unable to say more. I apologize, Housekeeper. But this is as it must be."

I groaned. "Amon's stupid rules?"

"Yes."

"So you can't help me at all," I said, sighing.

Sibeta looked pained. "It is so, Housekeeper. *I* may not interfere with Bayley's task in any way." She emphasized the "I," which I thought might be her way of implying that I could interfere, and was therefore on the right track. "Again, my apologies."

"Well, at least now you know what's going on. In case something happens, it's a good idea that someone knows what I've been up to."

I thanked Sibeta, then Fuzzy and I paid a quick visit to the Grack. After I made sure she and the Gracklettes were okay, I had Fuzzy help me explain what was happening and that I'd be unavailable for a bit.

When we got back in the kitchen, I put out a bunch of extra food for Fuzzy. "I don't think this will take very long, but given that the last time I tried strolling around my mental space I was unconscious for two days, better to be safe than sorry. Although, let's hope I'm not out that long this time, because I don't have Mari keeping me hydrated and healthy." I briefly considered going back to the basement to ask Mari to keep an eye on me again, but I really didn't think I'd need her, so I discarded the idea.

After a thorough check of my mental map, I said, "I think that does it for prep. Zav hasn't come back to the property, and nothing else seems out of place. All the lockdown protocols are still active, but if he shows up, please interrupt me, and I'll deal with him. So...I think I'm good to go for this little excursion. Now, where should I do this?"

I stared at the ceiling. "My bed is the obvious place—I'd be super comfortable there. Mmm. Maybe too comfortable. I want to maintain a meditative state, but I don't want to fall asleep—especially with Ailith around to waylay me. Maybe the couch?" I shook my head. "Right now, the sitting room makes me think of Ailith too much. I feel like if I'm in there, I'll be distracted, expecting her to show up."

Fuzzy hopped up on the kitchen table. "Meow?"

Looking around the kitchen, I nodded. "You're right. This is my happy place, where I feel strongest. Plus, the kitchen is the heart of any house—it's the perfect spot to try to reach Bayley from."

I sat in my favorite seat at the kitchen table, settling in and getting as comfortable as possible.

Fuzzy hopped up onto the table and sat himself right in front of me.

"I'm guessing you want to keep an eye on me."

"Meow."

I stroked between his ears and said, "Thanks. I appreciate the help."

Fuzzy chirruped at me.

"I don't know how long this will take, but if something goes really wrong, I left the door to the basement cracked. Go to Sibeta, she will help you."

Fuzzy's ears flattened to half-mast.

I held up my hands, placatingly. "I'm not expecting anything to go wrong, with me or the property, but I want to make sure you're taken care of, just in case." Especially with Zav lurking about. I didn't say that part aloud, but Fuzzy mumbled at me in a way that made me suspect he was thinking the same thing.

"Ready?"

Fuzzy leaned forward and nuzzled my face, his soft purr rumbling through me.

Putting my arms around Fuzzy, I touched foreheads with him. "Thank you. I love you too. Now, let's do this."

Chapter Forty-Nine

Leaning back in the chair, I closed my eyes.

My virtual avatar materialized in my mental space, and I zeroed in on my magical bond. Zooming alongside it, I quickly found myself standing in front of the dim spot that represented Bayley. But while the bond disappeared into the spot, I found I couldn't move forward. There was some kind of barrier separating me from Bayley, which made sense when I thought about it.

But I needed to get past that barrier and into Bayley's mind.

"Okay, Bayley. How am I supposed to get from here to you?" I didn't really expect him to answer, but talking to him made me feel better.

I turned to look at the bond. It had no problem crossing over to Bayley's side.

Because of the way the energy flowed back and forth, my mind saw the bond as a two-lane highway with a median strip down the middle, separating my side from Bayley's. The whole thing was encased in a sort of clear, iridescent tube, making the bond its own entity, separate from the rest of my mind.

Still, it linked me and Bayley, so maybe I could use it somehow.

Walking next to it wasn't doing me a lick of good.

"What would happen if I stepped into the bond, Bayley? I've been treating it like it's a separate thing, but part of it is mine. Maybe I can use it literally like a highway to your mind?"

I took a deep breath, which I realized was ridiculous in a virtual space, but helped me nonetheless, and pictured myself standing inside the bond, on the median in the middle of the energy highway.

For a moment, nothing happened. Then static hijacked my vision as my mind flailed about, trying to make visual sense of what I was doing.

Gritting my teeth, I struggled to focus on what the bond usually looked like. Darts of energy. An encased highway.

The static started to resolve into...a tube?

No, not a tube. A tunnel. I was standing in a tunnel with tiled walls that arched over and around me.

Looking down, I saw that I'd landed where I'd aimed for, on the broad, raised median that split the tunnel down the middle.

When I'd been outside in my mind, I could see into the bond. But now that I was inside, I couldn't see out.

"Interesting," I said, studying my surroundings.

On my right, dashes of green, blue, purple, red, and tan energy zipped by me like they were late for work.

"Ah, you're the part of the bond going from me to Bayley. Got it."

Lighting up the tunnel as they passed, the energy bursts caused the road below and the tiles on the walls to flicker with bursts of color. I tracked the bursts as far as I could see them, but they disappeared around a bend ahead of me.

All the dashes of color reminded me of the sprinkles I'd been putting on the sugar cookies I'd been making for the Samaras.

I shouldn't have started thinking about cookies. Now I really, really wanted sugar cookies. With sprinkles on top.

A golden dash of energy appeared in the distance. It made its way toward me on my left, traveling by me at horse-and-buggy pace.

"And you must be the energy coming from Bayley to me."

When I turned to watch it leave, it moseyed along until it disappeared into the distance behind me.

As I faced my side of the road again, my mouth dropped open. The energy dashes on my right had changed.

Into cookies.

Giant, glowing cookies, each the size of a big saucer sled,

and each topped with sprinkles. The cookies and their matching sprinkles were colored the same as the dashes had been.

"Ugh. I know better," I scolded myself. "I've got to pay attention to my wants in a mental space. I know this."

I considered trying to turn the cookies back into energy dashes. But they were just too cute. Besides, what fun was that?

"Okay, you magical-energy-boosting cookies—ugh. That's just awkward. I'm going to call you boosties. My boosties, you may stay as you are. Carry on," I said, waving at them.

Studying the tunnel, I said, "Okay. I'm not loving that I can't see either end of the tunnel. But at least I know which is Bayley's end and which is mine. That's something, right?"

Walking on the median, I followed alongside my stream of boosties toward Bayley's end of the tunnel.

After walking a short ways, I rounded the bend in the tunnel ahead and stopped short.

In front of me, a giant toll booth loomed.

"You look like a teenage boy after a growth spurt," I muttered as I stared up and up and up at it. The thing reached all the way to the ceiling. And even though it was way skinnier than most toll booths, it was exactly wide enough to take up the whole median in front of me.

Both sides of the toll booth had arms, but like the rest of the toll booth, they were odd. Twice as wide as normal toll booth arms, they were also longer, reaching all the way across each lane to the walls.

I stood there looking at the toll booth for a minute before I figured it out.

"Ohhhh. I get it. You must represent the barrier between me and Bayley." I peered at the booth before adding, "I don't see any place to pay a toll, so that means I get a free pass, right?"

As I studied the boosties zipping by, I realized that they stayed in the middle of the lane, and then passed right through the toll booth arm as if it didn't exist. Sticking close to the median so I didn't accidentally bump into any boosties, I stepped down onto my side of the highway and tried walking through the arm the way the boosties did.

It was like walking into a wall. The arm didn't budge.

Next, I tried ducking under the toll booth's arm.

It adjusted itself down to prevent me from going under it.

"Okay, how about over?"

Hiking up my leg, I went to swing it over the top of the arm, but stopped short as the arm raised itself to prevent me from going over.

Hopping back up onto the median, I reconsidered my options.

"Maybe you don't want me going on the right side because it's so busy?" I asked the toll booth.

It just lurked at me.

"Do you want me to try Bayley's side? My own side makes more sense to me, but I guess there's more space between the dashes on Bayley's side, and there's almost no chance I'll disrupt them."

The toll booth didn't say "no," so I decided to take its silence as a, "sure, why not give it a try?"

After waiting for Bayley's next golden dash to drift by on my left, I walked to the edge of the median and tried to step into the left lane.

Except when I looked down, I was still on the edge of the median.

Frowning, I took another step forward. Again, the left lane stayed just out of reach.

I stopped, turned, and faced the toll booth.

Keeping my eyes on it, I did a sidestep to the left.

I groaned. "Did you just move with me?"

No matter how hard I tried, I could get to the edge of the median, but I couldn't actually step into Bayley's lane.

Okay, maybe telling the toll booth my plans hadn't been a great idea.

I glared at the toll booth. "You know, I'm trying to help here. There's no reason for your bad attitude, mister."

The toll booth didn't say anything, but I felt like it was smirking.

I stomped up and down the median for a few minutes while I tried to puzzle it through.

The right side felt...well, right. The longer I stood there, the more I was certain that I needed to use it to get to Bayley.

So how did I do that?

First thing I needed to do was to get away from the watchful toll booth.

I backtracked the way I'd come, careful to stay on the median. Once I rounded the bend, the toll booth blinked out of sight again.

"Maybe 'out of sight, out of mind' will work here?" I mumbled to myself.

Turning sideways, I hopped down into the right lane, keeping as close to the edge of the median as I could.

A green boostie passed by me without slowing down, filling me with a little fizzy sensation as it slid by.

Releasing my breath, I started sidling my way back down the highway. Since I was walking sideways anyway, I put a little hip wiggle in my step, hummed a tune, and turned my side shuffle into a mambo.

I'd only mamboed a short distance when I rounded the bend again, and the toll booth reappeared.

Standing still, I studied the toll booth more closely. When the boosties reached the toll booth's arm, a section of the arm exactly as wide as the boostie vanished, only to resolidify the second the cookie had passed through.

"Huh."

I studied the boosties and realized they were coming at regular intervals.

"I have a terrible idea."

Before I could talk myself out of it, I ran toward a blue boostie and jumped onto it.

Well I tried to.

I couldn't figure how to hold on and slid right off, belly-flopping onto the road underneath it.

"Ow. You know, I really hate that things still hurt in the virtual world," I grumbled. "I mean, why is that a thing?"

Rolling over, I laid on my back and reassessed as I watched the extremely surreal sight of giant energy cookies floating over me.

"Eat your heart out Magritte," I murmured, grinning.

I crawled my way over to the median, careful to keep well under the boosties, and stood up again. I could swear the toll booth was somehow giving me the side eye, so I mamboed my way back down the tunnel.

When I'd rounded the bend and the toll booth disappeared from sight again, I climbed back onto the median.

"Let's try something different."

I turned to face in the direction of the toll booth and Bayley. Looking over my shoulder, I waited for the next green boostie to come along. When it was getting close to me, I started running and generating magical vines from my hands, made of the same magical energy as the boostie. As soon as it reached me, I leapt onto it.

This time, instead of sliding off, I lay sprawled across the top of the boostie like a really big sprinkle. Quickly, I twined the vines around me and my sweet ride, securing me in place.

Shifting my arms and legs so that none of me hung over the edges, I watched as the toll booth arm loomed in front of me.

Moment of truth…

I held my breath.

The arm approached. Then, one second it was there, the next it was gone.

"Yes!" I whispered, doing the best version of a happy dance that I could do while tied down on top of a fast-moving cookie.

Lifting my head, I looked around me and found that the far side of the tunnel looked the same as the side I'd just been in. After zipping along it for a short while, suddenly a light appeared in the distance.

The end of the tunnel! Bayley's brain! I'd done it!

I choked on my whoop of success as the image of the tunnel disappeared, and I found myself spiraling out of control.

Chapter Fifty

Flashing images, wind, and noise—so much noise—slammed into me. I couldn't understand any of it. It was like someone changed the channel on a TV so fast that I couldn't fully register any of the images, and each channel blared incomprehensible sounds, music, and words at me.

Instinctively, I curled up into a ball, ducking my head against the sensory onslaught so that the boostie was all I could see.

It saved me.

Inadvertently focusing on my own, familiar Foster energy gave me an anchor. I clung to that anchor, concentrating on the feel of my own energy, frantically yanking some of it from the boostie and wrapping it around me like a little kid hiding under the covers from a nightmare.

Once I was hidden under my boostie binkie, the visuals and noise became blurry and muffled, the same way they would if I had an actual blanket over my head. Wrapping myself in my own magical energy provided just enough distance from the chaos that I didn't feel like I was being shredded by it.

I realized I was chanting, "Don't panic, don't panic, don't panic." Hearing the sound of my own voice helped counter the bad karaoke happening outside. Maybe liking the sound of my own voice made me a narcissist, but it was helping, so I was going with it.

Aloud I said, "Okay think. What just happened? I jumped on my boostie here," I gave it a soft pat, "and everything was fine. Right up until I exited the bond and into what I'm assuming is Bayley's brain. Then, pandemonium." I shuddered as I contemplated the world outside the binkie. Looking down at the boostie again, I said, "C'mon, focus. Think it through. I got into Bayley's mind and…oh. I should've thought of this. I'm not in my own head anymore. No wonder everything seems strange. But yay! I'm in Bayley's mind." I sat up, carefully keeping my "blanket" over me. "Bayley!" I called.

No response.

"Bayley?"

Still no response.

Maybe he couldn't hear me. "BAYLEY!" I shouted as loud as I could.

My heart squeezed in panic as I realized I wasn't getting through to him.

Staring at my binkie, it dawned on me that while being covered in Foster magic was helping me stay sane, it was doing so by isolating me. If I were Bayley's brain, I'd just see another blob of Foster magic. He'd have no way of knowing that I was hiding inside.

But if I dropped it, I'd be overwhelmed again.

"Well this is a mess."

I peeked at Bayley's mind through the filter of the blanket. Flickering lights and unintelligible sounds rocketed around me. I could make out snippets of music and languages, none of which I spoke.

The languages tipped me off. I snapped my fingers. "I know what this is. It's a translation issue. Bayley speaks English, so he can relate to the words in my mind easily. But I don't even know what Bayley's native language is, never mind speak it, so no wonder his thoughts are confusing. I need a Babel fish to turn Bayley-speak into something my mind recognizes."

I took stock. I could tell that I was still moving, but it seemed like my boostie had slowed down.

Just as I thought that, my cookie bumped to a halt. A few seconds later, I felt something gently thump into my boostie from behind, and a few seconds later, an even softer thump. The thumps continued at regular intervals.

I needed to see what was happening.

I created a tiny peephole in my binkie, just big enough to see that the boosties coming up behind me were bumping into one another as they arrived.

Frowning, I closed the peep hole and made a different one facing in the opposite direction.

"Wow."

The view in front of me would make sugar addicts everywhere explode with delight—there was an ocean of boostie cookies. At the edges of the space, short walls corralled the boosties. Beyond the shortened walls, I could see the flashing images and hear the noise, but this space inside the corral seemed cordoned off just to stack up the energy.

In the very far distance, I could see that occasionally a few boosties would disappear all at once. I had to watch for a while, but eventually I caught on that Bayley was taking one of each kind of magical energy every time he "ate a cookie."

That gave me an idea.

Since it was my energy anyway, I could use the boosties too.

I spied blue, purple, red, and tan boosties stacked willy-nilly around me. At least one of every color was adjacent to me.

First, I "ate" the entire Foster boostie I was standing on, feeding all the energy into the "blanket," which I kept wrapped around me. As the boostie dissolved underneath me, I dropped down a short way onto a different boostie underneath it. Fortunately, the cookies were so packed together that I didn't have to worry about falling off.

Next, I poked a hole through the Foster energy blanket surrounding me and reached out to the tan boostie nearby.

I "ate the cookie," pulling all the tan Best energy to me. To my relief, it immediately reacted to my command, flowing toward me. Carefully, I wove the Foster and Best energies together. By the time I was done, I'd formed the brown and green into one single blanket arching over and around me.

One by one, I "ate" one boostie of each kind of magic. When I was finished, an energy blanket made of all five branches of magic completely surrounded me.

I waited to see if Bayley noticed—even calling his name several times—but still there was no response.

Worry pooled in my stomach. "I hope it's not a bad sign that you're so focused on what you're doing that you haven't noticed me yet." I sighed and chewed my lip. "Well, Bayley, if you can't easily notice me where I'm at, I'm going to have to make myself impossible to miss."

Pulling the energy blanket closer around me, I visualized a cross between a HAZMAT suit and colorful, hooded footsie pajamas. The blanket reshaped itself, and covered me head to toe. The covering blocked my vision though, so I imagined the magics forming a transparent helmet. I grinned as I looked out of the clear face mask, tinged iridescent with the shimmering magical energy.

"Magical HAZMAT footsie pajamas for the win!" I crowed, doing a fist pump.

I tried walking. The boosties were all crowded together, and I was able to easily move from one to the other. Quickly, I made my way to the closest wall, where I started jumping up and down and waving my arms.

I called, "Bayley, it's Finn!" and I sent a burst of combined magic outward toward the flickering images beyond the short wall.

I thought I saw a change of pattern in the flickering and tried again.

"Bayley, it's me, Finn. I'm not a figment of your imagination or a random memory. I'm actually here. In your head."

This time, I formed my magic burst into an image of a giant cup of coffee and shot it over my head, where it hung for few seconds before fading.

There was a noticeable drop in noise, and the flickering congealed into a single golden light.

"Over here! I'm here in the boosti—er, with the energy. Here!" And I jumped up and down some more, sending up another burst of magic, imagining fireworks bursting above me.

The golden light turned into a focused beam, like a spotlight, and swept over to me. When it hit me, I dissolved the magic gloves covering my hands and touched the light.

As soon as the light and I connected, I could feel Bayley again. And he could feel me because his shocked recognition at finding me there filtered through to me.

I nearly sobbed with relief. "There you are. Hi Bayley. I'm here to help."

Chapter Fifty-One

I could feel Bayley struggling with the reality of me being there.

"I know this is unexpected, but it seemed like something was really wrong."

A pang of fear stabbed through Bayley and into me, confirming my suspicions.

"Can I help?"

Worry, doubt, and hope slipped through to me as he wrapped his head around the situation. But I couldn't hear him speak the way I usually could when we talked in my head.

"Bayley, I can feel you now that I have your direct attention, but if you're talking to me, I can't hear you. I'm having trouble interfacing with your consciousness. At least I can focus enough to talk to you. When I first got here, I got totally overwhelmed by your brain—thus my killer outfit." I did a little spin. "My jammies here tune out the background gibberish. They're, uh, gibber jammies!"

I realized I was babbling, but amusement surged through Bayley along with some admiration.

"Bayley, I don't know how you manage to hang out in my consciousness without getting overwhelmed. Is it innate, or do you have some kind of universal translator thingy that allows you to plug in and interpret what you're seeing and hearing? Cuz I don't have that. If you've got the equivalent of a spare Babel fish hanging about, I could sure use it."

Understanding dawned in Bayley.

To my right, a glittering golden spark zoomed up and before I could dodge, splatted itself onto my gibber jammies.

"Uh, Bayley?"

The shimmery splat spread out over my entire outfit, then seeped into my energy, combining it. I felt a wave of dizziness followed by…

"Finn? Finn, can you hear me?"

"Bayley? Bayley! Is that really you?"

"Hello Finn."

"Oh man, I've missed you. How are you? Are you okay? Is it okay that I'm here? I'm not hurting you am I? Did I say that I missed you? I missed you a lot." My voice rasped from the tears I was holding back.

Bayley chuckled quietly, but fatigue leeched the joy from the sound.

I tensed, "Bayley, seriously, are you alright? You sound exhausted."

Bayley said, "This is as it must be."

He sounded so defeated that alarm bells clanged in my head. "I take it things are not going well?"

A wave of sadness and despair rolled over me as he said, "I'm afraid…this may all have been for nothing after all."

"Oh Bayley. What's happening?"

"I'm…I'm…" Bayley paused, then choked out, "failing. I'm failing, Finn. If I don't give up soon, I could damage us both."

Something about the way he said it made me suspect he'd already damaged himself somehow.

"How can I help?"

"I appreciate the offer—more than you know—but I don't think you are allowed."

"Says who?"

"There are rules." Resignation dragged his voice down as he said, "I must do this by myself."

I chewed my lip. "But do you want to do it by yourself? Because if you do, I will don my most awesome pom-poms and cheer you on from the sidelines. But if you want help, just say so. I'll do whatever you need."

Bayley said, "It's uncanny that you should be here. I was just thinking how the longer this process goes on, the more…

wrong…it feels doing this alone. But those are the rules."

"Are you sure? Who made these ridiculous rules?" A suspicion uncoiled in the back of my mind. "Wait a minute. This doesn't have to do with Amon, does it?"

I felt Bayley's surprise followed by uneasiness as he said, "You met Amon?"

"Yeah I did. There's a lot to catch you up on—later. But for now, let's just say I'm not going to be baking him cookies anytime soon."

I could feel Bayley's mix of curiosity and concern. But he sighed and said, "It's not just Amon."

"The, er, overseers of the houses?"

Stunned, Bayley said, "How do you—?"

"Again lots to catch up on. Suffice it to say I'm familiar with the fact of their existence but, unlike Amon, I haven't met them. I don't know about the overseer guys, but Amon's… tricky, and I can only imagine they're at least as bad."

Wryly, Bayley said, "That is accurate."

"Bayley, what do *you* want? If it were allowed, would you like my help? I know I'm really late—your time's almost up but—"

"Yes."

"Yes?"

"Yes, Finn. If it were my choice, I would be glad to finish this with you. Even if we don't succeed, there would be comfort in having you there."

"Oh Bayley. You sound like you've really been through it."

"As you said, lots to catch up on."

From the turmoil I was getting from Bayley, I imagined he'd been having as much fun as I'd been having with the hex.

"Bayley, I'm so sorry you had to do this alone this long. Let's see if we can change the rules. Or at least challenge their validity. We've stood up to big mucky-mucks before. We can do it again. We just need to channel our inner Nor."

I tapped my foot and tried to think like Nor. If I were a brilliant lawyer, what would I want to know? "Did anyone say, specifically, that your Housekeeper couldn't help you? Did you sign anything or take any kind of oath binding you to doing this solo?"

"No, but again, the rules are that I must pass the test myself."

I stopped short. "Yourself?"

"Yes."

I started smiling. Rubbing my hands together, I said, "I have an idea."

Chapter Fifty-Two

"First thing we need to do is to talk to Amon. Can we do that?" I wanted to kick Amon in the shins for how dejected Bayley felt, but I was going to have to try and be diplomatic.

"…Yes. But not here."

"By 'here,' you mean…?"

Bayley thought for a second and said, "I am unsure how my mind will appear to you. When I visit a Housekeeper's mind, there are different areas for different things. I communicate with you in one place. Your memories are stored in a different place. The Knack Shack is its own place."

"Makes sense."

"This is not my communication space. I interact with Amon and the others from a different area in my mind."

"Can I go there?"

"…I can try to lead you to the right place."

"Great! Let's go."

Bayley's spotlight moved forward, and I was relieved to find that I could follow along with it.

As soon as we left the boostie area, my brain tried to lock up again as it struggled to make sense of the next part of Bayley's mind. But after a brief bout where white noise filled my vision, my Bayley-enhanced gibber jammies worked their magic, and the next section of Bayley's mind resolved around me.

"Trees!"

Bayley's spotlight stopped short. "What?"

"Uh, Bayley, your mind, to me it looks like it's filled with trees! At least, I think they're trees." All around me, trunks, branches, and leaves formed the walls of a hallway. Beautiful arched door-ways formed by intricately interwoven branches dotted the walls. They were all closed, so I didn't get to peek inside.

"That makes sense." He resumed moving.

I said, "It does?"

"Mmm. What else do you see?"

"It looks like I'm in a long hallway with lots of closed doors. I guess my mind is interpreting the different sections of your brain as different rooms. Huh."

"What?"

"One of the doors way down the hallway seems like it's partly ajar—there's light peeping out."

"That's where we're going," Bayley said.

"Cool!"

When we reached the door, it swung open, and I followed Bayley through. The moment we were inside, the door closed behind us, then disappeared, replaced by an uninterrupted wall.

Looking around me, I saw that the room didn't appear to have any exits. It was completely walled off from the rest of Bayley's mind. And those walls, including the ceiling and floor, were super dense, formed of multiple layers of tightly woven branches and leaves.

"It's so…quiet." No flickering lights or sounds flitted around us. "The walls in here are so thick that this room feels totally isolated." I snapped my fingers. "Reinforced! They're reinforced, right? These are mental shields, keeping the rest of your brain safe from whomever you're communicating with?"

Bayley said proudly, "Correct."

I shook my head. "Good idea with Amon around."

"Amon is—" a blinking light appeared in the middle of one wall, and Bayley's attention jerked away. Tension laced his voice as he said, "I think they know you're here. I'm being summoned."

The amount of apprehension radiating off him had me looking around, glaring suspiciously at the shadows. I felt like the boogeyman was about to jump us.

"I'm ready if you are."

Bayley hesitated. "If you're sure. It's not too late. You can still go back."

"Not on your life. Not if there's any chance that I can help. Let's just go see them and see what happens?" I almost added, "What's the worst that can happen," but not wanting coffee to suddenly go missing from the universe, I restrained myself.

In front of me, an arched, open doorway appeared in the wall. A shadow flowed through it, and Amon resolved in front of us.

His face slackened, and his eyes widened slightly, which for him was the equivalent of a jaw-dropping gasp.

I wanted to say, *Hah hah. Didn't expect this, did you?* But I managed to keep my mouth closed.

He turned to Bayley. "What is she doing here?"

I gave him a little wave. "Hello Amon. Lovely to see you again too. And 'she' can speak for herself, thanks."

Amon's brows lowered, his eyes narrowed, and he said, "Again?" He took a step closer, "You remember me?"

I resisted the urge to back pedal a few steps and instead stood even straighter. "Yup. And by the way, I do not appreciate the hex. That was rude."

Bayley growled, "Hex?"

In a comforting tone, I said, "I'll fill you in later." To Amon, I said, "If you keep frowning that hard, you're going to give yourself a headache."

In a dangerously quiet voice, Amon said, "Someone broke the rules."

"Ugh, you and your rules. Which rules are you referring to?" I asked Amon.

"Someone broke the hex—"

"Yeah. Me."

Amon went still, studying me in a way that made me feel naked. "You're telling the truth. How…interesting. Be that as it may, you chose to break the hex on your own, and you must suffer the consequences on your own. Bayley is not available to help you heal—"

"You think I'm here to ask for Bayley's help?"

Amon looked annoyed that I'd interrupted him. "Yes."

"Wrong again." I shot Bayley a grin then faced Amon. "I'm here to help Bayley."

"Help?"

"Yes, help."

He gave me a long look. "Do you even know what Bayley is doing?"

I didn't know precisely what Amon was making Bayley do, but I wasn't about to admit that. Instead, I crossed my arms and said, "He's here to level up."

He stared at me. "And you think you can...?"

"Help." He just stared at me some more so I added, "Assist? Aid? Abet? Any of this ringing a bell?"

Amon said carefully, "While your offer of...assistance... is likely well-intended, it is beyond the scope of the current proceedings."

He might be speaking very formally, but I recognized a "no" when I heard one.

"Why?"

There was finality in Amon's tone, as he said, "It is not done." He took a step toward me and ordered, "Go." When I didn't move, he added, "Now," and took another step forward.

My lizard brain did not like the creepy danger dude stalking toward me like I was a mosquito he was about to squish. It didn't like it one bit. For a moment, I hovered between fight and flight.

Then I felt Bayley's worry and, underneath it, hopeless resignation.

No way was I going to let this guy bully us. I put my hands on my hips and glared at Amon.

Bayley said, "Finn," in a warning tone.

Too late. I'd already opted for fight mode. I took a step toward Amon and raised my chin. "Sibeta said you have to be honest. So then, tell me the truth Amon. Is it really up to you whether I stay or go?" I was playing a hunch, but I knew I was right when I saw Amon's lips flatten into a hard line.

"Didn't think so." Channeling all my pain-in-the-patootie

diner customers, I looked down my nose at him and demanded, "I'd like to speak to the people who actually make the decisions please."

He smoothed his expression back into its usual, annoyingly bland mask and said, "You insist on pleading your case before the...others?"

"I do," I said with a confidence I didn't feel. But standing there butting heads with Amon didn't seem like it was going to get me anywhere, so I went for option B.

Amon smiled, and I immediately started wondering if I needed a plan C.

His smile turned pensive, and he began tapping his lips with his finger. "This is going to take something special, I think." He eyed me, and his delighted grin made me want to duck and cover.

Did I want to find out what Amon's idea of "something special" was? No I did not. Was I going to do it anyway for Bayley's sake? Yup.

I resisted the urge to say, "Bring it on," because I'm not a total idiot, and instead pulled on my Polite Girl pants and said, "Thank you, Amon, for working with me and Bayley."

With a quiet, "Hm," Amon disappeared back the way he'd come.

I looked at Bayley and whispered, "Where'd he go?"

"I would guess he's gone to consult with the others. Finn, are you sure you want to do this? They are...different than what you've encountered before."

"Different than what I've encountered before? Please. That's every other Saturday for the past six months," I scoffed. "As long as it allows me to help you, in whatever way I can, then I'm up for whatever nonsense Amon is planning. And about these others—"

Amon reappeared.

I said, "That was fast. Jonesing for my company? If I'd known you found it difficult to be parted from me for long, I'd have come sooner."

Ignoring me, Amon faced Bayley and said, "Bayley, we

would like to change the venue from your mental space," he waved to the room we were in, "to a space that will better accommodate Finn's limited mental capabilities." Amon pretended not to see my eye roll and added, "But the decision is yours, Bayley."

Bayley said, "Will it hurt Finn?" at the same time that I said, "Wait, will this hurt Bayley?"

I felt Bayley's amusement and giggled, "Jinx! You owe me a coffee!"

Amon studied us like we were unusual bugs before saying, "Bayley, what say you?"

I raised my hand.

"Yes Finn?" said Amon with exaggerated patience.

"Will being in this new space hurt Bayley's chances of succeeding?"

"Can I take my mental shielding with me?" added Bayley.

To me, Amon said, "No, it will not alter his chances of success." He faced Bayley. "Nothing will have changed. We're merely translating the internal to the external. Your defenses, including your shielding, remain your own."

"And you didn't answer us. Will it harm either of us?" I asked Amon.

"That is entirely up to you both."

Chapter Fifty-Three

Amon might as well have waved a big, red, flashing "Danger Ahead" sign.

But if he thought his ominous vibe was going to warn me off, he had another thing coming. Not only was this not my or Bayley's first brush with danger, but also I'd come all this way—it wasn't like I was going to turn back now.

But this was Bayley's show, so I asked him, "You still up for this?" trying to reassure him with my best we've-got-this smile.

Bayley said, "Let's go."

Looking a little too pleased for my comfort, Amon said, "This may feel a bit…strange," and placed one hand on the golden light that was Bayley, and one hand on my shoulder.

The world warped.

My mind did not appreciate yet another round of weird input. Everything went black, and I felt like I was simultaneously being sucked through a straw while whipping around madly in a tilt-a-whirl. My stomach lurched, and I wondered if it was possible for a virtual avatar to throw up.

Then the world righted itself again.

As my head stopped spinning, I looked around and got my bearings.

It seemed Amon had a sense of humor after all.

We appeared to be in the desert.

Night blanketed the area, and though there was no moon, I could see clearly in the dark. Creosote bushes dotted the sandy area between me and a rocky cliff wall that stretched up to the starry sky.

My eyes widened in amazement. I could actually smell the earthy creosote and the warm sand scents of the desert. Cool night air nipped at me, and I found myself shuffling my feet to keep warm.

It was so real that for a moment I wondered if Amon had actually transported my physical body somewhere. But looking down, I saw I was still wearing my gibber jammies, which meant this was still virtual. My jammies had a new layer, too, like a shadow crawling back and forth across the surface.

I was betting that belonged to Amon.

While I understood that Amon had added his touch to my jammies to allow me to interface with this virtual reality, I couldn't help but feel squicked out at being coated in Amon's cooties.

On my left, I spotted Bayley. As usual, he looked like a glowing, golden light to me. But instead of an orb, he was an oblong shape, taller than I was.

I spun and faced Amon, arms crossed over my chest. Before I could speak, the rock face in front of me rumbled. A low hum vibrated through me, and I felt a slight pause as my gibber jammies tried to translate something. But instead of hearing words, I heard static after the pause.

It took me a moment to figure out what they were trying to translate. "Uh, did the rocks just talk?"

"You are seeing rocks?" Amon asked.

"Well, technically a rock wall—a cliff. And don't you know what I'm seeing? You designed this."

"I chose the general...scenario. But your consciousness is... filling in the details, so to speak, in its own way." Amon walked a few steps away. "If I may ask, what do you see this as?"

"Creosote. It's a shrub that grows in the desert."

"Just this one?"

"No. There's a few."

"But you see these," he pointed, "as a cliff?"

"Yes. What do you mean 'these'? There's only one cliff."

Amon looked intrigued. "How fascinating. Your mind has categorized the...creosotes...as separate individuals, but the... other group here...you see as one."

"Well, I can see the strata in the cliff. It's clearly not a single rock, but several different layers," I said. "Anyway, why do you care what I'm seeing? This isn't about me. I'm here to help Bayley."

"No one has agreed to that. You are here merely to petition us. And for you to do so, I must understand what you are capable of comprehending."

I couldn't tell if he was purposefully insulting my intelligence, or if he was just being honest. Given that I was dealing with beings above my pay grade, I tried to give him the benefit of the doubt and kept a lid on my aggravation the best I could.

Another long vibration came from the cliff.

The creosote bushes waved in the air, their branches rasping as they rubbed together. It was like there was a strong wind, except only the creosotes moved.

To my surprise, I heard the translator kick in. But again, the pause was followed by static.

Amon said, "Did you understand any of that?"

I shook my head.

"What did you just experience?"

"The rocks grumbled, and the creosote branches kind of whooshed against each other. Instead of a translation, all I got was static."

"Interesting. Your mind can only interpret so much, even with Bayley's and my assistance. Very well. I will translate for you."

I would much rather have had someone I could rely on translate for me.

Bayley, I asked. *Can you understand them? Can you let me know if Amon translates incorrectly?*

"We can hear you."

I glared at him. "Our individual thoughts or our conversations with each other?"

"In this space, only the latter." Amon sighed. "I suppose I should be offended that you doubt my veracity, but in your situation, I will allow that it is prudent for you to be cautious."

"Gee thanks."

The creosotes shifted their branches again, and this time I reached out with my Best magic, feeding more of it into the gibber jammies as the translator came online.

I still couldn't understand what they were saying, but I nearly smiled when I realized that I could sense an underlying feeling. "Are they laughing?"

Amon said, "Interesting," and then squinted at me. "I see." He nodded. "A proper application of your Best heritage. And yes, for some reason, they find you amusing."

Oh yippee. The weird "plants" understood sarcasm and found me entertaining.

Why did I feel like a trained seal in front of a crowd waiting for me to perform?

I stared at the creosote bushes and at the cliff, trying to figure out what they had in common. I was sure my brain was trying to tell me something by interpreting them this way.

Sure they both existed in the desert. But one was a plant, and the other was a weathered rock wall that reminded me of the Grand Canyon.

Something clicked in my brain.

Old. They were both really, really old.

Creosote bushes could live to be thousands of years old. And it'd taken millions of years for the Grand Canyon to be carved.

I suppressed a shiver.

We were dealing with impossibly old beings.

Forget feeling like a trained seal. To them, I was a toddler who, for the moment, amused the visiting great-great-great grandparents.

What happened if I annoyed them?

I found myself hoping these were the warm, cuddly kind of elders rather than the crotchety kind.

Amon snagged my attention as he moved toward me. Both here and in the real world, Amon looked human. Did that mean he was younger than the others?

"Now that we know how you are interacting with this environment, formal introductions are in order." With a sweep of his hand, he said, "Finley Foster, current Housekeeper of Bayley House, I present you to…" there was a delay while my translator tried to parse what he said, and then I got, "Mixed Nuts."

I stifled the snicker but didn't quite manage to squash a smile because Amon gave me the side-eye.

I coughed to cover the giggle that was trying to surface and said, "Could you try that again please? The translator seems to be having an issue."

Amon sighed. "What did you hear?"

"Mixed Nuts."

"Mixed Nuts?"

"Yeah, I know. I'm guessing that's incorrect."

Amon nodded, paused, then said, "The closest translation of the collective group name that I can think of is Those Who Watch All the Time."

"Because that's not disturbing at all," I muttered. Louder I added, "That's kind of long to say." I thought about it and said, "How about Thwats? Unless you think that sounds too close to 'twat'?"

"What is a twat?" asked Amon.

"Someone like you," I said sweetly.

Bayley groaned in my head, but I shushed him.

Amon frowned. "Like me or like them?"

"Aren't you all part of the same group?"

Amon tipped his head side to side. "Yes, but we are not all the same...level."

I guessed, "They're your bosses?"

Amon did the yes-and-no head tip again. "The, er, Thwats—both the creosotes and the cliff—are far different than I am. Still, if the name works for you, so be it."

I bowed in the direction of the cliff and creosote bushes and said, "Hello."

Amon turned to face the bushes and the cliff. His mouth didn't move, but I got the sense that he was speaking with them.

After a long moment, he bowed his head to them, and turned back to me and Bayley.

"You may address the Thwats."

Bayley started to speak, but Amon held up a hand.

"Since Finn has seen fit to interrupt these proceedings, and may not be here long, the Thwats would like to hear from her."

"Bayley, is that okay with you?" I asked.

"Of course. Thank you, Finn."

I took a moment to summon my inner Nor: cool, professional, and positively deadly in an argument. "First, I would like some more information, please."

Amon just stared at me, which I chose to interpret as permission to go ahead.

"We've established that Bayley is attempting to level up. Where is he in the process?"

"At the end."

"Does that mean he's completed the other, er, tasks that you set for him?"

"He has."

I nearly shouted, "Woohoo! Go Bayley!" but my inner Nor gave me a look, so I tamped that down to a more sedate, "Excellent job, Bayley, for making it this far."

From Bayley, I felt uncertainty, followed by a tiny spark of pride, and then an even tinier spark of hope.

It was really unlike him to have so little optimism. I suspected they'd been pummeling his self-confidence the entire time he'd been gone. By isolating him completely like this, they'd had ample time to whittle away at him.

Amon said, "Congratulations are not in order. Bayley has failed to obtain his objective. He is running out of time."

Like that. Amon squashed Bayley's little surge of pride, and I really wanted to squash Amon.

Instead, I focused on the problem. "Running out of time? You mean because it's almost my birthday?"

"Yes."

"Doesn't that seem kind of arbitrary to you? You'd think that you'd pick a fixed amount of time, like six months or a year, rather than whenever the current Housekeeper's birthday happens to roll around. What's up with that?"

Amon looked to the Thwats, who must have told him to answer me, because he sighed and said, "There is a magic in changing years. The magic is most potent in the first change. Each consecutive year, the Housekeeper birthday holds less power."

I frowned at him. "Is this some 'humans are less powerful as we get older' bullsh— er, nonsense? Because if that's the case, you're so wrong."

Amon said, "It is not age. It is the spark created by the newness of the connection between House and Housekeeper combined with the liminal space of transitioning years." He held up a hand, forestalling any further questions. "Suffice it to say that this is so."

"Fine. So we have a deadline coming up because of my birthday. Got it." I crossed my arms. "And Bayley only has one final thing to do for you?"

"Yes."

"You guys *have* noticed, haven't you, that he has completed all his tasks in record time—he'd normally have months, and he did it in weeks. Doesn't that count for something?"

"No."

"Is there some kind of partial credit, or is this an all or none kind of scenario?"

Amon and Bayley answered, "All or none," at the same time.

Well, that seemed like a really dumb system, but antagonizing the Thwats by telling them their system sucked didn't seem like the right play just then.

"You said he must do this whole, er, leveling up thing on his own."

"Yes."

"Could you please explain why?"

"It is how it is done."

I swallowed my frustration and tried a different angle. "Have others had to go through this same system to be able to level up?"

"Yes."

"Others like Bayley, or different kinds of others?"

"Yes."

I looked at the ground so he wouldn't see the "aha!" in my eyes and said, "For the purpose of this conversation, let's focus on Bayley's, er, people—the others like him. They were all bonded to someone? Like Bayley and I are bonded?"

"It is their way."

"And they all had to do the test alone?"

With a trace of exasperation, Amon said, "As I have said, this is how it is done. If you have a point, make it."

"Have any of them been able to level up?"

Amon looked to the Thwats behind him. After a moment, he faced me again and said, "No."

My gritted my teeth. "Nobody? *Ever?*"

Amon seemed to think that didn't require a response because he just stared at me. But Bayley felt as shocked as I was.

"And that didn't strike anyone as odd?"

In a talking-to-kindergartners tone, Amon said, "It is supposed to be difficult."

I shook my head, shifting my gaze between Amon, the bushes, and the cliff. "Has it never occurred to any of you that the reason no one can complete your tasks is because all the Bayleys are no longer truly single entities? They are bonded to the point that they literally can't live without their Housekeepers—and we can't live without them. So how is it fair that you isolate one part of the pair and force it to take the full brunt of this?"

Amon pursed his lips. "Were you not tested on your own?"

"Well yeah." I stopped him mid-smirk when I added, "But that was *before* we bonded."

The rocks shifted, and the resulting groaning and grinding didn't sound happy.

I plowed on anyway. "I mean, think about it. The outcome of this whole leveling up thing affects us both. So separating the bonded pairs doesn't really make sense. You're essentially chopping off a part of a person and expecting them to proceed as if everything is working normally." I looked past Amon to his bosses, did a quick head bow, and said, "No disrespect, but maybe if this has never worked, it's time to try something different."

Amon said in a silky tone, "What makes you think it's not working?"

I went cold as suddenly I understood. Bayley reached the same conclusion as I did, and he said quietly, "Oh. You want us to fail."

"We want you to be worthy," Amon said.

The bushes and rocks chattered in a way that I took as, "What he said."

I swept my gaze across Amon and the Thwats. "Why even offer the promotion if you're rooting so hard for them to fail? What's the point?"

"It's necessary," said Amon.

"It's cruel," I said. "And patently unfair."

Amon shrugged again, and Bayley and I had the same urge to whack him, though we both managed to behave ourselves.

Bayley said, "If you're making this nearly impossible, there must be a reason. What aren't you telling us?"

I chewed my lip and guessed, "Something about the leveling up.... It's a problem for you guys somehow?"

Amon cocked his head for a moment. "Not in the way you mean. Not the leveling up itself."

"I don't understand."

"You are not meant to." I gave him my stubborn face until he relented and added, "It may change things. Beyond you and Bayley."

I waited a little longer, but it seemed I wasn't going to be able to squeeze anything else out of Amon, so I said, "To sum up, from Bayley and my point of view, Bayley gets to grow. But the way you see it, if Bayley levels up, then there are other 'changes' that might happen. And they worry you enough that you made the leveling up process ridiculously hard. Am I correct?"

"An oversimplification but close enough."

"Just out of curiosity, how many others have made it as far in your tasks as Bayley has?"

Amon consulted with the Thwats and said, "None."

Chapter Fifty-Four

Bayley started to say, "I—"

But the Thwats cut him off with their whispering and grumbling.

Amon said, "Bayley, we know your thoughts. The Thwats want to hear what Finn has to say."

I addressed the Thwats directly.

"Look, your system may have worked in the past, but given Bayley's progress, it's obvious that this time things are different."

They didn't respond so I paced toward them and adopted my best lawyer-making-closing-arguments pose, ignoring how ridiculous I may have looked in my gibber jammies.

"I've made a strong case. First, it is illogical to separate us. You are, in effect, crippling Bayley."

As I spoke, Amon drifted over to stand beside me. I had the feeling he was trying to intimidate me, but he was outclassed by the bazillion-year-old beings I was arguing with.

I ignored Amon and continued my summation. "By your own admission, Bayley is the only one to make it this far in your process. I understand that up to this point, no one else has had their partner with them. But nobody else has made it to this final stage. For something this hard, and apparently significant, shouldn't the final round be fair? Shouldn't you equip Bayley properly to have a fighting chance to finish instead of making this an exercise in futility? Otherwise, there's no point in ever even offering a chance to level up, as there is zero chance anyone will ever be able to do so under the current rules." I turned to Amon. "Is that what you really want? No possibility that this will ever work?"

The creosote bushes and the cliff hissed and crackled.

"No," said Amon. "That...cannot be."

"Then I rest my case."

Though I dipped my head in a show of respect, the Thwats set up a ruckus. Grinding, whooshing, rasping, and rumbling ensued, and while I couldn't understand the exact words in the back-and-forth, it was clear that they were arguing.

Amon stayed where he was, head bent, deep in conversation with the Thwats.

While they argued amongst themselves, I sidled closer to Bayley.

Hoping the Thwats didn't hear, I whispered, "You okay?"

"I've been going nonstop since I left. And they haven't let me use much of the extra energy you sent." Barely audible, Bayley said, "I'm coming to the conclusion they wanted me so exhausted I had no chance of finishing."

Amon made a surprised noise, and we turned toward him.

After a moment, he nodded his head to the Thwats and walked over to us.

"Your request has been approved." He added, in a warning tone, "By a narrow margin. And against my better judgment."

"Good thing for us you don't get to decide then, huh?"

Amon quirked an eyebrow at me. "Is it? We shall see."

I didn't care if we squeaked by with a single extra vote in our favor—we won, and that's all that mattered.

Bayley said, "Thank you," to the Thwats, and I gave them one of my best deep bows.

Turning to Amon, I said, "Now what?"

"The final round will commence with a practical test of your supposed combined skills."

Bayley said, "Amon and, er, Thwats, before we begin, I request the right of access to my energy stockpile, for both myself and Finn. She is, after all, only human, and it would be counterproductive to deprive us of the very fuel we need to successfully complete this final phase."

Amon looked like he was going to argue, but the rocks

shook, and he bowed his head instead.

"It is so," said Amon.

I felt a surge of relief from Bayley, then I jumped a little as I felt my own energy shift. Smiling, I said, "I feel like I suddenly had a big cup of coffee."

Bayley said, "I shunted energy to you by adding it directly into the filter I have surrounding you."

"Clever," said Amon, and the Thwats murmured in agreement.

Bayley said, "I am ready."

Amon said, "You are certain? I cannot guarantee this will make one bit of difference, and it may result in some harm to one or both of you."

"What kind of harm?" I demanded.

"Who is to say?"

"Uh, you are. You seem to be managing this whole process." I looked at the Thwats. "Are you sure you've got the right guy for this? He seems kind of confused."

Amon did not look pleased, but the creosotes broke out in a bunch of laughing whispers again.

Amon squinted at us. "I assure you I am well up to the task."

The look he was giving us sent shivers down my spine. Maybe poking the test admin was a bad idea. I wouldn't put it past him to make things more difficult than they needed to be.

Amon spun to the Thwats. "Since Finn has insisted on joining, I think something…creative…is in order."

I tried not to wince but wasn't entirely successful. Yup, poking the teacher was a bad idea.

Then without permission I felt Amon probing my mind.

"Hey! Get out of my head!" I yelled, slamming my shields down around him.

Amon said absently, "We already scanned Bayley. I only required a moment. I am already done."

And suddenly we were back in Bayley's communication room.

At least I didn't have to go through the sucked-through-a-straw feeling again.

I looked at Bayley. "Uh that went well? I mean, we're not dead, they didn't say no, and Amon hasn't set fire to me yet, so…good?"

Bayley said, "At this point, I don't know what to think. Having them admit they want me to fail, it…well it doesn't really give me a lot of confidence that whatever they come up with next is going to be fair."

"Try not to worry about it. Whatever it is that they hit us with, we'll deal with it. At this point I think one of our biggest advantages is how much they underestimate you."

Bayley stilled. All along his determination hadn't wavered, but my heart hurt at how fragile his hope was. "You think they underestimate me?"

"Bayley have you met you? In the few months since I've known you, you have helped me survive magical attacks, gun battles, and power-hungry mages. I was brand new to magic, and you've helped me grow my knowledge and practical skills in record time. Not to mention that you put up with Gram on a regular basis. And that's just the tip of the iceberg! You are undeniably incredible. It's not your fault that these old fogey Thwats are too stuck in their own ways to notice the gem in front of them."

As I talked, the sass that had been missing returned to Bayley.

I grinned. "Now, do you want to hear my 'Once more unto the breach' speech, or are you good?"

"No, I think I'm good," Bayley chuckled.

"Excellent! They'll never know what hit them."

Amon picked that moment to appear before us. He didn't give us any notice, and I couldn't help the squeak that escaped.

"Maybe knock first?"

Ignoring me, Amon faced Bayley. "We are ready." He paused and stepped closer to Bayley. "This is my final offer. Are you sure this is what you want?"

I stepped back and waited. In the end, this was Bayley's decision.

Amon added quietly, "There is no shame in conceding and returning to your post. You have impressed us with your persistence and skill thus far. Why not leave it thus and go home now, on a positive note, while you can."

I support you either way, I whispered in Bayley's head.

Bayley sent me a pulse of appreciation and answered Amon. "This is my one chance. I came here because I believe it is my time. I choose to take it."

Amon looked tired as he said, "So be it." He slid a glance to me, and I thought I saw a flicker of condemnation in his eyes.

I held up my hands. "This is not my fault. I am not making Bayley do this. This is his party. My job here is to support him." I shot Amon a cheeky grin and a wink, "You know…Housekeeper keeping my house company. It's in the job description."

Amon wasn't amused. He nodded once to Bayley, turned, and strode away calling, "It begins."

Chapter Fifty-Five

Amon vanished, and everything went dark around us. My inner ear insisted that I was spinning again and moving very fast.

Then everything stopped.

The smell hit me first: wet pavement, moldering trash, and a hint of acrid urine, underscored by whiffs of car exhaust.

The blackness receded to gray, and a cold, wet drizzle slid down my neck.

Suddenly I could see, and an alley resolved around me. Light from a lone street lamp at the alley's entrance made a sad attempt to part the gloom, with mixed results.

Crammed in between two tall buildings, the alleyway harbored random mounds of trash that huddled against the walls. Some of the litter a few feet from me moved, and I caught sight of a long tail skittering away from me.

Sound kicked in along with the visuals. On the road at the front of the alley, cars rumbled and hissed past on wet pavement. The drizzle muffled the sound slightly, making everything even more surreal than it already was.

I felt Bayley behind me and turned to him as I said, "What is happen—oh! Oh!!! Bayley?!?" My hand flew to my mouth as I stared wide-eyed.

He nodded.

Bayley was a person. A man, to be exact. Dressed in a 1940s suit, he looked like he'd walked straight out of the movie we were watching the night he left. He was several inches taller than I was, probably a couple of inches over six feet. His pinstripe suit fit him like a glove, showing off broad shoulders and a long, lean body. The suit ended in shoes so shiny that they gleamed in the meager light. A stylish hat tipped at a jaunty angle topped off the outfit.

Under the hat, Bayley's brown eyes met mine. His eyes and hair were the same shade of brown as the wood of the house, and his skin sported a golden tan.

I whispered, "Wow. You look like a 1940s private detective from the movies."

And then it hit me. Bayley was here, in person form. I threw my arms around him and hugged him hard as tears filled my eyes. "I can finally hug you for real." Burying my head against his shoulder, I felt his arms go around me and hug me back. He still smelled like Bayley, somehow, the comforting scents of old wood and Bayley's magic tickling my nose.

"I really missed you. Life sucks without your best friend around," I said.

Holding me tighter, Bayley said, "I really missed you too," in the same warm British voice I'd been hearing in my head for months.

With an effort, I pulled myself together and stepped back. Surveying him, I shook my head asking, "Are you okay? This is…this is quite the transformation."

"I'm…fine?" said Bayley, shifting back and forth, then walking up and down the alley a bit, shaking his arms and hands as he went. "Actually, it seems I'm more than fine. I feel great. This is unexpected but delightful!"

"But why…why make you human?"

Bayley narrowed his eyes as he thought. "Best guess? To throw me off balance. See how I adjust to a form I haven't taken before."

"So, to make things more difficult. Well, joke's on them. You're adapting like a champ, and plus you look great."

Bayley stopped pacing to stand next to me and said in his best noir imitation, "You think I'm snazzy, you should get a load of yourself, doll. You're quite the dame."

I looked down and did a double-take when I caught a glimpse of my outfit. I was wearing a fitted hunter green jacket over a pale green blouse with a huge bow draping down the front. A fit-and-flare hunter green skirt with plenty of swing to it completed the outfit. Reaching up, I realized I had my own fancy lid, a smallish hat pinned to my hair at a rakish angle. Looking down at my feet, I laughed. "Heels! I don't even remember the last time I had heels on." I did a little twirl to try out the skirt and couldn't help but giggle as it swirled around me.

Bayley was playing with his clothes too. He unbuttoned his jacket and located the inner pockets. One at a time, he withdrew a bulging wallet, a pack of cigarettes, a notepad and pencil, and a sloshing flask.

"This is all very strange," I said.

Bayley opened the wallet and withdrew a business card.

"Bayley Detective Agency," he read. "Hey! I'm a private investigator."

"I guess that'd make me your assistant."

Bayley looked down at himself, then at me, brows furrowed in thought. He said slowly, "I think it's a directive from the Thwats on the roles they want us to play. If it's okay with you, I should take the lead here." He shifted back and forth, the creaking of his shoes reminding me of the creaking sound the house made when Bayley was uncomfortable.

"Of course! This is your party. I'm just here to provide support." I pointed to my outfit. "Just call me your Girl Friday."

Relief smoothed Bayley's forehead. "Thanks Finn."

I gave him an encouraging smile, "No problem. So what's the plan?"

"First things first. Let's see what kind of tools we have at our disposal," said Bayley, and then he stared at me.

When a few seconds had passed, and he didn't add anything, I said, "Why are you looking at me like that?"

He frowned. "Well, that's not great. You didn't get any impressions from me in your mind?"

It was my turn to frown. "No."

"Try to talk to me in your head."

Alarm speared through me as I said *Bayley, can you hear me?* When he didn't respond, I said, "I just asked if you could hear me. I'm guessing from your blank look that you couldn't."

Irritation flickered in Bayley's eyes. "Another part of the test, I'm sure—changing how we communicate." He paced a minute, head down in thought. "I can see why you people pace all the time. It's oddly soothing," he said distractedly. "So, we can't communicate the way we normally do. That takes away one advantage. Next question is, can we do magic?"

"It'd be pretty stupid of them to prohibit magic use when that's a big part of what we do as a team."

Bayley said, "Let me try something simple." He spun around and focused on a nearby pile of trash. A moment later the various bits and pieces began moving. The papers folded themselves this way and that, stacking and combining until a few moments later, a small replica of Bayley House stood before us.

"Well that's neat," I said.

Bayley smiled and with a swipe of his hand dismissed the magic, returning the pile to its former disarray.

"My turn," I said. After looking around the alley for a moment, I walked a few feet away and stared down at a clump of weeds that had shouldered their way up through a crack in the alley pavement. I reached for my Foster magic, relieved to find it ready and eager. With a gesture, I fed a little magic into the weed, then watched it change from drooping and scraggly to upright and healthy.

"Lovely," said Bayley. "Now both of us."

"I'm not sure how that'll work," I said, chewing my lip.

"I'll start. This might feel a little weird," he warned. "Usually I add my magic to yours when you need it. Here, I'm going to be adding your magic to mine."

"So more of a pull than a push?"

"Exactly so."

That sounded invasive in a way that made me a little uneasy, but I said, "Let's give it a go."

Bayley's magic touched my own, and my magic surged forward in answer.

Gently separating a strand of my Best magic, Bayley wove it with his. I let the magic flow to him as he directed it toward the wall. A moment later five rats lined up in front of him.

"Hello there," Bayley said in a warm voice. "Anything here in the alley that we need to find?"

The rats scurried away and then came back a few minutes later. All of them were empty-handed.

"Good to know. Thank you for looking," he said. I felt the moment he released the rats, then he released his pull on my magic, and asked, "Are you okay, Finn?"

I had to think about it. Did it feel weird? Yes. But to my relief, instead of feeling intrusive, it felt comfortable. "I'm fine with it." As I said it, I realized I was. "I mean, I trust you to mix your magic with mine all the time. This is the same thing, if you think about it."

"But you're letting me drive," said Bayley.

"Yes, well, sometimes it's nice to be in the passenger seat. Gives you a different perspective."

Bayley grinned. "Thank you Finn. For being here. For all of this."

"I wouldn't have it any other way." I looked around us. "Good thinking, checking with the rats," I said. "That wouldn't have occurred to me."

"Keep in mind I've been at this for weeks. There's been a lot of 'Is he clever enough to notice what we're hiding' from the Thwats in the previous rounds. If this goes the same way the rest of this process has, then nothing will be laid out for us. We will not only need to accomplish whatever the objective is, but we'll also have to identify the objective itself. And there may be more than one." He hesitated and then added quietly, "And keep in mind they are watching. They are always watching."

"Sounds fun," I said dryly. Looking around us, I asked, "What's next?"

"Let's get a better look at things." Bayley walked to the only door in the alley and tugged on it, but it was locked. As he led the way down the alley toward the street, I trailed after him, carefully navigating around all the rippling puddles and wiggling trash. I was a little more wobbly in my heels than I'd have liked, but I was hopeful I'd get used to them sooner rather than later. At least they had a nice ankle strap so I wouldn't have to worry about accidentally walking right out of them, leaving the shoes behind while I stepped on the muddy pavement.

At the end of the alley, Bayley stopped, so I stopped too. We both peeked around the alley's corner, taking in the street scene in front of us.

It was like looking at an antique car collector's dream. Beautiful 1940s cars sloshed by on the wet street. Given how water glistened on every available surface, it must have rained fairly hard before we arrived. But the rain had ratcheted down now to a grumpy drizzle, filling the air with a mist that gave everything a softened, hazy look.

I let out a low whistle, "It's like stepping onto a film noir movie set."

Bayley tilted his head, nodding slowly. "Yes. That's it. One of the last memories we share from before I left is watching that marathon of old movies. They must have pulled the memories from us." He gave me a nod of approval. "Good call, Finn. At least now we have an idea of what we're in for."

"We do?"

Bayley nodded again, eyes glinting. "Today's theme is film noir."

Given how many bodies turned up in film noir, I wasn't entirely sure I was happy about that. Sure the outfits were great and all, but I wasn't certain it was worth the violence we might encounter. At least Bayley hadn't shown up in mobster gear carrying a gun, so there was that.

"What would they have done if we'd been watching reruns of *Battlestar Galactica*? Would we be in outer space, and there'd be lasers and spaceships?"

Bayley shrugged. "Probably."

I wasn't sure if I was relieved or disappointed. Maybe a little of both.

Bayley derailed my thoughts by pointing to the wall we were standing next to. "This is a restaurant. Italian by the looks of it."

I peered around the corner to see what he was looking at. Big glass windows fronted the building we were hiding beside.

People clustered around tables with checkered tablecloths while waiters bustled in between tables, carrying brimming plates of food. I saw at least three plates heaping with spaghetti, sauce, and enormous meatballs. My stomach grumbled. To my surprise, so did Bayley's.

"You're hungry?"

Bayley said, "Hey I'm as surprised as you are." Pursing his lips, he said thoughtfully, "You know, I wonder if this is part of the assessment. I don't normally feel hunger this way. I feel a lack of energy, sure, which I regularly replenish. But this new form," he gestured to his body, "this is going to require some adjustment." Bayley's face lit up. "All part of seeing if I can adapt, I'd guess." He looked admiring. "You have to give them credit. That's clever."

"Is it?" I asked. "This seems like a lot to ask. Changing realities *and* changing forms? It's a little excessive."

"We did insist we were up to their tasks," said Bayley. Rubbing his hands together, a roguish gleam in his eyes, he said, "I'm going to squeeze as much fun out of this adventure as I can. How about you? Whaddya say, doll?"

Shaking my head, I couldn't help but grin at him. Looping my arm through his, I said, "Forget those lugheads and their games. Let's enjoy what we can."

"Now you're talking."

"So where to, boss?"

Chapter Fifty-Six

Offering me his arm, Bayley stepped out of the alley and onto the sidewalk. Together we strolled a few feet until we could see clearly through the window into the restaurant. As a couple exited, the garlicky aroma of really good Italian food wafted out with them and enticed us forward.

Bayley frowned. "Just a minute. That seems too…easy. Too obvious? Something. I don't think the restaurant is where we need to go."

"Well I trust your instincts."

He pivoted to take in the buildings around us, and I followed his lead, surveying the area.

On the other side of the street, opposite the alley, a sign announced an accountant's office, which was locked up tight. A quick look up and down the block showed a bunch of other small businesses, most also closed for the night. The lone exceptions were a laundromat, a diner, and a bookstore.

I looked at all three, but my attention kept returning to the bookstore.

An old sign hung crookedly over the worn door, the chipped letters half-heartedly announcing, "Books for Sale." A single, dirty window displayed a stack of faded books and allowed a hazy glimpse inside. I could see the clerk behind a counter just inside the door, and behind him, rows of bookshelves.

I loved bookstores, but something about this place seemed off. I frowned as I watched.

"You caught it too," Bayley said with a satisfied smile.

"Why are there so many people going into the bookstore?"

"Look at how they're dressed."

I studied a young couple about to enter the store. The woman was dressed to the nines, jewelry glittering as she moved. Her gentleman was also well-groomed, shiny cufflinks and pomaded hair glinting in the lamplight.

"Those are awfully fancy duds to be wearing into a bookstore," I said, as another, similarly attired couple entered after the first. "I suppose there could be some kind of event inside."

"But you don't think so, do you? Me either."

"I mean, look at that place. I can see the dust on the books through the window."

Bayley said, "I think we should do some shopping."

I looked down at my outfit. It looked snazzy, but I was not up to par with the swanky couples entering the bookshop. "Whatever is going on in there, I don't think I'm dressed appropriately." I gently whacked Bayley on the arm. "You men, all you need is a fancy suit, and you fit in everywhere. Not so for the ladies. I'm going to stand out like a sore thumb compared to everyone else we've seen."

Bayley smiled and said, "Let's see if I can help with that." He tugged me back into the alley and stood behind me, hands on my shoulders. With mischief lacing his voice, he said, "Close your eyes."

As soon as I did, a tingle started in my shoulders under Bayley's warm fingers. It rapidly spread across my whole body, then disappeared in a flash.

Bayley released me and stepped back. "Have a look," he said.

I opened my eyes, looking down at my outfit as I turned to face him. Made of shimmering celery green silk, the ankle-length dress had a fitted bodice that flowed into a long, column skirt of silk and chiffon, just flared enough to float around me and allow me to move freely.

"Oh Bayley," I chirped, spinning this way and that to watch the skirt sway and glitter in the light. I stopped spinning and threw my arms around him in a quick hug. "It's perfect! Absolutely beautiful. But, how did you do it?"

Bayley shrugged. "They want to see me use my skills. House

magic 101: transformation magic."

I'd seen Bayley transform himself and the property plenty of times over the last few months. "But this is different," I said in awe. "You usually change yourself and your environment. This seems like a whole other level of material manipulation."

"We're bonded, so this is just a natural extension of what I normally do."

"Well, you might not think it's a big deal," I said, swishing my skirt some more, "but I do. Well done, Bayley!"

Grinning, he held out his elbow with a, "Ma'am," and I took his arm. Crossing the street, we walked down the sidewalk and entered the bookstore.

It was even dustier on the inside than the view through the window had suggested. The desk clerk gave us a once-over, then a short nod.

Bayley gave the guy a nod back and said, "The dame just wants to look around a little."

The clerk looked dubious but said, "Certainly."

Bayley steered me to a nearby bookshelf that had the double advantage of obscuring us while allowing us to peek through the books at the desk and the door.

We pretended to browse, but we didn't have to wait long until a group of six came bustling in, all noise and laughter.

Bayley's gaze sharpened as he watched them.

The guy at the front of the group grabbed a random book off the nearest shelf and approached the clerk. Handing the book to the clerk along with a $20 bill, the dandy said in a stage whisper that carried across the store, "We're here for the...you know."

The clerk said, "Of course, sir," slid the money into a drawer, and handed the book back to the dandy with a receipt on top.

Bayley tugged my elbow, and I followed him quietly down our row as we shadowed the group moving through a different row on our right. There really wasn't that much need for stealth. They were making enough racket that a herd of elephants could've been behind them, and they wouldn't have noticed.

The group reached the wall on the far side of the bookstore and came to a stop in front of a partially-filled bookshelf. The book-holding dandy gave a cursory glance over his shoulder then stuck his book on a half-filled shelf, retaining the receipt as he did so. Then he reached for an orange book on the right side of the bookcase. The book tilted toward him, and the bookcase silently swung partway open.

Music and crowd noises spilled out, and the ladies in the group squealed with delight. The pack moved through the door, and the bookcase swung shut behind them.

Bayley turned to me, a huge smile lighting his face. "It's like a speakeasy. This day just keeps getting better and better."

His enthusiasm was contagious, and I couldn't help but grin back.

As we headed back to the front of the store, Bayley snagged a pink book off a nearby shelf. We approached the clerk, and Bayley handed him the book with a flourish, "Pink for the lady," and he handed over $20.

The clerk gave Bayley a bland look, stuck the $20 in the drawer, and handed the book back to Bayley with a receipt.

As we walked toward the back of the store, I realized it wasn't a receipt. It was a ticket. There were no words on it, just an embossed picture of a palm leaf.

When Bayley and I reached the back wall, he deposited our book on a shelf, then pulled on the orange book. I heard more people enter the bookshop behind us, but then the bookcase slid open, and the music drowned out the bookshop's sounds.

"Ladies first," Bayley said, handing me through the door before entering behind me. The door swung shut behind us, but I barely noticed because I was too taken by the scene in front of me.

Chapter Fifty-Seven

Standing on the landing of a broad, five-step stairway leading down, we took in the scene before us.

The landing where we stood was halfway between the circular main floor and an upper level that formed a semicircle above it. Left and right of us, short flights of stairs accessed the upper level, which was roped off. I could make out a few shadowy booths overlooking the action below. Where the main floor had golden-hour lighting, the upper level was cloaked in twilight.

I mentioned it to Bayley and he said, "Makes you wonder what they're hiding."

I snorted. "I imagine there's a fair amount of canoodling going on that's probably going to make me grateful for the dim lighting."

In front of us down the stairs, crowded tables filled the center of the dining area, which also had booths arranged in a semicircle around the edges, backed against the walls holding up the upper level. Beyond the main tables, a dance floor writhed with dancing couples. A big band orchestra played up a storm on a raised bandstand at the far end of the room.

To the left of the bandstand, there was a hallway. Judging from the number of women coming and going, it likely housed the powder room.

To the right of the bandstand, a line of potted palm trees blocked whatever was behind them from view. I caught motion through the palm fronds, and a waiter appeared carrying a tray. As another waiter left the floor and moved behind the palms, I realized that the blinking light I glimpsed through the trees was a swinging door, likely to the kitchen.

Another group entered behind us, so we made our way down the stairs where a hostess behind a fancy stand halted our progress.

Bayley winked at the hostess. As he slid her a twenty and the ticket, he said, "A table with a little privacy would be appreciated."

"Of course, Mr. Bayley, right this way."

As she took the ticket and disappeared the bribe, the hostess led the way across the crowded room.

"Looks like you're a regular here," I said in a low voice as we followed her. At Bayley's quirked brow, I added, "She knows you on sight."

Bayley scanned the room as we walked and said, "So we're in a scenario where we already have a particular reputation. People know us, but we don't know them."

"It's like in real life. People know you're the house, and I'm the Housekeeper, and they come with all sorts of preconceived notions about us both." I put my hand on his arm as I asked, "You think this test is about dealing with others' perceptions of us?"

Bayley nodded slowly. "That seems likely. But it won't be that simple."

The hostess guided us to one of the high-backed booths that were like little islands on the edge of the rollicking sea of party people in the center of the room. After depositing us in one, she hurried back to the hostess stand.

Bayley waited like a gentleman as I slid into the booth before sliding in next to me. We both scooched all the way to the back so we had a view of the club spread out before us.

Our booth was midway down the left side of the main floor, roughly halfway to the bathroom. From here, I could see that there were extra sets of stairs at the back of the club that led to the section above us.

"I think the upper level is for VIPs," I told Bayley, after watching a stunningly clad woman dripping with diamonds ascend to the upper level.

"Makes sense. They can watch all the action but only join the fray if they feel like rubbing elbows with the common folk."

"What do you think we're doing here?" I asked.

Bayley surveyed the scene in front of us. "I'm sure something will present itself. We just need to be really alert."

"Got it. In the meantime, should we order something to blend in better? Can we even eat in this world?"

Bayley tipped his head as he thought. "Could be another part of what they want."

"They want to watch us eat? Isn't that kind of...pervy?"

Bayley barked out a laugh. "If this follows the pattern of the rest of my experience, they want to see us identify and take advantage of available resources. Sure, we have access to our energy stockpile. But in this form," he gestured to his body, "eating shows that I understand how to access and stock up on different kinds of energy even when circumstances are...unusual."

"Jeez. That's a lot."

"It is. And everything we do here is like that." He signaled for a menu, and we poured over it together.

"Is there anything you've always wanted to taste?" I asked Bayley.

He grinned sheepishly. "How about everything?"

After some discussion, we decided to start with something simple and classic. While Bayley ordered for us, I looked around the restaurant. As soon as the waiter left, Bayley leaned in and asked, "May I borrow some of your magic again?"

"Of course! Under the circumstances, you have my permission to use my magic when you need to. Just, you know, give me a look or a quick pat to let me know what's happening if you can."

Bayley grinned, then I felt a tug, and this time, all my magic rose to answer.

Bayley murmured, "Not sure what I'm looking for, so best to sprinkle a little of everything into the search."

Nodding, I flowed my magic to Bayley, and he wove it into his own. Bayley sent the magic seeking, and I found I was able to feel what it was doing, just like when he fed his magic to me. The major difference was that he controlled the flow of my magic as well as his, steering the magic to his will.

Our invisible magical stream slipped through the club, ghosting from table to table, person to person, wisping against them like the faintest fog and then moving on.

"Light touches are best," said Bayley. "If there's anyone like us in here, we don't want them to notice."

Bayley finished the main floor and moved up to the VIP section.

"Whoa," I whispered.

The second our magic snuck into the VIP section, the magic started buzzing like a hive of bees that had just spotted a field of daisies. As Bayley deftly reeled our magic back, I scanned the crowd around us. "Can anyone else feel that?"

"Not likely," Bayley said squinting at the upper level.

"Why is there magic in the VIP section of a '40s nightclub? It doesn't exactly go with the genre."

"Good question."

The waiter picked that moment to arrive with our food.

"Do we have time to eat?" I asked glancing nervously at the VIP section.

"Absolutely," said Bayley. He took a bite of his burger, and a huge grin spread across his face.

Digging into my own burger, I was shocked to find that it was one of the best burgers I'd ever had. It tasted exactly like it should, juicy and flavorful.

"Good choice?" I asked.

"Mmmf sooo good," Bayley said around a mouthful of burger. "Wait till you get a taste of the fries."

Watching Bayley's face light up as he crunched into his first french fry almost made up for all the Thwat-induced stress.

As we demolished our burgers and fries in record time, we studied the people in the club and discussed what might be happening in the VIP section.

"That was as good as I imagined," said Bayley as our waiter cleared our plates. Bayley leaned over and murmured something to the waiter who nodded and left.

I burst out laughing when the waiter returned a few moments later with steaming, fresh coffee.

Bayley gave me a wicked grin. "What? You didn't think I'd miss out on your favorite food group while I have the chance, did you?"

Bayley tried it black first, then added cream and sugar. Like me, he preferred his coffee light and sweet.

"I could see where a person could get used to this," he said on a sigh.

A different waiter interrupted us. "You Bayley? The private detective?"

While I was slow blinking at the waiter, Bayley didn't miss a beat. "Who wants to know?"

The waiter nodded his head toward the VIP section. "Dame upstairs. Wants to see you. Now."

Bayley unhurriedly finished his coffee before saying, "My assistant, Miss Finn, will need to accompany me."

"No skin off my nose," the waiter shrugged. "But get a move on. She's waiting."

As Bayley helped me out of the booth, he asked, "What's the dope on the dame?"

The waiter shrugged and said, "Above my pay grade," and headed off toward the nearest stairs.

As we reached the top of the staircase, a beefy bouncer stepped out of the shadows. At a nod from the waiter, the bouncer opened the rope blocking the way and let us through.

The moment we stepped onto the VIP level, I sucked in a breath. Foreign magics swirled by me, permeating the whole section with a low-level magical vibration.

"I feel it too," murmured Bayley as we followed the waiter.

While we made our way around the level, we passed by several booths. After the first two, I realized that magics emanated from the booths. I couldn't tell what each magic did, but I could feel that they differed.

A third of the way down, we stopped in front of a deeply shadowed booth. Strange magic pooled toward the back, so faint I nearly missed it.

"Ma'am," said the waiter, and a diamond-braceleted arm handed him a folded bill. He nodded his thanks and made himself scarce.

We could barely see the lady in the back, but I was sure she was the source of the magic.

"I'm Bayley. This is my assistant, Miss Finn. You asked to see us?"

"Please, have a seat," said a low female voice.

Bayley gestured, and I slid into one side of the booth while he slid into the other.

The lady clicked a lighter, the flame slashing a bright light across her face just so, like we were watching Marlene Dietrich get her close-up. The woman was beautiful in the way of the 1940s starlets, with high cheekbones, arched brows, and wavy dark hair. The beads on her gown and the diamonds in her necklace glittered as she shifted to hold out a hand to Bayley.

"I'm Ms.," she paused just enough to make me suspect that she made up the, "Smith. But you can call me Dolores."

Clasping her hand briefly but politely, Bayley said, "How can I help you Ms. Dolores?"

She eyed Bayley for a second, then said, "You have a reputation for discretion."

I said encouragingly, "Mr. B is *very* discreet. Just ask anyone."

She blew out a plume of smoke and considered Bayley for a long moment before nodding and saying, "This situation is… delicate."

Bayley said, "What is it that you think I can help you with?"

"I need you to find someone." She reached into a jewel-encrusted clutch and slid a photo of a handsome, dark-haired man across the table, giving us just a few moments to look at it before tucking it away again. "He's gone missing. He's…special to me."

The husky edge to her voice suggested what kind of "special" this guy was. A quick glance at her left hand told me she wasn't wearing a ring, but if she were single, why the whole cloak-and-dagger thing she had going on?

"How long has he been missing?" asked Bayley.

"Oh, about a week. That may not seem long," she hastened to add, "but he's never been out of contact like this before. And tonight he was supposed to work at the club." She took a long draw off her cigarette. "There's a lot of tips to be made on a Saturday night. He wouldn't miss this shift for anything."

Now I understood the need for discretion. A fancy lady like

her stepping out with a waiter would not fly in this kind of society.

"Someone like you can ask questions," she said. "But someone like me, well, that would draw the kind of attention I can't afford."

"I see," said Bayley. "Unfortunately, I'm in the middle of another case—"

"The matter really is quite urgent. I need to talk to him tonight. We have…things…to discuss. Couldn't you please just ask around, see if anyone knows where he is?"

Dolores reached into her clutch and pulled out a wad of cash. "Will this cover your usual fee? I'm including a little bonus for expedited service."

Bayley took the proffered cash and gave a low whistle. "You really are in a hurry, huh?"

"Please," Dolores said, her voice cracking. Tears sparkled prettily in her eyes, "I'm just so worried."

Something about the way she'd whipped up those tears out of nothing had me wondering if they were crocodile tears or the real thing. I shot Bayley a glance to see if he was picking up the liar-liar-pants-on-fire vibe I was getting, but he was focused on Dolores.

"Sure doll. I can ask around a bit. No need to turn on the waterworks." Bayley pocketed the cash. "How should I get in touch with you?"

"I'll be here at my table for some time. Please check back with me before closing time at the latest."

Bayley nodded and rose, so I followed his lead as he said, "I'll let you know what I find out."

A waiter materialized and led us back to our booth in the club.

As soon as we were seated, I asked, "What did you think?"

Bayley signaled the waiter, "I think we're going to need more coffee."

Chapter Fifty-Eight

As Bayley and I sipped our coffee, Bayley sent our magic questing around the room again, this time looking for any sign of Johnny.

I felt my Best magic perk up, and Bayley tilted his head, deploying an extra pulse of his own magic. "Ladies' room," he said.

"Figures," I said. "What? A ladies' room is a hotbed of gossip. Give me a minute to check it out."

After Bayley released the magic, I slipped off to the powder room.

Like every ladies' room I'd ever been in, this one was busy. But it was much fancier than any I'd seen before. There was a big rest area complete with velvet couches and padded chairs that formed a sort of antechamber you had to pass through to get to the actual bathroom.

I went to a sink and washed my hands while I studied the women gliding around.

A group of giggling ladies departed in a herd, which left me as the only one in the room suddenly. When I heard a sniff, I realized I wasn't totally alone after all. Walking back into the rest area, I spotted a woman huddled in a dim corner, alternating between dabbing at her eyes and wringing her handkerchief.

Another damsel in distress. But the woman in front of me couldn't have been more different from Dolores. Where Dolores had been dripping wealth, this woman looked like she was wearing her only formal dress, not couture. And where I suspected Dolores might be playing some kind of angle, this woman's red eyes and dripping nose made me think she was genuinely upset.

As another gaggle of girls came through the door, I walked over to the crying lady and asked gently, "Are you okay?"

She tilted her head so she could see me more clearly from under the hat she wore. Her lip trembled, and she swiped at her eyes again as she said, "I'm fine."

The warbling in her voice and teary eyes said otherwise. "If you don't mind me saying, you don't look fine. What's your name?"

She looked down at her lap and said, "Millie."

"Hi Millie. I'm Finn."

"That's a funny name for a gal."

I supposed in this time it would be. "Parents? Whaddya gonna do?" I said with a shrug. "At least they didn't name me something really unusual, like 'Rainbow.'"

"Rainbow?" a surprised laugh escaped her. "Where are you *from*?"

I had no idea what city we were in, so I went with a vague wave and an, "Out West."

Apparently that was the right thing to say because she nodded and said, "Oh. I've heard they're a little wacky in the West."

Another group of women came through the door, and I sat down so that I blocked their view, giving Millie added privacy.

"So Millie, what's got you bothered? Is your fella being a heel?"

That was the exact wrong thing to say because more tears sprang to her eyes, and she started to cry in earnest.

I patted her hands as said, "Oh honey. It's going to be okay. Why don't you tell me what's wrong?"

Millie took a minute to compose herself before she responded. "Well since you seem like you really care," she said on a hiccup, and then it came pouring out of her. "My Johnny's gone missing."

Fortunately, she was too upset to notice the look of recognition on my face.

"I ain't seen 'im for nearly a week! I thought for sure he'd be here workin' his regular shift at the club, but he ain't here. An' that means somethun's definitely, really wrong. He'd never miss a Saturday shift! That's where ya make the big dough. He tried real hard to get a job here, said it was his big break. And he's been real proud to work here, ya know?"

Her voice caught on a half sob as she added, "I'm worried something terrible has happened to him. I even asked one of the girls here, and she says he's workin', but I been here an hour, and I swear I seen every waiter and bus boy here. Still no Johnny."

She was twisting her handkerchief so hard that I was worried she'd tear it. I said gently, "You know, I'm here with my boss. He's a private detective and a good one at that."

She gave me a worried look, shaking her head. "Oh I don't know about that. I've heard about them private dicks. Those guys are kinda hard, don't ya think?"

"Some are, sure. But he's not like that. He's a real gentlemen. I bet he could help you find your guy, no problem. Why don't you at least come talk to him for a minute?"

Indecision flickered in her eyes, but I could tell she was interested because she'd stopped strangling her hanky.

I pressed, "Hey, what've you got to lose? There's no harm in at least meeting my boss. If you don't like him, you're no worse off than before."

She sniffed delicately, then nodded at me. I held out my hand and helped her up off the couch, then led her back to our table.

Bayley slid out of the booth when he saw us approaching.

I wished I could talk to him mind-to-mind because by now I'd have filled him in. He didn't miss a beat though, assessing Millie's tear-stained face and giving her a gentle smile. "Who is this beautiful lady you've brought to see us?" he asked me before turning to a blushing Millie.

"Mr. B, this is Millie. Millie, Mr. B."

"Having a tough night, doll? Why don't you take a load off and sit with us a minute." He waved her into the booth, waited for me to slide in on the other side, then sat down next to me.

"Can I get you anything?" Bayley asked.

"No thank you," Millie said, shaking her head.

I quickly filled him in on what little I knew then added, "Do you think you can help her, boss?"

"I can sure try." He gave Millie a reassuring smile, and some of the tension left her shoulders. Her hanky was getting a break, which I took to be a good sign.

"Can you tell me about the last time you saw him?" Bayley asked. He pulled the notebook out of his pocket and started making notes.

"It's like I was sayin'. It was a week ago tomorrow."

Her voice was starting to hitch again, so I reached across the table and patted her arm comfortingly.

In a quieter tone, she said, "Last time I seen him, he was all excited, like. He said he'd be working a lot more for the next little while, and not to take it personal if I didn't see him as much." She sniffed. "But we was supposed to catch a movie last Wednesday when the club is closed, and he didn't show up. Didn't even call. That's not like him. I tried calling him, but he never answered. Then I started getting worried. I talked to the landlady at his building, and she says Johnny ain't been around in days. So I says to myself, no way would Johnny miss a Saturday shift at the club. But I came here and still no Johnny," her voice rose in despair, and she started in on the poor hanky again. "I got a real bad feeling. I think something awful has happened, I just know it."

The waiter picked that moment to top off our coffee.

"Sure I can't get you something? On the house," said Bayley.

"That's swell of you, but no thanks. I ain't real hungry," Millie said. When the waiter left, she turned wide, tearful eyes on Bayley. "So whaddya think? Can ya help me find my Johnny?"

"I can certainly take a look," said Bayley.

I interjected, "You can trust Mr. B here. There's nobody better at finding out what's what."

As the panic left her, Millie slumped a bit, exhaustion replacing the pinched look on her face.

I patted Millie's arm and said, "Hey honey, how about you leave this to us and go on home and get some rest?" She looked like she was going to argue so I added, "You wanna look your best when we find Johnny, right?"

She looked to Bayley who nodded and said, "Finn's right.

There's nothing more you can do tonight. Get some rest. Give me a call tomorrow, and we'll set up a time to catch you up on what we learn." Bayley extracted a business card from his wallet and handed it to her.

Accepting the card, Millie nodded. Eyes darting around uncertainly, she said, "Sure thing, Mr. B. Tomorrow then," and she left.

As we watched her head for the exit, I said, "For her sake, I sure hope this doesn't go the way of usual film noir."

Bayley said, "Why?"

"If it does, Johnny's probably already dead."

Chapter Fifty-Nine

Trying to shake my sense of foreboding, I said, "What do you think? We've got two women after the same guy."

"What's your impression of them?"

I shook my head. "There's something off about Dolores that I can't put my finger on yet. But I think Millie is genuinely upset. It's hard to fake that much snot. Still, we're dealing with the Thwats, so I'm not inclined to take anything at face value."

"Agreed. But I think it's clear we need to find Johnny." Bayley turned his gaze to the club as he sipped his coffee. I followed his lead and studied our surroundings. After a few minutes, he said, "What do you notice?"

"The staff seem to have free run of the place. But the patrons are confined to particular areas. VIP up above, bouncer at the top of each set of stairs, preventing the riffraff from bothering the special people."

Eyes narrowed, Bayley nodded. "Notice anything about the kitchen?"

I peered across the room at the palm trees screening the door to the kitchen. I saw waiters traveling back and forth at intervals. "Hey wait."

"Interesting huh?" said Bayley.

"Why are those fancy schmancy people from the VIP section sneaking into the kitchen?" I asked.

"They're not the first," said Bayley. "Every once in a while people will slip into the kitchen—people who aren't waiters. If they come down that particular set of steps from the VIP section, they land in the hallway behind the palm trees. It's really hard to see them."

"How'd you notice?"

"I caught the first one by accident. It's the ladies and their jewels. The sparkles caught my eye as a group was descending the stairs."

"Huh," I said. "I've been distracted watching the interplay on the main floor, not to mention the band, and the groovy dancing." I sighed, "That's the point, isn't it? The Thwats are trying to distract us, so we miss important stuff. With so much to look at, who's gonna care about the dark corner where the staff goes?"

"Exactly," said Bayley.

"Sneaky. Have you seen anyone come back out?"

"No." A spark lit Bayley's eyes. "Want to find out why?"

"Sure thing boss. What's the plan?"

"Look at the staff going up to the VIP section."

I clocked a waiter and a couple of cigarette girls going up and down the VIP stairs at the front of the club. I swiveled my head to look at the staff on the main floor, then back again. "Their outfits are different. It's subtle, but you can see the differences if you look. The VIP waiters' bow ties are black and red instead of all black. And the VIP girls' skirts are edged with black and dark, blood-red lace."

"Did you see the pins?"

I nodded. "A few of the VIP staff have black and red pins."

"I think we need to be VIP staff, don't you?"

Five minutes and more of Bayley's transformation magic later, I was tugging at the edge of my cigarette girl outfit, hoping my butt wasn't hanging out the back of my extremely short skirt. Bayley was tugging at the black-and-red bow tie of his waiter's outfit. Both of us were crammed behind yet another grouping of palms. I'd encouraged them to grow extra lush to provide us with somewhat of a screen, but we were barely hidden, like my butt. Bayley had decided to risk transforming us, and he'd just finished when another VIP waiter, one with a pin, came around the corner.

"Hey, you lug. No hanky-panky with the cigarette girls,

you know the rules." He gave me a once-over that lingered on my legs. "Not that I blame you. Look at those gams," he said, flashing me a cheeky wink.

I pasted a smile on my face and batted my eyes at him, while I surreptitiously tugged at my skirt and tried to cover more of my legs.

Bayley grinned at the waiter conspiratorially. "The gams *are* nice, but that's not what I was doing. I was just asking this cookie if she's seen Johnny. You know him?"

"Who's asking?"

"The guy he owes a pile of clams to, that's who. Word to the wise. Don't play cards with him," Bayley said.

"Everybody knows that."

Bayley shrugged. "I'm new. So sue me. You seen him or what?"

The waiter gave Bayley a pitying look. "You got about as much chance of getting your dough as I've got of owning this club. But yeah, I seen him just a little while ago. He's working at the end of the line tonight."

"Thanks," said Bayley.

"Good luck," said the waiter and with another wink at me, he was off.

I felt Bayley's magic tingle through me and looked down to find we were both wearing pins. They consisted of two black bars with a blood-red symbol on top. The symbol looked sort of like a rectangle with a lumpy top and it had a black line running diagonally across it. Something about it tickled my memory, but I couldn't put my finger on it.

"Any idea what the pin is supposed to be?" Bayley asked.

I shook my head. "It seems sort of familiar, but I'm not sure."

"What about 'the end of the line'? Any ideas?"

"The cooks in a fancy kitchen are sometimes called line cooks. Maybe he got moved to working in the kitchen?"

Bayley nodded. "The kitchen is our next stop then. Let's split up. See if you notice anything when you cross the club. I'm going to stop by Dolores's table and tell her we have a lead on Johnny. I'll meet you outside the kitchen."

"Uh, you can't see Dolores looking like that."

Bayley looked down, sighed, waved his hand and was back in detective garb.

I kind of wanted to see Dolores's reaction, but this was Bayley's adventure, so I held my tongue, and we split up.

I worked my way across the club, my disappointment growing as I neither saw Johnny nor heard anyone talking about him.

Eventually, I made it across the room and slipped behind the palms and into the kitchen hallway. It was even darker up close than it looked from a distance. I was surprised the waiters weren't constantly tripping and spilling their trays.

Hovering at the top of the VIP stairs, I could just make out the hulking outline of what I assumed was a bouncer. So far, he didn't seem to notice me, and I was hoping my luck held.

After a few moments, Bayley came down the stairs. He stepped behind the largest palm, I felt a whisper of magic, and he was back in VIP waiter garb.

I whispered, "How'd it go with Dolores?"

"For someone who says she's upset, she barely reacted. I told her Johnny was last seen at the end of the line, and she thanked me for the update then dismissed me. Told me my services were no longer needed."

"Really? What's she going to do? Storm the kitchen?"

"Who knows."

I frowned.

"What?"

Furrowing my brows, I said, "Doesn't this all seem a little too easy to you? We need to find out where Johnny is and, bam, someone tells us, then our client says 'see you' and that's it? Seems a little too cut-and-dry for a you're-doomed-to-fail kind of test."

"Agreed."

"Persistence?" I asked. At Bayley's questioning look, I clarified, "Do you think the Thwats are testing our persistence?"

"Almost certainly." His lips twisted like he'd eaten something bitter as he muttered, "You'd think by making it this far I'd have already shown that I don't give up easily."

I nodded vigorously. "No kidding. You've done awesome

so far. Maybe it's me they're worried will call it quits too soon. Hah. We'll show them. They want persistent? Once we set our minds to something, we're like a cat that's determined to get at the catnip."

I felt some of Bayley's frustration disperse, replaced by humor. With a small smile he said, "Just because Dolores says we're done, doesn't mean we are. I'd like to talk to Johnny before she does. Let's see if he's in here," and Bayley waltzed into the kitchen. I took a deep breath, tugged at my skirt, and followed after him.

Chapter Sixty

Controlled chaos reigned in the kitchen. A din of dishes clanking, people chattering, and grills sizzling provided the soundtrack as waiters hurried to and fro in front of counters loaded with food. Behind the counters, a double line of cooks chopped, grilled, and arranged dish after dish, slapping each completed meal on a counter.

I followed Bayley as he wove his way deeper into the kitchen. "I don't see Johnny," Bayley said.

"Me either," I said, scanning the cooks again. "What next?"

"Hey sister, where ya goin'?" a woman called to me.

I spun around to see another cigarette girl eying me. She was wearing the same VIP outfit and pin that I was.

"I, uh, I need...stuff," I said, pointing to my empty tray.

"Thought so. You're new, huh?" she said, gesturing me to follow her.

I glanced at Bayley, who murmured, "Go with it," and shooed me after her.

I was reluctant to be separated from Bayley, but I trusted his instincts, so I followed the girl across the kitchen, dodging chefs, waiters, and busboys until we arrived at a quieter corner in the far back right-hand side of the room. As we walked, she said, "This place is a bit of a maze back here. Don't blame ya for getting lost. I'm Wanda, by the way."

She stopped at a closet with a horizontally split door. The top half was open, the bottom closed. A middle-aged woman in a kitchen uniform leaned on the bottom half, chomping on a piece of gum.

"Got a fresh one here for ya, Lottie," said Wanda. Turning to me, she asked, "What's your name, honey?"

Given how well "Finn" had gone over with Millie, I frantically tried to come up with something a little less obvious. "Viv-ian," I stuttered.

"Like Vivian Leigh?" Lottie asked.

I nodded.

Lottie leaned on the door. "Ah, I loved *Gone with the Wind*."

"Me too," I said. "I just saw it again recently."

Lottie sighed. "Ooh that Clark Gable. I wouldn't kick that man outta bed for eatin' crackers, if you know what I mean," she cackled.

Wanda and I giggled along with her.

Since we were bonding, it seemed like a good time to get some info. "Speaking of dishes," I said, "either of you know Johnny?"

Lottie and Wanda exchanged a glance, and as Lottie started shaking her head, Wanda said, "Trust me, honey, you don't wanna go messing with that one. He may be a looker, but he ain't nothin' but trouble. 'Sides, he's already got a gal."

Lottie snorted. "At least one."

Wanda nodded. "Like I said, trouble."

I shook my head. "Oh it's not like that. We're related. Distantly. He's my uh, I think it's like third cousin or something? Anyways, my ma told me to go say hello when I got here. He's always been trouble—there's one in every family, am I right? But you don't want to mess with my ma when she tells you to do something. I, uh, haven't seen him around though."

Wanda said, "You can probably catch him downstairs."

"Downstairs?"

Mistaking my confusion, Lottie said, "Better show her the way, Wanda, so she doesn't get lost," and Lottie handed me and Wanda packs of cigarettes, gum, and candy to refill our trays.

"Sure thing. Headed that way myself, now I got my tray set," said Wanda, who gestured to me, and we started back across the kitchen, me trailing behind her.

"It's unusual for them to put a new girl downstairs. Did Johnny pull some strings for ya?" Wanda asked, shooting me a questioning look.

"Hah. As if Johnny would go out of his way." Wanda gave me a commiserating look, and I added, "Nah, my friend," I scrambled to think of a common '40s name, "uh Betty? You know her?"

Wanda shook her head.

"She didn't last here too long. Too much of a crazy scene for her. But she let me know they were looking for girls. And I'm not new," I said. "Well, new here, but not *new*. I've been waitressing since I was a kid."

Wanda looked over her shoulder at me and said, "Aw, then this'll be a piece of cake. It's easy. You just smile, maybe flirt a little. If they wanna chat, you chat. If they want you to scram, you scram. You get the idea. Just keep the customers happy."

As Wanda chattered, I tried to make sense of what was going on. She kept mentioning "downstairs," and I thought she was referring to the downstairs area of the main floor. But I was wearing the special skirt that was supposed to give me access to the VIP area upstairs. Had we been mistaken about what the outfits meant?

Frantically I looked around, but Bayley was nowhere to be seen. Though I couldn't talk to him through the bond, I could still feel his emotions, and he seemed all right. More than all right—he seemed energized.

Weaving through the kitchen traffic behind Wanda, I was confused to see we weren't going out to the main floor. Instead, we arrived at the freezer in the back left-hand corner of the club, and she stopped.

Wanda mistook my confusion for nerves. "Hey now. You're the nervous sort, huh?"

"Just the first day jitters," I said.

She gave me a smile and a pat on the shoulder. "Well look, honey, downstairs is the same as up here, mostly. Although you play your cards right, and the tips are better. Just keep a smile on and try to have fun."

She tugged on the handle to the freezer and went in with a, "Whew, that'll wake you up."

I followed her into a huge walk-in freezer. We zigged behind a shelf and came to a stop at a side wall with a door.

Wanda pulled at her pin and the red symbol came off. What I'd thought was a divot in the door was a slot in the exact shape of the symbol. Like it was magnetized, the symbol jerked toward the divot and slipped in with a little clink.

Magic flared, startling me. Once the magic was activated, I heard the clunking sound of door locks disengaging.

"Step back," Wanda said as she moved backwards with me. "These pins are weird little keys, I'll say that. It's amazing what they can do with magnets these days, huh?" she added, confirming my suspicion that she had no idea she was using magic.

With a last clank, the door popped open partway. Wanda retrieved the symbol from its slot and held it against her pin, where it clicked into place. Then she swung the door open, revealing a set of stairs descending into the darkness. Music drifted up from somewhere below along with the scent of cigars and alcohol.

"Ready for the big time?" she asked and shooed me forward.

Chapter Sixty-One

I started down the steps and heard the door thump shut behind me. Wanda passed by me, gesturing for me to follow her down a winding set of stone stairs. Cool air, dim lighting, and the gray stone walls created a ghostly vibe that was an abrupt shift from the bustle we'd just left.

As I followed Wanda, I let myself panic a bit. Where was Bayley? Were we messing things up by splitting up after we'd argued so hard to work together? The more I worried, the closer the walls felt around me. I took deep breaths, trying to calm myself.

I should've been paying better attention. Midway down, the stairs took a sharp turn, and I crashed into the wall with my tray. Hanging from my neck the way it did, the tray jutted out awkwardly.

Wanda stopped ahead of me with a giggle, "Happens to all of us. You'll get used to maneuvering that thing, I promise. You drop anything?"

"Nope, I don't think so. Thanks."

"Okay good then. Show time." Her face lit up with a flirtatious smile, and she proceeded around another sharp corner.

I followed her around what turned out to be the final turn in the stairs and got hit with a low hum of noise as I found myself on a wide landing overlooking another crowded room.

My mouth dropped open.

Wanda shook her head and said, "Don't tell me no one warned you? Figures. Well, welcome to The End of the Line."

"Name's a little on the nose isn't it?"

The whole room buzzed with magic, but that wasn't what was causing me to stand there and blink like a deer in the headlights.

The club was decorated in what I could only call "cemetery chic."

Decked in shades of gray and black, with accents of blood red here and there, the entire club resembled a graveyard the size of an enormous warehouse.

Instead of tables, tombstones littered the room, and they looked eerily similar to the ones in the Housekeeper cemetery, right down to the chips and cracks. Each tombstone's top had been flattened, and people blithely placed their drinks there. Cement statues and leafless, skeletal trees were interspersed throughout in such a way that the place looked eerily realistic.

Drifting fog hid the floor, swirling and pooling around people's ankles, giving the effect that everyone was floating above the ground like ghosts. From the laughter, it seemed like everyone felt more giddy than ghostly.

The facade of a massive stone mausoleum took up nearly the entire wall at one end of the room. Waving and chattering patrons pushed their way toward a wraparound bar that fronted the steps.

At the other end of the room from the bar, a band with a three-piece horn section played slow, bluesy jazz, underscoring the ambiance.

Whereas the upstairs club had booths arranged in a semicircle around the main floor, here small mausoleums created distinct little rooms along the walls. Red lights glinted from the interiors, bathing the occupants in blood-tinted shadows and making it impossible to see them clearly.

Not that I would've been able to see them very well anyway. All the patrons in the club wore masks in shades of gray, black, and red. Between the low lights, the fog, and the masks, it was hard to see anyone clearly.

Wanda said, "I know it's really somethin', but don't let 'em catch you standing here gawkin' okay?"

I nodded.

"Good luck," said Wanda, and she descended the final steps and disappeared into the crowd.

I scanned the room, looking for Bayley or Johnny in vain. I had a startled moment where I thought I saw Millie sliding into a group of people, but when the group shifted, I saw a blond lady with a similar haircut but a different dress. It quickly became apparent that if I wanted to see people clearly, I was going to have to dive into the fray.

Schooling my face into my best serving-customers-at-the-diner smile, I stepped down into the room. The cool fog slid along my legs, making me shiver as I edged my way over to one of the walls. With so many people, the room should have been hot. But the club was cool and vaguely damp. Like a graveyard.

As I took in the club, my pin suddenly made sense. The symbol in the middle was a tombstone. And the overall design was a take on the railroad symbol for the end of the line. Except instead of a red circle over two train tracks, they'd used a tombstone.

Bayley? I called in my mind before remembering that he couldn't hear me. I grimaced in frustration. Between the huge size of the room, the crowd, and the fog, there was no way I was going to see him even if he was in the club. I needed to try something different.

While I made a show of arranging the items on my tray, I reached out a tendril of magic through our bond and tugged at Bayley.

My face blossomed into a genuine smile when I felt an answering tug from the other side of the room. He didn't seem to be in any distress, but he was distracted.

Pushing off the wall, I stepped into the crowd, aiming in Bayley's direction. I had no idea how I was supposed to thread the tombstones and the glitterati without whacking into one or the other with my giant tray. At first I tried to gingerly weave my way around people, but after my third indignant, "Hey! Watch it sister!" I gave up trying to be subtle and wielded the tray unflinchingly, forcing people to move around me.

My newfound confidence attracted customers. People began stopping me every few feet to buy the cigarettes, gum, and candy I had on offer.

When the first group stopped me, I gritted my teeth as I smiled, aggravated that they were slowing my progress.

They didn't even really talk to me. They talked amongst themselves as if I wasn't even there.

I started smiling for real when I realized what an advantage that was.

As the next group stopped me, I put my best flirty face on.

"Would ya look at the landing gear on you," the guy said, looking at my legs. He slowly raked his gaze back up to my eyes and asked, "Got anything I want?"

I resisted the urge to roll my eyes and instead giggled and said, "Got some cigarettes. And if ya want something sweet," I batted my eyes and paused meaningfully before adding innocently, "got some candy."

He grinned and paid me for the cigarettes, tucking a little extra in my tray with a wink.

But while I flirted with Mr. Landing Gear, I kept an ear on the conversation continuing behind him.

That's when I noticed that magic wafted from everyone in the group. As I moved on, it became clear that all the club patrons were magical. There were so many types of magic that it was like being in a room where everyone wore a different type of perfume, none of which I recognized. Nobody was actively using their magic. But still, it seemed that this club was a playground exclusively for magical patrons. Only the staff were magic-less.

I eavesdropped my way across the room, and about halfway to Bayley, I struck gold.

"...not what I heard," a woman said, as I sold some gum to two guys in the group. She lowered her voice slightly, but she couldn't really whisper and still be heard in the crowd, so I could hear her clearly.

"I heard it's some priceless jewel, and they're doing the deal tonight," a woman said.

"Where'd you hear that?" another woman asked.

"From a bartender. Ya really wanna know the rumble, those bartenders hear everything."

One of the guys said, "You gotta be three parts fearless and one part crazy to do a deal with Virgil."

A different guy snorted and said, "There's a reason they called this place The End of the Line, you know. Virgil's nickname is the Grim Reaper."

Chapter Sixty-Two

By the time I was closing in on Bayley, it'd taken me a while
to get across the room. Although I still hadn't seen Johnny,
I couldn't help my satisfied smile. I'd heard two more conversations about the not-so-secret deal happening. Also, my tray was
empty. My parents had instilled a solid work ethic in me and,
regardless of the ridiculous circumstances, it still felt good to
do my cigarette-girl job well.

I rounded a knot of people and stopped short. Behind the
bar, a gaggle of bartenders mixed up drinks while they chatted
with the customers and with each other. Lurking behind them,
Bayley was bussing dirty glasses into a crate.

I tugged on our bond, and his head jerked up. Searching the
crowd, he smiled when he caught my eye, then he held up one
finger and nodded his head to the side, indicating a spot to the
side of the bar. As I made my way over, he finished loading the
crate, hefted it up, and then carried it out to meet me.

He glanced down and said, "Good that your tray is empty.
Gives us both an excuse to leave the floor."

Opening a door hidden behind the mausoleum facade,
Bayley ushered me inside. Once the door closed behind us, the
outside noise faded. The room was the size of a modest walk-in
closet. Stacks of crates with fresh glasses waited to the left, and a
dumb waiter took up the back wall. For the moment, the room
was empty except for us.

"I was worried," I said at the same time that Bayley said, "I
knew you'd find me."

We both laughed as he hefted his crate onto the dumb

waiter and pushed a button. As the glasses ascended, I said, "How'd you get down here?"

"Same way you did, I expect. I followed another waiter down."

"Good thinking," I said.

"I heard—" we both said at the same time, then started laughing.

"Ladies first," Bayley said.

"I got some eavesdropping in when I was crossing the floor. There's some kind of big deal going down tonight. One lady thought maybe it was some kind of jewel."

Bayley nodded. "The bartenders are gossiping about it too. But everyone seems to have a different idea of what's being exchanged. In addition to the jewel theory, I've heard people mention money, drugs, and even artifacts."

"So we've got some kind of big deal taking place. Do you think that has anything to do with why Johnny is missing?"

"Word from the bartenders is that Johnny has quite the sketchy reputation. What do you want to bet Johnny and the deal are related?"

I shook my head, smiling. "No bet. The ladies upstairs said he was trouble."

Bayley said, "From what I hear, Johnny is Little League compared to Virgil, the club owner. Did you hear about him?"

"You mean the Grim Reaper? Oh yeah. Everyone talks about him with part awe, part terror."

Bayley said, "I haven't seen either of them yet. You?"

"No. I looked for Johnny, but no luck. I, uh, I'm not sure I want to go looking for the Grim Reaper. Pretty sure he's someone we want to avoid."

"Good point. Let's concentrate on Johnny. First things first. Let's change back so that we're not working anymore." Bayley's magic tingled across my skin, and I found myself back in my dress, but this time wearing a mask. Bayley was back in his suit, and he was also wearing a mask.

I didn't have time to relish the lack of breeze on my butt because the door swung open, and a waiter glared at us.

"Hey. Staff only. Get your kicks somewhere else."

I gave my best drunken giggle, slurred, "Spoilsport," at the waiter, then pretended to drunkenly stumble out of there. Bayley followed my lead and staggered after me.

I came to a stop out of sight of the waiter, edging around one of the creepy angel statues so that we were half-hidden behind it. To anyone passing by, we'd look like a couple trying to get some privacy.

"I think we need to find Johnny. If I may," Bayley said, gently tugging on my magic. Mine was ready, leaping to go play with his.

Bayley sent our magic questing through the club.

No Johnny.

Bayley said, "Maybe I'm going about this wrong. Instead of looking for Johnny, maybe we should be looking for this deal that's happening."

I thought about it. "Everyone here has magic. What are the chances that this deal will use some kind of magic? Or that the jewel or whatever it is has magical properties?"

Bayley nodded. "That's clever, Finn." He looked thoughtful then said, "I have an idea."

This time, when Bayley tugged at my magic, I was surprised to feel my Guthrie magic answering.

Bayley mixed the Guthrie magic with his own and sent a wisp of wind snaking through the crowd. I could feel the magical wind drift up to the nearest set of people. To my surprise, the wind switched direction and blew back toward us. I jumped when a second later, a snippet of their conversation ghosted back to us.

"…heard she's been stepping out on him…"

"…not the marrying kind…"

I turned to Bayley. "Neat trick."

"Your Guthrie practice gave me the idea. Now that we know that it works, we'll track any magic that stands out and listen to what's happening," he said and added some of my Best magic into his concoction.

Bayley directed the small gust into the crowd, whisking it this way and that.

At first, all we found were people doing small feats of magic, like a guy offering, "Want me to chill your drink, honey?"

Bayley and I both stiffened a few minutes later. We'd found a magic that felt different than the others, somehow both more powerful and more static.

A man's voice murmured, "...that's right, c'mon you stupid hunk of junk, take me to it."

Bayley and I turned in the direction of the magic in time to see Johnny walk down the stairs. He tugged on a mask, then disappeared into the club.

"There he is," I said.

Bayley frowned. "I only got a quick look at him, but he was alone right?"

We listened as Johnny kept up a steady stream of chatter in the same whispering voice.

"I think he's talking to himself," I said. "Or to something he's holding. He looked like he had something in his hand."

Bayley nodded. "Too bad he's not saying anything particularly useful."

I could feel the wind moving as Johnny talked and realized it was following him as he made his way across the floor.

"Let's go," Bayley said, taking my elbow.

We followed our magic, trying to close the distance between us and Johnny without looking like we were rushing across the club. We were at the bar end of the room, and Johnny seemed to be heading for the opposite side, near the band.

As we were nearing him, suddenly Johnny's voice changed to a normal volume. "Hey, am I glad to see you," he said warmly.

There was a muffled cracking sound, and then he stopped talking.

Bayley and I hurried the rest of the way and arrived to find Johnny slumped against the wall between two statues, eyes open and empty.

Bayley bent down to feel Johnny's pulse.

"Is he...?" I asked.

"Dead. Yes," Bayley said grimly.

Then the screaming started.

Chapter Sixty-Three

A woman behind us shrieked an ear-piercing wail, and people started yelling, pushing, and shoving.

I froze. I understood that this was a virtual reality simulation, that these were not real people. But Johnny looked like a real person. And he was dead on the floor in front of me. I couldn't help but feel a sort of stunned horror as I looked at his lifeless eyes.

Amon and the Thwats had taken their simulation so far that they were killing people off? What did that say about me and Bayley?

Within moments, Bayley and I were surrounded by big, beefy bodyguards. It was like a hockey team suddenly materialized and formed a human semicircle around us, blocking the view of the club patrons and trapping me and Bayley. None of them wore masks, so there was nothing to blunt the threatening glares they aimed at us.

Bayley stood slowly from where he was crouching and stepped slightly in front of me, putting himself between me and the goon squad.

"Lose the masks," said one of the guys. It didn't seem wise to argue, so we took them off.

"I saw what happened," came a low, cultured voice behind the human wall.

A raspy male voice answered, "Is that so?"

Two of the guards parted and let Dolores and a man through before closing up again behind them.

Magic flared and the club racket went quiet. I could feel

the magic arching over and around us, forming a bubble. The silence should have felt like a relief after all the noise. Instead, I felt like I'd suddenly been shoved in a cage.

My attention snapped back when Dolores said, "They did it. I saw them. They killed Johnny." Her voice warbled, and she tugged off her mask to dab at her eyes.

I pursed my lips. If those were real tears, then I was Amon's biggest fan.

The man turned to me and Bayley. "I don't know you." Even without a mask, he was plenty creepy. He had a gaunt face, all sharp cheekbones and aquiline nose. He was average height with dark hair and dark brown, calculating eyes.

"I'm Bayley."

"The private detective?"

Bayley nodded. "And this is my assistant, Miss Finn. And you are?"

"Virgil Jones. I own this joint."

Great. Just what I was hoping to avoid—a face-to-face meeting with the Grim Reaper.

Dolores doubled down on the tears. "I hired Mr. Bayley to find Johnny. I didn't tell you to hurt him! How could you?"

Virgil nodded to one of the goons. "Take Ms. Smith here to the private bar." He turned to her and said, "I'll take care of this, doll. You go and calm your nerves."

It was clear that it was an order, not a suggestion, and after a slight hesitation, Dolores nodded and left with a goon. The remaining guys shuffled to fill the gap in their human wall.

Bayley said, "We didn't do anything. We found him like this."

Virgil didn't respond. He turned to one of the bodyguards and said, "Check the body." While one guy did a thorough search of Johnny, Virgil nodded to another guy and said, "Search them."

"Is this really necessary?" Bayley asked as a guy searched him roughly. My guy was slightly gentler, but no less thorough as he patted me down then checked my purse.

Virgil didn't deign to respond.

"Nothin' boss," said the guy next to Johnny.

"Same here," said Bayley's guy, and mine chimed in, "Nothin' here neither."

Virgil nodded to Johnny. "Get rid of him." He turned to us. "You two, let's have a little chat."

The goon squad rearranged themselves, two guys peeling off to shepherd me, Bayley, and Virgil through the club, while the remainder stayed behind to deal with Johnny and any lookie-loos. The patrons had backed off from the scene, but several were glancing our way, trying to catch the action.

The bodyguard in front led us into one of the mini-mausoleums. There was a door at the back, and magic pulsed as the guy opened it. We all filed through, and the bodyguard at the back swung the door shut, abruptly chopping off the sounds of the club and our exit.

Chapter Sixty-Four

We found ourselves in a gray, carpeted hallway. Really gray. The walls were alternating satin and matte gray stripes. The carpet was gray. Even the ceiling was painted gray. I had the odd impression that I was standing in a cave and half expected bats to come flying by.

The hallway had no doors or windows and ended in a wall. We followed Virgil and the front bodyguard, who about halfway down the hallway turned to his right and tapped the wall.

With a pulse of magic, a door appeared and swung inward, and we all went inside.

I nearly let out a whistle. The room reminded me of an English gentleman's study, complete with the scents of old books, rich tobacco, and a hint of whiskey. Cherry wood covered the walls in large panels that were detailed with delicate molding and wainscoting. Built-in bookcases took up most of the walls, and oil paintings dotted the remaining available space.

"It's like that movie," Bayley murmured, and I remembered that we'd watched an English historical drama recently.

Virgil skirted a beautiful antique desk, dropping into a leather chair, then pointed to the chairs in front of the desk as he said, "Sit down."

While Bayley and I took our seats, one bodyguard took up position leaning against a wall, while the other brought Virgil a whiskey and then came to lurk just behind us.

Taking a cigar out of a fancy box on his desk, Virgil fired up a gold lighter and took his time studying us while he got the cigar going. I didn't know if he was trying to make us squirm by making us wait, but Bayley and I waited patiently. It didn't escape my notice, though, that Virgil hadn't offered either of us a cigar or a drink. He was very clearly putting us in our place.

After taking a sip of his whiskey, Virgil finally spoke. "Where is it?"

I shot Bayley a confused glance then asked Virgil, "Where's what?"

Virgil's face hardened. "You can save the ditzy dame dramatics for some other yuck. You better get it through your head right now that I'm no one's patsy, sister."

I looked at Bayley who said, "She's not acting. We honestly don't know what you're talking about."

Cigar hanging from his mouth, Virgil deadpanned, "So you just happened to be standing there?"

Bayley shook his head. "No, we were there on purpose. Dolores hired me to find Johnny. We saw him crossing the club, and we followed. But by the time we got to him, he was dead."

"Convenient," said Virgil.

"Not really," said Bayley. "My client, Ms. Smith, was most eager to find him."

I could have hugged Bayley for keeping Millie out of it. I didn't care if none of this was real; I didn't want her to have to deal with Virgil.

Virgil said, "Well congratulations. You found him alright."

"Not in the condition we hoped," said Bayley dryly.

Virgil shrugged a shoulder. "You win some, you lose some." He leaned forward slightly. "Personally, I don't like to lose. Where is it?"

Bayley held out his hands, palms up, and said, "I still don't know what you're looking for."

Virgil swung his gaze to me, and I resisted the urge to flinch back from his cold, searching look. "You," he said. "You got no poker face. I'm only going to ask you one more time. Where is it?"

I shook my head. "He's telling the truth. We don't know what you're talking about."

Virgil tapped the ash off his cigar into a crystal ashtray as he said, "Let's say I believe you for a moment. And let's say that

Johnny delayed a...business transaction and took something that wasn't his."

My mind scrambled. Johnny must've somehow messed up the deal that the whole club was buzzing about. I still had no idea what he took though.

A glance at Bayley showed me he was doing a similar calculus.

Virgil speared me with another look. "You sure you seen nothing?"

Bayley answered. "The place was packed. We couldn't see anything till we practically tripped over Johnny."

A thought occurred to me, and it must have shown because Virgil pounced. Pointing with his cigar, "Out with it."

I glanced at Bayley, and he gave me a scant nod. I said slowly, "Well there was one other person who showed up awful quick. Did anyone search Dolores?" It was bad form to turn on a client, but since Dolores had fired us, technically she wasn't our client anymore, so maybe it was okay.

A smile glinted in Bayley's eyes, which made me feel better.

Virgil glanced at one of the bodyguards. He shrugged. "Don't know if Davey searched her or not."

"Well go find out," snapped Virgil.

We waited in tense silence for the bodyguard to come back. Stifling the urge to fidget, I found myself wishing more than ever that I still had Bayley to talk to in my head.

The bodyguard surged into the room and rushed over to Virgil. He whispered frantically to Virgil, whose face transformed into cold fury. Suddenly I had the feeling I was looking at the Grim Reaper, not Virgil anymore.

"Show me."

The henchman left again, gesturing for his buddy to join him on the way out. We spent a few quiet minutes watching Virgil silently seethe, and then the goons returned, one with Dolores slung over his shoulder, the other dragging Davey. Both Dolores and Davey were unconscious.

As Bayley asked, "What happened to them?" Virgil pointed at us and said, "Stay put," dumped his cigar in the ashtray, and stalked over to the bodyguards.

Magic buzzed through the room as Virgil checked first Davey then Dolores. "Fool," he muttered. He glared at the bodyguards and said, "Take 'em to the doc. I'll deal with them later."

As the bodyguards exited, Virgil rounded his desk again. But instead of sitting, this time he placed both hands on his desk and leaned toward us. "Looks like you were right about Dolores."

"I don't get it," I said. "What happened?"

"That," said Virgil, his posture radiating menace, "is what happens when you touch things that don't belong to you."

Unfazed by Virgil's tough guy routine, Bayley said calmly, "As I said, we had nothing to do with Johnny's death or your missing item. So are we free to go?"

Virgil smiled, but there was no warmth or humor in it. "'Fraid not." He shrugged. "You have the misfortune to be in the wrong place at the wrong time."

The henchmen reappeared.

"Put 'em in the garden," Virgil said, gesturing at us.

One of the goons blanched, and the other one flinched, but they both stepped forward, yanking us out of our chairs.

Bayley said, "I take it we're not going to enjoy your collection of heirloom roses?"

Virgil's predatory smile returned. "You think you're real cute, don't ya?"

Bayley shrugged. "I have my moments."

I wanted to warn Bayley not to poke the snake, but it was too late, and we were being shoved back out into the hallway.

Behind me, Bayley said, "We're going, we're going. No need to get rough."

The guys manhandled us down the hallway to the end, where they magicked the wall, and another door opened. Shoving us both through, they slammed the door behind us with an echoing thud.

Chapter Sixty-Five

Bayley let out a low whistle. I couldn't even manage that. I just stopped short and started gaping.

An enormous interior garden sprawled before us. I'd seen pictures of the conservatory in the New York City Botanical Gardens, and this place was big enough to give it a run for its money. But unlike New York's glass-walled confection, this garden's walls were boxed in by the concrete walls of several buildings that rose all around us, stories high.

I turned, and the door we'd entered through had disappeared. There wasn't even a wall there. Just a jungle of thick, leafy vines.

Turning back to face the garden, I couldn't see any doors anywhere. But above our heads, the walls all sported rows of dark windows that glowered down at us.

Despite the unease that the windows stirred in me, I couldn't help but feel a sense of wonder. Stretching out before us, lush and vibrant, the garden was so big that it boasted trees as well as plants. Looking up, I realized the garden had plenty of room for the trees to grow. The glass roof was hundreds of feet up.

A sigh escaped me, and I said, "So, what fresh hell do you think this is? I mean the garden's stunning and all, but did you see the look on Thug One and Two's faces when Virgil mentioned this place?"

"I did." Bayley turned to me, wrapping me in a hug. "I could feel how horrified you were when we found Johnny dead." Anger and sadness warred on Bayley's face only to be supplanted by grim resignation. "I knew this would be hard. If it wasn't, then everyone would get a promotion." He rubbed a hand across his face. "But this is…"

"Nuts?"

"Extreme."

I shuddered. "I guess I didn't realize they would take it this far, where they'd actually start killing people. I mean, I get this is a virtual reality, but still." I lowered my voice further and said, "Do you think they mean to kill us?"

Bayley squeezed me tighter. "We're not going to let that happen."

Determination poured through me and I said, "No we're not." But left unsaid was the thought that neither of us would put it past them to try.

Bayley stepped back from me and said, "Let's see what we're dealing with." He hesitated then added, "I'd suggest we be leery of who might be watching from those windows, but we know we're constantly under observation anyway, so what's the point?"

I nodded. "I had the same thought."

With a tug, he sent our combined magics flooding through the room. After a moment, he asked, "Do you feel that?" We both turned to the right-side wall. "There's some kind of structure over there."

"If we're going to hike all the way over there, we need another costume change," I said, picking up my foot and pointing to my shoe.

Magic tingled over me, and I looked own to see that I was wearing a safari adventurer outfit, complete with tan shirt and pants as well as hiking boots. Bayley was decked in the same.

I grinned. "Dr. Livingstone, I presume?"

Bayley laughed and said, "Come along, Stanley."

As we picked our way through the garden and headed in the direction of the structure, I couldn't help but reach out and touch the plants. They brimmed with energy, healthy and happy in their current home.

I touched the trunks of several of the trees and got the same response.

I told Bayley, "The plants are thriving. I was particularly worried about the trees, but they all seem content. Really well nourished."

The garden was so big that it took us a while to get to the wall. Finally, we rounded a set of shrubs and found ourselves facing a large garden shed.

Bayley and I looked at each other and then approached.

"Hello?" Bayley called out.

Nobody responded to us.

Peering around the area, Bayley said, "Looks like there's a clearing behind," and I followed him as we circled around the shed.

Two chest-high mounds of dirt in open wooden corrals greeted us.

"Compost," I said after a moment. "No wonder the plants look so health—what is that?"

The pile to our right had something white sticking out.

Bayley started brushing away the dirt, and my throat closed up in horror.

Bayley had uncovered the edge of an embroidered handkerchief. The same one I'd last seen in Millie's twisting hands.

"Oh no. Oh no no no," I said.

Rushing forward, I swiped away some more dirt and revealed a pale hand that was clutching the other end of the hanky. I felt for a pulse. Of course there wasn't one.

"I think I'm going to be sick," I said stumbling away.

Bayley looked stunned.

Fighting back nausea, I paced as I babbled, "I...I thought I saw her. When I first got to The End of the Line. I thought my eyes were playing tricks on me, but she must have stayed to do some investigating on her own and finagled her way into the club. Should I have gone after her? Is it my fault she's gone because I didn't trust my eyes?"

Bayley grasped my shoulders, causing me to stop pacing and to look at him. "Finn, in no way is this your fault. You didn't do this."

I could feel the reassurance pouring off of him, but guilt still dragged at me. In a small voice, I said, "Why couldn't she have trusted us?"

Bayley put his arms around me, and I realized I was shaking.

"I know it's not real," I said, sounding sick even to my own ears, "but is this really necessary? What is this supposed to prove?" In an officious voice loaded with sarcasm, I said, "'Oh, he's fine with dead bodies—we should definitely promote him! Har, har, har.'" I swept an arm toward Millie as I continued in my normal voice, "How can this senseless death possibly be helpful?"

Pulling away from Bayley, I stomped around some more then growled, "If they say something like 'Oops, client is dead, you fail,' I swear I will not be responsible for my actions."

Bayley was quiet a long moment then said, "If helping the client was the main goal, the simulation would have ended. We're still here, so I can't help but think there's more to come."

I shook my head. "So, what? Is this supposed to be a 'you're next' kind of warning? 'Cuz if it is, it sucks."

Bayley looked pale as he said, "If I had to guess, what we're facing here is a test of 'if there are casualties, can we go on?' Amon did say there were dangers."

I didn't have any response to that other than calling Amon a bunch of really colorful names, so I just huffed.

A noise made me turn my head. Soft, like a tiny cry.

Leave it to me to notice if there was even the slightest possibility there was a fuzzy beast in distress in a ten-mile radius. All the dismay I felt over Millie changed into anger. If the Thwats were hurting animals as well as humans, I swore I'd find a way to dump a horde of desert fire ants down each of their pants.

I heard the soft noise again, pulling me out of my revenge fantasy. "Did you hear that?"

"No," said Bayley looking around.

Closing my eyes and standing very still, I listened. I was just about to give up, when I heard it again. My eyes flew open, and I stared in the direction the sound had come from.

"Still no?" I asked Bayley.

"No," he said looking confused.

I started off in the direction of the sound, and Bayley

followed along after me, a concerned look on his face. As we made our way along a path leading deeper into the garden, I flowed my magic to him.

The sound came again, and this time, Bayley jerked.

"You heard it now?" I said. When he nodded, I asked, "Any idea what it is?"

He shook his head.

Frowning, I said, "We've both had more than our fair share of mind games recently, so let's be cautious."

This time the sound was much closer. If anything, it seemed to be moving toward us as we were moving toward it.

As we neared a bend in the path, I thought I saw the air waver a little, like there was a heat mirage dissipating, but when we came around the corner the air was normal. And there sitting on a rock was a—

"Uh, are you seeing this or is my brain having some kind of render error?"

Chapter Sixty-Six

"I'm seeing it," said Bayley.

We both looked down at the tiny gnome standing there waving at us. He looked like a very small ceramic garden gnome had come to life. He had white hair and a matching long white beard, a blue tunic belted at the waist, blue pants, black boots, and a pointy red cap topping the whole ensemble off.

Waving back at the gnome as I studied him, I muttered to Bayley, "Do we think the Thwats saw some garden gnomes in my memory and didn't realize they were imaginary creatures? If so, I'm gonna have to try real hard not to think about the Stay Puft Marshmallow Man."

"I can hear you," the gnome said in a surprisingly deep, gravelly voice. "And I assure you that I am real."

I was still shaken up by finding Millie, and now there was a talking gnome. At that point, I wouldn't have been surprised if a smoking caterpillar or a Cheshire cat showed up.

Bayley must've felt my fraying nerves through the bond because he gently placed his hand on my arm, grounding me, while to the gnome he said, "Apologies. We mean no offense."

I added, "I've, uh, never seen an actual gnome before, well not a real live one, if you catch my drift."

"I do not. But I rather think the explanation is going to give me a headache, and I really don't have time for that right now. I got dumped in this stupid place—without my consent, I might add—and now I can't get out. The characters in this place keep trying to catch me, but I keep getting away."

"Trying to catch you?" I said.

Bayley was ahead of me because he said, "You're what they were making the deal about."

The gnome said, "Yeah. They seem to think I'm a genie or some nonsense, and they keep trying to catch me so they can rub me for some good luck."

The "ew" popped out of my mouth before I could stop it.

"You're not kidding. So look you two, would you be willing to offer me assistance? I really need to get out of here, and so do you." He sighed and added, "I'm not going to sugarcoat it. They want me bad. If you want to leave me here, I completely understand. Having me with you is going to paint an even bigger target on your back than you already have. But you understand, I have to ask."

Bayley said, "Would you give us a moment?" The gnome nodded, and Bayley tugged me a short distance away.

"Do you feel that?" he whispered.

I nodded. "He feels...different than the rest of this place."

"His energy is different."

"Do you want to ditch him?"

Bayley slowly shook his head. "No. His energy isn't bad...it's just...not the same. I think if he's in our path, there's probably a reason. Let's go with it, but keep your eyes open."

I nodded, and we went back to where the gnome was glancing nervously around while he waited for us. Bayley said, "We haven't quite figured out how we're getting out of here ourselves, but if you want to take a chance with us, we'd be happy to help. I'm Bayley, and this is Finn."

"I'm Pierre." Touching his hand to his red cap, the gnome said, "Pleased to meet you."

As I smiled at Pierre, I took stock of the situation. Why would the Thwats put a gnome in our path? Were they testing Bayley's level of compassion? I'd think that his agreeing to help Millie would have proved that he was willing and capable of helping others.

A soft growling sound rolled through the garden, followed by a low bark that had the hairs on the back of my neck standing up.

"What was that?" I asked looking around wildly.

"Those," said Pierre, "are the tracking spells."

"Spells make noise?"

"They do when they have physical form," said Bayley, searching the garden. "There." He pointed to where some plants were swaying in the distance. "Whatever it is, it's over there."

I turned in a circle then stopped. "And there," I said pointing in the opposite direction.

Bayley nodded. "They're coming at us from both sides. Smart tactic."

I looked askance at him.

"What? It is. I can admire their skill and still not approve of their methods." Bayley looked down at Pierre. "Any suggestions?"

"Yeah. Let's leave."

Bayley snickered. "I'm fine with that suggestion, but something a little more concrete would be helpful. Do you happen to know where the exits are?"

Pierre sighed. "There aren't any that I've found."

"That doesn't sound good," I said, watching the swaying grass. "Well, one good thing is that they seem to be taking their time."

Pierre said, "Sure. What fun is it if you don't play with your food a bit first?"

Bayley and I gave him a look. He shrugged.

Bayley asked, "You've been successfully avoiding them. How about you help us do the same."

Pierre was shaking his head before Bayley even finished. "Won't work. The only reason I've been getting away with this so far is because I'm so small."

Bayley looked at me, calculating.

"What?" I asked a little nervously.

"I'd like to try something."

"Okaaaaay."

Bayley walked over to me and hugged me. When I hugged him back, he said, "Close your eyes."

Sighing, I forced myself to relax, closing my eyes as instructed.

As Bayley's took a sharp breath, his magic surged, combined with mine, and everything squeezed.

The magic dissipated. Panting, I cautiously opened my eyes,

and then promptly closed them again.

"What did you do?" I squeaked.

I could hear Bayley's grin as he said, "Aw c'mon Finn. Don't you want to let your inner Lilliputian out?"

I opened my eyes again, but the sudden change in aspect ratio made my brain melt. Staring up at the towering plants seemed to be too much overload for my brain. Shutting my eyes again and clutching at Bayley to maintain my balance, I said, "A little warning next time might help. My brain feels like it's a bunch of bread dough that's been roughly pummeled then stuffed back in the bowl to think about what it's done for a while."

"It's transformation magic, but I wasn't sure if I could swing more than just your clothes. Thanks for the power boost," Bayley said, stepping back, but keeping his hands on my shoulders.

My eyes popped open. "What if it only worked on my clothes?" I said indignantly.

Bayley chuckled, holding up his hands in surrender. "I wouldn't peek. I'm a gentleman."

Apparently being aggravated was helping my brain to cope because I was able to keep my eyes open this time without the world warbling around me.

Seeing that I was fine now, Bayley dropped his hands and turned to Pierre. "Now can you help us hide? Or at least buy us some time to figure a way out of here?"

"Sure," said Pierre sounding tired. "Follow me."

"What's the plan?" asked Bayley.

"We need to dodge this first pass of trackers."

I said, "*First* pass? As in there's going to be more?"

Pierre shot me a look over his shoulder. "You should always be prepared for more, Finn."

Chapter Sixty-Seven

Something growled, closer this time, and something on the other side of us answered.

"In here," said Pierre, pushing aside a huge leaf, and scooting under the rock we'd found him initially standing on.

We dove in after him, right as another round of growls rang out.

"Oof," Pierre said as we crammed in together. The area under the rock was plenty big for just him, but all three of us made it a tight fit. Pierre tugged the leaf back over the entrance, casting our cave in a green light.

Thudding footfalls hit the ground outside, and we could hear snorting and pawing.

I held very still, my heart pounding so loud that I was worried it would echo in the rocky space. After a few agonizing minutes, the thudding steps moved on.

We waited a few more minutes in frozen silence before Pierre relaxed and said, "They're out of range for now."

I could hear them growling, heading back in the direction that Bayley and I had come from.

We all crawled out of the hole and looked around.

I said, "Now what?"

Bayley said, "I've had enough of this place. Let's get out of here."

Pierre was staring up and to the right. Bayley and I turned to follow his gaze. Pointing to the closest wall, Pierre said, "I want to go over there."

Bayley assessed the wall, then gave a slow nod.

"As long as we avoid the compost pile, fine by me too," I said.

Bayley returned us to normal size. With Pierre's permission, Bayley scooped him up, and we double-timed it to the wall, staying well clear of the shed area.

Bayley set Pierre down in front of the wall, and Pierre looked up and stroked his beard as he asked, "What do you make of this?"

"The wall or the windows?" I asked.

"Both."

Bayley reached out and touched the wall, immediately jerking his hand back.

"Are you okay?" I asked.

"Do me a favor?" he said. "Touch the wall and tell me what you feel."

Tentatively, I stuck my finger out and touched the wall. When nothing happened, I put my whole palm against it. Turning to Bayley, I said, "Um, it feels like a bumpy, concrete wall?"

He looked down at Pierre. "And you?"

Pierre shook his head. "I am not touching that."

Bayley narrowed his eyes. "Do you know what that is?"

Pierre responded, "Do you?"

Bayley's jaw clenched as he reached for the wall again. His shoulders locked up the second his hand hit the surface, but he kept his hand where it was and closed his eyes.

"It's reacting to my magic," he muttered. Sweat beaded on his brow, but he held his stance, never breaking contact with the wall. After a minute, his eyes popped open, and Bayley dropped his hand from the wall, shaking it out. Wiping his face on his sleeve, he muttered, "That's one good thing about being a house. You don't sweat."

"Bayley are you okay?" I asked.

He looked up and said, "I know what we're doing now."

"What happened?"

"I interfaced with the," he gestured to the walls around us.

"The Not A House?"

He grinned. "Yes, that'll do. The, uh, Not A House is a fully interconnected set of all the buildings in this reality. I'm not sure if it was a side effect of the way this dimension was built, or if it was intended to be set up that way as some sort of test for me."

"Well either way, you not only managed to find it, you also managed to communicate with it, so go you," I said.

Turning to me he said, "It's quite dissimilar to me, but it was aware enough for me to interface with. By connecting with the Not A House, I was able to flow my magic through all the walls connecting the buildings in this realm, including the ceilings and floors."

"Whoa." No wonder he'd been sweating up a storm. "Are you sure you're okay?"

"I've been steadily using the stockpiled energy cookies, so I'm good," he said.

A pang of worry darted through me as I wondered if that huge stockpile I'd seen was really all that huge after all, and if it would be enough to last.

Bayley interrupted my thoughts. "Bottom line, I got the floor plan for this entire simulation we're in. I know what the layout is. And I think the final challenge is to exit the simulation successfully." He looked up again then pointed. "We need to go up there."

"To the windows? Why?"

"This," Bayley gestured at the walls, "it's like a super-array. If I'm right," and he sounded like he was pretty sure he was, "the windows are the gates, portals, whatever you want to call them, to other places. And the walls, the walls are like superconductors, funneling magic that fuels the windows. I don't know where all those windows go, but I know they go...elsewhere—outside of this simulation."

Pierre said, "As I suspected."

Mind racing, I looked up at the windows. "The nearest row of windows is way up there. And you're thinking—"

Pierre interrupted, pointing as he said, "We need to go look at that one."

We both stared at him.

"Why that one?" I asked.

"It's the right one."

Bayley said, "Are you certain?"

"I am."

I was going to ask questions, but then we heard voices at the other end of the garden.

"...better get them or else," growled Virgil.

I said quietly, "Not to be Captain Obvious, but we've got company." I looked at Bayley, who was staring at the windows, face pinched in worry.

"Bayley, what's wrong?"

Concern crinkled his eyes. "I can't even begin to describe the amount of magic needed to fuel one array like that," he gestured to our wall and its windows. "There are *four* here. Even if we get up to the windows, actually manipulating the magic fueling the windows is going to be..." he shook his head.

"A ridiculous challenge? Almost impossibly hard?" I said.

Bayley rubbed his forehead and said, "Yes. And according to the layout I got from the Not A House, it's our only option. If we keep going from room to room long enough, we'll wind up like Millie and Johnny."

"Not my first choice," I admitted. "Plus, the fact that it's so difficult to get out of the windows just confirms that it's the right way to go. Stupid Thwats."

"Agreed," said Bayley. "Window it is."

Pierre said, "Good choice." He took his cap off and twisted it in his hands as he said, "I would be grateful if you would take me with you when you try."

Bayley nodded, so I said, "Of course. It's not like we're going to abandon you to face the goon squad by yourself."

Speaking of which, Virgil and friends were making no attempts to hide themselves. Their voices were getting louder by the second.

Bayley looked around us and said, "Time to go. Finn, let's use the plants. We can use your magic for the growing, and my magic for the shaping." He nodded once. "Yes, I think that's the way to do it."

I smiled and said, "You're the boss. Tell me how I can help."

Pierre cleared his throat. "I can kick in a little extra oomph if needed." When I raised my eyebrows, he said, "I may look small, but I pack a wallop."

"Okay then."

"We thank you for any help you're able to provide," Bayley said formally. Reaching for my hand he said, "Ready?"

"You bet."

Bayley directed our magic to the grass under our feet. I felt my Foster magic helping the grass to grow rapidly while Bayley's magic knitted the grasses together. Within moments, we stood on a small but thick grass mat roughly rectangular in shape.

At the same time, the rose bushes next to us sent canes shooting along the ground.

"Really Bayley? Roses?" I grumbled.

He smiled and kept working.

The thorny rose branches wove together, both across and then up, forming a makeshift scaffolding under the mat. As they grew, they lifted us further and further off the ground.

Pierre sent a burst of magic into the structure, and the branches grew so fast that we shot into the air.

In less than a minute, we'd reached a height even with the first row of windows, and Bayley stopped growing our platform.

Unfortunately, being so high up in the air put us in the clear sights of our company.

"You'll come down from there and hand over the gnome right now if you know what's good for you," yelled Virgil.

I looked down to see Virgil, Dolores, and a group of henchmen approaching our scaffolding.

I groaned. "Dolores too? Really? She must have done some fancy talking to keep Virgil from adding her to the compost bin."

"Could be worse," offered Pierre.

One of Virgil's henchmen fired a gun at us.

Glaring at Pierre, I said, "You had to say it didn't you."

"Don't shoot at them, you idiot. You might hit the gnome!" Virgil hollered.

Peering over the side of our platform, Pierre said, "Good choice using the roses. Those thorns look wicked. That'll slow them down."

I looked over the side and saw that a thicket of extra long, extra pointy thorns had popped out of all the rose canes. Visions of the henchmen getting stuck with the thorns danced in my head.

I looked at Bayley who was giving me an "I told you so" smile. I couldn't help smiling back. "Okay, the roses were definitely the way to go."

Apparently, Virgil and Dolores did not agree. Virgil's glare was so hot that I half-expected our scaffolding to burst into flames.

The bad guys formed a huddle a short way from us, and after some gesturing from Virgil, the henchmen split up, heading into different sections of the garden.

"Oh that can't be good," I said.

Pierre said, "Bayley, boost me up to the windowsill please."

Bayley did as Pierre asked, placing Pierre on the window ledge, as Virgil shouted, "Last chance."

As Bayley and I turned to look at Virgil, Pierre said, "I can't let them catch me," from behind us.

Then everything happened at once.

Magic and light flared from behind us, causing me and Bayley to turn just as Pierre cracked open the bottom of the window a couple of inches. He called over his shoulder as he squeezed through, "This is my exit, not yours. Thank you for the help. I won't forget it." The second he was through, the window slammed shut behind him.

Virgil and Dolores could see him leaving and yelled, "No!" then started shooting at us.

The henchmen, who were mid-shimmy up the trunks of various trees, paused where they were and also opened fire.

While Bayley and I dove for the mat, we both hauled on our magics, weaving together a wall of rose branches to hide behind.

I lay on the grass mat panting. "Hah! And they thought limiting our communications would hobble us. The Thwats can suck it."

"Finn, you're bleeding!"

I looked down to see that my arm was, indeed, bleeding. It didn't hurt until I noticed it. "I must've gotten clipped. It's not bad."

I felt a tingle and looked down to find a bandage covering my arm.

"Thanks. See? All better." Taking in Bayley's drawn face, I patted his arm and said, "It's not bad, honest. Just a scratch." I looked behind me at the closed window. "What do you want to talk about first? Virgil and Dolores, or Pierre?"

"Pierre's gone. Let's deal with these two." Anger darkened Bayley's face. "We need to get rid of them so we can concentrate on getting out of here."

"Nothing like getting rid of a case of VD," I said. At Bayley's look, I shrugged and said, "Gotta find the humor where we can."

Shaking his head, Bayley sent our combined magics to scan our surroundings.

Our tower shook, and smoke started to rise. Peeping between the rose branches, I flinched back as I saw Dolores lob a fireball at us, while at the same time Virgil launched green goo in our direction. The tower shook again. When I looked over the side, it turned out that the green stuff was some kind of acid, so now our tower was being both eaten away and flambéed.

"Bayley, any thoughts?"

"Yes."

Bayley stared up at the glass roof overhead. Snagging some of my Murphy magic and braiding it with his own, Bayley aimed it upward. I thought he was arrowing for the roof itself, but instead he stopped just shy of it, pouring the magic along some pipes there. With a series of loud cracks, they broke open, and then Bayley wrenched hard, and they spewed water in huge torrents into the garden below.

Dolores shrieked, and Virgil swore. Judging by the yelps and thuds, at least a few of the henchmen got washed out of their trees.

Bayley pulled more, and the water cascaded down even harder. "Finn, wash them toward that end of the room," Bayley said, pointing, and then he slammed his hand against the wall. A loud rumbling began, and I peeped between the rose branches to see a big crack opening in the wall that Bayley had pointed to.

Summoning my Murphy magic, I shoved the curtains of falling water, forming waves that slapped into Virgil, Dolores, and the henchmen. Their shouts cut off abruptly as the waves submerged them, dragging them toward the crack in the wall.

When the last of the henchmen were through, I yelled over the sound of the rushing water, "Done!" and Bayley closed the gap in the wall.

"They can just come back in—"

"Not done yet," gritted out Bayley. With a series of loud clicking sounds, the walls around us shook, then went silent.

"You can let go," said Bayley, sounding slightly out of breath. As he released his hold on my Murphy magic, so did I.

Panting, we both lay on the grass mat. As Bayley and I collected ourselves, the water leaking from the pipes slowed from a torrent to a trickle, forming a gentle rain.

"I convinced the Not A House to recode the walls to prevent anyone from entering. At least temporarily. It'll buy us some time to deal with the windows." He eyed me. "Load up on as many cookies as you can, and I'll do the same. We're going to make a final push at this."

Chapter Sixty-Eight

Bayley and I restocked our energy to full, then we both sat up.

Bayley turned to me, held my hands, and said, "Finn, this is going to be a huge drain. By the time we're done, I suspect we'll have used all our energy reserves and may have to start tapping into our personal energy wells. I want to be really sure that you are okay with that."

I asked gently, "Are you?"

Hope and trepidation warred in his eyes as he said, "This is the way I prove myself. I know it."

"I'm all in if you are. And you've totally got this."

Helping me to my feet, Bayley stepped up to the window.

"I know what Pierre said, but we still need to check out his window—it's not like he's been totally trustworthy. If that really isn't our exit, then we'll need to get from window to window until we find ours."

Bayley rested his hand on the windowsill, and then poked his magic under the edge of the window.

I could feel it fighting him. But after an intense battle with him pushing up and the window refusing to budge, the window finally gave and groaned upward a few inches.

We stared at a bright, sunny field. It looked like a nice summer afternoon, except that the two suns were blue, and the grass in the field was purple. Pierre was nowhere in sight.

I said, "Yup. That's definitely not for us."

"Agreed," said Bayley. He stopped pushing, and the window slammed shut. "Plan B then. We need to find our window."

After looking around the room for a few minutes, Bayley said,

"I have a crazy idea."

"My favorite kind."

At Bayley's request, my Smith magic rose to meet his. At first, I thought he was flooding the room with it, but then I realized he was pouring it out in a defined band.

"Finn, can you see what I'm doing?"

I nodded. "You heated a section in the middle of the air."

"Good," said Bayley, "I want you to hold it in place."

Just a few months ago, I wouldn't have had the control for this. But that was then. Closing my eyes, I felt for the band of Smith magic heating the air. It took me a few tries to figure out how to grab control without separating my magic from Bayley's, but then I latched onto my Smith magic and told it, "Stay." And it did.

As I held it in place, I felt Bayley call on the Smith magic again and direct it down to the garden and then he…pulled.

Usually, I used my Smith magic to output heat. Bayley was using it to pull the heat from below and funnel it into the warm layer I was holding in place.

The garden temperature plummeted while the area up in the air around us stayed warm.

"I'm setting this to keep running," said Bayley.

"Like a robot vacuum cleaner, but instead of sucking up dirt, it's sucking up heat."

"And it's sucking up our energy, so just be aware that it's running in the background, feeding heat to the layer you're holding onto, until we dismiss it."

"Got it."

Next, Bayley called to my Guthrie magic and sent wind eddying around us, stirring the layer of warm air that I was holding over the cool room below.

As I felt the wind blow something damp against my cheek, Bayley said quietly, "Open your eyes."

The world had been transformed into a magical fairyland. Dense fog blurred the edges of the walls around us.

"This is so cool," I said.

Bayley grinned.

As I continued to hold the warm air in place, Bayley used my Guthrie magic to herd some of the fog, compressing and shaping it into a rough square. Then he wove his magic and the air magic together, under and through the fog, but I wasn't sure what he was doing.

"Time to go," he said.

"Go? Go where?" I asked, attention half on holding the Smith magic in place.

He gestured to the fog square before stepping onto it himself. When he didn't fall through, I just kind of gaped at him.

Holding out his hand to me, eyes twinkling, he said, "Think of it as a flying carpet."

I'd have to be nuts to turn down a magic carpet ride.

With a deep breath, I grabbed Bayley's hand and stepped onto the fog cloud.

It was a lot more solid than I expected, and my feet tingled a little from all the magic running back and forth beneath them.

"Well, this is amazing."

"Watch this," said Bayley. A surge of magic brought a gust of wind, and we started moving.

I nearly lost my balance and my grip on the Smith magic, but I managed to hold onto both. With a breathless laugh, I said, "Definite flying carpet vibes. Way to go Bayley!"

Sweat beaded on his forehead as Bayley concentrated on holding all the magics. I only had to hold onto the Smith magic so far, and I could feel the strain. Bayley was channeling his magic and mine in multiple ways. No wonder he was getting tired.

Concern squirmed through me. "We don't need the rose branch scaffolding anymore right? Can we let that go?"

Nodding, Bayley released my Foster magic, and both our shoulders slumped a little in relief. I did a quick energy check and drew in a quick breath in alarm. Bayley had warned me, but my energy level was dropping rapidly. Bayley was doing the bulk of the magical mojo, but he was still using me as a base.

"Annnnd next," he said, as he manipulated the wind and pushed our flying carpet cloud along the wall.

As the cloud moved, I realized why I was holding the Smith magic in place. We were keeping enough warm air moving over the cool air that we could maintain the fog without it dissipating. With our flying fog carpet, we now had the mobility we needed to move from window to window. Using the wind to steer us, we could go back and forth and even up and down

I looked at Bayley. "Wow Bayley, this is really clever."

He gave me a shy smile in return, and his shoulders straightened with pride.

Then, we both turned to study the windows.

Chapter Sixty-Nine

As Bayley and I hovered on the fog carpet, scrutinizing the windows, it felt a lot like they were inspecting us right back. In fact, the weight of their stares felt like a physical pressure, like the way a storm feels before it lets loose.

I had the urge to whisper when I asked, "What are you thinking?"

Bayley sighed. "This one is on me. I can't explain to you how I know this, but I need to do this alone."

I nodded, chewing my lip. "I have a feeling this is going to take a lot out of you. Why don't I take a whack at controlling the wind?"

Bayley gave me an uncertain look. "You're already maintaining the Smith—"

"And you're keeping our magic carpet cloud together," I said. "I can manage multiple magics too—you know I can."

What we both left unsaid was that the more magics we wielded, the faster we'd burn through our energy reserves.

Bayley bowed his head and said, "Thank you, Finn. I'm grateful for your help as always."

Calling my Guthrie magic, I directed it to blow the wind steadily under and beside our cloud. At first, I pushed too hard with the side wind, and we whomped into the wall.

"Sorry," I said, teeth gritted. "One moment." Closing my eyes, I got my nerves and my focus under control, easing back on the wind until I got the flow just right.

Bayley touched my arm. "You've got it," and he let his grip on the wind go.

Slowly, I opened my eyes. My brain felt like it was in overdrive. One part of my attention was maintaining the Smith magic while another part managed the crosswinds that kept us afloat. A third part of my brain was monitoring what happened in front of me as Bayley faced off with the windows.

After I steadied us under the next window in the wall, Bayley reached out one finger and gingerly traced the edge where the windowpane met the sill.

Magic crackled in the air like static electricity, sparking around us and making the hair on the back of my neck stick up.

The window jerked up a couple of inches.

"Uh," I said. "Not it."

Looking at the four moons and red sky, Bayley said, "Definitely not," and slammed the window closed. He looked at me, "Next please."

"Up or across?" I asked.

"Across."

I gusted the wind, and we slipped over to the next window to our left.

Either this one was easier to open, or Bayley had a better idea how to do it now. Bayley's magic surged, and the window slipped up halfway.

This window showed mountains silhouetted against a starry night sky. "That's the Milky Way," I said.

"Closer to home," Bayley said. Then he added almost to himself, "It feels wrong. It was easier to open, but it...it feels wrong. I don't think that's where we're supposed to be headed."

He shut the window, and we proceeded down the row.

When we'd reached the fifth window, Bayley said, "This is taking too long." He stared at the wall lost in thought.

"Can I help?" I asked.

Distractedly, as though he were talking more to himself than to me, Bayley said, "Did you notice the difference in the windows? It's subtle. But now that I know what to look for, I can see it coming. Hmm...I wonder."

Bayley put both hands against the wall next to the window. Leaning his weight on his hands, Bayley closed his eyes. After a moment, Bayley's magic began moving from one window to the next, touching the window, then moving on.

I got vague flashes of each window's character as the wave of Bayley's magic sampled it. Now I could see what Bayley had meant. Through his magic, I could feel that each window was slightly different.

When Bayley's magic had touched every window on the wall, he pulled back and said, "It's not here."

"Our exit? How can you tell?"

He shook his head in frustration. "I don't know. It's just not."

"No worries," I said, though my head was starting to ache and lots of me felt very worried. "Next wall?"

"Next wall," Bayley said grimly, gesturing to the wall perpendicular to ours.

It was actually a bit of a relief to move the cloud for several seconds rather than holding it still. I was able to let the wind flow more freely, which was what it liked best.

Both my Guthrie magic and I were slightly refreshed by the time we drifted to a stop in front of the first window in the next wall.

Bayley didn't even bother trying to open this one. He went straight to flowing his magic from one window to the other. He finished much more quickly this time, raising his head after only a few minutes to say, "Next wall."

I'd barely stopped the cloud before Bayley was reaching out to the wall. A few moments later, he raised his head and looked up. "This is very odd. I'm getting hits from two of the windows."

Bayley pointed to a pair of windows above us and down the wall a bit.

Going where Bayley directed me, I moved the cloud up and over to float between a pair of windows that looked just like all the others.

Bayley's magic surged, and he tried to yank the first window up a couple of inches.

It wouldn't go.

When he tried the second window, the same thing happened.

Panting, Bayley said, "I'm not sure if it's that we're both really low on energy, or if the Thwats designed this last bit to need us both. But I think we have to do this together."

Quickly, Bayley used our magics to sprout a huge mushroom, and we climbed off the cloud carpet onto it.

With a relieved exhale, I let go of the Smith and Guthrie magics, while Bayley let the flying fog carpet dissipate.

He faced the windows, held my hand, and said, "Follow my lead."

Bayley unleashed his magic, and I unfurled mine to join with it. Directing the magic toward the first window, we both yanked at the window with our combined strength.

It felt so stuck that it was like it had been painted shut. But finally, with a loud crack, it shot up a couple of inches, knocking us back slightly.

We found ourselves looking at the desertscape and the Thwats. I stared at them and had the definite sense that they were staring right back.

"So that's the exit back to the Thwats," murmured Bayley.

We let the window slide shut again and pried open the second window.

The kitchen at Bayley House blinked into view. My brain stuttered as I found myself looking at me.

I was slumped in the fetal position on the floor. I was pretty sure I was still alive because I was currently alive in this virtual space. Also, there was a giant puddle of drool forming under my mouth.

Fuzzy stood over me, front paws on one side of my torso, back paws on the other, my body sheltered under his belly. His fur was puffed out and his tail would have made an excellent feather duster, three times its usual size and swiping back and forth viciously. Ears pinned back, teeth bared, he looked like he was growling.

I couldn't say I blamed him when I swiveled my gaze up to see what he was defending my body from.

Ailith stood nearby. She seemed to be arguing with Fuzzy. Whatever she was saying, he was not having it.

My throat had gone dry, but after a couple of tries I squeaked out, "You're seeing this?"

"Ailith," whispered Bayley.

Surprise had me turning to him, but then of course he knew her. She was his first Housekeeper.

"She's been haunting my dreams," I said.

Bayley's lips thinned into a flat line. "She would know that you would be vulnerable if I tried for a promotion." He opened his mouth to say something when a dark look washed across his face.

I turned back to the window to see what he was looking at and said, "Oh crap. Not Zav too. How did he even get in the house?"

"You've been dealing with Zav? And Ailith?" He shifted his gaze to me, "Why didn't you tell me?"

Gesturing wildly with my hands, I said, "I didn't want to distract you. Plus, we've been a little busy! In my defense, I did tell you there was all sorts of stuff happening back at the house, and we'd catch up later." I thumbed toward the arguing pair. "These two idiots are part of the 'stuff.'"

Bayley swiveled back to face the unfolding scene. Now it looked like Zav and Ailith were yelling at each other instead of Fuzzy. Bayley said, "Fuzzy can't hold them off forever. You've got to get back there."

I felt the same sense of urgency, but we hadn't finished what we'd started yet. "I can't leave you. Not till we're done."

"None of this is worth it if you die," said Bayley, his voice gravelly with emotion. He let the window close and turned to face me.

I argued, "You only get one shot at this. So we have to make it count." I huffed and ran a hand through my hair, as I puzzled aloud, "So the Thwats are allowing us to see this. Why?"

Bayley said slowly, "It seems to me they want me to choose."

I nodded.

Bayley looked at me, sorrow in his eyes. "There's no real choice to be made here, Finn. Not for me. You're my Housekeeper, but more than that you're my best friend. Your safety is as important to me as my own. You have to go home." When I opened my mouth to protest, he cut me off with, "Hear me out." When I nodded, he hurriedly explained, "This is a practical decision as much as it is a sentimental one. If you are critically injured or if you," his voice cracked as he said, "die in the real world," he cleared his throat, "who's to say I could even return there? Even if I did manage to reintegrate my consciousness, how much would be intact with no Housekeeper to ground me after this ordeal? No, Finn. This is the way it has to be. You and I must go our separate ways again. I'll come back to you as soon as I can."

The sinking feeling in my gut told me he was right. "This sucks," I said. "I don't want to leave you to face the Thwats alone again."

Bayley hugged me, and I hugged him back, hard. "It'll be alright," he whispered in my hair. "Thanks to you, I've made it through this whole simulation. And, I've got my confidence back. I'll go to the desert, you'll go home, and we will handle whatever happens next."

I nodded and squeezed him tight.

After a moment, Bayley pulled away and said, "Time to go. Ready?"

No. No, I was not ready. I was suddenly terrified I wouldn't see Bayley again. Blinking back tears, I nodded.

We poured everything we had into opening both the windows at once. With a huge surge of magic, we shoved them both all the way open.

I was relieved to see that I was still in the same position, but the relief was short-lived as I saw that Ailith and Zav had split up and now stood on either side of Fuzzy, who had crouched low over me. It looked like they were getting ready to charge him.

"See you soon," Bayley said.

And we both dove through our windows.

Chapter Seventy

Everything went black, and I flailed against the spinning and falling sensations engulfing me.

Then with no warning, I landed on my side with a loud thud. Sucking in a deep breath, I said, "Ow," and pushed up off the floor.

Except it wasn't the wooden floor of Bayley House. Disoriented, it took me several seconds to realize where I was.

I was back in the desertscape, covered once again in my gibber jammies.

My mind scrambled to figure out what had happened. I'd gone through the right window, hadn't I? I knew I had. I was looking right at Fuzzy as I dove through.

The bottom edge of a long coat appeared in my eyeline, through the visor of my gibber jammies. I looked up to find Amon staring down at me. "You look confused," he said.

"Why am I here?" I asked, forcing myself to my feet. I tottered a little unsteadily, the magic drain making itself felt as my head spun and throbbed at me. Looking around, I said, "Where's Bayley? His window should have brought him here." I looked askance at Amon. "What games are you playing now?"

"No games," he said, hands up placatingly.

"Fine, then send me home."

"In due time," he said. "We have some questions first."

"Time is a commodity I don't have to spare, Amon. Thanks to your little buddy Zav, Fuzzy is in real trouble, not to mention what's about to happen to my physical body." I didn't actually know what Ailith and Zav specifically intended, but I had no doubt that it wasn't good. "I need to go home. Now." When he furrowed his brow at me, I groaned and rubbed my eyes. "Oh for the love of villains everywhere. Was this your plan all along? Wait until I was vulnerable and then prove some kind of point?"

If anything, Amon's brows furrowed even further. "I do not understand what you are talking about."

I threw my hands up in the air, which made me teeter again, but now I was too mad to care if I was stumbling around. "Don't play all innocent with me. You waited until I was unconscious to sick Ailith and Zav on me—and Fuzzy! What kind of person sics their bad guys on a poor little kitten?" Okay maybe Fuzzy wasn't so little anymore, or even a kitten, but the concept was the same.

The creosotes had been issuing the occasional swishing rasp, but now the sounds grew loud, crescendoing as though a big wind was whipping the branches into a frenzy. The rocks behind them joined in, rumbling in discontent.

Apparently I wasn't the only one who was pissed off.

"Peace," Amon said raising his hands to the Thwats before turning to me. "Is what you say the truth?"

I crossed my arms. "Oh, so it's not bad enough that you're keeping me here long enough for your henchmen to kill me. Now you're going to call me a liar on top of it? Wow, buddy. You sure know how to treat a lady right."

I knew I should be more respectful, but I just didn't have it in me. As the fatigue dragged at me, my headache was ratcheting up from throbbing to mildly pokey and if I didn't miss my guess, I wasn't a long way off from full-on stabby. I needed to get home while I still had some energy left to deal with Ailith and Zav.

Amon ignored my tantrum and said, "Zav is with you at the house?"

"Yes," I said louder than strictly necessary. I noticed that he didn't seem surprised about Ailith. Had he made some sort of agreement with her?

Amon turned to the Thwats, frowning. "This is...unexpected."

I snorted, "Right." Amon glanced at me over his shoulder. I pointed at him, "Don't look at me like that. Your boy Zav has been causing all sorts of mayhem, and you know it." My voice started to shake with fury, "And I know you're some kind of big advanced being, but it is a bazillion kinds of screwed up that you would let that sicko torture a kid." I looked over Amon's shoulder. "Did you guys know about that? Amon's pet Zav screwing with the mind of child? For funsies? A child! It's taken us months to try to put poor Neil back together, and the trauma of it will likely be with him for the rest of his life. Or were you in on it too?"

Suddenly, the only noise was me panting from anger. Everyone else had gone silent.

The red haze muting my sense of self-preservation disappeared, and as my reasoning skills came back online, the fact that I might just have gone too far was accompanied by the realization that I was too mentally, physically, and emotionally tired to care.

Amon looked at me and said quietly, "I know not of what you speak."

When I looked at him doubtfully, he bowed slightly and said, "I speak the truth."

Turning to the Thwats, he said, "I beg leave of you to investigate this further."

For the next few minutes, soft grumbles and whispers ensued, with Amon glancing over at me from time to time.

I used the time they were chatting to rub at my aching temples and try to figure out what they'd done with Bayley. When I reached through our bond for him, there he was, again at a distance, but still there.

Relief and worry fought for dominance within me.

After what felt like an eternity, but in reality was only a few minutes, Amon turned to me at last and said, "You may go."

He waved me off, and suddenly everything went dark again. I blinked and realized I was back in Bayley's mindspace room, but as soon as I realized that, I was racing back through his mind, through the now empty energy room, whipping down the bond, and bam, I was back in my own brain.

Chapter Seventy-One

I had a moment of confusion as my consciousness and my body greeted each other and reintegrated. The kitchen scents of coffee and old wood registered at the same time that my body started yelling at me about the amount of time it had spent on the floor.

I ignored my body in favor of listening to the sounds demanding my attention. My ears were ringing, sort of buzzing and chiming, but not enough to drown out the sounds of Ailith and Zav arguing, punctuated by the occasional deadly growl from Fuzzy, who was still standing over my body.

I called *Bayley?* in my mind.

No answer.

Although I was back where I should be, Bayley wasn't.

When I peered inward, Bayley was still a dim spot in the corner of my mind. While I was glad he seemed more or less okay, I was not looking forward to dealing with Ailith and Zav on my own.

Worried about what else might have happened in my absence, I pulled up my mental map of the property, and relief poured through me when everything looked as it should. So the only emergency I had to deal with was in the room with me.

Only.

I sighed and tried to move my body.

Zav and Ailith cut off abruptly.

Cracking open my eyes, I blinked until Fuzzy's paw swam into focus a few inches from my face.

Leaning down, Fuzzy nosed my face, making anxious noises.

As I reached a shaking hand to pet Fuzzy, Zav's disgusted, "She's awake," greeted me.

Ignoring him, I croaked, "Hey Fuzzy." I swallowed, then swallowed again, trying to bring some moisture into my parched throat. Apparently I'd drooled it all onto the floor.

Fuzzy shifted to sit beside me, and I pushed myself up slowly into a sitting position in time to see Ailith throw up her hands and stomp a few feet away. But although she looked solid, she mustn't have been totally corporeal, because I couldn't hear her footsteps. Unfortunately, I could hear her start shrieking at Zav, who yelled right back.

Ailith noticed me staring, motioned to Zav, and the two of them scuttled over to the corner, huddling together as they whispered and gestured furiously.

Squinting, I looked at them again. Why were they pink? Looking around the kitchen, I realized that everything had a pink tinge, except for Fuzzy. Had my vision been damaged somehow?

I didn't think standing was a good idea yet, so I stayed seated, using my arms to brace myself.

Fuzzy scooted closer, pressing himself tightly against my side. I took the hint and threw an arm over him, leaning into him. He responded with a small trill of affection.

Burying my face against his fur for a moment, I had the strong urge to sit there and count Fuzzy's stripes until I felt better.

Zav stalked closer to us, snaring my attention. However, he was looking at Ailith, not me, and when he stepped too close, I heard a crackle. Zav hissed and jumped away, throwing an "I'm going to kill you" snarl at me and Fuzzy before returning to his whisper party with Ailith.

The crackle clued me in.

Looking above me, I realized I was sitting under a pink dome.

"Fuzzy," I said, barely making any sound. "Am I seeing things, or is there a big pink protection bubble around us?"

Fuzzy nodded.

"Did you do this?"

Fuzzy nosed my chest. To my surprise, under my clothes my necklace was in its usual place.

Leaning into Fuzzy's fur, I whispered, "Did you fetch Percy?"
Fuzzy nodded.

Once before, Fuzzy had used Percy to help when I was unconscious, so he must have done the same this time.

"Percy," I said quietly, barely moving my lips. "Did you make the pink protection bubble?"

So softly I could barely hear him, he said, "I had help." Before I could ask him to clarify, he added, "Your pocket. Fuzzy's tail."

My ears weren't ringing after all. The steady chiming I was hearing was coming from Stella in my pocket.

Blinking a few times, I tried to get my brain in gear. I'd totally forgotten I had Stella with me. When I reached into my pocket, Stella pulsed against my hand. I had the sense it was pleased to see me.

Trying to be subtle, I looked at Fuzzy's tail, only to have the Samaras stare back at me. They were spaced along his tail, blending into the lighter gray stripes in his fur, and they were vibrating their wings to form a buzzing sound that harmonized with Stella's chime.

I could feel the energy from the buzzing and chiming and realized they were both feeding into the dome, which was also lightly humming.

What had Zav and Ailith done while I'd been waylaid in Thwatland that had caused the need for this makeshift extra protection?

I knew I should be paying attention to whatever Ailith and Zav were whispering about in their mean girl huddle, but I was so happy that Fuzzy seemed okay and that I was home that it was hard to focus on what they were plotting.

With a sigh, I picked my head up and looked at the evil divas. I had to wave my hand to get their attention.

"How about you two take this," I waved vaguely at them, "whatever it is, outside?" They both stared at me. I wasn't sure if the looks were because I was so exhausted I sounded a little drunk or because I probably looked like hell. Or maybe whatever they'd expected me to say, that wasn't it. I get that a lot.

"Speaking of outside, how'd you get inside the house, Zav?"

For a second, I thought my slurred words were too garbled for them to understand because neither responded.

A shift in Ailith's eyes gave me the answer. I groaned. "You let him in, didn't you." Making an effort to speak clearly, I said slowly, as my brain worked it through, "You're a former Housekeeper. You're dead, so I'm guessing no one thought to revoke your privileges or whatever." I frowned. "But you *are* dead, so how are you," I made walking motions with my fingers as I said, "walking around here—oh," I turned my exhausted glare on Zav. "I bet I have you to thank for that."

Zav gave me a little bow. "As amusing as it is to watch your meager intellect try and figure things out, I really don't have the time to waste on this right now." He faced Ailith. "It would seem that you are not as formidable as you once were." He sneered at her as he looked her up and down, "Or, your 'skills' were never actually impressive in the first place."

I pursed my lips in a silent "ooooh" and raised my eyebrows in an oh-no-he-didn't look. I'd just met Ailith and even I knew it was not a good idea to poke that bear.

Ailith flushed, but her face went flat and her eyes cold. I was betting axe murderers looked just like that before methodically chopping their victims into teeny tiny bits. Not that I'd mind having one less Zav around, but I really didn't want Ailith messing up my kitchen.

Zav, who was either oblivious or completely lacking in self-preservation, kept on going, saying, "If Finn is back, then it's only a matter of time before the House returns to its full—and potentially enhanced—status. We're out of time."

"That," said Ailith through clenched teeth, "is not what you promised me."

Zav shrugged. "It was worth a try. It didn't pan out for you. Time for me to go."

He turned to look out the kitchen door, which is when I noticed that a glowing green light was leaking from the hallway into the kitchen.

Gasping, I stumbled to my feet. As soon as I stood, the chiming and buzzing stopped, and the pink dome disappeared. My extra protection was gone.

But at the moment, I didn't care because I had a bigger problem.

I teetered my way over to the counter and peered out into the hallway.

My stomach sank.

DeeDee was cracked open.

Chapter Seventy-Two

"How did you get DeeDee...?" Hanging onto the counter to steady myself, I turned to Ailith, "You. You helped him do this."

Ailith folded her arms across her chest. "*I* fulfill my bargains."

I could see the moment when Ailith and Zav noticed my missing bubble because they exchanged a calculating look. I thought they might rush me, but they flinched back instead when Fuzzy hopped up on the counter beside me and did his best *Aliens-Cujo*-hybrid impression. While showing them his fangs, Fuzzy unleashed an unearthly hiss that had all the hairs on my arms standing up.

Boy was I glad he was on my side.

Clinging to the counter with one hand, I used the other to rub my forehead as I tried to work things through. Part of me wanted to cry. All I wanted was a super-sized Shake-It-Off and to get Bayley home safely. I really did not want to deal with this.

Forcing myself to concentrate, I said, "Let me see if I can get this straight. You," I pointed to the Ailith, "are trying to open the door for Zav. And you," I pointed to Zav, "are messing with me for her in return. To what end?"

Zav smiled. "A spirit needs a host. Although your," he used air quotes, "'intellect' is useless, there's nothing wrong with your physical body."

I looked at Ailith. "I said no to sharing my brain, so you... what? You were going to go all *Invasion of the Body Snatchers* on me?"

Ailith sniffed. "I am the First."

As if that explained everything. I looked at her and said, "I don't think that means what you think it does." With a sigh I felt down to my toes, I added, "Well sorry, not sorry, things didn't work out the way you planned. I'm still here." Shifting my gaze, I studied DeeDee. And started smiling. I couldn't help it. "Had a little trouble with the door, I see."

I sent a silent thanks to Mila. When we'd gone over the physical security of the house, Mila had insisted on running "what if" scenarios.

I'd told her she was being ridiculous.

She'd folded her hands on the table. "Yeah, sure, it sounds nuts. But bear with me. What if someone tries to open the door without you and Bayley?" I started to protest, but she held up a hand. "I know it's highly unlikely. But that's what we're doing here. Trying to imagine the outlier scenarios and prepare for them. So, in this scenario, you and Bayley are both...otherwise occupied. Someone with a boatload of power gets in—"

"Past Bayley? Past the containment circles you made me build in front of the doors?" I said, skepticism dripping from my voice.

"Yup. Let's posit that anyone powerful enough to get past you and Bayley *and* to pry open the door by themselves is powerful enough to dismantle our backup security circles as well."

She had a point, so I nodded.

"What's a little extra something-something we can put in place to mess with them?"

We'd brainstormed all sorts of crazy magical possibilities until Mila came up with something so simple I'd laughed.

She'd shrugged, "Basic is often best."

Now, as I stared at DeeDee, who was open, but only a crack, I couldn't help smiling.

DeeDee was caught on a doorstop.

Mila had instructed Bayley to put a wedge-shaped lump in the floor—a magically reinforced lump that couldn't be moved by anyone other than me or him. If someone tried to open DeeDee without us removing the lump, then DeeDee got stuck on the doorstop. The harder they tried to pry her open, the more stuck she would become.

Peering at DeeDee now, it looked as though they'd been prying at her really hard. She looked totally jammed in place.

Zav did not like my grin. He snapped at me, "Don't get smug Finn. You're not out of the woods yet." His sneer slid into an arctic smile. "In fact, I think that you being awake might actually give us what we need."

Eyes brimming with suspicion, Ailith turned to him. "How so?"

"She's one hundred percent here now. With her full consciousness back, I can wreck it once and for all, with just enough shreds left to keep her bond with Bayley intact. But she'll be gone, for all intents and purposes—gone for good. You can move right in, and you'll never have to worry about her returning. And with the bond intact, there's nothing anyone will be able to do about it."

Greed replaced the suspicion in Ailith's eyes. "When I'm in control, I can force Bayley to open the door fully." She nodded. "Our bargain will then be met in full."

Rubbing his hands together, a spiteful glee lighting his face, Zav said to me, "Well, this is going to be so much more fun with you here to realize what I'm doing as I destroy you."

He was so over the top, I couldn't help but giggle a little.

Nothing takes the wind out of a bad guy's sails more than having their potential victim refuse to cower in fear. Zav stopped monologuing to try and glare me into submission.

"No," I said.

Zav cocked his head at me. "What do you mean 'no'?"

He looked poised to lash out at me. Calling on the last of my reserves, I started frantically building up my mental fortifications.

Buying myself some time to wall off my mind, I waved a hand dismissively, using my talking-to-small-children voice to say, "No to all of this. No, you may not fry my brain." I looked at Ailith as I said, "No, you may not body snatch me." Turning back to Zav, "No you may not use DeeDee."

He grinned. "And how do you think you're going to stop us? One of us, maybe, if you got lucky. But both of us? Oh please." He leaned forward and with a twinkle in his eye, he said, "Give up now, and I'll make it painless. Well, mostly painless. Gotta have a little fun." He said that last bit with a lascivious grin that turned my stomach.

If I ever saw Amon again, I was going to have strong words with him about the ethics of letting a sociopath wander around unchaperoned.

Thinking of wandering around had me furrowing my brow at Zav. "Why do you want to open DeeDee anyway? You're not sick are you?" I didn't mean to sound hopeful when I said that last part, honest I didn't.

The change in topic startled Zav. He abandoned his menacing posture and adopted a nonchalant one. Too nonchalant. He might as well have held up a sign that said, "I'm hiding something."

Taking a shot in the dark, I said, "Does Amon know you're planning on using the door?"

When Zav's gaze flickered, I knew I'd hit the bullseye. Ailith shifted back and forth, her fidgeting giving away her nervousness.

I crowed, "Oh ho ho. You're sneaking around behind Amon's back? I suppose I should say you're doing *more* sneaking around behind Amon's back, since he doesn't seem to keep very close tabs on you. He had no idea about what you did to Neil."

Zav went still as a rock. "What?"

All innocence, I said, "Neil. Teenager. Sweet kid. Well, until you messed with him—"

With no warning, Zav attacked me with a thrumming screech that should've zombified me in seconds.

I slammed my mental shields down. But at the same time, Stella chimed and the Samaras buzzed their wings together while Percy hummed and a pink wall went up in front of me, forming a sound barrier that clashed with the noise Zav was making.

Even with our combined efforts, the attack Zav leveled at me was crazy strong, a no-holds-barred rage-filled shriek that made my brain vibrate in a way that told me he was trying to liquefy it into a bowl full of gelatin.

"No!" hollered Ailith. "What are you doing? Intact! I need her brain intact!"

Zav responded by redoubling his efforts.

With a growl, Ailith flung out a hand. A chair flew through the air and slammed into Zav, breaking his concentration.

He staggered, raising a hand to his head that came away bloody. At least I thought it was blood. It was clear with a sort of sheen to it.

"You dare?" hissed Zav at Ailith.

"Think!" she yelled at him. "We can still salvage this."

"I think the time for salvage has long passed," came a voice from the hallway.

We all turned to find Amon walking calmly into the room, his coat swirling around him.

Chapter Seventy-Three

I didn't know if I should be relieved or not. But Percy, Stella, and the Samaras apparently thought Amon's arrival was a good thing because my pink shield had disappeared the second he'd spoken from the hallway, before he'd even made it into the kitchen.

I relaxed my mental shields slightly but not all the way.

Then, a wild spark of hope lit in me when I realized if Amon was here, maybe Bayley was back.

Bayley???

Still not home.

Worry wormed through me, and I couldn't help the plaintive, "And Bayley?" that I asked Amon.

He raised an eyebrow. "All this," he gestured to Zav, Ailith, and DeeDee, "and your first thought is still of Bayley? How interesting."

"I mean, duh." I suppose I should've tried to say something clever, but I really didn't see how he could have been watching me this entire time and still not get very basic facts about me.

Amon didn't take offense. He merely nodded and said, "As you say." Studying me he said, "You look unwell Housekeeper."

I realized I was swaying again and made an effort to steady myself against the counter. "Been a long day. And these two asshats are keeping me from getting the nap I deserve."

Amon pursed his lips. "This will not do. I need you functioning." Suddenly he was standing in front of me. I jerked, which didn't work so well with all the swaying, and Amon grabbed my shoulder to keep me from falling over. "If I may help a little?" he asked.

"You want to *help* me?"

"It is expeditious."

Ah, he wanted to help me to help himself. That I could buy. Besides, at that point, I was about five seconds from falling over on my face so I said, "Sure why not."

Coolness flowed from Amon's hand on my shoulder, spreading throughout my body. It had the same effect as stepping outside into the frosty air, refreshing me and making the fatigue recede. It was still there, but the cool kept it at bay.

"This is temporary," warned Amon, before dropping his hand. Turning, Amon looked at Zav and said, "You have been busy."

Ailith said, "I—"

But Amon lifted a hand, and a column of shadow slammed into place around Ailith, cutting her off. "We will speak in due time."

She looked frozen in place, except for her face. I could see her lips moving, but the grayness containing her muted whatever she was saying. Her eyes spit fire at us, but Amon didn't seem the least bit bothered.

Having dismissed Ailith, Amon faced Zav again and said, "It seems as though you've omitted some things from your recent communiqués."

An array of feelings flashed through Zav's eyes. He finally settled on defiance, crossing his arms and smirking at Amon. "You prize my initiative. That's one of the reasons you rely on me. Let us speak in private away from," he gestured dismissively at me, "her, and I can explain things in full."

Amon raised an eyebrow. "Rely on you?" He sighed. "I suppose from a certain vantage that could seem so." Amon turned to look at DeeDee, lips pursed. Very calmly, he said, "You were planning to leave."

Zav shrugged. "You weren't planning on keeping me here forever. Come, let me show you what I've been working on," said Zav, walking toward the back door.

Amon walked with Zav as far as the kitchen door then motioned for Zav to wait. He did, though he didn't look happy about it, keeping one foot in the kitchen and one in the hall.

I released the breath I'd been holding. As much as I wanted Zav gone, I didn't trust him to tell Amon the truth. Having Zav here where I could counter his story was better than letting him sequester Amon and fill Amon with whatever lies he'd concocted.

Amon approached DeeDee, scanning the area around her until his gaze caught on the floor. Chuckling he turned to me and said, "The simplest solutions are often the best, aren't they."

It was my turn to shrug. "That's what Mila said."

"I have a feeling that I might like this Mila."

My stomach twisted at the thought that I had just put Mila on Amon's radar. I hoped real hard that he was just making a passing comment.

Pressing a hand to DeeDee, Amon murmured something under his breath. With a whisper, DeeDee swung shut.

Amon turned his attention back to Zav, who was smart enough to smooth over the look of fury he'd been wearing as Amon shut DeeDee. "I misspoke. You were planning to leave. *Without permission.*"

A muscle ticked in Zav's jaw, whether from anger or fear I couldn't tell. But his voice was smooth as butter as he said, "Again, initiative. And I didn't say I wasn't planning on coming back."

"Mmm," said Amon.

Percy snorted softly, so softly that I should have been the only one to hear him, but Amon's head snapped up. "You have something to add."

Percy said nothing. Which, in his defense, was his go-to response, but Amon glowered at me.

He flicked his fingers, and my necklace jerked out of my shirt to land out in the open on my chest.

"That was not a request," said Amon. "Report."

Zav said, "I wouldn't," with such menace that I nearly took a step back.

Amon flicked his fingers again and Zav went flying and slammed against the kitchen wall, remaining pinned there as

Amon strode toward me.

Percy sighed. He sounded oddly resigned. "You didn't ask him if he was planning on coming back alone."

Amon stopped, a blank look on his face as he said, "Oh?"

Uh oh.

Pivoting to face Zav, Amon asked casually, "You were planning on entertaining guests?"

"Something like that," gritted Zav.

"I see," said Amon. He studied Zav for a long moment then said, "Let us discuss this…Neil."

Zav swallowed. "What about him? He's a pawn. Using pawns is well within my purview."

Amon pursed his lips again. "You think so? Pawns are used to remove the king, is that not correct? And in this case, the 'king' you chose to depose was the Housekeeper?"

With a harsh laugh, Zav said, "She's no king. She's useless."

"And yet, there she stands, despite your," Amon shot a look at Ailith, "considerable efforts."

Zav clamped his mouth shut.

"Let me see if I understand," said Amon. "Using your 'initiative' you decided to harm a child, mount multiple attacks on the Housekeeper, and then to leave? Oh yes, yes, with plans to return. *With guests.*"

I said, "Wow." At the look Amon gave me, I said, "Well when you put it that way, it really does sound bad. Don't get me wrong, I'm not defending him. It's just having it laid out like that makes it clear that he one hundred percent belongs on the naughty list."

"As you say," Amon said thoughtfully.

For the first time, I saw fear skitter across Zav's eyes.

"What about him?" Zav said, jerking his head toward me.

It took me a second, but I realized who he was referring to, and said, "Leave Percy alone," as I covered my necklace with my hand.

"That won't help," said Percy and Amon at the same time.

I let my hand slowly fall away.

Amon said to Zav, "I see you are trying to redeem yourself.

Very well. What is it?"

"He's been opening doors for her."

The scary stillness came over Amon again. "Has he indeed?"

My hand came up to cup my necklace again, wrapping around it and rubbing the bump in the star in a motion that was both protective and comforting. "Percy is a valued member of this household," I said, raising my chin to stare Amon down. "He has selflessly assisted both the House and the Housekeeper. Both Bayley and I are grateful to him for his aid. We think of him as family." I gave the necklace a little squeeze to let Percy know I meant it.

"Even though he's been spying on you?" asked Zav.

He wasn't telling me anything I didn't already know, but I had to suppress a cringe. I'd had two spies on the property this whole time, and I'd had no clue.

I turned to Amon. "How many others are there?" I asked.

"Others?"

"How many spies do you have wandering around the property?"

"I have no spies, although I suppose I could see where you might think that. There have been…monitors in place."

I scowled at Amon.

Amusement lit up Zav's face. "Feeling paranoid Finn? You should," and he started chuckling.

Amon studied Zav's laughing face with a sort of detached curiosity before turning back to me, and saying, "Are two not sufficient?"

"You didn't answer my question."

"You are correct. I did not."

That made Zav laugh even harder and meaner.

Amon turned to him. "Interesting that you find your position so amusing."

Zav's laughter died immediately. "What do you mean 'my position.'"

Amon quirked his eyebrows. "Oh come now. Let's not play games."

Amon silenced whatever Zav had been about to say by

waving his hand and encasing Zav in another column of shadow. Turning to Ailith, he said, "Let us hear from you."

With another wave of Amon's hand, Ailith's shadow cell disappeared.

She growled, "How dare—"

Amon raised his hand and said in a cold voice, "Think carefully before you speak, Ailith. I allowed your presence here." The "and I can send you back" was left unspoken, hanging over Ailith's head like a guillotine waiting to drop.

It looked like it cost Ailith some effort to choke back whatever vitriol she'd been about to fling. I saw the moment she realized that she needed a different approach because her hateful expression dissolved, and she gave Amon a respectful bow of the head.

I looked to see Amon's reaction. He couldn't be buying this, could he? But he seemed appeased by her sudden change in demeanor.

"Explain," Amon said.

Ailith shrugged. "I am the First. By rights, this house has been, is now, and will always be mine first. I acted accordingly."

"Do tell," said Amon.

"She is weak," said Ailith flicking her fingers at me like she was flicking off a bug. "A fluke of fate gave her the gifts she possesses, nothing more. They are wasted on her. It makes the most sense to let the right person wield them."

"And that right person is you?"

"Who better?"

Understanding dawned. "The gifts I possess? Is this about the balance thing again?"

Zav didn't need his voice to express himself. His eye roll spoke volumes.

Ailith gestured at me as she said to Amon, "You see, she proves my point. She's barely aware."

"Mmm," said Amon. "And you think her incapable of learning?"

"Who has time for that?" demanded Ailith.

"Let's say you were successful in taking control of her body.

That was the plan, was it not?"

As Ailith nodded, I raised my hand and said, "Just for the record, I don't agree to that. At all."

Amon ignored me, continuing, "Given control of her body, you would gain the powers of the balance," he narrowed his gaze at her, "that you yourself lacked."

Ailith ground her lips together as though it were costing her not to reply.

"What Ailith," he said in a mild tone, "would you do with them then? Have you, perhaps, pledged yourself?"

Ailith's glance flickered to Zav. She had an even worse poker face than I did, and that was saying something.

Amon smiled. "Ah, I see."

Zav's gray cage disappeared.

His bland mask in place, Amon said to Zav, "It is you who have done the pledging. And to whom have you pledged yourself? Other than me, that is," he added silkily.

Zav's eyes flared. "I was pledged to you. I did not pledge myself."

"You were given a choice. Pay your dues in service or time."

"I've paid. Oh I've paid alright. I've been stuck on this backwater nothing of a planet *for years* with these *stupid, ridiculous,*" he spat out, "*humans*! And now this, this," he gestured at me, sputtering as he tried to find the right word, gave up and just went with, "*Finn.* It has to be some kind of joke. This whole time, all these wasted years, *pointless,* because *look at her!* It'll be over in a second." He snarled, "I'll give that to him. He chose well. No one in their right mind would think this idiot Housekeeper in this remote house was the place—"

Zav cut off with a choking sound as Amon said, "That is enough."

Finding his voice again, Zav said, "He's coming one way or the other. You know it; I know it. The difference is that I'm smart enough to see how this will play out." He sneered at me. "She doesn't stand a chance."

"And therefore…?" asked Amon.

"I choose his side."

Amon nodded, a genuine smile on his face. "There it is. Now it all makes sense. Alas, there is a flaw in your plan. You were not here for the first several Housekeepers. You should have studied the history of this place." He looked at Ailith. "Unless something has changed?"

"Nothing has changed," said Ailith, hate dripping from her voice.

Amon looked like he was truly enjoying himself as he smiled and shook his head at Zav. "Who do you think originally helped the house remain free?"

Zav locked eyes with Ailith. "You."

Anger and pride warred for position as Ailith sneered at Zav and said, "Me."

Anger marred Zav's face as he said, "You never intended to let me leave."

"Of course I did. A bargain struck is a bargain kept."

Understanding dawned on Zav's face. "You want him to come. You want to be the one—"

"To end him once and for all? Yes. It is my right," said Ailith, and I thought I heard an old hurt under all that anger.

Zav howled with laughter. "They say hell hath no fury like a woman scorned. Ah this is priceless. It'd almost be worth it to hang around to watch him ruin you. Again."

Ailith opened her mouth to respond, but Amon said, "You're leaving?"

Zav said sunnily, "I am. You can't leave me here now. You don't trust me with this situation. Either you let me leave on my own, or you reassign me elsewhere. Either way, I win."

Chapter Seventy-Four

Amon frowned. "You are not entirely wrong." Amon glanced at my necklace. "You are also not the only monitor at fault." Amon looked at me. "Your...Percy is it?"

I nodded.

"He must come with me."

"Why?"

"He has violated the terms of his service."

A suspicion formed in my mind. "When you talked about Zav's 'service' you made it sound like a punishment."

"That is so."

"Is Percy being punished?" A horrifying thought crept its way into my mind. "Are you the one who stuck him in the necklace?"

Amon looked pleased. "I am."

"That's, that's," I sputtered.

"Leave it, Finn," said Percy.

"Awful," I finally got out.

"You do not know his crimes," Amon said.

I hated to admit it, but he was right.

"I don't, but it seems awfully harsh," I said.

"That was the intent," Amon said smiling, as if I'd complimented him. "You may be pleased to know that the same fate awaits Zav. Different container of course."

I shuddered and looked over at Zav, who looked like he was contemplating murdering Amon.

I said, "I'd prefer it if Percy stayed."

Amon steepled his hands. "You demanded satisfaction for the

actions of Zav against the child Neil. Is that not still the case?"

"Oh he absolutely should be held accountable for that," I started ticking things off on my fingers, "and for his collaboration with Ailith to zombify me, and for his plans to let loose on my planet whatever terror it is you guys have been talking about, and for whatever other havoc he's been wreaking while you weren't paying attention."

Amon nodded.

"But," I held up a finger, "that doesn't mean that Percy doesn't deserve some leniency. Percy has been imprisoned for centuries, so he's paid—in both time and service. And I can honestly attest that he's actually done some good for me and Bayley. Don't get me wrong, he's got the personality of a warthog with a thorn in its paw, but he still helps out here. In his own way, he's taken good care of Bayley and me."

Amon looked at the ceiling for a long moment. "Choose."

"Choose?"

"For the wrongs Zav has committed, you are due one boon. One. Not two. You must choose. I punish Zav as I have the... Percy, or Percy may stay here."

"A moment please," I said.

Doing my best to tune out the menaces in front of me, I held my necklace in front of my face and said, "Percy, given the opportunity, would you want to stay here? If you'd rather go off and try your chances somewhere else, I understand. I'd miss your surliness, but I get it. But if you want to stay here, you're welcome to do so."

When I looked up, Amon was viewing me with puzzlement.

After a long moment, Percy said, "You'd let me choose?"

"C'mon Percy. You've been an active member of this household for the last six months. How is this a surprise to you? Of course you get to choose. I don't want this place to be a prison."

I couldn't tell if Percy was speechless, being his usual recalcitrant self, or just thinking really hard, but he was quiet.

A warning in his voice, Amon prompted, "Percy."

And Percy replied, "I choose to stay here."

I let out a long breath and said, "Then I choose to keep Percy over punishing Zav." To be honest, although Zav definitely deserved some kind of retribution, the idea of imprisoning anyone, even Zav, in some kind of physical object gave me the heebie-jeebies.

"Interesting," said Amon.

"You keep saying that."

"You keep providing points of interest."

I didn't really have anything to say to that, so I left it alone.

Head tipped to the side, Amon stared at me for a long moment. "Are you certain that is the boon you wish to claim?" He held up a hand forestalling me. "What if I offered you another option? The chance to speak with your parents perhaps?"

My heart stopped. When it started beating again, it felt like Amon had ripped the scab of my grief and sent a torrent of pain gushing through me. I hated how transparent the heartache in my voice was as I said, "My parents?" I swallowed against the lump in my throat. "That's not possible."

Amon shot a meaningful look at Ailith and said, "Obviously it is."

"I..." I couldn't think what to say, and I looked at the floor to hide the tears in my eyes. The part of me that was desperate to see my parents again was crying so loudly that it made it almost impossible to think.

I could tell them about Bayley, and we could laugh together at my crazy adventures.

I could finally ask them all the questions that had been plaguing me about why they'd hidden so much from me.

Maybe I could even hug them again.

And they could hug me.

If I had doubts before about Amon, they'd tripled now. The kind of choice he was offering me was awful. Condemn a live being so I could have one of my deepest desires? If this were *Dungeons & Dragons,* I had a suspicion Amon might be lawful evil rather than the lawful neutral that he seemed to think he was.

A small voice in my heart asked me, "What would your parents do?"

I knew the answer without having to think about it. It didn't change the fact that I wanted to vomit at what I needed to do.

With all my sorrow plain in my voice, I said, "They're dead. Percy is alive. There's no choice, really."

Percy said, "Finn—"

Shaking my head, I said, "No Percy. This is the right thing." Tears choked my voice, but I nodded my head to show I meant it.

Amon turned to Zav. "It seems you get your wish. You will leave this place. However, your terms of service have not been fulfilled. You're being reassigned." With a wave, Amon disappeared Zav.

Taking in my disgust, Amon slid me a look. "Getting what we wish is not always what we expect."

Given the vengeful satisfaction in Amon's voice, I got the feeling that Amon had done something like stripping Zav down to his speedo and sending him to an ice planet. At least I could hope so.

"Amon?" Percy asked. "What are the terms of my stay here?"

Amon clasped his hands behind his back. "They have a term for this here." He looked as if he were searching his memory. "Patrol?"

"Parole?" I asked.

"Ah yes. That's it." He looked at Percy. "You are not truly free, not yet. But you have some freedoms."

"And the doors?" Percy pressed.

Amon slid a glance between Percy and me. "Opening and closing only. And you still may not speak of…things. Am I clear?"

"Yes."

In a dangerous voice that gave me chills, Amon added, "We will know."

I said, "Uh, speaking of which, what's the deal with Percy's spying job? Is he, uh, still on the payroll?"

"Let's call it a condition of his parole. He must still make regular reports."

I sighed inwardly but decided not to push it.

Movement made me switch my gaze to see Ailith flickering in and out of focus.

Amon said, "Zav's stasis spell is wearing off now that he's

not here." He did something with a wave of his hand, and Ailith stabilized.

"What are we going to do about her?" I asked.

Amon leveled his gaze at Ailith. "Have you completed your assignment?"

"I have not," she said defiantly.

Amon looked as though he were searching for patience and coming up short. "This was a grave mistake, Ailith. Had you truly wished to accomplish your goal, you should have done as you were instructed. Now it is too late."

"But—"

"Bayley returns. You know the rules. Only one Housekeeper in the house at a time. It is time for you to go."

Frustration and anger darkened Ailith's face. "You should let me have her!"

Amon shook his head sadly. "Perhaps the mistake was mine to think you could temper your anger with reason. Regardless, the time has passed. Come along Ailith," and he once again encased her in shadow.

Amon headed for the back door, and Ailith floated across the room and out into the hallway.

After opening the door, Amon sent Ailith ahead of him outside. Pausing on the threshold, Amon said, "Housekeeper Finley Foster. It has been—"

"Interesting?"

"Indeed."

And then he walked off into the night, blending into the shadows as he went. Still, I knew what to look for. I tottered back to the kitchen table, collapsing into a chair as I watched Amon on my mental map. I wasn't surprised to see him head for the cemetery.

There was a moment of silence, then my protectors started talking all at once.

Chapter Seventy-Five

Fuzzy meowed and jumped up, cramming himself onto my lap. At the same time, the Samaras launched themselves from Fuzzy's tail and darted toward my face. And to top it all off, Stella began chiming in my pocket.

As I wrapped my arms around Fuzzy, the Samaras all chattered at me.

"Housekeeper Finn! Housekeeper Finn!"

"The Orret said you were away!"

"You were on the floor!"

"Do you have brain damage again?"

I snorted out a laugh. "Hi guys. I'm fine, thank you. I just need some rest."

I reached into my pocket and gave Stella a reassuring pat. It let out a loud, happy-sounding chime, then went silent.

The Samaras landed in a row on the table in front of me and Fuzzy.

Corey hopped forward, wringing his hands. "Are you sure you are well? You were gone a long time. You would not wake."

In a reassuring voice, I said, "Yes, I am sure. Thank you so much for your help. Uh, how did you even know I needed assistance? For that matter, how did you get in here?"

Corey said, "We were flying by the house—"

Shay said dourly, "There was no food outside—"

Jet said, "We looked in the window—"

"You were on the floor," added Rou helpfully.

Shay said, "Maybe you hit your head—"

"She did not hit her head!" said Corey.

"Well we know that *now*," grumbled Shay.

Corey said, "We could not get inside."

Jet said, "But we tapped on the window. The Orret came."

Corey said, "He told us that you were away."

I clarified, "You talked to Fuzzy through the windowpane?"

They nodded.

Giving Fuzzy a squeeze, I looked down and said, "Thank you."

With a trill, Fuzzy nuzzled my face.

Corey hunched his wings as he said, "Then the bad noise came."

All the Samaras nodded and shuffled nervously.

"Zav?" I asked.

They all shook their wings, like trying to shake off bad vibes, and repeated, "Zav."

Trying to follow along with all of them was making my head ache, so I said, "Corey, can you tell me what happened next?"

He hopped another step forward, bowed quickly, and said, "Yes Housekeeper. We thought the bad noi—Zav would be trouble. Since you were away."

"Well you were right. That was good thinking."

All the Samaras smiled and fluttered their wings, causing them to pop up off the table, and they started twirling and diving like a bunch of seeds scattered by the wind. Corey signaled, and they all landed on the table again.

I prompted, "And what happened next?"

Corey continued, "When we saw Zav enter the house, we followed quickly."

"We stayed up by the ceiling!" Rou said.

"He never saw us!" said Jet.

"Not as smart as he thinks," mumbled Shay.

Corey shot them all a quelling look and said, "I am telling the Housekeeper!"

They all settled down, and Corey continued, "Once inside, we waited, then went to the Orret."

Shay said, "Stupid Zav did not even see we were there," and Rou and Jet tittered.

Corey smiled at me. "It is true. Zav did not see us. We stayed with the Orret." Grudging admiration in his voice, Corey added, "The...Fuzzy protected you well."

All the Samaras murmured and flapped in agreement, and Stella let out a chime.

Leaning down, I pressed my forehead to Fuzzy's and whispered, "Thank you."

Corey said, "But then Zav made the bad noise."

Repeating "bad noise" like a series of echoes, the Samaras all shivered their wings again.

Corey said, "The Orret said we must help protect you. That if Zav used his bad noise, we must all help."

Now it made sense to me why I'd come back to find myself surrounded by the protection bubble. While I was trying to get back, Zav must have gotten frustrated and tried a sonic attack like the one he'd tried when he got mad after I woke up. And my impromptu team had protected me.

"Thank you, Corey, Jet, Rou, and Shay. Thank you, Stella," I said patting the star in my pocket. It vibrated in response. "Thank you, Percy," I said, patting my necklace. Percy, of course, was silent. But then again, after the night he'd had, I didn't blame him. We needed to talk, but not now. Finally, I tightened my hug on Fuzzy and kissed his head. "And thank you, Fuzzy, for coordinating it all."

As Fuzzy purred, I lifted my head to see that Corey was looking down, wringing his hands again, while the other Samaras mirrored him. They looked like a bunch of guilty children.

"Why do you look like you think you did something wrong?"

The Samaras exchanged a look and said, "We are not supposed to make the..." my translator stuttered, and I got, "penguins."

"The what?" I asked.

Corey said, "The penguins. The bad wing noise. It is not allowed."

Rou said, "Unless Zav attacks us."

Jet added, "Or the others."

Shay repeated grimly, "It is not allowed."

Slowly, I said, "I see. You helped, and you are worried you will get in trouble because it's against your rules?"

They nodded.

"If that's the case, have your, er, parents or elders or leaders—whoever—have them come and talk to me. You have done a great service to the Housekeeper and Bayley House, and therefore by extension, to your people because we are the ones who keep them safe. If they have any issues, they can come talk to me."

All the Samaras perked up at once, taking to the air in a series of dives and darts as they uttered a flurry of thanks.

Pausing in midair, Corey looked out the window and said, "We must go."

I put Fuzzy down and dragged myself to the back door. Amon's energy boost was wearing off, and my fatigue was returning with a vengeance. "Thank you again, you guys. Come back soon, and I'll make you a pile of treats to celebrate."

On a loud burst of cheers, the Samaras all gusted out the door and into the night.

Closing the door, I stumbled back to the table and flopped into a chair.

I was watching Amon's shadow when the house squeaked around me.

My head whipped up and tears filled my eyes, as I cried out, "Bayley!"

And in my head, I heard, *Hello, Finn.*

Chapter Seventy-Six

As I cried out, "Bayley you're back!!!" Fuzzy let loose a string of meows, pacing in excitement.

Bayley chuckled.

I said, "And you're talking to me! Do you have enough energy to be talking to me? Oh no, are we in more trouble?"

No, it's part of my new skills, said Bayley. He added shyly, *A birthday present, of sorts. It's one of my new powers that I grabbed access to first.*

It took a second to kick in. "Part of your—you won! You got your promotion!" I did a little happy dance in my seat, immediately regretted it, and slumped back in the chair.

Despite my exhaustion, Bayley's laughter filled me with delight. *WE won my promotion.* In a more serious tone, he said, *But that can wait. What's been happening here? Are you okay?*

I shook my head. "There's too much to tell. I don't even know where to start."

Hesitantly, Bayley said, *I know you dislike it, but would you mind if I did a quick scan of your memory to catch us up? It'll be fast, I promise—much faster than you trying to fill me in.*

I waved my hand in the air. "Go for it. I'm going to just put my head down while you rummage around."

Fuzzy hopped up on the table and lay down next to me, purring softly while Bayley did his thing.

After just a few minutes, Bayley said, *You weren't kidding.*

You have done exceedingly well on your own, Finn, pride rippled through his voice. *Thank you for taking such good care of me.*

"You're welcome," I said. It came out a little garbled because my head was pillowed on my arms.

A fresh burst of energy flowed into me. I felt like a flower getting rain for the first time in months. All of me started perking up immediately.

Raising my head, I asked, "What was that?"

Part of my new skills. I'm going to be able to replenish my energy quicker now and that means I can also help you to recharge.

I shook my head experimentally. It didn't hurt anymore. I was still tired, but my energy wasn't dangerously low any longer. "I think I'm going to like this promotion a lot," I said.

Me too.

"I'm so happy you're home, Bayley. I can't wait to hear all about what happened after I left—"

About that...

I sat up a little straighter at the concern in his voice. "Oh no, what now?"

The Thwats imparted an...interesting bit of knowledge when I got there.

"From the sound of your voice, this is going to be the bad kind of interesting."

Not necessarily, Bayley hedged.

"Just tell me."

Bayley blurted, *We weren't quite as close to the deadline as we thought. We have an extra day left.*

I frowned in confusion. "But it's almost the end of my birthday—have I lost track of the days? Isn't today the 28th?"

It is. Bayley paused, then said gently, *Your birthday isn't when you think it is.*

"It isn't?" I said with a sinking feeling.

Bayley took a deep breath then plunged ahead. *It's off by a year and a day. You're a year older than you think you are.*

"WHAT?!?" I stared at the wall. "I mean, a day I can understand, but a year?"

I think it's because you were a leap year baby. You were born on the 29th.

"Wow. Just wow. What the hell were my parents—"

I choked, staring at Ailith, who had appeared in the middle of the kitchen.

Fuzzy leapt up onto all fours, hair standing up, and hissed.

Ignoring us, Ailith said, "Bayley." She was flickering in and out.

Jumping to my feet, I demanded, "How are you here? Amon said he was returning you to...wherever it is you came from."

Dismissively, Ailith said, "Amon is detained."

A quick check of my mental map—now back in high-def and full color, hooray!—showed me that Amon's shadow was in the same spot in the forest as it had been the last time I'd looked. Except now, I could detect some kind of magic around him. It looked familiar.

"Zav," I said. "What'd he do, lay some kind of trap?"

Ailith nodded.

I whistled. "That must be some trap to hold a being like Amon." No wonder Zav had tried to get Amon to go outside to chat. By trapping Amon, Zav would've had a chance to escape.

Ailith ignored me, her gaze focused on the nearest wall. "Bayley, I am the First. My bond supersedes them all. I claim my right as Housekeeper."

"What?!?" There was so much wrong with that statement I couldn't figure out what to latch onto first. So I went with the obvious. "Lady, not to be rude, but you're dead. D-E-A-D. Dead. You can't even hold your form without Zav or Amon here to stabilize you. You can't be Housekeeper."

"I can. My bond with Bayley is special. First and best. He may choose me over you."

"You think Bayley is going to what, help you body-jack me?" I asked. I could feel the disbelief crinkling my face.

"I am the First."

"No, really?" I said, voice dripping with sarcasm.

In my head, I said, *Oh Bayley. I'm so sorry. This must be hard for you.*

Bayley said, *I've got this.*

I know. It's just that after everything else you've been through, you shouldn't have to deal with this too.

Ailith's and my attentions were caught by movement in the wall. The wooden boards shifted and blurred until a head popped out of the wall.

I laughed. I couldn't help it. I was looking at a wooden version of the way Bayley looked in the simulation.

The wooden eyelids popped open, and the face began to speak with Bayley's voice. "Ailith," he said, "you do not belong here anymore."

Ailith looked startled, then hunger creased her face into a terrible mask. "You have become more powerful at last. Excellent. Think of all we can do together. Let us be as we were before. But this time, nothing will stand in my—our—way."

Nice catch there.

Bayley shook his wooden head. Gently, as though speaking to a child, Bayley said, "No, Ailith."

She flickered in and out faster, agitation tinging her voice as she said, "I am the First. My bond comes before all others."

Bayley said, "It is true that your bond was first. But you can no longer command me the way you once did."

"You are mine!"

"I am not. I never was. That is something you never understood."

I said, "It's time for you to go Ailith. Bayley has spoken. You must respect that."

Ailith turned on me, eyes narrowed. Then she dove at me, hands outstretched.

Instinctively, I yanked up a protection circle around me and Fuzzy, and I felt Bayley's magic join mine, reinforcing the circle.

Ailith's magic was nothing compared to our combined magics. As she pounded on the circle, she screamed with rage.

I pushed at her, the circle sizzled, and Ailith flew back.

As she stared at me, mouth open in shocked silence, I said, "Out of courtesy for the fact that you're a former Housekeeper, I've been more than polite. But that's enough. Your access to Bayley House is now revoked. You are no longer welcome in the house or on the property."

"You can't do that."

"Sure we can. Right Bayley?" I wasn't actually sure if we could do that, but it was worth a try.

Bayley said, "Goodbye, Ailith," at the same time as I sent him a mental image of what I wanted to do. Watching Amon had given me an idea.

Pulling on Bayley's magic, I poured it with mine into a bubble that snapped closed around Ailith.

"No!" she shrieked, pounding at the bubble with her hands. I found myself missing Amon's mute function.

Ailith fought the bubble, but it did no good. She was well and truly trapped. Her image dimmed further, and she began to flicker more unsteadily.

Then without warning, Amon appeared in the kitchen. One look told me he was furious. "Ailith," he said in a deadly voice. He pointed, and she disappeared, ball and all, then so did he.

I checked my mental map. I saw his shadow reappear in the cemetery. Moments later, it was gone.

"Ailith?" I asked Bayley.

The wooden face had sunk back into the wall, but Bayley said in my head, *Gone.*

"I'm so sorry Bayley. For all of that."

I felt a little wistfulness from him. *Ailith was so very long ago. I was very new, and my memories of the time are blurry. It... it might have been nice to visit after all this time.*

I reached out and patted the wall, and the house sighed around me. "They say you never forget your first love. I imagine your first Housekeeper is somewhat the same. Truly, I am sorry Bayley."

Truly, I am happy with the Housekeeper I have.

"I love you too Bayley. It's so good to see you!!! I wasn't sure how long it'd take you to get back—what happened after we split up?"

While I fed Fuzzy and made myself a Shake-It-Off, Bayley said, *When we went through the windows, I wound up exactly where I thought I would, back in the desert. Except, it seemed like it took a while to get there, which I'm guessing was because they wanted to see you first. But when the desert resolved around* me, *Amon was there briefly, long enough to tell me I was being promoted with provisos—*

"What provisos?" I stopped making my Shake-It-Off, frustration making me frown.

Not to worry. It's not all that bad, said Bayley. *After Amon disappeared, I was left to talk to the Thwats, who explained everything. One of them, one of the ones that looked like creosote bushes to you, spoke for the group. They said I'd passed, provisionally.*

I leaned on the counter, frowning as I sipped my Shake-It-Off. "You earned your promotion fair and square. There shouldn't be any strings attached."

It's just that there will be a sort of probationary period where they see how I settle into my new powers and which of them take. I have the opportunity to grow, but how I grow is up to me. Like you, I'll have to do a lot of experimenting and learning to see what I can do.

I perked up. "That sounds like fun! I love me a good experiment. Hey, you and I can have practice time together," I added with a big smile.

Excitement laced Bayley's voice as he said, *I can't wait!* His voice shifted, and he said more tentatively, *There's one more thing. This probation period comes with a…I guess you could say a probation officer.*

Dread curdled my stomach. "No…please don't tell me it's—"

Amusement and wariness tinged Bayley's voice as he said, *It'll likely be Amon, yes.*

"Awesome. Well, it's not like we have any choice. And I suppose the devil you know…."

That was my thought as well.

I slugged back my shake and tried to force myself to look on the bright side. "Well, look, at least you've got the go-ahead to grow—and I gotta say I'm loving your new skills already. It's going to fill me with glee every time I hear your voice in my head! And you're home safe! I have zero doubts that you'll pass your probationary period with flying colors. We'll make sure of it."

Thank you. For everything. And happy birthday, Finn.

I looked at the clock. It was just after midnight. "Hah. Having a new birth date is already an advantage—I get to spend my first birthday as Housekeeper with you after all. And having you back is the best present ever."

The house settled around me and sighed in contentment.

Chapter Seventy-Seven

The next evening, I was drinking a cup of coffee, when I felt Zo blip onto my mental map, followed shortly by a knock on the door.

Letting her in, I said, "I was wondering when you'd show up."

I had texted her to let her know Bayley and I were okay, and she'd said, "Good to know," and nothing else.

Zo made her way into the kitchen, where she stopped, put her hand on a counter, and looked around.

"I see," she said after a few moments.

"What do you see?" I asked.

Zo moved to the stove, grabbed the kettle, and went to the sink. As she was filling it, she said, "Bayley has changed—is changing."

I nodded. "I told you he won his promotion."

As she took the kettle to the stove, Zo snorted and mumbled, "Won."

Brows furrowed, I said, "You don't sound happy."

Sighing, Zo rubbed her forehead, looking tired. "It is as it should be, I suppose."

"Well look, if you're worried about Bayley having a bunch of power all of a sudden, it's not like he's going to level up overnight. He has to grow into his powers over time, which I still don't totally get—"

"You ever seen a tree in a pot?"

I blinked trying to adjust to the abrupt change in topic. "What?"

"A tree. In a pot."

"Uh, yes?"

"If you take the tree out of the pot and put it in the ground, does the tree sprout into a giant oak overnight?"

"Er, no?"

"Right."

I said slowly, "You're saying that you can remove the pot, but it takes time for the tree's roots to spread out, for the tree to grow—new roots, new branches, new leaves, and a trunk to support it all. And, in this analogy, Bayley is the tree?"

She nodded. "And they took away his pot." She bustled around the kitchen getting herself a teabag and mug as she added, "But for all our sakes, he better not take as long as a tree to grow into his new power—that actually goes for both of you."

She gestured for me to sit down, and she joined me.

"What do you mean for all our sakes?"

Zo sipped her tea. "What did Amon," she sounded like she was chewing a rotten egg when she said his name, "say about the consequences of Bayley winning?"

I thought back. "Something about ripples."

She grunted then sipped her tea. "That's all?"

"Pretty much?"

"Bayley?" she turned to the wall. "Do you have anything to add?"

To my surprise, like he had done for Ailith, Bayley popped his head out of the wall and answered Zo, "No."

Zo showed no reaction to Bayley's new ability. She merely sipped her tea. "Well, at least you know there are potential 'ripples.'" After grimacing into her cup, she said, "Now tell me everything that happened." She looked at Bayley and added, "You too."

We took turns filling Zo in on our adventures.

When I got to the part about Amon making me choose between Percy, Zav, and my parents, Zo slammed her mug on the table. "He offered to bring your parents back?"

I shook my head, blinking back the tears that were threatening. "I don't know if he meant to bring them back, or just to let me talk to them. We didn't get that far."

"Oh Finn."

I looked up to see true sorrow in Zo's eyes warring with fury. In a small voice, I asked, "Could he really have done it?"

Zo put her hand over mine. "Does it matter? What's done is done."

A tear slipped down my face, and as I brushed it away she squeezed my hand and said, "You made the only possible choice that allowed you to remain true to yourself. Your parents would be proud."

She let my hand go and gave me a moment to get myself under control, then said, "Tell me the rest."

"Well speaking of my parents," and I told her about them hiding my birthday from me. Something sparked in her eyes, but instead of commenting, she prompted me to tell the remainder of my tale.

When I finished, Zo smirked. "Ailith was planning to double-cross Zav."

I nodded. "Zav said 'hell hath no fury like a woman scorned.' But how was she scorned? What happened?"

Zo looked into her cup. "Bayley, what do you remember from that time?"

Bayley said, "Very little. It's…oddly blurry."

Zo said, "Hmpf. Do you remember anything at all?"

After a moment, Bayley said, "I remember flashes of Ailith as the first Housekeeper and not much else."

Zo said, "Ailith was…angry."

I nodded, "Yeah I got that—newsflash, she still is. But about what exactly? Who is this Guest Guy? If Zav was going to bring a buddy, I'm assuming it was to cause trouble."

"Understatement," Zo muttered.

A chill slithered down my spine. "What do you know about this Guest Guy? He must have been here before if he knew Ailith—"

"Don't."

I yanked my necklace out of my shirt and looked at Percy. "Oh *now* you decide to speak? What do you mean 'don't'?" I looked at Zo and said, "Bayley and I have been trying to talk to Percy all day, and he wouldn't respond."

Ignoring me, Percy said, "Zo, don't."

Zo gave my necklace a look that made me worried it was going to burst into flames and melt into a puddle of goo. "Do not presume to lecture me. I'm aware of my responsibilities...*Percy.*"

And I was suddenly sure that Zo knew Percy's real name. Which made me wonder, "Do you know why he's in the necklace?"

Zo said, "Yes," and Percy made a sound like he was sucking in a sharp breath. After letting him worry a moment, Zo said, "But it's not my place to say." Looking at Percy, she added, "Not for now."

I shook my head. "I'm not asking you to tell me—I was just curious if you knew. I can wait for him to tell me on his own." I took a deep breath. "I ask because if you know that, then did you know he was spying on us?"

With no hesitation, very matter-of-factly, she said, "Yes."

"And you didn't tell me because...?"

"It wasn't relevant."

I gaped at her.

"Has it harmed Bayley? Has it interfered with you being Housekeeper?" When I shook my head, she said, "Not relevant."

Bayley shifted his head toward Zo and said, "How did I not know?"

When Bayley and I had talked, I'd found out that he didn't know about either Percy or Zav keeping tabs on us. He'd known Zav existed, but not what he'd been up to.

Zo said carefully, "The monitors...are part of Amon's... thing. Think of being monitored as part of the cost of being Housekeeper and House, and let it go."

The house grumbled around us, and Bayley's frown matched my own, but we let it be for the moment.

Zo finished her tea as I asked, "Zo...the way Zav was talking...it made it seem like his buddy is going to come here no matter what. Like it's inevitable."

Zo took her cup to the sink but didn't say anything.

"Well?"

She looked at me. "Well what? You haven't asked a question."

"Is it true? The Guest Guy, the 'going to make trouble is an understatement' guy, is he inevitable?"

Zo didn't answer. But her clenched fists and grim face said it all.

"How long?" I asked softly.

"I honestly don't know. It partially depends on how long it takes for word to reach him—and word *will* eventually reach him—that Bayley has access to his full power potential."

"Who *is* this Guest Guy? Can't you tell us anything else?"

I thought I heard Percy suck in a breath.

Zo looked at me and at Bayley. She patted the counter and said, "Don't dawdle." And then she left.

Epilogue

"Thanks again!" I waved at Nor and Mila as they climbed into their car and drove off.

Shutting the front door, I couldn't stop smiling.

After Bayley had lifted the lockdown protocols, my cell phone had gone bonkers, dinging and pinging with a week's worth of messages, many of which were from Nor and Mila.

When I'd called Nor and Mila and filled them in on my adventures, they were both speechless.

Finally Mila whistled and said, "Looks like we have some more 'worst case scenario' plans to make."

I groaned, "I'll say. I don't know what we can do against someone like Amon, but we need to at least think about defenses against him."

Nor said, "Hmm."

I asked, "What?"

Nor said, "It's just that Amon let Zav reveal a lot of information about your 'Guest Guy' when he didn't really have to. He could have had it out with Zav in private."

I asked, "What are you getting at?"

Nor said, "I could be wrong, but it was almost like he was warning you."

Mila said, "Or testing you—seeing if you were smart enough to pick up what he was throwing down and to act on it while there's time."

I grumped, "That sounds like Amon."

Nor said, "In any event, we need to do some planning and soon. But before that, we have other matters to attend to."

Nor had then insisted on doing a belated birthday. Mila had added that since I was suddenly an extra year older, that I should have twice the birthday celebration. I was so excited to have Bayley home that I'd actually been in the mood to celebrate my birthday for the first time in a while, even with all the weirdness.

We'd planned to meet in a few days, so I'd spent the time resting, catching up on missed calls, and doing chores, including ordering a pile of groceries.

Bayley and I had also started in on our magical studies. Between Zo's "don't dawdle" and our own excitement about Bayley's new potential, Bayley and I were super motivated and had already started working together on his new skills.

Yesterday, Bayley had asked me to meet him in the Knack Shack.

I'd closed my eyes and gone to my mental space. But I'd nearly jolted myself back into reality again when I saw the surprise Bayley had for me.

I'd expected to find Bayley the way he usually was, a glowing golden orb.

But there, standing in the middle of the Knack Shack, stood the Bayley I'd come to know from the simulation.

"You're...you're here!" I squeaked.

Grinning from ear to ear, he said, "I am. And I will be. I can keep this form now." And he held open his arms.

Half-worried he'd disappear, I'd stepped tentatively into the hug.

He felt warm and solid and real, just like he had in the simulation, just like my own virtual avatar felt real.

He wrapped his arms around me, and I hugged him back.

"Practice time is going to be *so* much more fun," I mumbled into his shoulder.

His chuckle rumbled low in his chest. "You bet. It's a whole new world for us both. I can't wait to see what kind of trouble we can get into."

As if that wasn't enough of a birthday present, Nor and Mila had come by earlier this evening and created the perfect birthday celebration.

They'd picked up a ton of food from the diner in town, along with a ginormous cake, and we'd had a lovely girls' night, catching up. The two had showered me with a pile of thoughtful gifts, including a set of cross-country skis and a pair of ice skates. We had plans to go outdoor adventuring next weekend.

Now, as I made my way back to the kitchen, I couldn't stop grinning. After the last few weeks of isolation, I snuggled into the warmth and love being heaped on me.

After I piled some treats in Fuzzy's bowl, I cut off an enormous hunk of cake and left it outside for the Samaras.

When I got back inside, I brewed some coffee and checked on Stella. Rather than sticking it back in the attic, I'd kept the star in the kitchen. Since Bayley had gotten home, Stella didn't have the same separation anxiety it had had while Bayley was gone. When I'd asked if it minded hanging out on the windowsill with my lavender plant Sprout instead of being in my pocket all the time, it had chimed happily.

Since then, Stella had been quiet, but I had the sense that it was awake now and quietly watching. That's why I'd put it someplace with a view.

When I'd asked Bayley about Stella, he'd hesitated then said, *I always felt there was something special about Stella. But since I got back…I can't explain it. I just know Stella is important.*

We both decided to keep an eye on Stella and see what happened.

My coffee maker burbled, so I poured myself a cup and made my way to the table. I was eager to brainstorm a list of goodies to bake for the Samaras now that I could get groceries again.

Fuzzy jumped up on the table, and I put my coffee aside to give him chin rubs.

I have one more birthday present for you, said Bayley. *Think of it as an extra gift for the extra year that just got added to your age.*

"That's not necessary, Bayley, really. You being able to talk to me easily is already the best present ever. Not to mention that I get to see you in the Knack Shack!"

Bayley chuckled. *Oh I think you're going to like this present just as much. It's actually an offshoot of the one I already gave you—well it comes from the same power-up. It took me a few days to figure it out—it'd just be easier if I showed you.*

Curiosity made me bounce a little. "Yes please!"

I'll need your permission to work a little magic in your mind. It's a sort of...unlocking.

"Of course."

I stopped petting Fuzzy, who sighed and started grooming himself.

Then I closed my eyes and held still. I felt a tingly feeling in my head, like someone had poured seltzer water in there, and it was gently bubbling. The sensation faded quickly.

Bayley sounded positively giddy as he said, *That should do it.*

"Do what?"

Fuzzy stopped grooming his paw, looked up at me and said, *Hello Finn.*

I jumped so hard that I nearly knocked over my coffee cup.

Bayley laughed, and I heard a gruff chuckle along with it that I realized was Fuzzy's.

Happy birthday, Finn, Bayley said, his voice sparkling with joy.

"Oh Bayley! This is the best birthday ever!" I cried. I shifted to the Knack Shack so I could hug Bayley. I may have also jumped up and down and squeeed a few times before I returned to reality and looked at Fuzzy.

Fuzzy wore a very smug feline expression. He shifted so he could give me a gentle headbutt, then sat back in cat pose in front me.

Fuzzy said, *I can't wait for our next adventure. It's going to be even more fun now.*

Acknowledgements

First, a sincere thank you to the readers who've been waiting so patiently for this book to arrive. It took longer than expected, but I hope you feel it was worth the wait.

It may seem like this book was inspired by or is a comment on the 2020 COVID-19 pandemic and ensuing lockdown isolation. While the pandemic did affect how long it took me to write this book, it was not the inspiration behind it. That honor goes to my friend Morgan. After beta reading Book 1 in the series, *A House for Keeping,* Morgan said something along the lines that she was curious to see how the choice to remain isolated on the property would impact Finn.

That gave me the seed of the idea for this book. For years I've been planning on dealing with Finn's isolation in Book 4— since before Book 1 was even published.

But when I started writing *A Season for Solitude,* blammo— the pandemic hit.

A lot of creatives used the pandemic as an opportunity to go into creative overdrive. Unfortunately, that is not how my brain works. I can write under a lot of trying circumstances, but the pandemic and the chaos it caused (lockdowns, layoffs, etc.) put the kibosh on my creativity, effectively putting this book on hold until things settled down.

So while the pandemic definitely impacted this book, it's not perhaps in the way people might think—the pandemic delayed the book rather than inspiring it.

That said, I'm so delighted to finally get this book to you, my readers. I can't thank you enough for the encouraging messages you've sent me and for hanging in there to see what's next with these characters.

Being an alpha reader might be its own special sublevel of hell—they're constantly left hanging while I dole out chapters a few at a time, and they have to deal with an anxious writer who's wringing my hands at showing my work for the first time. So a huge thank you to Michael Duhan and Steven Elliott for stepping in to alpha read for me when my usual alpha reader was unavailable. I was super nervous to finally share this book for the first time, and they made it so easy and fun. Their thoughtful feedback and enthusiastic support helped so very much. In fact, they have been unflagging cheerleaders during my entire writing journey, and I'm so grateful and fortunate to have them in my corner. Thank you, gentlemen.

When I was trying to name the Samaras, I knew I wanted to derive their names from dance terminology because of how they look when they fly. A big thanks to Kim Prentice for creating and explaining a list of dance terms that helped me name my guys.

Thank you to my beta readers for your invaluable comments. You guys rock.

As always, thank you to Michael Tangent for the excellent editing and brilliant cover design, not to mention for all the random plotting discussions and for the repeated reassurances during the extended process of writing this book.

Well, that's a wrap, at last, on *A Season for Solitude*.

Looking forward to our next adventure together!